Susan Shwartz was born on New Year's Eve, 1949, in Ohio in the American Midwest. She became interested in fantasy and science fiction when she was seven years old, and a cousin gave her Edith Hamilton's *Mythology*; her father, who grew up on *Planet Stories*, subsequently introduced her to Robert Heinlein, Andre Norton and Isaac Asimov's books at about the time that Alan Shepard went up in his suborbital flight – and she has been hooked ever since.

She was educated in Massachusetts, at Mount Holyoke College. During that time she spent two summers on exchange, living in Trinity College, Oxford, in a programme sponsored by the University of Massachusetts. She studied Shakespeare, paleography and medieval romance. She went on to take a Ph.D. at Harvard University, and was a specialist in Arthurian romance.

For three years she taught at Ithaca College, in upstate New York. Then, wanting a business career and to be closer to the New York publishing scene, she moved to New York City. After switching jobs too many times, she went to work at BEA Associates, an investment firm for which she managed electronic mail, a few other databases, personnel functions, and much of the in-house communications. She now works on Wall Street. She daily courts overwork with a heavy writing schedule, too. She has written a good deal of non-fiction for major US papers, and is also active on the circuit of fantasy and SF conventions.

Susan Shwartz has written a mass of short stories (one of which has been nominated for a Nebula Award), numerous articles and essays (including an essay on 'Women in Science Fiction' for the *New York Times Book Review* and an article on Jean Auel for *Vogue*), and several science fiction novels, including *White Wing* with Shariann Lewitt, writing as 'Gordon Kendall'.

Queensblade is the concluding book in the trilogy *Heirs to Byzantium*. The first two books, *Byzantium's Crown* and *The Woman of Flowers* are also available in Pan.

Susan Shwartz

Queensblade

Volume Three in the
Heirs to Byzantium
trilogy

Pan Original
Pan Books   London, Sydney and Auckland

First published in Great Britain 1988 by
Pan Books Ltd, Cavaye Place, London SW10 9PG
9 8 7 6 5 4 3 2 1
© Susan Shwartz 1988
ISBN 0 330 30401 1

Phototypeset by Input Typesetting London
Printed in Great Britain by Richard Clay, Bungay, Suffolk

Dedication

In memory of Morton W. Bloomfield, Professor of English and American Literature and Language at Harvard University

Surely there is a vein for the silver, and a place for gold where they fine it.
Iron is taken out of the earth, and brass is molten out of the stone.

But where shall wisdom be found? and where is the place of understanding?
Man knoweth not the price thereof; neither is it found in the land of the living.

Job 28:1–2; 28:12–13.

Acknowledgement

Much of what is now Chapter Twenty-one originally appeared as 'Dagger Spring' a short story written by Susan Shwartz and published in *Greyhaven*, an anthology of original short fantasy stories edited by Marion Zimmer Bradley (DAW Books, 1983). It has been substantially rewritten. I am grateful for permission to use the material.

Notes

Any writer who attempts alternative history owes a great debt to many sources of information. In *Byzantium's Crown* and *The Woman of Flowers* (the first two volumes in this trilogy), I have listed a great number of such sources, all of which were influential as I researched and wrote *Queensblade*. Chief among them for Egyptian ritual are *The Egyptian Book of The Dead*, translated and transcribed by E. A. Wallis Budge (Dover, 1967), and Joseph Campbell's *The Masks of God: Oriental Mythology* (Penguin, 1986). I am indebted to Gareth Knight's *The Secret Tradition in Arthurian Legend* for his account of Stone King (The Aquarian Press, 1983), though any transmogrifications of his work are wholly my own responsibility. And, if we're getting back to first causes, I am vastly obligated to the *Anathemata* of David Jones (Viking, 1965) and, of course, to Sir J. G. Frazer's *The Golden Bough*.

Chapter One

Midwinter snowdrifts tumbled outside Queen Olwen's hall, almost to the eaves. Within it, huddled forlornly on limp straw, lay the Queen's white bear. Its harsh breathing rustled and rattled in its wattled throat until its fur, thinning and yellowed with age and firelight, shook. The elegant head, with its long, pointed muzzle and the crafty small eyes that were filming over now, lay in Queen Olwen's lap; and her own gaze was very far away.

At harvest, the bear had started to weaken. Already it was old, almost as old as the Queen's son, Mor, now half a world away while his father drilled him to rule an empire and forget his home in the Isles of Mist. It was older than Mor's sister, Gwenlliant, whose long, wayward hair the fire touched with a splendour that her mother did not see. At times, Gwenlliant thought that Queen Olwen had not seen much of anything since her return from Byzantium to take up her crown here, in her home, once again. Except, of course, her lands. And now her bear. It was twenty, and it was dying.

The harvest had been meagre, the stalks and husks dry. When the farmers came to cast the Straw Man into the fires that blazed on every hill, they had burned high, and will o' the wisps had danced down the slopes and disappeared in the depths of the forests.

Queen Olwen's amber eyes stared past the dying bear into the firelight. How fiercely the needfires had blazed that autumn. Their glow had made the ancient trees of the hawthorn nemet seem so sere and dark of leaf. *A dreadful place!* Gwenlliant had said, and, grown woman though she was, refused to enter. Olwen's bear had groaned, and crept into this corner of her hall, spurning food, turning its head away even from Princess Alexa, who had dwelt among the great bears, and who loved them.

The bear will regain its strength with the snows, she had reassured Olwen, her sister by marriage. But even when the silent, gentle snow fell, softening the harsh stubble that pierced

1

each field in Penllyn of the Mists, the bear grunted and moaned. In winters gone by, the years when Mor and Gwenlliant were young, the bear would race them through the snow, pretending to nip at their legs. Now, the children were gone. Elen, Alexa's only living child, had withdrawn into her studies, her mother's daughter even to her silences. Of Olwen's own children, Mor had left for his father's city; Gwenlliant, though she remained in the land the Goddess had destined her to rule, was so remote that she, too, might as well be in Byzantium. Except, of course, when she tried to quarrel with Elen.

What had become of the loving children who had wrestled each winter with a bear the colour of snow?

Winter came, but now the bear refused to go outside. It lay in the straw, twisting and groaning as if its very bones ached. Its white fur dulled and fell out in patches. Yet it continued to follow Olwen about with its eyes until sight too began to fail, overwhelmed by the firelight, the shadow, and the ageing of a queen who had once been so fair that bards sang that where she walked, white blooms fell and the fragrance of spring rose up to greet her.

Now the Queen smelled of faded petals. *Weeds, most likely,* Olwen chuckled dryly to herself. Her hall, bare now of feasts, smelled not of flowers but of ashes and the pungent herbs burned to purge the air of the smells of the bear's old age. No one complained. No one would. For the bear had been brought to Olwen as a cub by Audun Bearmaster in token of her right to govern; and it was dear to all who knew her.

The fire roared up as the hall's doors swung wide.

'Gereint!' Alexa leapt from her bench. Though her daughter Elen was older than either the Prince or Princess, and silver streaked Alexa's long black hair, she was as supple as any girl as she darted towards her husband. He embraced her with his good arm; with the other, which a wound, taken three years ago on top of an older injury, caused to stiffen each winter, he smoothed back the strands, the dark and the silver, which always slipped free of her braids. He kissed her, and the way Alexa went pliant in his arms made Olwen glance away. Despite the season, her face heated. *Marric,* she thought. *Even when I am angriest at you . . .*

Alexa reached up to grasp her husband's shoulders, her eyes anxious until she saw that he wore his golden torque, but no circlet of kingship. 'How long have you lived among us?' he asked her between kisses on her mouth, eyes and hair, 'and still will not remember that to be a king among the tribes, a man must have no blemishes?'

Alexa's green eyes blazed, bringing a memory to the hall of more fruitful summers than the last. 'With four generations of their royal line to choose among, the Brigantes have found no heir. We send them our finest, and they spurn you?' Even after half a lifetime in Penllyn, she spoke with an accent, for she had been born a princess in Byzantium.

She stamped her foot, then clung to Gereint like a bride, laughing. 'It is true that I see no fault in you. So I am angry that they are fools and do not choose you. Yet truly, I have no wish for some tribe to ask you to rule, and for us to leave our home.'

Alexa's rippling, relieved laughter made Olwen raise her head and smile. Briefly, as sunlight might transform a dried flower, the Queen's smile reminded the others in the hall of her youth. Olwen's hair had been the colour of the harvest; and harvests had been golden then, far richer than now, when her hair had faded to russets and strands of frost. But still she possessed more than a ghost of her former splendour. She was thinner than she had been; her pale skin moulded itself over the strong, fine bones like goldwork on a harp. She had been this feeble once before, when she had miscarried and *Alexa dragged me from the battlefield and saved my life then, and afterwards*, Olwen thought, forcing herself not to flinch at the old memories. But she had been younger then, younger and able to recover and to conceive again.

'What of the other tribes? What of my sisters and cousins among the Iceni?' she asked.

Gereint turned towards the fire, making elaborate play of warming his hands as Alexa herself hastened to the tripod where the wine jar hung. Even Gwenlliant, who had been dreaming in the leaping bronze light, shifted restlessly. Her eyes met her cousin Elen's: golden eyes against blue; it was the golden eyes that glanced down first.

3

'Do not try to distract me, Gereint,' Olwen began, her voice deceptively low.

'He is cold, Olwen. It makes his arm hurt.'

'I know my brother. He has never complained of the cold. Or of anything else.'

The bear stirred and muttered in its uneasy waking dream. Elen knelt beside it and smoothed the matted fur on one wasted flank. 'It is too young to die like this,' she murmured.

Tenderly, Olwen laid the bear's head down and strode towards her brother, her green skirts swinging with her long steps. Anger brought back a shadow of her youth; the odour of flowers which yet clung to her grew stronger.

'Brother, I will have your answer.'

Gereint looked at his sister, then lowered his eyes, the same blue as his daughter's, though red-rimmed now from his long, icy ride back to the queen's hall and maenol. Alexa pressed against his side, offering comfort and support.

Gereint swallowed, then found voice. 'There will be hunger by spring.'

'Ah, no!' The cry came from Princess Gwenlliant. Her cousin Elen hissed in warning and reproach. Olwen eyed her daughter reprovingly. Well enough for Gwenlliant to lament hunger, when she sat warm and well fed, and shuddered at what she must do if she were to ward it away from the land.

The glances silenced Gwenlliant, though she glared hard at her cousin who had been heir before Gwenlliant's birth displaced her. Elen – who, except perhaps her mother, could guess what that one thought? Dark haired like Alexa, though with her father's blue eyes, she was usually silent, which made her easy to overlook in a hall full of Celts, who laughed when they had something to laugh at, and talked loudly whenever possible. It was too much to expect that, also like Alexa, she would be content with a place near the throne from which another woman ruled. But she listened, she studied, and she obeyed. Had she been the daughter of any woman but Alexa, Olwen would have worried.

Alexa is the one Imperial I can trust, and wouldn't the Goddess know it? She would have to be the sister of the man I trust least of all.

4

'We could ask aid,' Gereint said slowly, 'from the Empire. After all—'

You rule there too, if you would but trouble yourself. Olwen could all but hear Gereint's thought, which was all but a reproach to her. Gereint and the Emperor Marric were friends, Olwen thought with the usual stab of irritation that that reminder brought her. Man-like, they thought well of one another; and, once they had made the decision to respect one another, they did not trouble to reconsider. *I will not lower myself to ask*, Olwen thought. There were other things, however, that she had to ask.

'I do not think that you have told me everything,' Olwen said. 'I can see it on your face.'

Gereint looked down. 'I didn't want to tell you. There have been raids on the Saxon Shore against the Iceni. They lost their queen.'

'My brother finished Jomsborg twenty years ago!' Alexa cried, then hid her face against her husband's shoulder.

'Twenty years ago . . .' Olwen paused to let the time sink in. 'I was younger then, and the fields were bright. I remember.'

'No,' Alexa cut in. It had taken her many years to learn to interrupt the Queen like a proper Celt, but she relished the privilege. 'You do not remember. *I* remember. You had had a miscarriage, and until you conceived again, you made our lives miserable with this same lament about the wretched harvest.

'Despite her lack of control, I agree with Gwenlliant,' Alexa said, her voice as calm as the Queen's daughter's had been distraught. Olwen suspected that Alexa found rudeness in a queen's hall the next thing to blasphemy. 'Bad harvests can happen any time in a queen's reign. Wait until spring. It is too early.' Alexa broke off with a gasp. 'Too early.'

Her eyes went huge and blank. *Would she prophesy right now?* Olwen wondered. There had been years in which Alexa fell into trance as easily as into her husband's arms, which were wrapped about her now, warming her, supporting her. Alexa shuddered, fighting against the burden of vision. Finally, she drew a long, shuddering breath.

'What is too early?' Olwen asked. When Alexa was a girl, she had touched darkness. Like a woman who was poisoned by toadstools and therefore shunned all mushrooms, Alexa feared the darkness, yet found herself drawn to it, more sensitive to evil than even the ArchDruid Amergin.

Alexa shook her head. 'It's gone now. Just flickers of vision, and no more. But it is too early for what you plan, sister. Audun will come in the spring; and Audun will bring advice and perhaps a new—'

Olwen shook her head, as if the dying bear could understand this talk of the Bearmaster who would come in the spring and might bring Olwen a young, virile bear to replace the one that faded now, hour by hour.

'And if he does not?' she asked. She laid hand to the rough hilt of her long dagger, its black blade hammered from metal smelted from a fallen star, the crude, ancient blade hidden by wrought silver and fine leather and art.

Alexa glanced from Olwen to Princess Gwenlliant, then over to her own child, taller and sturdier than she, with a ruddy cast to her dark hair. Though Elen had her father's blue eyes, she looked no more like a Celt than Alexa herself.

'If he brings you no bear, then—' her voice broke – 'then, sister, that will be time enough to think of what you must do next.'

Alexa's eyes lit on her daughter, still kneeling by the bear. Olwen could see questions rising in those eyes like fish in a green pool, the speculation and the curiosity that were even more Alexa's heritage than the crown that she had renounced half a lifetime ago. 'Too soon for it to die too?' Olwen heard her mutter. Then she shook herself free of whatever question still troubled her and glanced at Olwen.

The two older women nodded at one another. Very carefully. They did not glance at their daughters. After so many years of wars, connivance and, at the last, peace, they hardly needed words to understand one another. *We may need that time*, Olwen knew Alexa was thinking. Knowing Alexa, Olwen would have wagered her emeralds that the smaller woman had already begun to spin a scheme that would embroil crowns and countries for the next ten years. Though she had exiled herself from her home half a lifetime ago, Alexa still had Byzantium in her blood. She could barely walk without considering the ramifications of each step: crush this blade of grass, or stumble over this rock; near this warrior, or avoid this merchant – each act had its separate meaning and consequence.

Life was simpler when I was a girl, Olwen sighed. The bear wheezed, and she lifted its head on to her lap once more to ease its breathing. *Simpler and richer*. The world had been filled with men and women she loved – Gereint, of course, the memory of their father Aillel . . . *my mother, and Rhodri*.

Even after twenty-five years and two children, Olwen's memories of her Druid lover and the daughter she had miscarried on a battlefield made her eyes smart as if she had walked through smoke. The Jomsborgers had cut the blood-eagle on him when he had ridden out alone to explain Penllyn's law to men who delighted in violating all law. Olwen had run mad then and would have died, except that Alexa pulled her back and healed her: Alexa, who had fought magic and madness herself and had declared herself unfit to wear the moon crown of Isis on Earth. Olwen's Greeks . . . first Alexa, then her brother Marric: first Olwen's enemy, and then, in a rite half-blood and half-prophecy, her husband, the Emperor of the Rhomaioi who ruled in Byzantium.

Perhaps that was the strangest thing of all, that their marriage lasted as long as it had. It had produced two children and, had either of them dared consent to remain for longer than a season every year or so in the other's realm, it might have produced more. Always, they welcomed one another passionately – and were just as passionately relieved when it came time for Marric to return East, or Olwen to leave Byzantium. *If we lived together more often, we would realize how badly suited we are*, Olwen mused. By the end of such a meeting, she and Marric invariably said that to one another. By now, it was almost a joke. Olwen winced. It *had* been a joke.

Strange lands and stranger crowns and, strangest of all, the gods and the customs. As a younger woman, Olwen had adapted; and it had been easier yet for her when her mother, Blodeuedd the Queen, had lived. Her fading, even the Beltane when she would choose to pass within the hawthorn nemet, turn queensblade against herself, and return her life to the Dark Goddess, had been long known, long planned for – not in the tortuous manner of the Byzantines, but forthrightly, as befitted a woman who was the Goddess' child.

That last year of Blodeuedd's life, Olwen had ridden with her about the land, had stood in the grove for the rites or entered the Druids' temples with their pillars marked with skulls. She had contemplated queensblade, the dagger of black iron that her mother took off only to bathe or sleep. On Beltane Eve, Blodeuedd would draw it to pierce her heart and let her blood flow upon the land. And then queensblade and the land itself would pass to Olwen until she, too, grew too old to bear them.

Olwen had listened to her mother and the Druids, had listened and raged, wept, but finally accepted, as she knew she always would. In the end, as she knew she must, she had stood by her mother in the nemet when her mother finally drew the blade for the land's sake. She had even watched the rite, though the Druids had assured her that she would lose neither power nor honour if, at the last moment, she glanced away.

I wanted to hurl it from me, but when Rhodri knelt and cleansed it in the earth, and offered it to me, what could I do but accept?

What could she do? She had accepted the dagger and wept; and he had comforted her. If Olwen had not miscarried, Rhodri's daughter would have been her heir.

Gwenlliant, who was her heir, had stormed and protested when, earlier in the year, Olwen had begun to speak of entering the grove. 'Barbarous', she called the very idea, until Alexa slapped her. Doubtless, she had learned the word from her father's court: Olwen remembered the stares and the whispers whenever she appeared robed and crowned beside the Emperor Marric as the Goddess Incarnate whom his people called Isis.

In the rituals, Marric was the God, Horus Incarnate, ruling for his father on the Horizon. But he rebelled against the royal magic and always had. *Do not push Gwenlliant*, Alexa had warned. *What if she tells my brother what you plan?*

He knows, Olwen had replied. *I told him . . . that night. When you joined our hands and prophesied we would conceive Mor.*

But Alexa had shaken her head, her eyes wise with her own knowledge and that of her inner guide, a seeress who was one reason that Marric feared the powers of the Horizon. He had not been able to prevent that woman's death. What would he do to stop Olwen's?

Praise the Goddess, his restraint has held. So far. The Isles had power to repel invaders, and Marric knew it. But if those powers had failed to stop Jomsborg, they would hardly restrain the man whose wife was the Goddess' favoured child. Let his patience snap, and Marric would call out his army, invade Penllyn, and fail magnificently – at least, she hoped that he would fail. She could not risk, however, that any of the punishment for his presumption fall upon her land: already it was gaunt and strained.

Though it hurt not to be able to confide in her own daughter, and to rely upon her as Blodeuedd had been able to rely upon Olwen, Alexa was right as always. Gwenlliant might look like Olwen, but in spirit she was her father's child – and Marric, Olwen thought with a smile that even now had twenty years' reluctant tenderness in it, spoiled her.

Once again the doors burst open with a gust of icy air that made everyone in the hall recoil. Sparks exploded from the central firepit, and Elen rose to fan them away from the Queen and her bear. As the smoke and fire sank down, there emerged first the Druids' long shadows, then the Druids themselves. The cold air had reddened their faces and frosted their hair; they wore only coarse robes of undyed wool. Amergin, who had survived at least eighty such winters, stood barefoot and oblivious in a puddle of snowmelt; the others wore light sandals.

'The rites?' Olwen asked. She expected, and received, no answer. 'I cannot come now.'

Amergin took a step forward. Olwen knew what custom and ritual demanded: she must enter the nemet; she must gaze into the Water of Vision, which did not freeze even in the deepest of winters; she must plead with the Horned King not to harm the land and intercede with the Lady that the sun come again, and the year turn back towards light and warmth. *Withered as I am, why should he heed me? I can neither command nor seduce him*, she told herself. *I am of more use here*.

But regardless of what Marric thought, Gwenlliant was *her* heir, young and lovely. Surely the Horned King would hear her prayers.

'Daughter,' she used the tone that meant that she would brook no opposition, 'you will go to the nemet in my place.'

Her daughter leapt up, her hands upraised as if to ward off the order. Her mouth opened on the usual protests.

The bear groaned and shifted. Olwen stifled a sigh. Gwenlliant's colouring, her tall slenderness, even her quick, impulsive disposition much resembled her own. But her rebelliousness and – a serious problem for a land in which the Queen was the Goddess' favoured child – her aversion to magic were gifts from her father. *Sweet Goddess, give her time*, Olwen prayed. *She will learn, she will learn to submit*. At least Gwenlliant *had* the magic in her blood. Olwen very much suspected that it slept in her son Mor (as the royal magic sometimes did for a generation), and she knew that his father was relieved.

'Go on,' whispered Elen, flicking back one long, thick braid. 'Move. Perhaps the Water of Vision will show you your next lover. What are you afraid of?'

Gwenlliant cast her cousin a look that should have charred the darker girl to bone. Seizing up the nearest plaid cloak, she strode stiff-backed from the hall, taller and more splendid than the Druids who turned her attack of temper into a procession.

Chapter Two

The sickle moon looked like the ArchDruid Amergin's knife, sharp and bright and cold. Gwenlliant laid her hand on the hilt of her own blade, brighter than her mother's sacred dagger and far less powerful. The chill of the night wind against her face, heated by rage and hearthfire, stung her cheeks and eyes. She took deep breaths of the sweet air, battling for the serenity that her mother, her aunt Alexa and Elen, that counterfeit of perfection, put on and took off as easily as she changed her bracelets.

She pulled the cloak tightly about her shoulders, grateful for the heavy warmth of the oily wool. It was not cold that made her shiver, but power. Tonight, the shortest night of the year, power quivered throughout the Isles of Mist like threads of living silver stretching across the icy fields, shimmering from ley line to ley line, to enmesh the land the way an armsmaster wraps a dagger's hilt in wire, or a jeweller binds an emerald in its setting.

The power reached out to enmesh her, to possess her, draw her into the ritual. She tossed her head as if to shake it free of a noose, and her ruddy hair floated about her face, as full of sparks as an amber necklace rubbed against silk or wool.

Think of the powers of the sun, she told herself. Sun on the harbour her father had taught her to call the Golden Horn. Sun on her hair, on green grass, sun on her mother's hair and crown and gems . . . no, don't think of that! Think of anything else, anything but the darkness and the cold towards which the Druids guided her, and towards which Olwen hastened as if running to an assignation with a long-absent lover.

One might, as Elen had jeered, see such a lover in the Water of Vision. But just as easily, one might see one's own burial place. And Gwenlliant had no desire to die. Not yet – and certainly not in that nemet where her grandmother had died, and to which her own mother, with terrifying earnestness, had ordered her to go.

They were all going to die! she thought, furious. Like that mangy bear, which had crept to the comfortable, warm hearth. Or like her Uncle Gereint, who might have ruled, but refused many offers until, finally, one last battle rendered him unfit to be a king. Or Alexa, born Imperial, who spent half her time in retreat to whatever otherworld adepts and priestesses might choose for their meditations. All of them, Gwenlliant assumed, equally harsh; all of them places in which Gwenlliant was as unnecessary as she was untalented. *This* world was enough for her, as it had been – *as it still is!* she protested – for her mother. But the world was changing. It was Olwen who should have been the centerpoise of this ritual as she was of their land.

But then (Gwenlliant tossed her head again) Olwen herself had betrayed them. She had admitted that she was growing older, and accepted ageing and death. She even made plans to hasten them, and Gwenlliant was part of her plans. And, for all the courage that had won Gwenlliant her father's cheers during a chariot race, she was afraid now.

It was too soon, Alexa had said, and her eyes had gone strange. All her life, Gwenlliant had seen her elders heed Alexa when her eyes went strange like that.

She stamped her foot and snow rose up about her boot. *She was not so fair that white blossoms fell upon her footsteps.* She kicked at the drifts, not quite daring to launch a kick strong enough that it would send snow flying at the backside of the Druid who ushered her towards the nemet. Maybe he would slip. Now, that was a thought that would make her father's eyes warm even as he fought to look stern. It was not that he scorned the gods. Far from it. But their priests – ah, that was another matter.

Gwenlliant almost laughed, but she knew that the very idea of laughing now would horrify her mother, her aunt and her cousin. Who would all probably know the instant she did it. *She had none of her mother's power to heal . . . not yet . . .* she remembered her Aunt Alexa's saying time after time, nor the interests that her aunt had shared with Elen. Hour after hour, they studied with the Druids, memorizing Goddess-only-knew what.

But what are my *powers?* When Gwenlliant realized that there would be no such hours for her, no descent into the shrine below the sacred mound, she had asked that of Olwen. *The land*, her mother had replied, *and you will know them when it is time*.

It was a pity Elen could not have remained Olwen's heir. The eldest of the three royal children in Penllyn, she had enjoyed being *Princess* Elen, had queened it royally over Mor, a year or two younger, and Gwenlliant, three years younger yet, until they grew taller than she and allied to prevent the tyranny. When had Elen realized that though she bore a royal title, she would have no realm to govern? Her mother must have warned her. That would have been like Aunt Alexa, who had spent her life as a princess when she might have ruled Byzantium. She had guided her daughter towards the magics, the silences and the discipline so important in her own life. Elen, though: Gwenlliant couldn't see her in a homespun robe, living in a grove. It was a shame that her father Gereint's arm made it impossible for him to be summoned to rule another tribe. Then Elen could be heir *there;* and Gwenlliant would not feel diminished and gawky by the elder girl's poise and knowledge.

Or, if Elen were heir to Penllyn, Gwenlliant could go free, could race her father's ponies in Byzantium, ride out with him, and play at ruling a court that was ready to worship her simply for being young and lovely, her father's daughter.

And her brother's sister. His bride, if the customs of the Pharaohs were to be followed. Gwenlliant suppressed a snicker that her father would have criticized as unworthy of a princess, the harshest reproof he ever needed to use. The Emperor Marric might wear the robes of Horus on Earth, but her father was a sensible man, and his true faith was bound up with his empire. An empire, Gwenlliant had long noted, that did not demand the sacrifice of his life while he was still in his prime. She had only to fall in with her father's plans and she could call that empire, and the moon crown of Isis-made-manifest, her own.

So why didn't she? Granted, her brother Mor was handsome enough. He looked like their father, whom everyone but Aunt Alexa thought was the most magnificent man in the world; and Gwenlliant suspected that he had learned early how best to please a lover – if not in Penllyn (which was where she herself had learned), then in Byzantium, where Mor's titles and wealth, if not his person, would draw women as a direction-finder from Ch'in drew iron filings. Mor never spoke or stepped wrongly. It was hard to call a youth docile, but when Gwenlliant thought of her brother, that was the word that came to mind.

Such a decision to marry would make her father rejoice, but it would pierce her mother's heart just as surely as the black dagger. Perhaps if she had grown up in Byzantium, had grown up thinking that it was right and normal for an imperial brother and sister to wed one another . . . but Olwen had visited her husband's capital as briefly as she dared, and had made sure that Gwenlliant grew up more Celt than Byzantine. And there was another problem. *What do I tell you, my father? That my mother would slay herself and would expect me, in turn, to turn the knife on myself; and that I prefer to wed my brother and leave my home than suffer that?* It was cowardly, unworthy of a princess who must learn not to rely upon her father to solve her problems for her.

She had no desire to see an eastern – a foreign – army in her home, even if father or brother led it. Not even invasion would save Olwen, her daughter was sure, if the Queen decided to sacrifice herself. And an attempt to do so would surely bring doom upon them all – as her father probably knew.

The hawthorn grove loomed before her. Though torches made the snow thick on the boughs glisten like memories of Olwen's hair in summer, nothing could lighten that place. Not even her memory of her last visit with her mother to Byzantium. Gwenlliant doubted that even the *bardd teulu*'s satires could have captured the zest and the fury of the quarrel she had overheard between Olwen and her father. That argument had been worse than a quarrel, Gwenlliant thought, less noisy and more passionate. It might have been war, or led to it. As always when she thought of it, her eyes filled. Tears spilled over and she blinked them away, glistening as they sank into the snow.

She had eavesdropped, of course. Olwen would have condemned that as typically Byzantine, and her aunt might have applauded, then demanded a report on what Gwenlliant had overheard.

'Not *my* daughter,' Olwen had spat at Marric. 'Look you, Alexa revolted from the idea of wedding her own brother—'

'Revolted? Lady, I thank you for your choice of words. Yes, Alexa abdicated. Her stubbornness – and yours – came precious close to making you lose a war,' her father had pointed out. 'Isis and Osiris are one flesh. Since the very pyramids were built, brothers have wed sisters, and ruled as Pharaohs.'

'Your parents were not brother and sister,' Olwen snarled. Gwenlliant's father was the only man who ever made her that angry, the only man who ever dared.

'And look how Alexa and I turned out. She, a dabbler in necromancy; I, a priest-king but no true priest.'

Shrinking against the cool marble, Gwenlliant had sweated and trembled. Her father never spoke of magic; for him to speak of it now, he must be as furious as her mother. *Please the Goddess they do not see me.* The voices rose again, rousing Gwenlliant from her trance of guilt and fear.

'That is the true wedding, the royal match . . .'

'No!' Once more, Marric's calm had infuriated her mother, and she stamped her foot, much as Gwenlliant herself did when she was angry, on the marble. Her voice rang out and echoed in the vast, high-ceilinged room with its mosaics of Isis, moon crown glowing, her white robes shining, standing between her son, Horus, the very sigil of the Falcon, and Osiris, splendid in the gravewrappings that only testified to his rescue by his sister-queen and his subsequent rebirth.

'Do you hear me, Marric?' she had cried.

'I should think,' Marric replied with the irony that always drove Olwen into a shouting rage, 'that the sailors in the harbour can hear you. And very instructive for them too, I should say.'

'Not my daughter! A son cannot inherit, so I freely agreed that Mor should be your heir. You have your son, *Emperor*. Leave me my daughter. Gwenlliant rules after me in Penllyn.'

Marric's irony deserted him. His hands tightened into fists, and his lips thinned and turned white. Hiding behind a door, Gwenlliant shivered as her elegant, powerful father sprang from his chair, erupting into the rage she knew that his soldiers marvelled at, and that he usually regretted once it had burnt itself out. In one such rage, he had even killed a Druid.

'Rules after you? *Dies* after you, lady.' He gestured at the dagger that Olwen never removed. 'If that filthy thing were lost, or you could not get to the grove . . .'

'Do not dare to speak of that,' Olwen hissed. 'Don't even think it! Unless, of course, you have decided that it has been too long since your last sacrilege.'

'By all the gods, lady, you try me too far!'

'By all the gods, husband, you have no right to call on the gods when you refuse them their due. You go through the rituals, I have seen you; but it is a service of the mouth, not of the soul.'

She turned angrily, and Gwenlliant shrank, head down, against the wall lest her mother see her. Despite that, she saw what her mother did not: her father's face, stricken and older; the way his mouth soundlessly formed her mother's name; and the way he flung out a hand as if to ward off a cunning, cruel blow or to pull her towards him.

'You will not stop me, Marric. Or – I swear it by my own blood – I shall turn the dagger on myself in the inmost shrine of Isis, and your Empire will abide the consequences.'

For a moment, Marric's hand, wearing the heavy ring of his office, trembled. Then, slowly, he withdrew it.

'Shall I alert the Autarch of the Fleet?' he asked; his voice harsh and hoarse.

'I think that would be best,' Olwen had replied with equal caution. 'It should not take long to prepare to leave.'

'Olwen, even an officer's wife travels with more ceremony than you, the Empress!' Her father had seized on an old, much safer quarrel with relief.

'Perhaps an empress requires it. But for the Queen of Penllyn . . .' Olwen shook her head. She moved past him, but he caught her by the shoulder. Gwenlliant could see how the fight went out of her, and she embraced him.

'I used to think that all the strength and pleasure of the world were in your arms,' she said. 'But it won't work.'

'I know,' Marric said; and kissed her once. It was a reverent kiss, such as one might give the feet of an image; and they both knew it. Withdrawing herself, Olwen left the room.

'Get in here! I know you're listening!' Marric shouted, and Gwenlliant almost fainted. But, as the doors were flung open and a veritable legion of logothetes scurried in, she knew he had only summoned his staff. She shrank into deeper hiding, knowing that this time, she had overheard things that were probably unforgivable. Their farewells at the ship were constrained. Olwen's face was white, the Emperor's like that of a statue, except for his eyes, which burned because, cursed as he had been, he was unable to weep.

The last time. Never again to see her rooms, or the sun on the harbour of the Golden Horn, the snarl of silk and gems in the markets, or the mad dashes to and fro of exotic, strangely garbed people. And you, too. Farewell, my . . . love.

Gwenlliant, crossing from dock to ship, reeled and almost fell. She had heard Olwen's thoughts. *If I tell her, I shall be as trapped as she, never to be free, and to die young.*

No, that was no memory with which to dispel Gwenlliant's fears. In entering the hawthorn grove, she walked towards their cause, and their core. The snow-laden branches sprinkled heavy, wet snow upon her head and shoulders as she brushed by them into the clearing. On the *gorsedd*, or royal mound, the snow lay softly, except upon the rock plug that guarded the entrance beneath the mound where Druids walked from this world into the next. Alexa had done so and wished her daughter Elen to do the same. Gwenlliant thought, at times, she might like to try it.

Before the rocks and snow, the Water of Vision shimmered unfrozen, untouched in the night. Gwenlliant drew a shuddering breath as the Druids guided her to kneel by it as if she were the sacrifice, and not the Princess whose vision was to complete their ritual.

Amergin approached her. No longer was he the kindly old man who had always been the grandfather that neither of her parents could provide. Stealthily, as if he had stolen it, Amergin drew out of his long, coarse sleeve a sprig of mistletoe. Sharp leaves and hard, poisonous berries should have gleamed like enamel on gold, but the leaves were fissured and cracked, the berries half rotted. Nevertheless, he presented it to Gwenlliant as if it were a treasure. She pricked her fingers on the barbs of one leaf. Three drops of blood fell on to the snow and the Druids murmured their satisfaction.

Amergin held out his hand to Gwenlliant. Though she backed away, nursing her wounded finger against her breast, she could not resist gesture and glance. Obediently she knelt on the icy rim of the Water of Vision.

The water bubbled, appeared to steam and cloud faintly. Alexa had never warned her of that! Unfit, inept, Gwenlliant scolded herself. She looked up, expecting Amergin's eyes to reproach her. But the old man frowned, not at her, but at the younger Druids, who muttered of barriers and perturbations.

'Try again,' Amergin told her. Dutifully, Gwenlliant stared into the water once more, making her will into a spear. Goddess knew, she was stubborn enough. A sense – there! – of furious resistance! She slashed out at it, and her will slipped past the barrier, much the way a lucky blow from a novice warrior might fell a man vastly more seasoned.

The water bubbled. Then it changed. In its depths gleamed

lights, icy rainbows shimmering on mountains of ice upon which white bears played; and each of the bears wore a crown. Gwenlliant blinked and the vision shifted, replaced by shining, long-bladed hawthorn leaves. Pushing his way through them – ahhhh, the young man Gwenlliant saw had fair hair and eyes the colour of sunlight on indigo. His eyes met hers and, despite the winter's cold, she felt the heated bemusement of desire.

She smiled and put out her hand to touch his face but, 'Do not destroy the spell!' Amergin ordered in an urgent hiss, and once again, Gwenlliant obeyed.

A white bear appeared behind him. Then man and bear disappeared, replaced by another of the damnable visions of the hawthorn grove. And in this one, the snow in the quiet aisles and corridors of the wood was spattered red, and a black dagger steamed on the ground.

'No,' Gwenlliant despised the whine she heard in her own voice. 'No. There has to be a better way. There has to be another way!'

She put out her hand as if she expected to part the hawthorn leaves she saw quivering in the water, part them and touch the face of the fair young man of her earlier vision.

'Do not touch the water!' hissed Amergin.

With a choke of surprise and fear, Gwenlliant started to withdraw. She had no desire to touch that water.

Abruptly, a gust of wind howled through the grove and sent Gwenlliant three steps forward, just as the resistance she had met earlier gathered itself and struck. The vision faded and the water steamed, then turned red and foul. Amergin stepped forward to catch her, lest she stumble into the pool. He chanted a few syllables that seemed to quiver up Gwenlliant's spine, and the red tinge of the water faded. Even as she collected her wits and her courage, the gust twitched the branch of mistletoe that she held into the pool. Then, as quickly as the wind rose, it died away.

'I'm sorry, I didn't mean it!' she whispered, hot with guilt.

'That was not your fault,' the Druid told her. 'Now, we wait for a token.'

Waves rippled from the pool's centre, threatening to lap over the icy stones that bordered it and flow down the *gorsedd* itself.

Water splashed Gwenlliant's feet. She had expected it to be icy, but it was warm. That very warmth drew a gasp from her, a thing of indrawn breath and frost in the lungs; and then the vision and the warmth dissipated at once.

Once again the water rippled and a vision formed in the pool. 'A test,' murmured one of the Druids. 'Princess . . .'

Gwenlliant wanted to whimper, but her pride forbade. Her mother was a warrior queen, her father almost a god. Whatever feeble thing she was, she would not be a coward.

Before her gleamed a weapon she knew well. How not? Every day, her mother belted queensblade about herself and removed it only to bathe or to sleep. It had been her mother's before it was Olwen's; and one day, as Olwen intended, it would pass to Gwenlliant as it had passed to Olwen, warm from the heart's blood of the woman who had worn it.

Then the earth rumbled. Several Druids went sprawling. With a crack, a tree buckled and toppled. Someone screamed as it hit him.

Amergin shoved Gwenlliant back from the pool. 'Run, child!' he ordered. It was not his command but the fear in his voice that made her panic. Her feet tangled in her heavy plaid skirts and she fell sprawling in the heaving snow among the Druids. She thrust herself back to her feet and bolted from the nemet, even as the ground rocked underfoot.

Outside it, a pony stood haltered and she ran towards it, snatching its reins and hurling herself on to its back before Amergin or his followers could forestall her.

'Come on, little sister,' her voice was harsh and breathy, as if she had wept for hours, 'let us be gone from here.' Her mother must be told of these things, she knew. But before Gwenlliant faced her, she needed time . . . she needed freedom . . . clean, safe air . . .

The pony ran as if it could understand Gwenlliant. Mile after mile it ran, its breath and sweat steaming in the cold air, until finally the night winds assuaged Gwenlliant's fears. The pony staggered, forcing her back to a consciousness of the animal she rode. By the time she reined in, the pony was badly lathered. Its head drooped and ropes of froth dripped from its jaws. Whispering praise and reassurance to the poor beast, Gwenlliant removed her cloak and draped it over its back, then walked back and forth with it, slowly, until its sides stopped heaving and she thought it might be safe to allow the pony to stand in a place sheltered from the wind.

For a wonder, she herself was not cold, as if she drew warmth and comfort from the land itself. Then she looked up at the stars, blooming against the blackness and the clouds of the winter sky. Below her the maenol lay huddled in upon itself. Gwenlliant's eyes watered, and her tears made the stars seem to wax and wane each time she blinked. The thrum of the blood in her temples combined with the wind and her fears, even the rough breathing of the pony, to produce a feverish music.

Abruptly, two ravens shrieked and swooped down towards her. Starlight glinted off their claws and beaks. Gwenlliant screamed and threw up her arms to protect herself from them. But they had no intention of striking. Instead, they perched on the nearest tree and watched her. Boldly, she met their eyes.

'And so you flee me, daughter?' The woman who spoke to her was heavily cloaked, a fold of cloth pulled over her head and overlapped so deeply that Gwenlliant could not see her face. Nor did she desire to do so. She raised her arm, and one of the ravens flapped over to use it as a perch, for all the world as if the raven were a fine hawk and its bearer a princess, rather than a hedgewitch who usurped the guise of the Goddess.

'I flee no one,' Gwenlliant told her.

'Then you admit that you endangered your pony's health because of your courage?' the woman's scorn cut deeply.

'I admit nothing!' Gwenlliant threw up her chin. 'I rode out for air. I need no help.'

'Do you not?' asked the woman. 'I think that the time will come when you beg for it. Nevertheless, I will leave you a gift, if you have the strength to take it.'

'No!' Gwenlliant snapped, and the tall woman faded into the trees.

'Well spoken! I think I may enjoy this one,' declared a voice that was deep and resonant, but oddly hollow.

A tall figure, dressed in dagged leathers of browns and ochres, strode from between a cleft in the tumbled rocks of which the hill was made. The blade he bore and the helmet upon his head shone bronze. Upon the helmet also gleamed traces of ivory, wrought in the shape of the horns that a stag in its prime might display to all his lesser fellows.

'You will not flee me, will you?' that voice asked. Gwenlliant found its tone irresistible. Wordlessly, she shook her head. Despite her fears and her good sense, she realized that at some point, she had begun to walk slowly – but not slowly enough – towards the man who stood with his hand outstretched. Beyond him came the stamping and whickers of a herd of horses, tended by men whose forms and faces flickered in the pale light. In an instant longer, Gwenlliant would have no choice but to grasp the King's shadowy hand, no choice but to remain here, in the darkness, the cold, and the peace.

He drew closer and she could see the reddish gleam that seemed to be all that he had for eyes, like firelight glowing through a skull. His face was long and lean, his skin very pale.

'Skreeee!' Like a flash of sunlight after a long, violent thunderstorm, a hawk dived from the clouds, flying between Gwenlliant and the shadowy King. The man backed off, but the hawk took up its perch on the branch of a tree that Gwenlliant remembered and watched her closely.

Now that Gwenlliant could study the hawk, 'A falcon,' she whispered.

'Let it go,' said the man or the King, whichever he was. 'We have other concerns. You have ridden far and hard. Are you perhaps hungry?'

What was that sudden savour in the air? Gwenlliant sniffed once, then again. Her mouth was watering. Mead, rich with herbs and honey, and roasting meat – a veritable feast. Oppressed by the smells and the ghosts in her mother's hall, she had eaten very little that night. Now, she found that she was ravenous.

As she turned towards the source of the delectable odours, half a hundred men and women emerged from the grove and laughingly surrounded Gwenlliant and drew her towards the food.

'Go away!' cried a tall, pale figure to the man crowned with antlers and bronze. 'This is not your time!' He flung out an arm in a warding gesture between Gwenlliant and the dark King, who laughed and held out his hand to take hers. The red gleams that were his eyes shone more brightly; the warmth and savour of the food Gwenlliant smelled brought tears to her eyes.

'Touch that food, and you will never return to the world of men,' said the stranger. 'Child, you should have remained where you were safe,' said the figure. A light gleamed about it . . . no, about him . . . and he seemed fairer than human. 'You are your mother's child, daughter of the Goddess. How should I permit you to come to harm?'

Gwenlliant shook her head. *But it is permitted that my mother contemplate death*, she thought. For the first time in her life, she understood her father's rage when magic intervened in his life and warped the fabric he had struggled so long to weave.

'I realize that this is the worst of all times to ask, but will you trust me, Princess?'

Trust: she had trusted her father, who planned to wed her to her brother Mor. Trust: she had trusted her mother, who ordered her off to the Druids' grove, from which she had fled – straight to this field of unknown, potentially deadly, powers. Trust: she might, still could, blindly have follow the Horned King into whatever realm he governed during the days of the year when he was not free to roam the haunts of mankind. That had been done before; once, when Alexa was in the mood for confidences – *or when, more likely, she thought that some advantage was to be gained by them* – she had spoken of a friend who had so chosen.

To ride with the Hunt . . . perhaps that would release her from her mother's plans for her to rule after her, yes, and die after her too. She took a step forward, holding out her hand for that of the Horned King.

'It is not *your* time,' the King told his rival. 'Nor will it ever be.'

'Princess, fight for yourself!' gasped the man. A sudden memory of the Water of Vision, lapping out towards her feet, leapt into her thoughts, then was overwhelmed by a memory from childhood . . . *she had waded out too far, and the undertow caught and tripped her. Even as her cousins screamed, 'Stay calm!' her father had shouted and hurled himself after her. Despite the water, his skin was warm and his heartbeat quieted her fear.* If she rode with the Horned King, she would never see him again. The King laughed. *I can do more for you than a father.*

'Princess, think of the grove!' The urgency in the pale stranger's voice whirled her around to look fully at him for the first time. The blighted mistletoe, the resistance in the water, the fallen tree, the heaving earth . . . and now this Horned King. She had a sudden, flashing image of Alexa flinging up a hand and slashing out with all her craft at the Horned King. *You* had *your chance, and now you are old*, he told her, and she fell back, white, upon the furs of her bed, her eyes glazed with exhaustion and despair.

If Alexa feared, if Alexa sought even at this distance to protect her . . . Gwenlliant withdrew her hand – the one she had pricked with the mistletoe, and stood, clasping it to her breast. The Horned King, emboldened, caught at her shoulder. His touch felt more like bones or branches than the warmth of a human hand, and she shook it off.

'Princess, thank all the gods,' breathed the newcomer. His hair was fair, his face and the clean lines of his shoulders fairer still. And his eyes were the fitful blue of the summer sea, stirred by wind and cloud. He was a creature of her own world, of daylight, of health: beside him, the Horned King and his creatures grew pale, and the odour of the feast they had laid to tempt her seemed over-rich, almost charnel.

'Are you afraid now?' asked the newcomer.

Gwenlliant brushed a hand over her face. The unease that had dogged her all night, even in her mother's hall, was gone. The wind that made her shiver and impelled her towards the other's warmth and welcome was sweet and fresh, without the tension and the miasma of some brooding and angry power that had plucked at her nerves for – how long? Gwenlliant could not tell. But for the first time, perhaps since she had heard her mother and father quarrel so fiercely, she felt warmed and at rest.

'I will trust you,' she promised the newcomer. 'But I do not know what to do.'

'Just follow me.'

The pale Prince held out a hand and drew Gwenlliant towards

the hill. The Horned King and his followers had vanished. In their place was a ring of splendidly garbed men and women, all of whom appeared to float upon the ground rather than dance.

A moment later, she too was singing, laughing and dancing, as if she had known the people who swung her from hand to hand all her life – until her partner accepted a gold-trimmed drinking horn from one of the dancers, drank from it in salute and in token that it was safe, then offered it to her. He watched as she took it, his eyes bold. Deliberately, Gwenlliant took and turned it so that when she drank, her lips rested on the horn where his had touched.

The mead it held was thin, very sweet, but fiery-potent. Gwenlliant gulped at it, gasped, then drained the horn. She could feel the liquor it held burn in her throat, heat her belly, and make her feel simultaneously as if she could fly, and as if she dared not move. Overhead, the ravens screamed a song, and the falcon that had saved Gwenlliant watched.

'Well?' asked the Prince.

Gwenlliant shook her head. The heavy plaits of her braids constrained her, and she raised her hands to pull her hair loose, down about her shoulders as the Prince watched, appreciating the lines of her arms and breasts as she unbound the tresses that swept almost to her knees. Again, she tossed her head, held out her hand imperiously, and led the smiling man back into the dance of which he was master. Its figures became more and more frenzied until, finally, her partner snatched her from the figure that they had completed and lured her from the dancing circle into the woods.

He drew her close and kissed her, not considering the possibility that she might dislike or fear him. Nor did she. The touch of his lips almost stung, and she trembled in his arms. Her lips warmed under his, and she let him lead her to a patch of ground where the snow had melted. He shrugged off a cloak which shone with colours in patterns which Gwenlliant knew she would never remember, and laid it on the damp soil. Embracing her, he lowered her to lie upon it.

Though it was scarcely the first time she had lain with a man, surely it was the strangest, she thought, before all thought left her. His caresses made her cry out and arch her back against the earth and his knowledgeable hands, but their joined bodies were just one more figure in the dance which went on outside their resting-place. She knew that she had cried out, and she thought that her lover had too. Afterwards, he had sighed and hidden his face between her breasts while she stroked his hair and rubbed his neck until his breathing slowed.

Finally, they lay staring up at the vault of the stars, and the stranger who loved her pointed out the patterns of their dance. She spared them a glance, preferring to see them reflected in her lover's eyes.

'Will I meet you again?' she asked. Her voice came out plaintive, too girlish. *Now he will think I am a child.* But he did not seem repelled.

'Do you want to?'

She nodded, rubbing her face against the warmth of his chest.

'Then you will. I cannot promise when, or in what guise. But for now, sleep in peace.'

He turned her chin up in his long, unscarred fingers, and kissed her eyes. Gwenlliant slept – and woke alone, except for the beasts, wild cat and deer, who couched peaceably nearby and watched her as if they were a guard of honour. Though it was winter, the morning after the longest night of the year, Gwenlliant lay on green grass, covered by a cloak she had never seen before. But all around her bed lay snow, unmarked by as much as a bird's tracks, let alone a man's footprints.

As the pale sun finally rose, Gwenlliant rode back into the maenol. Handing the reins of her borrowed pony to the grooms, she strode towards the dining hall, heavy with the scents of ashes and incense, the feral reek of the dying bear and the flower-scent of the ageing queen.

Only Olwen remained in the hall, sitting in the straw. In her lap lay the bear's heavy head. Idly, absently, her fingers stroked its straggling fur. Now it fought to breathe, a sound so much like sobbing that Gwenlliant wanted only to flee.

'Mother?' Gwenlliant called. Would Olwen blame her for fleeing the nemet? What else would she know of? Her words with the Goddess, the test of will with the Horned King, or the dance on the hill, and the strange, fair man who had rescued her and been her lover throughout the longest night of the year?

Perhaps she knows already. She sent me out to the grove. She was willing to risk losing me for the land's sake. If I had not met . . . she had no name for the youth who had been her lover on the cold hillside *. . . the Wild Hunt might have taken me. Was it a test, or a gift from the Goddess?*

The odour of dried flowers rose over the flatness of ash, age and illness as Olwen rose and came towards Gwenlliant. She knew how she must look, her clothing stained from her wild flight from the nemet, the dancing, and from being tossed aside, her hair tumbled, most probably with twigs caught within its coils, her eyes a little wild from the night's fears and passion, and deeply underscored by nightshadows.

Olwen reached out to touch the girl. From Gwenlliant's hair, she drew a white blossom and showed it to the girl before she kissed it. 'It appears that you fared well,' she shrugged. 'I remember . . .' her eyes warmed at an old memory. 'This rose, child. May I keep it?' At Gwenlliant's puzzled nod, she tucked the flower into her belt.

Behind her, the great bear shifted and whined in the straw.

'He is dying,' Olwen's voice came thickly. 'Do you remember how, when you were little, Alexa and I would set the bear to guard you, and Mor, and Elen?' Tears rolled down her face and splashed on to her hands as they caressed the beast. 'I thought he would want to see dawn just once more. Not that he can see much any more. But he is old, and earth-wise. He knows when the sun rises.'

Gwenlliant caught her breath. Forgotten, or almost forgotten, was the ecstasy of the night just past. But perhaps Olwen knew of it. *Perhaps her sending me with the Druids was a gift, not a command. She must know what rides the hills of her realm.*

'What can *I* do?' asked Gwenlliant as her mother dashed a hand across her face.

'What can you do?' Olwen echoed, as if from a vast distance. Suddenly and incongruously, she smiled.

'What can you do besides what you have already done, and done well? You overcame the Horned King and met . . .'

The Prince who had saved and wooed her was magic, some

fugitive from the hills or the Otherworld, and hence no fit husband for her, or any other daughter of earth, Gwenlliant started to protest.

Olwen smiled, a pale, weary shape of the lips. 'Go to sleep, my dearest. Just go to sleep. I must care for my bear.'

Gwenlliant flung her arms about her mother and kissed her. Then she bent to stroke the dying bear's muzzle.

'Go quickly,' Olwen whispered; and Gwenlliant saw her draw queensblade. One shrewd stroke across the throat, and the bear could be released to run free in the forests of which, doubtless, it dreamed, or to slide on the ice floes of whatever realm might receive it when its soul was released from its flesh.

Outside the hall, the air was cold and sweet. The bear made no outcry as the Queen ended its burdensome life; but the Queen did. Gwenlliant heard her; and she, who had feared neither the Horned King nor the lover who had snatched her from him only to cast her into more strangeness, fled, lest she hear her mother's hopeless weeping.

Chapter Three

Spring came late to Penllyn that year. 'But look how far north we are,' Gwenlliant whispered hopefully to Elen, who had just returned from several twelve-days on Deva, the Druid Isle. She had returned even more silent than usual, almost clinging to her mother's skirts as if she were a much younger girl. She looked thin and pale, so worn that she started like a bird that reapers frightened from its nest in the fields; her mother and Olwen were unusually tender with her *as if*, Gwenlliant thought, *she has fought a battle no one bothered to tell me of*.

Gwenlliant and Elen had spent their lives squabbling and competing. But now, Gwenlliant was surprised at how much she had missed her cousin, at how important a task she was finding it to make her smile. She pointed out the health of the fieldworkers, the way the cattle were fattening, and that leaves and buds were rich and green throughout the land until Elen's raised eyebrows made her aware that her voice had become shrill and over-eager. She looked again and saw bruises on the leaves, blight on the buds; many of the flowers blossomed, true, but their petals were pale and stunted.

'Stop trying to make things look all sweet and safe!' Elen told her, and her eyes flashed with their old disdain for Gwenlliant's opinion. Their familiar antagonism shattered whatever momentary kinship might have grown up again between them. *At least, though, Elen no longer cowers as if she expects a beating. I have done that much.*

When Elen quirked an eyebrow – *well, aren't you going to insult me back?* – Gwenlliant only laughed and ran off. Byzantines, Gwenlliant thought, turned to melancholy even more quickly than did Celtoi. And Alexa always had had a talent for discerning shadows even in the brightest sun. It appeared that Elen had inherited it. For Gwenlliant herself, well, she had an hour's leisure, and she planned to spend it on the hillside where she could watch the riders who took Sarn Elen, the road built by the wise Queen for whom her strange cousin was named, up to the Queen's door.

Though the morning had been cool and overcast, by noon the sun was warm enough for Gwenlliant to shed her cloak. She freed her hair from its clasps and smoothed it out, pleased with the way that the sunlight rippled in its deep, russet waves. She lay back on her cloak and stretched, one hand going out to touch the grass as if it were the fur of a much-loved animal.

The sun shone through into her eyes until she closed them and saw bright coins and gems of light inside her eyelids. Did she think she was her father's sigil, the hawk, to stare into the sun without flinching? She wriggled her shoulders against her cloak, under which she could feel the cool dampness of the earth. It was a great pity, she thought, yawning, that no man stood watching her . . . *pale hair, pale skin and a touch like fire*, she remembered from her winter night spent dancing on the hill. After that night, she had been sure that she would conceive, young as she was, but . . . very few lambs or calves had been born yet, either. Spring came late in Penllyn, regardless of Elen's gibes.

The sun grew warmer, and Gwenlliant drifted into pleasurable reveries, then into sleep, until a bird's cry jerked her upright. Even though this place was guarded by blade and by magic, she drew her dagger with a speed that her father and brother would have approved, and crept to the crest of the hill. The Iceni had hurled back raiders, she knew, and strange men had been seen riding north, leaving trampled fields and fire and blood behind them before they were destroyed. If any had reached this far north, she told herself, she would have heard of it. But a long train of men and horses wound up Sarn Elen towards the walls of the fortress. Who could it be? Gwenlliant squinted against the bright sunlight. There! Leading the parade, mounted on the largest horse Gwenlliant had ever seen, was the huge figure of Audun Bearmaster.

A shadow fell upon her face, and she looked up to see a hawk circling. Sunlight glinted on its feathers, making head and wings glow as if it wore the crown and necklaces of an emperor.

'Gwenlliant!' A wind brought Elen's call, high-pitched to carry far, up the hill as the girl ran towards her.

'It's Audun!' Gwenlliant cried. 'Come up here, where you can see him ride in!'

After winter, followed by the spring rains that made travel by land a muddy impossibility – and about as pleasant as the sea voyage north to the Orkneys – Penllyn, and especially the young people, rejoiced when the first traders came. Laughing and breathlessly anticipating what goods Audun might bring, Gwenlliant and Elen flung themselves down on the ridge to watch the procession.

'Wait,' Gwenlliant put a hand on her cousin's shoulder. Suddenly chilled, she wished she had not left her cloak lying behind her in the grass.

Elen nodded, biting her knuckles thoughtfully. 'It's all wrong,' she declared.

'What's all wrong?' Gwenlliant snapped.

'Let's not fight for no reason. You see it too, don't you? Look at Audun's train. Those aren't all Aescir, don't you see? Some of them are Imperials, your brother's troops, maybe, plus a few . . . no, I can't place them. But look again. Anywhere in that train, do you see a single hint of a white bear?'

Gwenlliant muttered a few words she had learned from her brother, and covered her mouth with her hands. Elen was right: that was why she had shivered; that was why Audun's train of armed men and merchants looked subtly wrong. No half-grown white bear frisked behind the Bearmaster's horse; no bear cub bounced along in his arms, or with any of his men.

'And there're wounded men, too,' Elen mused. 'Mother was right . . .'

'About what?'

'She says I can't talk about it. Not yet.'

Avoiding one another's eyes, Elen and Gwenlliant rose and brushed grass and dust from their skirts. Gwenlliant hooked her foot up under her cloak, lifting it towards her hand, and dragged it after her as they started down the slope.

'There's mother!' Elen hissed.

'We'd better run to greet them,' Gwenlliant agreed. 'We always did, remember? And we had better smile, too, or they'll see it!'

They had barely time to smooth their clothing and stop gasping for breath before Audun and his men rode into the maenol itself. Alexa awarded each of them a narrow-eyed glance, but said only, 'Each year, Audun looks more and more like one of his bears. And so much older.' She sighed. Before Alexa had come west to the Isles of Mist, she had lived among the Aescir.

Audun had grown even more massive than Elen and Gwenlliant remembered. His hair and beard were so long that his heavy gold chain tangled in the thick white strands. Ponderously, he dismounted, let out his breath in a long, long *whuff* of relief, and, when Elen, anticipating Gwenlliant's task, brought him a horn of ale, drank gratefully until he emptied it and handed it back to her.

She bowed properly and turned to leave, but he held caught her hand and drew her to stand close to him. 'You look much like your mother,' he said, and beckoned to Alexa. She ran to him and flung her arms about him, as far as they would go. He patted her back, then tugged her hair lightly to compel her to raise her head.

'Tell me I chose wisely for you, daughter,' he commanded her, smiling. Audun always greeted Alexa with that question. Long ago, Gwenlliant and Elen had agreed that it was an odd question to ask Alexa, who had the courage to contradict Olwen and Amergin the ArchDruid, and come out the winner.

But Alexa only laughed. 'You know you did,' she told Audun, as she always did.

'You think my daughter looks like me?' Alexa asked Audun. 'I think that she is far prettier. She is not as thin, and, see, she has her father's height, his eyes . . .'

To Gwenlliant's surprise, Elen grimaced, her usually pale cheeks flushed.

'Crying again, Alexa? I thought that you wept out all your tears on your way here, so many years ago.'

'It is just that I am so glad to see you, and so re—'

'So relieved? Indeed, I have got much older; no, do not contradict me, child. I know I have got older. My joints ache now when I am near water, which means that they ache almost all the time. I am too old, I fear, for the long trip to Finnmark . . . But do you think I would leave without saying farewell to you?' He kissed Alexa's cheek. 'Which I am, most definitely, not doing now.'

To Gwenlliant's surprise, the older woman not only permitted the caress but returned it warmly. 'Olwen waits for you in the hall,' she said, and linked her arm in his. Before she led him up the well-worn path, she leaned forward.

'Princess,' she told Gwenlliant formally, so she knew she had incurred another minor disgrace with her tardiness, 'if you need Elen's help to make the Bearmaster's kinsmen comfortable, you have only to ask. There are injured men to set at ease, too.'

– *I know how to welcome my mother's guests!* – Gwenlliant bit back her sullen thoughts. – *And I was about to do it!* –

– *See that you do*, – Alexa retorted. To Gwenlliant's surprise, her lips did not move, and a definite satisfaction coloured her thoughts.

'Since when,' Alexa asked, 'have Imperials and Romans joined the *var*?'

Gwenlliant blinked her eyes at Elen, hoping that the other girl would not disappoint her. 'The *var* is the pledge that all Aescir make to one another through the Bearmaster,' Elen whispered. 'Once, before she was married, mother almost took it, but . . . hush! I want to listen!'

'Your nephew Prince Mor asked if I would guard them on their way north, since they are so small and feeble,' Audun said, his eyes glinting slyly.

Alexa laughed and pretended to cuff at him. 'Those weaklings look as though they put up a fight,' she remarked. 'Or perhaps two fights. But you would know that better than I.'

Audun nodded gravely. 'The land is full of reavers,' he said. 'The Druids say that their cone of power has weakened.'

Alexa shook her head. 'I think that what you must say is best saved until the Queen, too, can hear it.' Deliberately, she closed her eyes and drew a deep breath, as if pulling strength up from the earth through the soles of her feet and into herself until she had mustered energy enough to smile. It was a fine trick, Gwenlliant had always thought, a trick that Elen had mastered but that she found all but impossible.

'How is Gerda?' Alexa asked, 'I want to hear all about Staraja Ladoga and my friends there.'

'Staraja Ladoga thrives,' said Audun, 'You may not believe it, but the girlchildren coax until their fathers build them model catapults; and then they quarrel over whose turn it is to be Alexa and save the town from Jomsborg pirates.'

'Oh no!' Alexa laughed, her hands rising to her cheeks.

'Have I ever lied to you, Alexa? Aside from that, Ingebjorg has a grandson; and Gerda . . . well, this autumn our first great-granddaughter came. She is named Halldis. Yes, I thought that would please you.'

Smiling (despite that beard of his, one could always tell when Audun smiled) and trading stories with Alexa, he strolled up towards the hall. Olwen appeared at its doors, a great honour to her guest, and embraced him. She had to notice that he brought her no new bear, but her smile was as wide and unforced, her manner as warm and unconscious as if such a beast capered at Audun's heels.

Gwenlliant glared impartially at the fine day, Alexa's back and Alexa's daughter.

'You saw,' Elen said, softly, as Elen usually spoke. 'No bear.'

'I see that if we do not welcome the Bearmaster's people, we will hear of it,' Gwenlliant retorted. She gestured at waiting servants and gave orders for ale to be brought, for guest housing to be made ready, for fires to be kindled, and hot water and fresh linen to be left there. 'And I do not want to be scorched by my mother's tongue. Or yours.'

In the next instant, Gwenlliant could have bitten her tongue. That was the perfect opening for too-perfect Elen to rebuke her for speaking so of either woman. To her surprise, however, Elen wrinkled her brow. One of the tall Aescir walked by, and quickly she smoothed her expression into a smile; but it was a smile of anger.

'They treat us like children,' Elen observed. 'Did you hear them? "She is even prettier than I." I hate it!' She stamped her foot, and the gesture made her look absurdly like her mother.

'And telling us how to welcome guests,' Gwenlliant flashed her cousin a smile that was closer to their old comradeship than she had done for years. ' "See that you do it," ' she mimicked Alexa.

'What?' Elen gasped.

'You heard what your mother said, didn't you?'

'Yes,' Elen said. 'I heard it. She and I speak mind-to-mind. I didn't know you could do that too.'

Gwenlliant dropped a horn of ale and stepped back before it spattered her skirts. 'Neither did I.' Elen spent much time in the Druids' groves, learning their arts, a chore that Gwenlliant had always feared and shirked. It was natural that she would learn to touch the minds of others. But Gwenlliant herself? She had received a queen's schooling in law, arms, language and healing, not in the powers which Elen studied.

'Your power is coming upon you,' Elen said. Her blue eyes filled, and she squeezed them shut, opening them, finally, with a fine imitation of her mother's curiosity. 'I wonder if you can heal, yet, the way your mother does.'

'If I have power, does it disappoint you?' Gwenlliant snapped. 'I assure you, I did not expect to learn magic. Beyond the fact that my mother is the daughter of the Goddess, I thought that any power in my line slept in me—'

'As it does in your brother Mor? My mother and Amergin both say that sometimes it sleeps for a generation in the royal line. They think that that is so with Mor, because your father . . . because the Emperor will not . . .' uncharacteristically, Elen stammered.

Gwenlliant gestured impatiently. She had pieced together her father's story. Cursed the night he won back his throne, he mistrusted magic, yet was plagued by it, fated to love and to lose the people it touched.

'I know,' she said. 'Father is glad about it too. But it's different for me. I need to heal, but . . .'

'Like your mother, you will be the Goddess' favoured daughter. That your power wakes now . . .'

'Simply means that now Penllyn has two Princesses that share it, you and I,' Gwenlliant flared. 'But you never have forgotten that you were heir before I was born – or forgiven me for it! Have you?'

The smaller, darker girl laid a hand on Gwenlliant's arm, but she shook it off. 'Cousin, do you truly think I envy you your mother's crown and queensblade?' Elen asked. 'You have been trained in logic. You should know better than that.'

Then what is it that you do want?

Elen stepped back, wincing, her hands covering her ears. 'I wish I knew, cousin; indeed, I wish I did. But one thing is true,' she said, and turned away, 'I do not want your place. I shall fetch the healers – unless you want to try healing the wounded yourself.'

Her quick footsteps made her seem to flee. And this strange new understanding of hers warned Gwenlliant not to press Elen further. Though Elen kept her own counsel, if she were provoked, she would speak her mind. And suddenly, Gwenlliant did not wish to hear it. She had sensed that the tears in the other girl's eyes were not tears of anger or chagrin, but of pity.

She turned towards the wounded men whom warriors had lifted from their horse-litters and placed on furs upon the ground. One had fainted, but the other watched her as she bent to examine the gash in his arm. As she laid a hand on the arm to hold it steady, the air quivered and she smelled flowers. She raised her head – *where is mother?* and the scent faded.

The injured man blinked at her. 'It doesn't hurt,' he murmured, then grinned in astonishment. 'Not any more.' White teeth flashed against his olive skin. His accent was strange, and he had neither the height of the Celtoi nor the fine-boned grace of the Egyptian-born.

'I thought a warrior never admitted to pain,' Gwenlliant could not resist saying. She had removed his pain; that much was true. But she could not heal him. Judging from his pleasure in simply being freed of pain, he had not expected to be healed. Only one people in the Empire were that pragmatic, she realized. The man whose arm she bound up must be a Roman, one of the hard-headed engineers, traders, soldiers and sailors who bustled throughout the West. Before Gwenlliant's ancestors ruled, she knew, the Empire had belonged to Rome, not Byzantium; and Imperials still occasionally called themselves Rhomaioi. But the city built on seven hills was a trade city now, not a centre of religion or military might.

You cannot heal. Not yet, came a treacherous voice from within her, and she shivered.

'I am a sailor, but no warrior, Princess,' the man told her. He gathered himself to rise, then sank back. A dark flush crept up along his cheekbones. 'Of your kindness . . .'

Gwenlliant lifted his good arm over her shoulder. Slowly, carefully, in order not to jar his injured arm, she stood. The man staggered forward an uneven step or two, then steadied himself against her.

'Why do you stare at me?' Gwenlliant asked.

The man blinked at her and then laughed. 'Girl, if you do not yet know why a man would stare at you – but it is not just the fact that you look like something that a poet, not a trader, whose words falter like my arm, might describe. You remind me of someone . . . have we not met before?'

The old, foolish question drew a laugh from Gwenlliant. 'Not that I know of. But I will gladly let you try to convince me,' she told him.

He looked down at his bandaged arm. 'Lady, I regret I cannot offer you a hand to escort you into your mother's hall,' he said.

'You are, I suspect, more than a handful. But . . .' lifting his uninjured right arm from her shoulders, he gestured her forward.

' . . . almost completely rebuilt Birka,' Audun was saying as Gwenlliant entered. 'With the trade in fur and amber resumed, they expected pirates . . .'

Gereint leaned forward. 'We've had attacks in the Isles, too. The Iceni have borne the brunt of them.'

Gwenlliant's Roman winced. 'Does your arm hurt?' Gwenlliant asked, and guided him to a seat. *I should cut his meat for him*, she thought.

'Thank you,' he whispered.

'Do you need help?'

'Certainly not!'

Stung, Gwenlliant withdrew. She should have known he would refuse.

'We eliminated Jomsborg as a fighting force twenty years ago!' Alexa cried. She held out her hands and reddish light began to rise from them, to form into a nimbus about her. 'What must we do this time? Attack, take the place and burn it, then sow the land with salt?'

'Alexa,' Gereint laid a hand on her arm, and she subsided.

Standing beside Gwenlliant, Elen sighed. 'That was twenty years ago,' she whispered. 'We have to think of *now!*'

Gwenlliant nodded. Quietly, they seated themselves as close to their elders as possible in order to listen.

'Fortunately,' Audun cut in, ignoring Alexa's outburst, 'the Empire has taken a hand. I had presented my two youngest sons to the Emperor, so I was in Byzantium at the time. Prince Mor has been sent into Gallia Belgica with two moirae and the auxiliaries. He should be coming north, too . . .'

'How is my son?' Olwen asked.

Audun shook his head, grinning reminiscently. 'Lady, he is much like his father at that age. His personal guard would follow him to . . . you call it Tuat, Princess?' he asked Alexa.

She nodded, grimacing. 'His guardsmen are your kin, I suppose? Then Mor is probably brave to the point of insanity, and beyond that, he is probably drunk.'

When at least three people shouted her down, she laughed, drank, and subsided.

'Go on,' Olwen demanded. For the first time in many months, she looked happy.

'The Emperor says that his son is a better driver than he was at that age. I believe he was *very* pleased with some horses that Prince Mor purchased last year, when he was stationed in the Eastern themes. He claims they come from the land called the Roof of the World, and have more endurance than any other breed.'

'Did you see them?' Gereint asked.

Olwen paused with her drinking horn halfway to her lips. 'I have not seen my son for over a year. This autumn, I thought that I must go to Byzantium to see him. But perhaps I could simply visit my kinswomen to the south, then cross into Gallia to meet Mor.'

'He sent soldiers north with me to serve as your guard,' Audun told her.

'I thought perhaps that was the reason,' Alexa mused. '*Would* you go to Byzantium once more?' Alexa asked. Gwenlliant had never heard such caution in her voice.

'I am too old for the journey now,' said Olwen. 'Yet, I think that I should.'

'I am too old for the trip to Finnmark and over the Great Ice,' Audun said. '*I* am the one who is old, while you are blossoming.'

'Audun, that is the first lie I have ever heard from you,' said the Queen. 'My bear died at midwinter.'

Audun bowed his head. 'I knew that. Alas, I have no other bear to bring you. We had but one, a female, and she went to the new Queen of the Iceni.'

'As well she should. Actually, it is not quite the whole truth to say that my bear died. It was old and sick, it took no pleasure in food and would not even look at the snow. When I saw that its life was a burden to it, I . . .' she touched the black dagger belted at her side.

'It is the royal death,' said Audun. 'But it came too soon. As it always does.'

The food before Gwenlliant suddenly tasted like wood-shavings forced down past a lump in her throat. Elen seized her hand and squeezed it.

Suddenly Gwenlliant winced, but not from the pain of Elen's grip. *It is a terrible thing when the old outlive the young. But she and I will fare together.* Empathy tore at her, great sorrow, and even greater guilt. *This cursed age of mine! I could make the trip to Finnmark well enough. I could even shift my form . . .*

– *This is Audun thinking!* – Elen's consciousness flared into fear and curiosity.

– *Hello, pretty spies*, – came Audun's thought, greeting them despite their intrusion into his thoughts. – *You need not steal morsels of news. Not from me, at least. And would you know more?* –

Chapter Four

Assent flowed out from Gwenlliant and Elen, like ripples in the Water of Vision before the water clears and new places emerge. And then they saw.

Audun wore the consecrated white pelts as he danced to summon his brothers and sisters in fur. Power flared down Audun's spine and out along his ribs. Behind him danced and chanted others of the Aescir. Despite his concentration, he could hear as the change came upon each one of them.

It was taking too long! He wanted to shout in rage, but it came out a growl. He focused his anger, his frustration and – yes – his fear, and aimed them at his own body. He would change. He was Audun Bearmaster, and whatever kept him from his kin on the White Ice must give place! When it came, the change forced him whining and panting to the ice, as his body thickened and extended. He rose on his haunches and extended massive forepaws, awed, as always, by the speed and strength of his bear-form.

But where were the others? Audun realized that of all the

Aescir who had made the journey north from Staraja to the land where the sun stood in the sky all summer, he alone remained on the threshold of the Great Ice. Always before in Finnmark, others of his brothers and sisters in fur had come down from the Great Ice to meet the Aescir and guide them back to the assembled kindred. He studied the snow, then sniffed: in this guise, his nose was keener far than his eyes. No scent of the brothers in fur nor, temptingly, of the sisters. And no tracks either. The Aescir had all gone before him. He bellowed out a prayer for their safety and started off.

For days Audun wandered alone on the ice, scooping up whatever fish he could find, using all the craft of his humanity and his borrowed form to escape when great chunks broke free and toppled down to crash upon him, or tore off from the main ice and drifted away on grey-green currents. His paws were ponderous and slow with age now, his haunches sluggish. The teeth in his great jaws had been too worn to chew as quickly as once they had.

He must have made a thousand false starts as he attempted to find easy passage among the cracks and ridges of the shore upwards into the ageless silence of the ice, and all about him, shimmering lights cast rainbows on the snow and hail as they fell and formed into icy little crystals that slashed at the pads of his feet.

Up ahead . . . he bellowed with rage as his numbing paws broke through a thin crust of ice and into the water itself. How old was he? Surely old enough to know when the ice was rotten. A huge chunk of it toppled into the water near where he floundered. Ice and sea rumbled. It was not the cold he feared, even at his age, nor the water: in this guise, he was a swimmer, and his blood still ran hot. It was the heaving of ice and sea which might send more ice down upon him, grinding his powerful body to pulp, or might prevent his climbing out of the water and into the safety of the inner glaciers.

Finally, he clawed himself out and lay panting on the ice as it rocked beneath him. He knew rage then, but not his own. What had sent the ice toppling? And why had he that sense of a momentary retreat? He too would have to retreat, he thought; but not yet. He crawled over to a fissure and dug himself into it. For now, at least, he was unable to go further, fearing himself unable to clamber free, and return to the shore and his proper form. He roared with sorrow. Never again would he wander among his kindred-in-fur. He might not even return home. The man in bear's guise wept at that. But Gerda would manage. And Audun's eldest son would be Bearmaster in his place. Only, it was still too soon!

Never again would the females choose to send their children south with him to be the cherished companions of kings and queens. Never again, he thought, would he see any of his kin.

Enraged by hunger and longing, he wore himself out struggling. When he awoke, a young male bear crouched nearby, and a large fish lay by Audun's muzzle. Audun glanced at the newcomer, sniffed, and recognized him as Arinbjorn, the youngest of his sons. Even in bear's guise, his height was unmistakable, though he had yet to fill out in his full growth.

Go away, he wished it. *They wait for you.*

The younger bear shook his head and lay down beside his father. Though Audun hated to admit it, he was grateful for the warmth. He gobbled the fish, and slept. When he woke again, there were other fish. Gradually, he rebuilt his strength.

Three days later, he woke to see two more bears crouched nearby: one a female, the second, her half-grown cub. With encouraging pushes and nips, the female aided him to rise. He started forward, up towards the Great Ice, but she cuffed at him. Go back, she was telling him. You are not fit to walk here any more. She swung her head to stare at Arinbjorn, who tossed his head, then laid it down, denying any interest.

Audun nudged at him with his muzzle, then cuffed him. *Go on.* Still Arinbjorn crouched sullenly by his father's bulk. *Go on!* Audun roared and cuffed him again, this time with real strength. Moaning, Arinbjorn rose to follow the female.

Audun lumbered to all fours and prepared to return to the shore. But as he turned to go, she cuffed the cub at her side, who trailed after Audun all the way to the shore. She would be the last cub he would ever foster with a ruler.

The transit from bear to man came slowly, and more painfully than Audun had ever known. He did not think he would have the courage, or the endurance, to submit to it ever again.

'The bears?' asked the men when he returned to his ship, the cub beside him.

'The others made the Change. It was I, only I, who could not make the passage,' he told his sons. 'Henceforward, another must be your Bearmaster.'

Had I been younger, braver, Audun reproached himself, I might have had more companions, and this good Queen might well decide to live. One land; one law – and this land has a harsh one.

Audun abandoned his recollections. His thoughts grew more brisk and decisive. – *Do your mothers know that you have the underhearing?* – he asked Elen and Gwenlliant.

– *Mine does not.* – Gwenlliant replied.

– *Perhaps it would ease her heart if she knew.* –

Gwenlliant studied her mother, seated among the people who meant the most to her. Olwen was beautiful, Olwen was serene, Olwen was so brave that she could plan calmly for a ritual that – were it a hundred years in Gwenlliant's future – made her numb with terror. Perhaps she should simply tell her mother that she was not fit to be her heir. That had worked for Alexa hadn't it?

'Olwen, perhaps you should go to Byzantium,' Alexa mused. 'Make your peace.'

Tenderly, Olwen laughed at her. 'Even after so many years you are still scheming. I can hear it. You are telling yourself, "Olwen will go to Byzantium, Olwen – since like all Celtoi, she blurts out whatever is most important to her – will tell my brother Marric that she is old, she is barren and it is time to relinquish crown and queensblade to Gwenlliant; and Marric will think of a way to stop her." You have done all you can, Alexa. Let it go.'

Alexa dashed tears from her face. 'I cannot,' she whispered. More tears came. 'Forgive me! I did not mean to weep like this.'

Go on, Gwenlliant told Elen, giving her hand a push. She knelt beside her mother and laid her head in her lap. Alexa stroked the dark hair that Elen wore hanging loose down her back with the gentleness she displayed so rarely that it seemed shocking. 'After all these years,' she mourned. 'I am just as bad as my brother. I cannot accept . . .' her eyes grew wide and entranced. Gwenlliant leaned forward to catch each slurred or strangled word.

As she had at midwinter, Alexa slumped against Gereint's shoulder, and much to Gwenlliant's surprise, she shook her head wearily and smiled. 'The visions elude me. A sense of the dark, of hunger . . . and it is gone. I dare not go further into the dark for my own soul's sake. But I have been reminded,' she said. 'Do you remember the night before we fought Jarl Grettir?'

Olwen nodded, flushing in the firelight so that she appeared ten years younger.

'Marric will remember that the bard Kynan died for his stubbornness. I know what I promised you. I know what is right to do. And, thus far, I have helped you, backed you, Isis spare me, I have even tried to argue your daughter – who is as stubborn as you and my brother combined – into submission. But now that the moment comes . . . Olwen, both of us love you. You cannot expect us not to try to keep you with us. It is against our natures, my brother's and mine. And Audun is right. It is just too early.'

Olwen thrust herself to her feet, her patience clearly at an end.

Even her mother's rages were royal. Gwenlliant's were simply bad temper.

'You never leave it alone, do you, you and your brother? Alexa, it's been twenty years! Did you think that the stories you heard about queensblade were just a story, some custom of the *barbaroi*' – her accent scornfully fine, she used the Greek word – 'that you can set aside with one of your clever plots?'

'I've been patient,' she told them. 'When my own mother could no longer bear children, she told me. I went to the hawthorn nemet with her – *and I watched!* Goddess strike you all, do you think it was easy for me?' Her eyes sought out Gwenlliant. 'And do you think it will be easy for me to pass that on to Gwenlliant? Already, she is frightened – and I know why. My son – his loyalty is to Byzantium, as his father and I agreed it should be. Mor is Marric's heir. But Gwenlliant is mine. One day this land will be hers, my crown will be hers – and queensblade will be hers, too. Or do you want the Goddess to unveil her dark face and loose the Wild Hunt to trample down the land?'

Alexa laid her hands on her daughter's shoulders, pushing her gently away before she rose to her feet to face the Queen's anger.

'You have lived here for more than twenty years, shared my bread and my counsel – and I have loved you, Alexa,' Olwen's voice almost broke. 'You have been my sister. Was all of that a lie? After half our lives together, do you suddenly turn on me for your brother's sake?'

Alexa opened her mouth to speak, but Olwen overrode her. 'I shall know your loyalty, sister. And your obedience.'

Elen cried out, a sharp, wordless thing, and ran from the hall. 'Go after her,' Alexa whispered to Gereint.

As clearly as if Alexa had whispered it in her ears as well, Gwenlliant heard her, felt the quick, intense clasp of a hand with which Alexa dispatched her husband after her daughter. She found herself staring into Alexa's face, noting the delicacy of the bone, the way the fine skin creased about her eyes, and her lips dried – *how frail she looks, and how much older!* – before sharing Alexa's thoughts. *Why put Gereint to a choice that would break his heart? Or shame him and Elen, worse than they might feel already? I simply pay for the folly of my candour. Celtoi or Byzantines, a court is a court. Alexa, will you never learn?*

'Sister,' Alexa said in nearly the voice she used when she prophesied. When she spoke thus, the hall had always fallen silent. This time was no exception. Even the Queen broke off her speech.

'My love you have always had. My obedience – I should have thought that after twenty years, you would need no proof of it. Still, if proof is what you require . . .'

Alexa walked towards Olwen's high seat, a tiny woman among the much taller Celtoi. Her light dress rustled about her, and the sunlight glanced off the gems that she wore and the white strands that threaded through her long, dark hair. When she stood directly across from the Queen, she paused.

Then, with great deliberation and the hieratic grace she had learned as a child in Byzantium, Alexa dropped to her knees, then lowered herself until she pressed her forehead against the rough floor in the formal prostration she would use before the gods, or that a commoner would use before the Emperor.

Slowly, Alexa raised her head and lifted herself to her feet. 'May the Queen,' she said quite distinctly, 'live forever.'

She looked up at Olwen, meeting the Queen's eyes as her own kindled into vast affection. 'Are you content now, sister?' she asked. To Gwenlliant's surprise, her voice lacked irony. Finally, she smiled. Then, with no abatement of her dignity, Alexa turned and walked quietly from the hall.

Chapter Five

Alexa burrowed herself further into a cloak lavishly woven in indigo and Tyrian purple and berated herself for being unable simultaneously to concentrate on Aristotle and listen for footsteps. *I could* will *her to come*, the thought, too faint to be temptation, whispered in her mind. She bit her lip, assessing her niece. *Assuming that I could.* The mind that she had touched while underhearing Audun had been untrained, that much was certain, but there was a definite strength to it . . .

Alexa shook her head. Of course, she would not coerce the girl, or even try; and she had known that all along. Irene had tried to coerce an empire and lost son, empire, life and soul for it. Alexa, infected with the same vice . . . she grimaced. She had lost too much herself by using proscribed methods to risk them. Besides which, Olwen's child – and her brother's! – was safe from her always.

A distant warmth told her that Stephana-within, her guide and companion, was present and that she was smiling. Stephana, her constant inner companion for most of her life, had deserted her, or so it seemed. *Or cannot reach me.* Except at times like this. What it had cost Stephana to pierce whatever veils that now blinded Alexa to the magic, she did not know. *I thought that perhaps she had simply gone free, risen another step on the Way. I would have missed her, but I could not hold her back.* Marric had not hindered the seeress either, Alexa remembered, and blinked fiercely. If we could set Stephana free to embrace her fate, why can we not relinquish Olwen?

– *Olwen's gift, like your brother's* – tenderness wreathed about Stephana's words as always, faint though they were, when she spoke of Marric – *has always been for life. It is hard to lay such a gift aside, or let another do so.* –

Stephana's presence faded and Alexa sighed. She laid down the *Politikoi* carefully, beside the fragile papyri she had stored against the prevailing damp in their leather tubes. Shutting her eyes, she launched her will south and winced as she encountered a barrier where should have been resistless aether. If she were stronger, she might use mind and spirit to batter that down. She smiled, wryly. If she were stronger, she never would have listened to Irene, her long-dead, long-damned stepmother; and she would rule now as Isis-on-Earth, her brother's Empress and wife.

And would never have met Gereint, or borne Elen, she thought. Her smile, this time, was tender. Her race had been old, unhealthy: for the proof of that, simply look at the troubles she and her brother . . . both brothers (she winced at the ugliness of her half-brother's ugly death, which she had devised) had caused. She had strength enough for one child, and Elen, thank Isis-Hathor, was without flaw.

Alexa cocked her head on one side, her eyes flickering to the cloth-hung door. It was hard to find or make privacy even in a queen's maenol, but what privacy there was, Alexa had managed to find and claim for herself years ago. Otherwise, she would have gone mad, she knew, among so many Celtoi so much taller and noisier than herself. Her privacy served her well now. Some there were who might have resented her after Olwen demanded her obedience; even after twenty years, and marriage to the Queen's brother and warleader, she was still an outlander, an outsider. And now, it appeared that her star was falling. In such a case, it was best to disappear for a time, to retreat strategically, and to plan.

Were those footsteps? After several days of 'planning',

however, restlessness set in. Gwenlliant had to come! Alexa glanced about the room she had transformed into some replica of Byzantium as she recalled it: the claw-footed chairs, glass bowls like so many rainbows, an image of Isis. Homesickness washed over her. In twenty years, she had not permitted herself to return to the city, not even once. When Olwen travelled there, Alexa stayed in Penllyn, regent for her sister. *Best not look upon what you have renounced*, she told herself. The brazen light on the Horn, the glimmer of braziers in the Temple of Isis (the new one, she had heard, was almost complete), the coolness of marble in the women's quarters in the summer, and warmth underfoot when the winds swept west from Scythia . . . *if I were exiled, I could go there. Would Gereint . . . ?*

'Aunt?' A gentle voice, a gentle touch on the door's curtaining fabric, and a faint, faint fragrance. It was late, to be sure, but Gwenlliant was finally coming into her powers. The child was cat-footed, certainly.

Alexa straightened, reluctantly shrugging out of the warm cloak. Now that the moment was upon her, she hated the way that her breathing quickened and the light swam in her eyes.

'Enter,' she said, and drew a deep breath.

As the girl entered, blinking into the sunlight at Alexa's back, she rose and bowed very slightly. 'Princess,' she said. 'How may I serve you.'

Gwenlliant raised both hands to her cheeks. Her shock was the reward Alexa wanted. She paused long enough to gaze up at her niece. What a beauty the girl had become! She had her mother's hair, like the richest, reddest gold from Ophir, but her father's look in her eyes, dark and secretive. Her height and her wilfulness she had from both parents, and she walked with the long-legged ease of a child still unconscious of her own power.

She paused a moment, long enough for Gwenlliant to take in the uncharacteristic splendour of her violet dress and the aquamarine, amethyst and gold earrings and necklace, wrought in clusters of blossoms, that she had chosen from her mother's jewellery for luck. The girl shifted from foot to foot (and Alexa would have wagered gold that her sandals were a minor disaster), feeling too tall, awkward and unfinished. Which was precisely how Alexa wanted her to feel.

Forgive me, Gwenlliant, Alexa thought silently. *It is not only my brother who is shepherd of the Two Lands.* 'May I offer you wine, or mead?' she asked, gesturing towards the pitchers and cups on a nearby chest, as careful not to turn her back on Gwenlliant as she would have been in her brother's court. *Damn her quivering voice! Twenty years' wait, and she was afraid.*

Gwenlliant accepted watered wine, and a seat in a chair that had come by boat and packtrain all the way from Alexandria, and that Alexa had draped with the purple. Her eyes were too wide and too bright. And why not? Alexa thought wryly. She comes to ask her aunt, who is in disgrace, how she can evade her mother's will and not take up her power – or her death, and how she can thwart her father's wish to wed her to his heir. And that same disgraced aunt accords her the welcome of an empress.

Alexa wet her lips from her own goblet and smiled lovingly at the girl. *You don't ask for much, do you, child?*

'Elen is not here,' she told her. 'I can have her sent for, should you wish.'

Ill at ease at Alexa's deference, Gwenlliant stroked the purple cloth that decked her chair and stammered. No, she would hardly wish to see Elen; they were not good friends these days. And how should they be? It was hard for Elen to see crowns, fortunes, power, and know that all of it belonged to her younger cousin; and hard, too, for Gwenlliant to see that the elder girl saw it, and knew herself at least as fit as she to hold it all. *Would* have had it, had Gwenlliant not been born.

You know little of how fortunate you are, niece, Alexa thought as she brought out the chessboard. *Elen is free of the taint of ambition. I learned that, at least, from my own fall.*

Gwenlliant gazed about, clearly hoping for a safe topic. Her eyes fell on Alexa's book.

'The *Politics*,' Alexa said. 'When one is adviser to a queen . . .'

'I thought . . .'

'That your mother is furious with me?' Alexa asked, her arched brows arching further. 'She was. Perhaps she still is. And

47

not for the first time. In either case, I felt it best to make myself small and difficult to find. Not that that has troubled you, my Princess. Perhaps . . .' again, the delicate brows arched in question.

'Is that why you read Aristotle, and wear purple?' Before Gwenlliant could stop herself, she blurted it out and flushed.

Alexa made herself sigh and shake her head. 'Twenty winters, and still . . .' she shivered, but disdained the warm wool of the cloak that had tumbled from the back of her chair. 'I am cold here. In the summer, the light on the Horn was like hammer on anvil; in the winters, at least the hypocausts kept us warm.' She heard her own voice shake. *Something in this child compels the truth. She is much like Olwen in that.*

'You miss it,' Gwenlliant put in. Tears rose in her eyes.

'I must miss it,' said Alexa. 'Penllyn has been my home for those twenty winters, and I have loved it well. Served it well, or so I think. But I always remember that I was born in Byzantium. Sometimes the memories overpower you as you grow older.'

This time, Gwenlliant tried to arch her brows in inquiry.

Alexa's eyes flared emerald the way they usually did when someone did or said something that she considered imbecilic. 'I may not always be a queen's adviser,' she said, low voiced. Again, the tremble in her speech: Gwenlliant did not think she was reading that into what she heard.

She fears me *?*

Alexa nodded. Gwenlliant's underhearing was strong, then; her empathy stronger yet.

Ah, then. As long as her mother thought she had no powers, Olwen would remain alive, praying that Gwenlliant might mature into her birthrights of empathy and healing. As delicately as Alexa might stroke a rare old silk, she touched Gwenlliant's consciousness. *To spare Olwen, she would block those gifts forever, Isis smile upon her.* But that would prevent Gwenlliant from becoming the woman that she could be.

But it was past time to answer, or the girl would think Alexa mocked her. 'Aye, I fear you. It is why I hoped – much as Penllyn has been my home and I have loved it – that Gereint might be chosen king elsewhere. A young queen needs a young court.' *And there is Elen, too. What sort of life will she have when her younger cousin queens it over her?* Carefully, she set that thought in the forefront of her consciousness and waited until she felt Gwenlliant's mind brush towards it.

'How long have you had the underhearing?' she demanded, choosing to attack. 'Audun told me that you had it. Your mother should know that your powers come upon you, finally.'

Gwenlliant nearly choked on her wine. Her rejection was instant.

'The empathy, too. I could teach you to bear that kinship with those about you. I could help you, as I have helped your mother all these years,' Alexa pointed out.

'What good would it do?' she asked.

'For a start, it might be bargaining coin when you go East. You do not wish to go, do you? Is it that you do not wish to leave Penllyn right now? Or do you fear your brother Mor? What do you find to object to in him?'

'What did you find to object to in my father?' Gwenlliant retorted.

Alexa smiled, then suppressed it quickly. Gwenlliant was more than a Celt, as Byzantines saw them. As was Olwen. They had cunning of their own, and vision. But Gwenlliant was also her brother's daughter; Alexa must be on guard for subtleties.

'The gods are sly,' Alexa said, and watched her niece's eyes darken with shock. 'They give my brother a son after his own heart – and a daughter according to his nature. That question was well asked, child.

'No woman alive could object to my brother,' Alexa declared. 'But then I had made myself unfit to rule, and then I saw Gereint. I had made myself unfit. Were I not, do you think that your mother would think herself failing and fading? Do you think, for one moment, that I would not plunge after whatever this power is that shakes the earth and makes all our power wither?'

Desire to pierce that barrier to the south, to slash through it and shrivel whatever forced Audun to lay down his power and tempted Olwen to put aside her life made Alexa reel, almost as if she entered a trance. A gentle touch, loving, but mildly reproachful, steadied her. 'Even my guide of twenty years . . . Stephana speaks but faintly in my mind now. She is blameless;

perhaps it is time that she journeyed on. But I have long known that I was too weak to rule as Isis and wield the full magic of the moon crown.'

For what seemed like half a day, Alexa let Gwenlliant stare at her, let her draw the conclusions she had set out. Then, finally, she took pity on her. 'You did not come here to discuss magical powers, I feel sure. In fact, you conceal what power you already have, whether out of fear for yourself or your mother . . .' Tactfully, she let her voice trail off. 'Perhaps, you might find it easier to speak if your hands were full. Chess?' she suggested. 'Or senit?'

Gwenlliant had little skill in senit, a game favoured among women in the Empire. She took up a chess piece and admired it.

'From Audun,' Alexa said. 'These pieces are old friends. When I first sailed north with the Aescir, I played for hours each day. At times, that was all that kept me ali— . . . I am very fond of this set.' She smoothed her sleeves down over her wrists, where the purple slid gently over the thin, white scars. The slashes she had inflicted on herself were scarcely bandaged when Audun had brought out that board, and she had played chess the way a beaten soldier drank: to drug herself into forgetfulness.

'I hope I will not be an unworthy opponent,' Gwenlliant said politely.

'Ah, like you, Princess, I have known the temptation to relax into less than one might be,' she retorted.

Gwenlliant's eyes flared. *Stop calling me Princess! Three days ago, you scolded Elen and me like children!*

Alexa bent her head to conceal a feline smile.

'Your move,' she pointed out, and waited. It was gratifying to see how good the child's control was. She would make a fine queen – but of whose realm? Footsteps pounded down the hall, the long, hasty steps of a Celt in even more of a hurry than normal, and she prayed that it was not Gereint, Gereint who would instantly know that she played a game (if not one of chess), but would not understand why it must be with his sister's child. Gwenlliant tensed too. Better and better yet.

'Aunt, what can I do?'

'What do you want to do?' Alexa challenged.

'I don't want mother to enter the grove. And I don't want to wed my brother.'

'Those are things you don't want,' Alexa told her. 'What do you want?'

Gwenlliant's head drooped and her hair dropped about her face, glistening in the light.

'Surely,' and Alexa's voice was gentle, 'you want to see your father. And,' she continued ruthlessly, 'your brother.'

The waves of her hair rippled as she shook her head.

'No? They are warriors, Gwenna. If you miss them now, only the Goddess knows if . . .'

A tear splashed down on to one of the chessmen. 'Mor will do as our father wants, he always does. But I . . . I do not want this. I do not know what I want.'

Alexa dared to lean forward, to touch Gwenlliant's mind in the very act of brushing the girl's hair tenderly from her face.

'You fear you cannot stand against your father, is that it?'

She waited for the headshake, half ashamed, half sullen, before she laughed.

'Dear heart, your mother is at least as stubborn as your father, and I can tell you that she has her heart set against that match as much as he . . . ah, I see. You know that.' Alexa laid her fingers, a gentle touch, on Gwenlliant's wrist, and the girl shrank back, guiltily. 'Byzantine enough to eavesdrop, but Celt at heart, to be shamed.'

'They fought as if they hated one another,' Gwenlliant whispered.

Did I do right? Marric had knelt aghast before the body of the Druid he had slain . . . Kynan, that was his name, of the order of Bards. When he pulled his hands from his temples, his face was marked by the Druid's blood. Olwen's face was ashen, and she glanced about as if she expected the Jomsborgers to fall upon the maenol, fit recompense for sacrilege, right then and there. But Alexa had joined their hands, had snatched Olwen's black dagger and slashed first her own wrist and then theirs, pressed the tiny wounds together to make them all brother and sisters in blood.

Alexa caught up the girl's hands. 'I assure you, Gwenlliant,

51

you are at least as stubborn as either of them. I promise you.'
She tried to coax a smile from the girl. 'It is a family sin.'

It had been prophecy, she told herself after the fact, remembering how she had quivered, how the rightness of what she was doing roared through her brain – *had it really?* Or had she simply seen the banked fires that smouldered between the Queen and her brother, and used that passion to control them both? Despite the consolations of Stephana-within, she had prayed and wept over that until the birth of Mor, a healthy, sturdy child with no taint, then or ever, of magic about him. She could not say the same of Gwenlliant, born three years later in the aftermath of a particularly violent argument. The potential in the girl for magic – a potential that must remain latent – set Alexa's own talents to aching. She might train her own child to sorcery, might guide her to levels from which Alexa herself was forever banned. But Gwenlliant's powers were not those of ritual but those of the self. Too-long study might stunt them.

Gwenlliant raised her head from her cup. 'Aunt,' she asked in a low voice, 'do you ever regret it?'

'Well played,' Alexa told her, not referring to the chessboard on which a pawn attempted regicide. 'For a time, very much. And then I met Gereint.' She knew she was flushing like a green girl. 'Even then, however, I hoped that Marric would forgive me that I had chosen . . .' she shook her head. 'Yes. I have regrets. What of it?'

She is old, old! and still she thinks of Elen's father as her young lover. While I, I never saw him but that once, and I half believe it was a dream. The onslaught of Gwenlliant's angry jealousy made Alexa's temples throb.

Not Mor, then, but some vision? she asked silently, and Gwenlliant flushed.

'I had such a vision once,' Alexa said. Abruptly, she found herself enjoying this, and poured herself and her guest more wine. Gwenlliant suddenly looked up at her and flashed her a grin, evidently pleased to sit in midday with a somewhat scandalous aunt, drinking and discussing men. 'When I first came here, it was Samhain, and I saw the Hunt . . .'

Gwenlliant caught her breath. 'So did I! That too must be a family failing.'

Alexa flung up a hand. 'Little one, it is not the Horned King, I hope?'

'No!' She tossed her head in scorn. 'But – no, I cannot talk about it. But he promised I would meet him again.'

Alexa smiled. 'Kinswoman, do you know what I would do, if I stood in your shoes? I would go to Byzantium. See your father. Hide, if you must, behind your mother's skirts. As you know, no one could be more opposed to your father's plans for you and Mor than—'

'Mother – oh!' Elen ran into the room and brought herself up short. 'What are you – Princess,' she ended with a good deal more wariness. *Not so hostile, daughter*, Alexa thought. Elen had flushed, and the colour made her lovely, with the long dark hair that she had from Alexa, and her father's deep blue eyes. She was taller than Alexa, *and far, far lovelier*, thought her mother.

Would Gwenlliant suffer Elen to serve her as I have served Olwen? Alexa asked herself. *If Gereint had won a crown, at least she might have ruled in a new country. I have not done well by her. Not yet.* She took a deep, and, for her, a reckless draught of her wine.

'Elen, you are not very gracious, are you?' she asked mildly.

Elen looked down at her hands, which were white, if ringless, then raised one to twist at the neckchain that was her uncle's birthgift, and which she always wore. She murmured something inaudible, which Alexa translated as, 'She resents my being in disgrace, you see. I do not fear, Gwenlliant. Your mother and I have quarrelled before.' *But never before have our powers been blunted by what lies to the south. I must know, I must! But I myself dare not.* It had been years since she had been greatly tempted, and she dared not test herself.

Not herself. But Elen. Elen might well go south, protected as carefully as Olwen – and all the warriors of Penllyn and Byzantium – could manage, Elen with her unsullied, growing power, her clarity and her innocence. And who knew?

Alexa reached out and took each girl by the hand, joining them as once, years before, she had joined Marric's and Olwen's hands. 'You are not now the sisters I would have you be,' she said. 'Forget about me, I beg you. Soon, Gwenlliant goes to Byzantium, and I would not have you quarrel before then.'

Guilt flamed in Gwenlliant's cheeks, and Elen glanced away. Alexa cast a carefully earnest glance at the younger girl, who flushed further, stammered, then breathed deeply and blurted out, 'Cousin, would you care to join us?'

'To study with the priestesses of Isis?' Elen asked. 'Oh yes, I should like that!'

Gwenlliant, shocked out of her guilt, laughed. 'Is that all you can think of to do in Byzantium?' she asked.

'What else is there for me?' Elen asked. Unlike Gwenlliant, Elen lacked the fitful charm – and the crown – that drew the local lords to her side. *She is too sombre, as if touched by my own frost – but where I have Gereint, what has she? Her studies. No, I must do better altogether for her.*

'Gwenlliant, that is a wonderful idea!' Alexa cried, and flung her arms about both girls. Over Elen's head, she managed to nod meaningfully at Gwenlliant. *This might be your solution*, she thought at her, though the girl looked doubtful.

Alexa pulled her necklace over her head and threw it over her daughter's shoulders. 'First we must pierce your ears,' she said, 'and then you shall have the earrings too. Or whatever else among my jewels that you admire. I shall not let you go to your uncle's City looking like a novice.'

The gems caught the lustre of Elen's eyes, and she began to kindle with excitement. *You shall have every chance that I renounced*, Alexa promised her.

Gwenlliant drained her cup and rose, somewhat unsteadily, to go.

'But the game!' Alexa pointed at the board on which the chess game lay muddled past repair.

Gwenlliant shrugged. 'I shall resign it to you.' She turned as if to leave, satisfaction warring faintly with unease in her dark eyes.

'That is unwise,' Alexa told her. 'You should always play the game out. Always.'

Elen raised her head, puzzled for once in her too-clever, too-studious life. It was time, Alexa thought, and past time, that she escape it as the silkworm breaks free of its cocoon.

Suspicion flickered in Gwenlliant's eyes. *I know she has manipulated me. But how?*

Alexa rose on to her toes to kiss her niece in farewell. For once, her smile was broad and unfeigned.

Alexa tipped over Gwenlliant's king. 'I should not permit that,' she told her. 'You should always play the game out. Always.' *But the practised player almost always wins.*

Chapter Six

As the procession of guards, packhorses, traders, Druids and Princesses followed Queen Olwen down the hill, Gwenlliant twisted in her saddle for a last look at the queen's maenol where she had spent most of her life. It was an action more scapegrace than royal; and more desperate than either. If she could not discover what she wanted . . . if Olwen lost the usual battle of wits with her father . . . if Alexa was outmanoeuvred, anything might happen! So she took what might turn out to be a long, last look at her home.

Standing at the gate was Alexa, flanked by Gereint and, much to everyone's surprise, by Audun. 'I am too old, too fat to venture south again in all this heat,' he had said. 'If the Queen will have me as a guest in her absence, I shall rest here, then continue north to visit my kin in the Orcades.'

Despite the heat, Alexa wore a cloak woven in the heavy pattern and many colours permitted only to rulers, and her torque and circlet were massy gold in the Celtic style, not her usual wear at all. The summer sunlight, filtered through the hot, moist air, struck fire from them and from the golden apples and the silver threads that adorned her long, dark braids. She held her chin high, her eyes blank, and only the quivering of the naked sword that she held before her, its point stabbed into the ground, showed that she was more than a life-size statue.

Gwenlliant heard a gulp and a sniff to her right, and counted ten before she turned to see Elen, her face blotched, craning in her saddle to catch a last glimpse of her parents. Gereint had embraced her as if she were as precious as the jade flowers from Ch'in that Gwenlliant's father had once brought her mother, but Alexa had hugged her in farewell, an unusual gesture for a woman who took court rituals as seriously as must an erstwhile heir to Isis. Finally, she turned her face up and looked into it long and lovingly.

'The Goddess make you lucky and fruitful. I have done my utmost,' she whispered and kissed her daughter's eyes.

Play the game out. You must always play the game out, Gwenlliant remembered Alexa saying. Her unwelcome empathy awoke in protest at the tension of that parting, and she turned to toy with the flowers woven into her horse's mane.

'The horned god take it!' Olwen had flared up that morning when she had seen the flower-caparisoned horses, 'this is no wedding procession!'

'No,' Alexa retorted. 'It is a triumph. Your triumph, Olwen. *Try* to remember,' she brought out the old words with a smile, 'that you are the Empress of the Romans, Isis-made-manifest, and that you are travelling to your capital to meet your consort. Just try, will you, Olwen? I know you would rather wear your oldest cloak and drive your chariot, but little things like this please Imperials . . .'

Olwen had snorted in a most unqueenly (let alone un-imperial manner) and laughed at the woman whom she had named regent once again.

'I shall submit,' she said haughtily. 'But see that you . . .'

Alexa had bowed her head. 'As indeed I do,' she murmured. Before they left, there had been some rather loud – Gwenlliant could not call them arguments – exchanges between her mother and her aunt. Oddly enough, none of them had concerned Elen's accompanying mother and daughter to Byzantium. Instead, when Alexa had approached Olwen in open court and requested that as a favour, Olwen had merely narrowed her eyes, a gesture borrowed from her sister-in-law, and assented. Inexplicably, the request had put her in good humour, all too rare these days, and when several of the men who had left the Emperor's army years ago to marry and to settle in Penllyn begged leave to guard the Queen, she nodded. It was those men, the Byzantines turned Celtoi, who had adorned the horses of the Queen and her daughter with flowers fit for a bridal. *They* had no doubts at all that Gwenlliant was ripe to marry, and, Goddess knew, they had a candidate in mind.

Their wives, though, Olwen thought, by now their wives should have dinned into their ears how terrible it was for sister to wed brother. Would no doubt have done so, had the emperor whom their husbands had served been anyone but Marric. Even her own clansmen and -women loved the songs that the bards had made of his fight against Jomsborg. Of course, no queen could silence a bard, but when that last one had started to compare her far-from-flawless husband to Arktos himself . . . 'Goddess, give me strength,' Olwen murmured, and knew that she would say that many times in the next few months.

Though some of the Celtoi might have wished that Olwen had not left Alexa in charge, she had been doing so for twenty years – 'and none of them,' Elen muttered at her side, 'would dare to quarrel with her. *Or* with my father.'

She sniffled again, then squared her shoulders. 'Would you wager,' she asked Gwenlliant in a voice that was deliberately offhand and cheerful, 'that my mother cries in his arms like a maid younger than we right now? So fond are they that I have often wondered why I have no tribe of little brothers and sisters.'

'Wretched girl,' Olwen overheard and called back at her, glad when Elen forced a smile.

Olwen plucked white roses from her horse's bridle, then hesitated, reluctant to throw them away in the presence of so many men who marched or rode wearing twenty-year-old imperial uniforms. They and their wives, she knew, had adorned her horse with blossoms and given wreaths to Gwenlliant and to Elen.

I promise that I shall bring them both back safely, she had told Alexa. But the other woman's eyes blanked and flickered with prophecy the way that heat lightning and thunder grumbled in the summer sky. Granted, it would be hard to withstand Marric, especially on his own ground. But Olwen had held him to a stand-off these past twenty years. She was a match for him.

And this would be her last journey to Byzantium, the last

time that she and Marric would shout at one another about their children, now all but grown, about arms, statecraft, spies or ritual – or just for the pure joy of shouting at an equal, whom, after all was said and done, one loved, in some strange fashion.

Which was worse: to bid farewell to an affectionate disaster of a husband or to a daughter whom the idea of marriage terrified and revolted? Olwen was certain of one thing: the very idea of leaving either of them, or her son, hurt worse than the thought of dissolution or the pain of a death blow. She maintained her own blades with oil and stone, and knew how sharp queensblade was, edge and point.

Alexa's eyes widened and went blank. She flung up her hands and her mouth worked.

'Alexa?' Olwen had steadied the smaller woman, amazed at how little she weighed. But Alexa had pushed free with astonishing strength.

'Shadows again, sister,' she had said, forcing a smile. 'Nothing more. You should have good weather and clear sailing for your journey south. And you shall have Romans and clansmen for your guards. Go in health, and may the Goddess smile upon you.'

Then, finally, it had been time for Alexa to stand back and let her and her train pass; better than anyone, Alexa knew that. But still the two of them lingered. Their last quarrel had been a hard one. *What would I have done had Alexa not yielded?* Olwen shuddered, remembering. *I cannot fight her and her brother.*

'Have you any message I can give your brother for you?' she asked.

Alexa embraced her fiercely. 'I have sent him my last, best message,' she said.

'I shall take care to deliver it.'

But Alexa's eyes had gone blank and formal, and she stepped back, to take up her position as regent and defender of the queen's maenol, her hands poised formally upon the hilt of a sword that reached almost to her breastbone. Had she believed her? Olwen still wondered that.

She glanced behind her at Elen, as she rode down Sarn Elen, the road that, centuries ago, her namesake had ordered to be built after her marriage to another emperor. The promise of a journey to her uncle's fabled city, her first in ten years, had shaken her from her usual dignity – *I would my Gwenlliant had some of her manners* – and she laughed and waved at soldiers and shepherds alike. Someone had given her a wreath of red roses, and she had bound her dark, wavy hair up beneath it. Her eyes and smile flashed. *Why, she is lovely*, thought the Queen.

Then her eyes shifted to her own daughter, blinking a little at the brightness of the sun upon Gwenlliant's hair, which streamed out behind her like an imperial banner as she laughed and raced down the track, tossing flowers from her horse's trappings to the men who hailed her. Olwen snorted, a most un-queenlike sound that made her laugh. What if she did that in Byzantium? Impatient of custom as a youth, Marric had bowed to it in public all his life. He might frown, not that Olwen cared a whit, *or he might laugh and sweep her up into his arms, middle-aged as they both were.*

It would be easier, it would always have been easier, if only their bodies had joined and she had found nothing to love in him. Affectionate disaster of a husband though he might be, he would be bereft – Gwenlliant rode whooping past her. *They are children, all children. Perhaps Audun and Alexa* were *right, and it is still too soon.* Any woman could miss a month of her courses, or even two or three, yet later on, resume them, or bear a child, even at her age.

She made herself wave gaily and kick her horse into a gallop as the guardsmen cheered.

At the first night's halt, they camped by a stream, and Olwen grimaced as the men whom her son had sent joined with her own Greeks to set up the elaborate tents and guardposts that imperial guards considered minimally appropriate to shelter an empress. She had never been able to convince them – or Marric either – that she neither liked nor required such things. Had she a choice, she might have preferred to fall asleep looking up at the sky. It had been years since she had slept out of doors, and only then . . . *we were outside the city* she recalled, *in that whitewashed villa Marric maintained as a refuge. We walked by*

*the fountain and I seduced him beneath the trees. Afterwards, of
course, he told me that he had seduced me.*

I do not want to remember such things!

Further south, they would guest with kings and queens. There
were weeks, however, until the first storms of autumn; Olwen
fully intended to use her journey to learn for herself what no
spy – and no brother, biased as Gereint could not help but be
– could tell her: the weal of all Prydein. The fields and flocks:
Well, she had seen worse summers than this one. Barley flour-
ished in the fields, the leaves overhead were wide and glossy,
and the air was heady with the sweetness of clover, somnolent
with fat bees.

But the tents were pitched, the firepits dug, and she and the
two girls ushered within, when the rumbling started. All that
day, humid as it was, there had been no clouds in the sky.
Gwenlliant put by a flap of the tent to stare into a sky in which
not even heat lightning flickered. Elen, who stood at a light
table mixing wine and water, stumbled, and some water spilled
on to the ground. Deftly, she reached out to steady the wine
bowl. Her eyes, when they met Olwen's, were troubled, and
her lips moved soundlessly.

'Earthquake,' she said. When she had assured herself that the
table would not tip over, spilling the wine, she knelt to rummage
in her pack. Olwen glanced politely away from what Elen pulled
out.

Again came a rumble. This time, more than the table rocked.
A stream of burning oil flashed from the polycandelon hanging
from a wooden strut and drizzled down on to the carpet.
Gwenlliant cried out and dashed water on to the blaze. When
that failed, she kicked the rug into a roll to smother the fire
before it grew. Smoke and the stink of scorching wool filled the
tent.

Outside, horses whinnied and the guardsmen shouted.

'Quiet out there! Have some respect for the Empress!'
shouted a voice with what Olwen recognized as an Italic accent.
One of Mor's auxiliaries, perhaps? she wondered even as she
helped her niece and daughter kick the smouldering carpet out
of doors where the guardsmen attacked it as viciously as they

would an assassin. The shouting grew louder as soldiers, priests and attendants crowded about.

'A lamp spilled in that last tremor,' Olwen told the crowd. 'The Princesses . . .' she made herself laugh . . . 'Goddess bless them, I do not know how young girls can move that fast. They put out the few sparks before the rugs could catch fire. So you see, there is no problem and nothing to fear.'

The Romans, pragmatic as they were, departed first, muttering of meals and guard-duty. Mor's guards took up their stations. Elen walked over to the nearest Druid, spoke to him quickly and urgently, then came back to the tent, which still smelled of smoke.

'Aunt,' Elen's voice was admirably level, 'will you let me touch your dagger?'

Bemused, Olwen drew queensblade, its serpent-carved handle warm in her hands, and handed it to the girl. Elen took the knife in both hands with great respect and stared at the ancient blade as if seeing visions in its dark, mottled surface. Then she raised it. Chanting, she saluted north, south, east and west, warding the tent, before she nicked her thumb on the blade and allowed the blood from the tiny cut to drip on to the ground where the burning carpet had lain. Finally, she returned the dagger to the Queen with a bow.

Almost before Elen reeled, Gwenlliant was at her side, easing her into a chair that Olwen had condemned an hour earlier as self-indulgently cushioned, and holding watered wine to her pale lips.

Usually oil and water were nothing to the way that those two girls quarrelled, Olwen thought. Now, however, Gwenlliant held her tongue until Elen regained as much colour as she ever had in her cheeks. Then she unleashed a torrent of abuse. 'Playing Druid, were you? My mother vowed to Aunt Alexa that you'd be safe. How can she keep that vow if you play with sorceries you cannot handle?'

Fear, Olwen noted with a secret smile, not of the tremors in the ground not of the fire, but for Elen's safety put the bite in Gwenlliant's voice. In just the same way, she quarrelled with Elen's mother. The scolding went on and on until Elen wearied of it and held up a hand.

'Enough,' she said, and her voice was but a thread of its usual softness. 'Gwenlliant, I have known how to ward a place since before my women's cycles began. But this time . . .' she shook her head, 'this time, something fought me, and it took not only learning but strength and blood to bind the wards.'

She laid her head down upon the chair's armrest. Waving away at least two serving-women, Olwen herself aided Elen out of her clothes and into bed. Despite the heat of the evening, the girl was shivering, and Olwen covered her warmly, then sat, stroking her hand until she drifted into uneasy, whimpering sleep.

Outside, the rumbling was heard once more. 'At least,' Olwen told her daughter, 'no lamps spilled this time. We have had all the excitement that we require tonight, don't you think?'

Once again, Gwenlliant peered out from the tent flap. The wind whirled inside, dousing one of the lamps so that they stood in a reddish half-light. Lightning crackled and, finally, true thunder pealed, and the rain poured down.

Exclaiming at the freshness of the air, Olwen laid Elen's hand down on her breast. She slept silently now, without the little whimpers of fear and exhaustion that had concerned Olwen earlier.

'I hope that the storm will not distress her,' Olwen murmured. Then, not at all softly to her daughter, 'Do you want to drown us all?'

Gwenlliant laughed as the lightning turned the night sky the colour of an imperial robe, and rain drenched the light tunic that she wore. 'The Hunt!' she cried. 'On a night like this, the Hunt rides forth! Maybe I will—'

With a speed that surprised herself, Olwen leapt for the tent flap and jerked it closed. The Hunt? Was her daughter still dreaming of the time she had met it and its dark master last winter? She reached for her fading gift of empathy, fading as her own spring and summer gave way to autumn, then fell back on shrewdness instead. Alexa would have been proud of her.

'You know, once your aunt met the Hunt and fled it.'

The wildness in her daughter's dark eyes flickered and banked itself. 'It wasn't just the Hunt, mother . . .' Gwenlliant sighed and unbound her hair to shake the rain from it. Then she walked over to look at her cousin. The light tangled in it, and about her wreathed the scents of honeysuckly and clover. 'Not the Hunt,' said Gwenlliant. 'Not the Horned King, though he wooed me.'

She flung up a hand, and Olwen forebore to press her.

'Elen may be a fool, but even she knows better than to fear a natural storm,' Gwenlliant remarked. Almost casually, she turned away once again towards the tent flap and the storm without.

'You knew!' Olwen accused. She spun her daughter around with a hand on her shoulder. So Gwenlliant had the under-hearing, the empathy of her line after all! How long had she concealed her gifts – and why?

At first Gwenlliant flinched from her mother's furious but furiously delighted gaze. Then, drawing composure from *somewhere*, she met her mother's eyes with a dark, stubborn gaze that reminded Olwen all too strongly of Gwenlliant's father, Marric, who claimed to disdain magics of any kind, but feared them, and used them only whenever he had no other choice. Olwen started to shake the girl, and Gwenlliant braced herself. Not to resist her, Olwen realized, shocked, but to endure the shaking in the hope that Olwen might lose interest. Her daughter was as tall as she now, and wiry from hours of riding, wild as the Huns whom her father, who should have known better, treated as fellow-tribesmen.

Abruptly, Gwenlliant laughed. Olwen stepped back, clasping her hands against a most unqueenly itch to box her daughter's delicate ears. 'Aunt Alexa says that the gods are sly, that they gave my father a son according to his heart, and a daughter according to his nature.'

It *was* empathy, Olwen exulted. How else could the child have known that Olwen had just compared her (albeit in unflattering terms) to her father?

'Your aunt should know better than to blaspheme, especially in front of a girl your age,' said Olwen. How pompous she sounded – and she hadn't set foot outside her own lands yet, let alone subjected herself to the officiousness of Byzantium.

Gwenlliant contrived (more of Alexa's training, no doubt) to look abashed. Then, abruptly, she yawned and stretched, the very image of a guileless, tired and irreproachable daughter.

Olwen sighed. What else could she do now but let Gwenlliant go to sleep, or pretend to? But the yawn was real, and so was her daughter's fatigue from the excitement of departure, the long ride and, finally, the earth tremor and the burning rug. Moments later, Gwenlliant lay asleep beside Elen.

Olwen the Queen stamped in frustration, but softly, in order not to wake the sleeping girls. The air that poured in from the opened flap was sweet with the scents of rain and moist earth, and a triangle of moonlight shone into the tent. Pulling a chair into the light, Olwen sat and watched the enigmatic, sleeping faces of her daughter and her niece as she had when they were infants. Her bear had been a cub then, and now it was dead. But these children, whom it had romped with, were become grown women now – or almost. In sleep, Elen's face lost the discipline that her training had imposed on her . . . prematurely, Olwen had always thought; Gwenlliant's face softened out of the fear and sullenness that Olwen had too often seen it wear, of late. She was very much her father's girl, questioning, restless, obeying only under compulsion . . . and just barely. She was not ready yet to be a queen or mother. At least, Olwen sighed to herself, at least for a little longer I can safeguard her. Her father and brother would never allow me that.

She realized that seated as she was in the light of the moon, she was a target. *So then*, she thought, and drew the black dagger of her queenship. *Very well, then. If attack you must, attack me openly. Attack me now*. But she doubted that whatever set the earthquake and the flame upon them had the honour – or the strength – to strike openly and unafraid. Alexa had spoken of something dark, something secret, draining away her powers, the land's virtue *and my own life with it*. Olwen ran a careful finger down the mottled blade of her dagger.

As if daring some unknown power, she sat in the opened tent flap, until the moon set and she wearied of the fragments of vision and half-formed thoughts that interlaced like the serpent chasings that she traced upon her dagger's hilt.

Whatever had caused the storm, and for whatever reason, the rain had freshened the air and laid the dust. The cool, damp wind brushed the day's febrile heat from her forehead. At the farthest reach of the horizon flickered the last pallid sparks of lightning. Their energy quivered in the air, and Olwen shivered, feeling suddenly younger and more . . . somehow more taut than she had felt in a year. She glanced over at her daughter.

Perhaps it is *too soon for me to leave you.* One other time, she had felt her strength forsake her and made her plans to die; she had been proven wrong that time. *Sweet Goddess, let me be wrong once more!* she prayed.

But it was almost dawn before she could sleep.

Chapter Seven

Gwenlliant stared into water that glinted and flashed like a heated mirror. Not even a cat's whisker of wind teased the ship's sail. Even the oarsmen's strokes seemed to slash into the water, rise, then cut back down without ripples spreading out to blur what she saw: a ship, a limp sail, and standing by the rail, one girl – herself – with red-gold hair and a look of discomfort and dissatisfaction in her sulky eyes, a second girl seated nearby, her dark hair pinned up on her neck.

For coolness, she and Gwenlliant wore the light, pleated linens and cottons of imperial dress. Elen might be unconscious of how the sailors' eyes followed them about, but Gwenlliant had flushed as she dressed that day, shamefacedly certain that she had somehow omitted several layers of clothing. Then she tossed her head and squared her shoulders defiantly. After all, the sailors who watched them with desire candid in their eyes – when they were not working off their excess strength (she thought slyly) at the oars – were no clan-kin of hers. Many were Romans, that swarthy, pragmatic race from the south of Italia who had ruled the Empire before Antony Cosmokrator and Divine Cleopatra took it for their own.

Unlike their own line, Gwenlliant remembered her father

saying, the Romans had no magic. How could one rule an empire without the god's favour, without the rituals that linked the heavens with the earth, yoking them in one endless dance? Though her father might distrust magic, it was in his blood. In their blood. The gods had loved Antony. But because of Cleopatra's descent from Alexander, the gods were her ancestors. Thus, they were Gwenlliant's ancestors too, if only she would claim them, as her father wished.

But then brightness burned upon the water, and Gwenlliant heard the sailors gasp and mutter as Olwen walked by. Awe had purged all the lust from the Roman's voices. She wore thin cotton brought from Hind, and her body shone within it like flame in an alabaster vessel. Compared with her, Elen's unconsciousness looked childlike, and Gwenlliant's annoyed modesty seemed only awkward.

All that long trip south from Penllyn to the Canti's port, that same glow had surrounded Olwen, as little akin to the poverty of the once-rich lands through which they had passed as the Horizon was to the lands of the living. The storm that they had encountered had been the last, Olwen mused, blinking up at the cloudless sky and at the glare of sunlight on water. The Isles of Mist were misty no more. In some places the soil seemed to be burnt away to the bare rocks. Facing the death of herds and the withering of crops, many people had despaired. The Saxons dwelling in Penllyn had a word for it: *wanhope*. People who suffered from it did not complain; but they did not thrive, either. It was as if they lost all interest in life. Very often, they ceased to care where they walked or rode, what – or whether – they ate and drank, and thus they took sick, and thus died of fevers and chills that a healthy man or woman would have set at naught.

But as Olwen rode by, the wanhope faded. Dobunni, Catuvellauni, even a few Iceni (who had a fine young queen of their own) appeared at whatever hall in which she guested, to greet her, to exchange news of blighted crops and poor hunting, of raids or brave defences, with a semblance of good cheer that, at times, was transmuted into genuine merriment. But mostly they sat, content to watch Olwen, perhaps to touch her hand in greeting as if the glow that hung about her, mingled with the odour of flowers, could somehow heal them. Even the soldiers whom Mor had sent as an honour guard stood rapt and silent in her presence – but then they regarded her as their Empress.

How strange it was, Gwenlliant thought. Her mother was but queen of one small realm; since the flight of Ganhumara the Faithless from Prydein, no high queens had ruled, and never again would any woman rise to do so. But after a winter and spring of fading and indecision, Olwen was once again the women of flowers of whom a nation of bards sang. Once again, she was beautiful; once again, she seemed young; and people's hearts rejoiced to see her, the talisman of the land's health.

Now, as Olwen walked by, the Romans faded into the shadows, abashed at her presence, murmuring of shifts at the oars or other such duties. How not? Caesar and his troops could not withstand the Celtoi, either. Pragmatists all, they could not watch the daughter of a goddess without amazement or alarm. Only one sailor remained to salute her in the manner of warrior to ruler. Gwenlliant studied the water very intently, hoping that Elen would not notice the flush on her cheeks. She had noticed that man standing by the cabins when they boarded the ship that Mor had despatched to bring them to Gesoriacum in Gallia. Taller than the Romans in the crew, he had the unruly dark hair of some Celtoi, and black eyes. Was he of the clans, then? Certainly his tunic was plain enough and coarse enough to allow him to look like his fellows, but Gwenlliant noted that he wore rich ornaments – a heavy chain, armlets, an ornately hilted blade.

'You are staring,' Elen whispered.

'I think I know him' Gwenlliant mused.

'From where?' her cousin asked, reasonably enough. Then she laughed behind her hand, shaking her head affectionately. 'But I trust you, Gwenlliant. If you do not know him, and you wish to, then you will. I wish I knew how you did it.'

Olwen cried out in pleased surprise as the sailor greeted her in familiar, courtly words and a well-known accent. 'But you are no Roman! To which clan do you belong?' she asked.

There was a long pause. 'To no clan any more, lady.'

'What nonsense!' Olwen stated firmly. 'You are of the Celtoi and will remain so until you die. Of which clan?' she asked, this time, more slowly, but with the authority of a woman entitled to an answer.

'Lady,' said the sailor, 'I was of the Iceni, but I have not lived among them for many years. It was for no crime of my own, you may trust in that; and many live there still who might speak kindly of me. I pray you, how does their queen?'

'Queen Luned fell this winter against invaders,' Olwen told the man, whose lips tightened and whose hands gripped the rope that he was mending, twisting it as he stood facing her.

'I have been in the south,' said the young man. 'When no word came, I feared that.'

Gwenlliant raised an eyebrow at Elen. Not just a man of the Iceni, but kin to their former queen.

'She was always rash,' the man continued, his voice husky, 'and I know that she had reached the age when even the fiercest warriors slow down.'

'I grieve with you. But since you claim Iceni blood, you have grounds for joy as well as mourning. Queen Luned's line runs true. Her daughter Mairedd is newly come to the throne,' Olwen told him. 'Audun Bearmaster has brought her a white bear; she should do well. Gwenlliant, Elen, come meet a kinsman! What is your name, warrior?'

Gwenlliant turned to greet the man, then shut her mouth on her words. 'Do not call me warrior,' said the tribesman. As he walked towards Gwenlliant, she saw how severely he limped, his left leg moving back and forth stiffly, 'I cannot earn that honour, and now you see why. As a child, I had a summer fever. When I rose from my bed, my leg had withered. The Druids call it a mark of the Goddess' favour that I am able to walk at all.'

Beside Gwenlliant, Elen raised her head, a familiar outrage smouldering in her eyes. If her father, Gereint, had not had a stiff arm, Gwenlliant recalled, he might now rule a tribe and kingdom easily Penllyn's size, and Elen would again be a royal heir.

'We are less than gentle, less than kind to those of us who are less than perfect, we Celtoi,' Elen said in a low voice. Like most of Elen's words, however, her comment carried over the water. 'Aren't we?'

The bite of irony in her voice made the young sailor's eyes flicker towards her. The light on the water was intolerably bright. It made Gwenlliant blink fiercely and seemed to hurt her mother's eyes too.

'More likely,' Elen addressed the sailor directly, a strangeness because Elen was slow, usually, to speak among strangers, 'the Goddess' favour lay not in your being able to walk, but in the stubbornness that made you master your limbs to walk again.'

'That being the case,' Gwenlliant put in, in rare agreement with her cousin, 'I call you not kinsman and warrior, but kinsman and victor.'

After all these years, she thought, amazed, she had found a use for the Plato that Alexa had insisted that she read when she would much rather have ridden or roamed the hills. The body was a prison-house for the soul – and this man was living proof.

The young Iceni flung up a hand and half turned away, deep crimson flaring along his cheekbones. But Olwen stood waiting for the young man's name, which he could not deny her without open rudeness.

'The Iceni called me Dylan the Halt,' he said in a low voice. 'And so, when I was old enough – and my leg had grown as strong as the Druids thought it might ever be – I left them.'

'For the sea . . .' Olwen let the words fall, her tone gentle, sympathetic. 'Your mother named you well.'

No one, though, spoke of the young man's father. That in itself was not unusual: parentage followed the mother. A lady like Queen Luned would have taken no unworthy men to her bed. If Dylan had not been cast out, no shame lay upon him.

'There are no cripples in the water,' said Dylan. 'For that reason alone, I would love it; but ever since my childhood I have loved the sea, and I have always wished to sail.' He had a thin, delicate-boned face softened only by a smile that flickered out, like noon light upon a fine blade, transforming an embittered young man, familiar beyond his years with pain and denial, to one who . . .

Gwenlliant smiled, then flushed. Alone among the men of that ship, he had not hovered about her and Elen, but, instead, had chosen to speak with the Queen. Despite all the easy flow of his speech, Gwenlliant wondered if he were not at least half

Roman. Certainly, he dressed like one. And he was serious, dignified. Romans, Alexa had told her once, called that type of dignity *gravitas*.

Gwenlliant called it a nuisance.

Finally, he cleared his throat and looked away, adding only, 'I went to the shore and offered myself as a sailor to a Roman trader. The Romans care not whether a man is a king or slave before he joins them, save only that he commit no crime while he takes their coin, and that he earn it fairly. Since I joined them, I have risen from sailor to officer, and finally to master of a vessel. Next season, I can buy my own ship.'

So you are content? Clearly, Olwen forebore to press that point, and Elen, rummaging through her bags, clamped her lips together, enjoining silence.

'I contrive,' said Dylan, though Gwenlliant was certain she had heard no one speak. Royal blood *and* the underhearing too. If Dylan had not steadied himself for balance against the mast, if his leg had not been twisted, he would have been very tall. He was one of the dark Celtoi, black hair, black eyes, and skin with a satisfyingly smokey tone.

'My daughter and my niece.' Finally, Olwen introduced Gwenlliant to the young clansman. Dylan bowed, his hand against his heart, but looked only briefly at Elen and at Gwenlliant. His fingers curled about whatever medallion hung from a heavy chain and lay beneath his tunic, then relaxed.

'Your pardon, Majesty,' he requested, bowing with a grace unlike either Roman or tribesman, the grace of a swimmer and of something else that Gwenlliant could not place but that fascinated her. 'I must excuse myself to see to my ship. I merely came to tell you what you yourself can see. Because we are becalmed, and the men must row, our crossing will be slow. I beg you to consider this ship and all aboard it as yours.'

Olwen smiled at him, amused at his formality. 'You are most gracious.'

'Not gracious, lady, but obedient to duty. The imperial Prince, your son, has given us our orders.' Another bow and, abruptly, Dylan withdrew. His limp, as the ship rocked gently, did not appear to be that pronounced.

Elen looked up at Gwenlliant, one eyebrow raised, her blue

70

eyes glinting with sly mirth. 'Caesar may have crossed to Britain overnight. We will cross to Gallia a good deal more slowly. We may as well take the captain up on his kind invitation to consider his ship ours. Shall we explore? Not, of course, too close to the captain, who seems to be so occupied with his duties. Or would you prefer to play Sirens and try to lure him with our music?'

Gwenlliant simply glared at her. No warrior should ignore her; and certainly no Iceni renegade who gave himself airs on account of a limp and a shipboard title. But she hadn't thought that Elen would point out her failure to attract him. Suddenly, her cousin choked off her laughter and became grave.

'Cousin,' she asked gently, 'was this one of the men of whom you dreamed that night you fled the grove?'

Only the presence of Dylan prevented Gwenlliant from slapping Elen the way that she deserved. But Olwen was watching them. Gwenlliant contented herself with a headshake and a glint in her eye that would have promised future vengeance had she seen any triumph in Elen's glance. But she did not: to her astonishment, the elder girl's gaze was grave and warm.

'What has come over the two of you?' asked Olwen. 'Think of it. For once, both of you are quiet. Gwenlliant, I suppose, is dreaming. But Elen, sister's daughter, are you meditating on the way of the gadfly?'

Gwenlliant smiled, laid aside the harp over which she had been dozing, and curled up on an outspread cloak beside her cousin, whose laughter turned into a yawn.

'The way of the gadfly, lady?' she asked. 'A useful creature in courts, I believe, though hemlock makes it horribly ill.'

Gwenlliant chortled, then yawned and stretched herself out more comfortably.

'And I thought that I would miss your mother when I travelled east,' Olwen commented.

Elen tapped Gwenlliant on the shoulder, then patted her lap, assuming that Gwenlliant trusted her enough not to pull her hair as she napped. Oddly enough, she did. Gadfly Elen might be to her, just as Alexa was to her mother, but daughter and mother were faithful.

'That hair of yours,' Elen murmured. 'It's like a ginger cat.

But a cat would groom it.' Gwenlliant purred sleepily as Elen lifted the sweat-dampened masses of curls from her neck.

'I think I have a comb about somewhere,' Elen told her cousin. Why had Gwenlliant never noticed how sweet her voice was? she wondered. *Because she generally says such sour things with it, that's why*.

'Do you want me to coil it up, so you'll be cooler? What did you say? Was that "hmph" a "yes?" ' Vehemently, Gwenlliant nodded her head.

Elen's touch with the ivory comb was gentle. The sunlight that poured over them from a cloudless sky felt like the baths in the women's quarters in her father's palace. A breeze touched her heated face and she shivered with pure pleasure. The strokes of ship's oars and Elen's comb merged with the gentle rocking of the ship. Gwenlliant remembered naps from her childhood, out under the blossoming trees of summer, cradled in her mother's arms, lulled by the plump bees that buzzed near Olwen's face, fascinated by the woman who smelled like a flower, but never stung her or her daughter. She could almost smell the flowers once again.

Lazily, she blinked. Yes, there stood Olwen by the rail, gazing back at Prydein. The chalk-white cliffs were veiled in a haze of heat and moisture; beyond them lay only a hint of the violent green through which they had ridden. The light glinted about her as if she were her own mosaic portrait, wrought all of white and gold tesserae, standing in a garden in which all the flowers were wrought of tiny, brilliant squares of glass. Compared with the living original, that mosaic was odourless, cold – and immortal.

'Do you think she will be all right?' Gwenlliant blurted in a sudden whisper.

'Hush,' urged Elen, stroking her hair. 'Just lie back now.'

When they were children, Elen might have ordered Gwenlliant and Mor about as an older child will dominate those younger than she, but it had been Elen, often, who had gone to Gwenlliant in the night if she wept from a nightmare or an ache; Elen, who bound up battered knees and elbows, stole herbs to minister to aching bellies, and never told adults what they had eaten to ache that much. Elen's tongue might sting like nettles, but if Elen said not to worry, then it was probably safe not to. Comforted, Gwenlliant slept, cradled between the sea and the sky.

Gradually, a shadow spread over her the way that Daphne, who always tended her in Byzantium, might draw a fine silk sheet up about her shoulders as she slept. Gwenlliant felt the muscles of her face smile. Elen sat dozing too, her hand stroking Gwenlliant's hair. Above them, the shadow darkened. Abruptly came such a blast of chill hatred that both girls blinked, as if slapped into awareness. Then Elen's fingers tightened once almost too briefly to be noticed, then resumed their steady motion through Gwenlliant's hair.

– *You felt that*, – came her voice in Gwenlliant's mind. – *Can you tell where it is?* –

Mentally, Gwenlliant winced. – *It's on this ship.* –

Elen's fingers tugged in her hair, then relaxed.

– *Wake up!* – Gwenlliant sent frantically at her. – *It* wants *us to sleep.* – With acting skill that astonished her even as she used it for the first time, she yawned and rolled away from her cousin, freeing both of them to act, if need be. Simultaneously, she cast the empathy that she still found so fearful and new about the ship . . .

. . . and recoiled almost instantly from the cold, the anger that she touched. What felt like a shield flashed between her and the rage that might have burnt her mind out, casting it away before it withdrew.

– *Let it think it won.* –

That went against her grain. Nevertheless, Gwenlliant set her teeth and feinted, letting her mental 'self' cry out and crumple, as if overwhelmed by the anger and the hatred, and felt their sender gloat over the tiny victory.

– *It's coming closer . . .* – came Elen's 'voice'.

Gwenlliant let her eyes flutter open. She sniffed the air and fought not to gag . . . *myrrh, mitre, ammonia, rot . . .* smells of the necropolis assailed her, but all that she saw from the restriction of her vantage-point were sailors tugging on lines, and the rise and fall of the 'wings' of oars against which Olwen stood, in a minbus of light both real and of Gwenlliant's imagination.

The gust of foulness came again, oozing out like a viscous wave of ink, thickened with blood and foulness; and it lapped out towards Olwen!

Frantically, Gwenlliant cast about with eyes and mind, and saw only a sailor, older than some, smaller than many, darker than most, approaching the Queen. – *Elen . . .* –

– *He doesn't look Roman. Or like the Celtoi*, – Elen responded. – *Egyptian perhaps.* –

'Majesty?'

Wrapped in her own thoughts, Olwen began slowly to turn towards the voice. The man started to bow, but . . .

In that instant, Gwenlliant knew how it would be done: how the respectful bow would turn into a lunge and a stab, and how the man would then hurl her mother, dead or dying, into the water. And meanwhile, *they* – Elen and herself – would be screaming, too distraught for anyone to believe what they saw until it was too late. Assuming that the assassin thought that that blast of hatred had not stripped them of their wits first.

Then Gwenlliant saw a light glint from the man's left hand, which held a blade with a blackened edge.

'He has a dagger!' Gwenlliant shrieked, as she snatched at her own. 'Elen, quick!'

She screamed for help with mind and voice, and launched herself at the assassin, Elen just behind her.

'Bring him down!' Elen gasped, hurling herself at the man's feet, her blade slashing for the man's hamstrings as Gwenlliant came up against his left arm, slamming the hand with the dagger against the guardrail. His grip held. Panting with rage and fright, she forced his hand down again and heard Elen cry out as he kicked her in the side. She swore, but held on in a sort of stubborn fury that Gwenlliant sensed and drew strength from. Gwenlliant felt the man stagger as her cousin's dagger sliced viciously into the man's leg.

Good! Now he would fall and now they would slash his throat, she thought. Or perhaps they should wait until Olwen questioned him.

'I can't make him fall!' Elen gasped, dodging another kick. 'Guard yourself! Don't let him cut you.'

Gwenlliant bent lower. Perhaps if she *bit* him . . . but his

74

right hand tangled itself in her hair, and she reeled from the foulness of his breath.

'Let her go,' Olwen spoke in a cold voice that Gwenlliant had never before heard from her. 'You don't want her. You want *me*.'

With a contemptuous push, the assassin hurled Gwenlliant against Elen. She struggled up, only to see Olwen, queensblade in hand, face the man. 'I am Isis on Earth,' she spoke almost ritually. 'I it was who returned from the mouth of hell. You cannot stand against me.'

'You are no Isis, but a barbarian wench raised beyond your highest dreams!' spat the man. He was bleeding, and he lurched unsteadily; Elen had most definitely cut the hamstrings of his right leg, but still he advanced, dragging it behind him in a hideous parody of Dylan's limp.

Gwenlliant crept forward with some hazed notion of tripping the man and tossing him overboard; Elen simply screamed with mind and voice until, after what seemed like ten winters, she was answered.

'Get away!' Dylan shouted. Gwenlliant flung herself to one side as the captain charged assassin and queen. He seemed to fly across the deck, striking the man in the chest with his shoulder as he grappled for the poisoned dagger with one hand and, with the other, thrust at the man's belly with a long knife, almost a sword. The man swerved with preternatural speed. 'Dylan – oh *no!*' cried Gwenlliant as the young captain took a slash across his palm from the assassin's blade. Something clattered, glinting, to the deck and was kicked aside.

Dylan cried out from the anguish of knifeblow and the acid pain of whatever venom had coated the blade, but struck again. This time his blade thrust threw the man, who fell so suddenly that both he and Dylan plunged into the water.

The screams of battle and that final splash broke what was left of the rhythm of the oars.

'Your captain's fallen. Bring the ship about!' Olwen shouted. 'Quick,' she commanded the girls. 'Elen, get your herbs. Gwenlliant, that line. Bring it. I can see him . . . help me throw him a line. No, he was injured, he can't hold on. Let me tie it in a loop first. Dylan! Catch this!'

The rope snaked out and slapped into the water near the captain, who swam towards it with the ease of one all but born in the sea. Abruptly, his eyes went wide, his mouth opened in a gasp for air or help, and he began to flounder, then to sink.

'He's poisoned!' Gwenlliant cried and threw herself over the side. There, in the shadow of the boat, the water was colder than any she had ever swum in, and its swells threatened to overpower her. She glanced about frantically. There was the rope loop, but where was Dylan? *Sensation of pain, of terror, as once again his body betrayed him and he went stiff, then limp.* Gwenlliant swam towards that fear and outrage and saw Dylan's face just as it sank into the swell of a wave so gentle that a child might have withstood it. She seized his hair and pulled until his face was out of the water. Then, holding her breath, she dived beneath the unconscious man until she could lash the rope about him.

She surfaced, gasping. The distance between herself, paddling frantically with one hand, and her mother and cousin, tugging at the rope, seemed to be the height of Mount Sinadon and getting higher by the instant as the ship drew away.

'Hold on!' cried Elen. Two sailors hurtled into the water and Gwenlliant recoiled, first from their splashes, then from their hands, outstretched towards her and their captain.

'*We* won't hurt you, little lady, Goddess love you,' one of the men said, as the other took charge of Dylan. His face lay against the crewman's shoulder. It was pale and the lips were pinched and blue.

'Is he breathing?' Gwenlliant coughed as she asked it.

'Just about . . . all right, I have him! Hoist us up!'

'See to him first, I can wait,' she gasped, glad now of the other sailor's grasp. Reaction from the battle began to set in and her limbs felt leaden.

As she collapsed on the deck, Elen ran to her and flung a cape about her. Gwenlliant saw the angry rope burns that slashed across her palms. For one precious instant, she and her cousin were hugging one another and crying. Then they turned towards Olwen, as she knelt above Dylan. The sweetness of flowers hung about her like a veil, mingling with the scent of brine.

'Poison on the blade. At least the salt water will have flushed the wound,' Olwen mused. 'Bring warm cloaks,' she ordered the nearest girl. Then she drew a deep breath, knelt and laid her hands upon Dylan's pallid face.

The air, which had been freshened by a cat's paw of wind, suddenly trembled and was still. Gwenlliant tensed, aware of the strain which made Olwen go rigid as her spirit sought for its old power, demanded it, and drew strength from her, mind and body.

'Roses,' whispered one of the sailors. 'She is like spring.'

Again the air trembled, wreathing about Queen and dying man. Olwen bent over him, her hair falling loose, concealing him like a shield. Her breath came quick and short. Now, she snatched his hand and all but fell.

Her garments and hair dripping, shivering from the impulsive plunge into the sea, Gwenlliant crawled over to her mother's side and wrapped her hands about her mother's.

– I cannot heal. Not yet. But take what you need. –

– Not your job, child. Get yourself clear. –

For a third time, Gwenlliant had the sense of the air wrapping about Dylan and Olwen, enshrouding them, bearing them the way she had supported him in the water. Then, abruptly, the cocoon of air fell apart. Olwen gasped and sagged on to the deck.

'Mother!' cried Gwenlliant. Olwen raised a hand, then head, and smiled. Though her lips were pale with exhaustion, that smile was bright with victory.

Beside her, Dylan groaned. Elen knelt at his side with herbal salves and linen.

Behind the women was a scuffling of bare feet. 'Do we take his hand off, lady?'

'No . . .' Dylan's voice was hoarse and full of dread. 'I'm crippled already. Take off my hand and you may as well take my head with it.'

'You don't need to,' Olwen spoke in a low, weary voice. She lifted the hand that the poisoned dagger had slashed. Only a thin white scar remained to mark the wound.

'Elen, come here and I will see to your hand.'

77

'No!' Elen whipped it behind her back. 'Don't waste your strength on a little thing like blisters.'

'Gwenlliant, my brave one,' her mother ordered, 'dry clothing for you, my dearest. Now.'

Gwenlliant pulled the cloak about her and refused to be ushered away. If defiance could work for Elen, it would work for her too. Now that her mother was safe and Dylan would live, the saltwater that stung her eyes and dripped from her hair made her shiver in delight, and the sea air affected her like undiluted Falernian wine.

Olwen clung to the nearest railing, visibly suppressing shudders. She was always exhausted, always drained after major healings. Gwenlliant pulled her mother's arm about her shoulders to support her.

'What was it?' Now, finally, others of their train joined them.

'Some sort of attack,' Olwen said. 'Didn't you feel it?'

A Druid novice bent his head. 'I did.'

'Very well, then, who would want to take my life?' she observed. She turned and looked out over the sea, back at Prydein. 'How foolish, when I was so close to giving it back,' Gwenlliant heard her muse. 'Perhaps, after all, it is still worth something.' She lifted her voice to allow it to carry over the slap of waves and the voices of men who began to return to their duties. 'Who among you knows anything about that man?'

All of the sailors seemed to protest at once and at the tops of their lungs, denying that they had ever seen him before. Olwen held up a hand for quiet.

'Dylan?' she asked. From where did she draw strength so that her voice did not quiver from exhaustion?

'Lady, I am crippled in mind as well as body. Call myself captain of a ship? What sort of captain does not search for stowaways?'

'A captain preoccupied with receiving a queen,' Elen retorted. For once, Gwenlliant was grateful for her cousin's acid tongue. In the next moment, Elen suppressed a yelp and an oath as the young Druid rubbed salve on to her blistered palm.

'My niece is right,' Olwen said. 'This self-hatred is a waste of time and spirit.'

'Ladies, you put me to shame,' Dylan said. He started to

lever himself up from the deck, carefully, favouring his withered leg. The clear sunlight of late afternoon slanted down into a tiny fire.

'What's that?' he demanded, and all but overbalanced as he reached to scoop it up.

'Don't touch it!' Olwen snapped. She wound linen about her hand and only then picked up the blaze of light.

'What is it?' Gwenlliant drew closer.

Olwen held out her hand, on which rested a bloodstone cut in the shape of a beetle, and deeply incised with the pictographs of the Two Lands.

'A scarab,' breathed Elen.

'Whose signet is this?' Olwen demanded. 'Elen, I know that your command of these signs is better than mine.'

Elen bent over the scarab, which was perhaps the size of the first joint of her thumb. 'Scarabs are not always signets, Aunt,' she said cautiously. 'Sometimes they are simply signs. And sometimes,' she looked more closely at it and went very pale, 'sometimes, priests and embalmers hide them in the linen that they used to wrap a mummy, or place them in its case.'

'Well,' Olwen asked the reasonable, logical question, 'which type of scarab is this? I can read some of the symbols. Here is one that means peace.'

Elen's eyes narrowed. Abruptly, she pounced, pushing at Olwen's hand, sending the scarab glittering to the deck.

'Don't touch that, at least not before you ward it,' she hissed. 'It was a funerary gem, that much I could sense, but it is also a signet, the cartouche of one who is dead and should have been forgotten.'

Her eyes were wide and wild, like a horse's just before it runs out of control. Abruptly, tears poured down her face. 'My mother's enemy and my uncle's the whole Empire's. You should be dead,' she sobbed at the scarab. 'My uncle saw you executed. You tried to drive my mother mad; she almost killed herself. Why couldn't you have just died and been damned? Why do you have to come back now?'

Olwen grasped the smaller woman by both shoulders and shook her.

'Enough of that, Elen. Your mother would be ashamed. Whose name is on that scarab?'

Elen looked down, then met Olwen's eyes resolutely.

'It belongs,' she said, with a sort of frozen calm, 'to one who tried to take the Empire for itself and who almost destroyed it all. You read the symbols yourself,' she said, and pointed. 'Only you read them wrong. See here? You read "*eirene*", the Greek word for peace. But it's also a name.' Elen gulped back a sound that was half sob, half appalled laughter. 'A less peaceful woman never existed. That scarab belongs to Irene, sorceress and usurper.'

Chapter Eight

Gesoriacum grew larger and larger as the ship neared its thriving harbour. From her vantage point a deferential two paces behind the Queen, Elen could see that the town had been built on the Roman model, with paved, ordered streets leading from the docks to the town itself. Much of it looked newly built, the result of twenty years of relative peace and definite prosperity as the Emperor had regained many of the Gallic lands that had been gnawed, in the past centuries, from Byzantium's holdings. Stretching out beyond the town, half obscured by the haze that rose by the sea on a summer's evening, were the high arches of the aqueducts that the Emperor had commanded to be built to carry water from the north to the much dryer southlands. Near to them gleamed the stonework of a hippodrome in which, Elen knew, Celtoi and Rhomaioi betted on their favourite drivers. Another of her uncle's schemes for drawing the two peoples together.

The Emperor: hard to think of her uncle, who petted her, spoiled her, and had given her, when she was a baby, the pearl-and-gold necklace that she always wore as the eidolon, half warrior and half god, of the Horus rituals and the glittering mosaics she remembered from her own few trips into the Empire.

Without turning her head, she contrived to watch preparations for their landing, even as she wondered where her cousin – in full, cumbersome splendour of torque, circlet, cloak (even though the sun was setting, the hot air pressed in upon Elen until she fought the urge to pray for a breeze that never came, or gasp for more air), bad temper and all – had disappeared to. Olwen, however, seemed serenely unconcerned, either with the heat or her daughter's absence. No one, Elen thought, would ever believe that, only hours ago, some fanatic who bore the cartouche of a woman long dead and justly accursed had tried to slay the Queen.

Swaying only slightly, with the ease of a woman long accustomed to chariots, Olwen stood on the ship's deck. The complications of her white undergown and pleated, transparent linen overgown were so carefully arrayed that they did not appear to move beneath her cloak. The last rays of the sun struck the silver crown she wore, a circlet set with two horns and the moon disc held between them, and blinding light flashed out from the crown over the water as if blessing the town.

'Where is Gwenlliant?' Olwen whispered, barely moving her lips.

'She left while you were being robed but said that she would be here when we landed,' Elen replied, with a spasm of guilt that she had not stopped the younger girl. She had been distracted by that Dylan since the instant that she had seen him.

An exasperated gesture, hidden in the careful folds of Olwen's purple cloak, let Elen know what the Queen thought of that – not that she could blame her. Bad enough that her wretch of a cousin had all but drowned herself to rescue a ship's captain who might, just might have known something about the assassination attempt on Queen Olwen (it had not escaped Elen that Dylan had managed to kill the assassin and to let his body sink beyond hope of interrogation or death-examination by priests), but for Gwenlliant to miss the landing!

'I see Mor!' Olwen's whispers rose. 'Look, Elen! The officer on the bay horse at the head of the column. He's grown so serious-looking. Oh, damn these ceremonies! All I want is to leave this ship and kiss my son. Why must the Empire make such a simple thing so complex? They would do better to drape our robes on statues and move them about as they wish.'

Because Elen's mother had always taken the inconvenience of ceremony for granted and trained her daughter to expect no better, Elen held her peace . . . and her smiles.

As if surprised by her silence, Olwen turned about fully and looked Elen over. She actually reached out and straightened Elen's circlet, a gift from Alexa, and enamalled with blue and white lotus blossoms, then beckoned the girl to stand beside her, holding her by the hand and pressing it tightly for sheer excitement.

Though Elen's hands were damp with excitement, at least they no longer ached from the rope burns she had suffered while trying to rescue Gwenlliant. Despite her mother's many warnings on how Olwen must not waste her strength, the Queen had healed her.

They had been dressing in haste for the landing when Elen fumbled at the heavy clasp of her necklace of amethysts and aquamarines set in gold flowers, and hissed with the pain of her rope burns as the metal pressed into the skin. Pain was simply pain, however. She overrode it, raised her arms to fasten the necklace about her throat, and winced as the movement pulled muscles bruised by the assassin's kicks. Carefully, she drew a deep breath. No sudden, lancing pains followed, and she sighed in relief, despite the twinge that cost her. At least none of her ribs had been broken.

'Elen.'

'My Aunt?' Elen realized that her voice sounded snappish from the pain. Unwise, indiscreet, to snap at the Queen on whom one's welfare depends. Even her mother did not dare to do so, as far as she presumed upon her own privileges.

'You realize, do you not, that you are being absurd?' Olwen's voice was as cool as her mother's could be. That tone always made Elen wince. What had she done this time, or, just as heinous, not done?

Not trusting her voice, she looked up interrogatively just in time to see Olwen settle the moon crown of Isis upon her head, silver gleaming upon the silvered gold of her hair, which looked like electrum in the cabin's dim light, and walk towards her, swaying in the confines of the tiny cabin. She caught her breath in admiration, even awe, that Olwen, who looked now as if she ought to live at the Horizon, not in a maenol of timber and stone, would address her at all.

'Give me your hands,' ordered the Queen. 'You are in pain; I will heal you.'

Elen clasped her hands behind her back, ignoring the sudden, burning ache as two blisters split. 'Healing takes too much of your strength, Aunt,' she said. 'You are already weary from transmuting the poison in Captain Dylan's hand; you should not waste strength on what will heal in its own time.'

Olwen embraced her as if she were, once again, a child rather than a problem. 'You have been listening to your mother, haven't you?' she asked warmly. 'Well, so have I. When the cleverest woman I have ever met tells me that she has sent her brother her best message, then loads her daughter with her own jewels, one need not have studied with the Druids or in an academy to know what that message is! Child, healing you will take no great strength, and may even restore me. After all, you are my own flesh and blood.'

Olwen held out her hands and smiled. 'Come now. Do you want to ache during the welcome that they have prepared for us? Is it fair, after all Gesoriacum's hard work, not to give them your most gracious smiles in return? They have a right to see Princesses who are beautiful and happy. How can you expect to smile if you are in pain?'

It was not Olwen's reasoning that made Elen's eyes well with tears and let her rest her sore hands in her aunt's – despite Alexa's warnings not to let Queen Olwen overspend her strength – but the gentleness in her voice. *Perhaps*. Elen thought, *perhaps she is right, and healing me will not harm her. She must stay well, oh she must. Gwenlliant wants it so.*

Once or twice, in Byzantium, Elen had smelled jasmine. Now the heavy sweetness of that scent wreathed about her, mingled with the freshness of roses and lilacs. Elen's palms tingled, then went blessedly cool as Olwen pressed them between her own hands, and the air twisted, went opalescent the way it did whenever Olwen worked a healing –

'Now the ribs,' Olwen ordered. 'I do not think that you need to undress.' She set her palms to Elen's side. 'Such a brave girl,' she crooned as, despite Elen's best efforts, she flinched at the touch. 'He kicked you so hard, but you never let go. In a moment you will feel easier.'

Warm met the unnatural heat of Elen's bruises and spread up and down her side like balm scented with roses. The pain disappeared so suddenly that she swayed to one side, almost giddy with relief. Olwen supported her.

'There you are,' Olwen said. 'Now tell me that you would have rather stayed in pain.'

For once Elen forgot that Olwen was a queen, and she a princess of a collateral line and no great future, long enough to fling her arms about her aunt in an impulsive hug, which Olwen returned. For a moment, the elder woman leaned on her. Elen tried to will her own strength, her own youth into the queen but –

'You'll wrinkle us both!' Olwen cried in mock horror, pretending to push her aside.

'Straighten your dress,' she ordered, then waved Elen's hands away and refastened the bands that bound her light gown about her waist and breasts. 'The way your ribs must have hurt, no wonder you tied it so loosely. Yes, I know. Before you tell me, I know that you are no child. I know to the day just how old you are. Remember, I was there when you were born.' She smiled at Elen, shaking her head. 'Besides, in that dress – now that it is properly laced – anyone can see that you are no child. Just look at yourself! What a little beauty you are.'

Over Elen's protests, which were only half sincere, she set her own silver mirror for the girl to look into. She gasped, and her hands, upraised to push the mirror aside, fell, then clasped themselves loosely in her white linen lap. The dress, in the classic Greek style, belted across and between her breasts and thrice about her waist, emphasizing the delicate curves of her body and setting off the faint colour that days in the sun had given her. The blue of the gems she wore made her eyes look darker and more lustrous. And, against her protests, Olwen had insisted that Elen line them in the Egyptian mode.

'You look as though you were born and raised in the women's

quarters of the Palace,' Olwen smiled. 'Oh, how pleased Alexa would be.' Tenderly – *as if I were her own daughter* – she stroked Elen's hair. 'Elen, if you knew that you could look this lovely, why, oh why, did you insist on muffling yourself in homespun robes?'

Elen shrugged. The girl in the mirror, jewels gleaming at brow, throat and bodice, was a revelation to her, too. *What need had I of beauty? No prince sought me, I had no wealth, or none to speak of, to attract a king; and Penllyn was for Gwenlliant, who is beautiful. No need even to try. Had I been beautiful, I should have been the more wounded.*

Everything was for Gwenlliant, beauty and land and royalty and healing; while Elen, who would have been heir to Penllyn had Gwenlliant not been born, must stand back, just as her mother had had to *because of Irene*. Damn Irene! Elen thought, then grimaced. It was far too late to damn a woman who was long dead, condemned by her own sorceries. *She has robbed us, mother and daughter, of our futures.* Irene had induced Alexa to study proscribed magics; Irene had all but driven her mad; Irene had separated brother and sister, setting them on their own courses until client-princess, wife to the Queen's brother, was the best fate to which Alexa might aspire. She had been bred to be Empress!

Instead, it was prostrate yourself to Olwen, speak humbly to your aunt, remember that Gwenlliant must come before you in all things . . . More than once, Elen had clenched her fingers into her palms until each bore a sigil like a bloody half-moon. It was hard to sense strength in oneself, growing grace, an awareness of people and events that might grow to statecraft if it were permitted, as it never would be.

Mother told me that she never craved a throne, Elen told herself. *But what she wants, she has. And I? What is the nothing that I am to be permitted?* Anger gave way, later, to disbelief. *Mother is imperial down to her rings*, Elen had thought. *She lies about her ambitions. And if she lies to me about that one thing, why should she not lie about other matters as well?*

The one time, however, that she had allowed her fury and powerlessness to rise to the fore in her conscious thoughts in Alexa's presence, her mother had flinched, then wept. Elen had never seen her weep before. When Gereint strode in, demanding to know why Alexa wept, she had simply shaken her head. Not once had either of them turned on her with *What have you done?*

No, people like that would not lie.

What *did* Elen want? Not what Gwenlliant had. For one thing, despite their frequent quarrels, she loved her cousin. It was hard not to love anyone that high-hearted, even carefree despite a future that, Elen admitted quite candidly, would have daunted her: to see her mother sacrifice herself; to know, as she aged, that she must one day contemplate death in the Druid's grove. Even the powers now maturing in the girl – the Queen of Penllyn *should* be a healer, and the Goddess knew, Elen was no such thing. Her own talents – *such as they were* – were less conspicuous: a taste for learning, a gift, as she had demonstrated just that afternoon, for enduring, for holding on when all else failed. How else had she held on to her loyalty and her love for her family when it robbed her of anything that a girl who knew herself to be talented, vital and lovely might consider a proper future? In all ways, she was thwarted.

What, would you have done, Elen, had Irene whispered to you of love, hope and power? Could you have conquered where your mother, with all her strength and vision, faltered and fell?

She was honest enough to admit that she did not know.

As she had drilled herself over the years of enforced patience and lowliness, Elen sat quietly, hands folded in her lap, before the mirror that reflected a woman who was born royal and beautiful. *This one day*, she thought. *Just this one day, it can do no harm to pretend.*

Now, adorned as a princess of a ruling line, Elen stood beside a queen, and her palms sweated with excitement.

'The ship is about to dock,' Olwen swayed from side to side, then steadied herself. 'I thought you said that Gwenlliant would meet us on deck.'

At least, Elen had good news to give of the young cousin whom, she must serve, one day, as her mother served Olwen. 'She slipped away to thank Captain Dylan for saving you. There is the captain now; she must be nearby.'

Olwen nodded almost imperceptibly, her eyes on the shore, where lines of soldiers and dignitaries formed up to greet her. 'Well enough. I hope that she has not decided to throw herself at his head. Life will be hard enough . . .' she sighed, and Elen remembered just how much she opposed her husband's plan for a dynastic match between Gwenlliant and her brother.

'I am not too late, am I?' Gwenlliant slipped through the mass of Olwen's attendants to her mother's side and turned to whisper to Elen.

'Where were you?'

'I told you that I wanted to thank Captain Dylan,' Gwenlliant said with some sharpness. 'He was busy.'

So, why did you not come here immediately? Elen started to ask, but, seeing Gwenlliant's eyes which threatened to brim with tears and ruin the careful lines of kohl that encircled them, choked back the question. *My aunt wastes her healing on a boor. If he has insulted my cousin* . . . she thought, her hand reaching for the dagger that she did not wear. She took Gwenlliant's hand and her own mood softened. *He has made her cry. So little time to have seen him, and already she cares. How does that happen?*

That was a greater mystery than any in the learning that she had mastered years ago. She suspected that it lay beyond the bounds of her power.

'What happened?' she asked gently, and saw her cousin's eyes begin to well over.

'Later,' Olwen whispered. 'Behave yourselves.'

The ship lurched as the sailors threw lines to the waiting docksmen, who made them fast. Abruptly, Elen's knees went weak, and her newly healed palms began to sweat again.

Leaving the ranks of Hetaeria guardsmen and Varangians who were drawn up, swords and axes in salute, on either side of a row of importantly robed and jewelled local magistrates, Prince Mor marched forward, his face set in the expressionless mask that was imperial propriety, and saluted his mother as he would a senior general. Behind him, his men raised their weapons in homage.

'You are seen, Prince,' Olwen called, then waited as Dylan and his second-in-command made fast the walkway to the dock.

Mor beckoned to an aide, who set aside his helmet and hastened forward. The instant that the planks touched the ground, Prince Mor, formality set aside, all but bounded up them and held out his hand to his mother.

His eyes and grin flashed as Olwen took his hand. Elen saw how she held still for a long moment, squeezing it. His eyes flickered over Gwenlliant and herself; they were the colour of barley, or amber, surprisingly light in a face tanned by a summer's campaigning. As soon as Olwen, graceful as her own daughter, stepped lightly to the shore, Mor dropped to his knees. Clearly, he intended to 'kiss earth' in the ancient manner, but Olwen forestalled him with hands on his armoured shoulders.

'Is that how a son should greet his mother?' she asked, drawing him up on to his feet and into an enthusiastic embrace. Then she held him at arms's length and looked him over, laughing with pride. 'You . . . oh Mor, you *glow!*' she cried, and laid hands on his dark hair, curled and matted from his helmet, to bless him before she kissed his forehead.

Definitely, Mor was worth looking at, Elen thought, then corrected herself. He was worth looking at now. Even Gwenlliant was staring unabashedly at her brother. They had been apart for many years, while Mor trained under his father's eye to rule the Empire that would one day be his. The last time but one that Elen had seen Mor, he had been a dark, robust boy, slow to get his growth; the last time she had seen him in Penllyn, he wore several years' rapid growth awkwardly, as if he had yet to fill out around his long bones. She had spared him a glance and quick greeting, then retired, dividing that summer between Deva the Druids' Isle, and the grove, while Mor had spent his time among Olwen's warriors as if eager to prove himself a man and their peer. Before that? She supposed that Mor must have played with her and Gwenlliant during the seasons that Marric brought him to spend in Penllyn, but her actual memories of that time were blurred, fragments of warmth and sweetness and far-ago laughter.

'Greet your sister and your cousin,' Olwen turned in Mor's strong, braceleted arms and held out her hand. Mor gestured, and his aide came up beside him, leaner than he, and lighter-skinned, crimson across the cheeks and throat with sunburn.

'Most Sacred Majesty,' began Mor, to be interrupted by a stamp of Olwen's foot. 'Mother,' he started over, then shook his head admiringly. 'You look as if my sister and my cousin could be *your* sisters. This letter' – he produced a sealed scroll from his belt – 'is from my father. Now, may I present my aide, Flavius Marcellinus?'

'That is Flavius?' Gwenlliant whispered. 'When I last saw him, he had spots!'

Elen stifled a nervous laugh and vowed to pinch Gwenlliant if she made another such comment. She recalled that the Emperor's most senior general and, when he left the city, his regent, was this youth's father, Caius Marcellinus. This Marcellinus was his youngest son, perhaps five or six years older than herself. As befitted the companion of an Imperial heir, he too had the manners of a prince as he bowed in reverence to his Empress and Isis made manifest on earth.

'Now,' demanded Olwen, laughing, 'greet me as my son and friend. You are most welcome, Flavius. Is your father well?'

The aide flushed, then swallowed twice before he could stammer assent. devotion shone in his eyes. Elen chuckled at how easily Olwen had succeeded in reducing a young and noble officer to adoring boyhood with a simple question. He stared at her until she raised an eyebrow and glanced back at the ship.

'Good!' Gwenlliant murmured. 'I was beginning to fear that Mor had decided to leave us here.'

Elen stifled a laugh. Flavius Marcellinus bent and murmured something confidentially to Mor, who laughed, setting his hands on his hips and looking up at Elen and Gwenlliant.

'You are quite right,' he told Flavius Marcellinus. 'But I enjoyed admiring them as they stood there.'

'But did they enjoy standing there, my Prince?'

'An excellent question, conscience of mine. Come and help me remedy my oversight.'

Again Mor advanced up the ramp with a lithe stride and had out his hand for Gwenlliant's. For a moment, brother and sister measured one another with a bold, challenging stare. Then he laughed and swung her up in his arms. For a wonder, Gwenlliant did not laugh, fume or try to kick her brother. Finally he set her down on the dock beside Marcellinus.

'I'm certain you'll be happy to see to Gwenlliant, Flavius!' he told his friend, who grinned and bowed to the Princess. Elen blinked. Surely that could not be his whole greeting to his ' sister. He ought at the very least to kiss her, but no, he started up the planks once again, his hand outheld for her own.

He smiled down into her face as his hand took hers in a firm, almost possessive grasp that jolted her. She remembered that grasp . . . no, it was gone . . . but for a moment, her hands ached, and her mind sought memories as her tongue might have probed for a bad tooth. She could not take her eyes from Mor. Why had she thought that his eyes were the colour of barley? There was an undertone of smoke in their depths. Elen shivered, hoping that finally the night winds had come to cool her cheeks.

'I remember you,' he said, in a voice softer than he had used either to his mother or his sister. 'Oh, I do remember. But . . .' his voice went gentle, coaxing, 'I see that you do not. Let me remind you, cousin. We were climbing in the hills when I tried to take a cliff that was too hard for me. Of course, I fell and twisted my ankle. I thought it was broken, and Gwenlliant was shrieking like a horde of Huns . . .'

Elen flung up her free hand and stepped forward somewhat unsteadily as the memories, hidden for so many years, leapt from her mind like a trout, to surface in the sunlight with a splash that, just for a moment, blinded her. 'Yes,' she breathed. 'You caught yourself,' she whispered past a lump that, unaccountably and to her infinite mortification, rose in her throat. 'I remember.'

What had made her forget, all these years? As Mor fell, Gwenlliant had screamed, sharing his pain and fear; Elen, who hated heights but, as the eldest, refused to show cowardice, screamed once, certain that her cousin had fallen to his death on the rocks far below. Then, with a courage she had not dreamed she possessed, she flung herself down at the cliff's edge, where Mor clung not a yard below her to a rock spur. He tried to swing himself up, but his injured leg touched the rock and buckled, and he fell back with a sharp cry of anguish.

'Go away, Elen,' he gasped. 'I don't want you here, watching when I fall.'

Elen had laid her head down in the dirt, fighting off giddiness and sickness at the hateful drop below for one self-indulgent moment. Then, 'Don't try that again, Mor. Just hold on!' she ordered in a calm voice that sounded like a queen, a Druid, or anything but a twelve-year-old scared past tears. 'Gwenlliant, you run for help. Stop crying, or I'll slap you! Just run and bring help.'

As she looked down at Mor, tears falling on to her grimy hands, suddenly her terrors faded. What lay on that ledge *changed* suddenly from Elen to a being far older and more self-possessed, a being that studied the way Mor clung to his hand-hold and calculated coldly and precisely that her twelve-year-old strength was not sufficient to let her climb down and rescue him. Instead, she inched out until she looked down into Mor's upturned face, white with pain and terror. If he cried out at all, she realized, he would panic and fall.

'You're going to be safe, Mor,' she called down. 'Hold on. You heard me. I sent Gwenlliant for help. Hold on!'

For what felt like years, and might, in fact, have been an hour or so, she had lain with her head over the abyss, staring down into what she feared most, as she crooned encouragement to Mor, sang to him, prayed with him, afraid to shut her eyes lest he lose heart, afraid to keep them open lest she see him fall.

'I can't,' he gasped. 'Tell my father . . .'

'No!' Elen screamed it and, before she could think about it and pull back, inched forward until she could grasp his hands. 'Hold on,' she gasped. 'Hold for both of us.'

Her nails left marks in his hand as she clung to him and pleaded with him for both of their lives . . .

'Can't hold . . .' he muttered.

Then a raven had swooped down from the heights, shrieking as it passed Mor's head. 'Hide your eyes!' Elen had called.

Once again it attacked. Mor cried out in protest, and his voice sounded remote, feeble . . .

'*NO!*' Elen remembered screaming at the bird. 'Get away!' She dared not remove her hands from Mor's to flap them at the creature. She lay there crying and screaming until another scream sounded from overhead, the cry of a hunting hawk as it stooped on its enemy – and theirs.

'A hawk, Elen!' Mor sobbed with relief. 'They'll come, you'll see, they'll come.' But she was past reason, except for the imperative 'hold on'. Time faded into an anguished blur until finally, running feet, panted breath and Gwenlliant's cries assured her that adults had finally come to save them both.

It was the Emperor himself who swung down beside his son. The raven swooped and dived at him, but he flung out an arm that sent the bird careening into the rock face and then, stunned, into the abyss. Blood welled and dripped from the slash that its beak had opened in Marric's arm, but he ignored it as he hoisted the boy up to safety, then scrabbled up beside him. Tenderly, he pried his son's fingers free of Elen's, then flung his arms about the boy in a hug tighter than even the Queen's white bear could give. Even then, Elen had known that Marric, unlike men of the Celtoi, did not weep – *could not*, she had heard the adults whisper, but not when they knew that she was present. His lips were white, and a muscle along his jaw twitched until he buried his face in his son's matted hair.

If Marric could not weep, Mor would not, and Gwenlliant was too little to hold in her tears. Accordingly, Elen bit back her sobs. As Marric sat there, shaking with relief, she tore a strip from the hem of her skirt and bandaged her uncle's arm. Then, as Marris lifted his heir in his arms and headed back down the slope towards Olwen and healing, she followed, clinging to his leg wherever she could, Gwenlliant clutching at her hand.

'I had nightmares all that summer after,' she told this transformed and vital Mor. 'My mother took me to Deva for the Druids to heal.' *Where*, she thought, *they must have made certain that I forgot what made me so ill. Was it simply seeing my cousin in peril of his life? Or had I over-strained, over-used . . . wasn't that the summer I first had my women's cycles?*

Why, however, had she forgotten all of that, only to remember it now? Her mind raced down paths that opened like roads from which guards had rolled away the barriers. Once or twice, she remembered being able to reason as quickly as now she did. Then Mor's voice broke the spell of her logic and lured her back to him.

'I looked for you,' Mor said. 'I hoped you would come to see me. I even dreamed about you. But you were gone.' He looked at their joined hands and smiled. 'Mother healed my leg, but said that the scratches you put on my hands could heal by themselves. They stung, though.'

Elen laid her free hand over the one that Mor held and smiled at him. 'I didn't want to hurt you,' she said. The boy whom she had cried with and comforted had become a man whose nearness warmed her as he drew her towards him, down the planks to the shore, one arm about her shoulders. He kissed her cheek as he had not bothered to kiss his sister's. Elen blushed, certain that the Queen would frown.

But Olwen was smiling. Abruptly, Elen trembled and tears started in her eyes. *Tell my brother that I have sent him my best message*, her mother had said.

She herself was, had to be, that message. Oh, it made sense. Alexa had renounced the moon crown, had wed – and been happy in wedding – Gereint, finding contentment in serving his sister as confidante and regent. But she had never forgotten her old ambitions or her home. Instead, she had simply transferred her dreams to her child so carefully, so subtly, that Elen had never guessed why the long years of training when Gwenlliant was permitted to run wild over the hills, why the attention to manners, the careful sheltering from most of the casual, fumbling loves of her age-mates, why the long, much-loved conversations about a city that Elen had been permitted to see but once or twice. Finally, Alexa had made her move; and her gamepiece was her daughter.

'Mother,' said Mor, as he came up beside Olwen, 'because my father told me, "see that your mother travels as befits an Empress" ' – he laughed as Olwen grimaced – 'I ordered a litter prepared. But I remember how, when I was a child, you drove me in your chariot, and now, if you permit, I shall drive you.'

He gestured, and men approached with a cushioned litter, its delicate silk curtains stained a rich purple. Flavius assisted Gwenlliant to recline on the lavish pillows, and Mor himself helped Elen to settle herself, his eyes meeting hers frankly before his gaze slipped down to her lips and over the rest of her body.

Then, he turned away.

'Captain,' she heard Mor say, 'you have my . . .' he stammered, then corrected himself ' . . . our thanks for Her Sacred Majesty's safe passage. Perhaps you will join us after sundown for a glass of wine?'

As Dylan's voice, raised to a military cadence, assented, Gwenlliant bit her lip. She was flushed, more flushed than a day in the sun might explain.

Elen could hear his call to his horses, the clatter of their hooves as they turned to lead the way from the docks.

'You're trembling,' Gwenlliant observed.

Elen felt a surge of pride for the way she turned that question aside. Yes indeed, her mother had trained her well. 'You know how I hate heights. I was afraid of falling into the water in front of all those people. And I cannot swim as well as you do – as you did today. Where were you? I thought that the Queen would order the ship to be searched. And when you finally arrived, you looked as if you had been crying. What happened, Gwenna?'

The baby name brought more tears to her cousin's eyes. Even as her eyes filled, however, she waved to the townspeople who lined up on either side of the Roman road to cheer the Queen.

'I went to talk with Dylan,' Gwenlliant began. 'Smile at them,' she hissed at Elen. 'Didn't your mother teach you *anything* about greeting townspeople? Smile and wave!'

Elen waved, smiled and suppressed a small moan of dismay. 'Your mother said, in so many words, "I hope that Gwenlliant will not throw herself at his head." Gwenlliant, must you make trouble?'

It was all for Gwenlliant, kingdom, crown, even . . . even her brother Mor, little as she thought of that. *I have to say it,* Elen told herself. 'You know what your father wants this trip to mean, don't you?'

Gwenlliant gestured in disgust, then turned her gesture into a greeting to four little girls who hurled clusters of overripe crimson blossoms into the litter. 'What does my mother have against Dylan, I want to know. He is of the Iceni, close to the Queen, from the way he spoke. If he cannot be a warrior, he is at least a fine sailor, soon to own a ship. And he saved my mother's life.'

'So he did,' Elen agreed, 'and contrived matters so that no assassin survived to be put to the question. I wonder about that. And cousin, I saw a chain that he wears beneath his tunic,' Elen observed. 'That has to be Byzantine work; you do not buy a chain that heavy for copper in a dockyard stall.'

'He is honest!' Gwenlliant protested. 'You too, you turn against him without cause.'

'But you are crying,' Elen retorted, 'which means that, apparently, he agrees with your mother. I don't know which astonishes me more, that you are interested in him, or that he refused you.'

'I hate you!' Gwenlliant snapped, then smiled at a blacksmith and his wife. Elen waved, then, once they were safely behind the litter, wrinkled her nose at the offal, buzzing with flies, that she had seen lying in a narrow alley.

'If you hate me, why do you want to tell me about Dylan?' Elen asked reasonably. Her own smile came unfeigned.

The litter had jounced and tumbled for at a least a thousand feet before Gwenlliant spoke again. 'You are right,' she said in a low voice. 'But it is not just that my pride is hurt. Dylan . . . I saw you look at Mor, oh yes, I did, cousin, and I saw him look at you.'

'Gwenlliant, for the love of Isis!' It was hot in the litter, even with its draperies pulled back, hot and oppressive. Even the salt of the sea, so bracing in the northern waters, had an over-ripe, almost rotten smell.

'Well, I saw it!' retorted the Princess. 'And I would have sworn that Dylan watched me in precisely the same way. Besides, even after mother healed him, I sensed that he was in some pain; and you know that I *can* do that, too.'

'At least, now you admit it,' said Elen.

'So I went to him and offered to remove the pain. He refused. Refused and told me to run about my business . . .'

'He never said that!' Elen cried softly.

'No. What he said was that I must keep my distance from the likes of him. Because I was young, and kind, and lovely – and because he must stay away from me.' Gwenlliant began to weep quietly.

'Wipe your eyes,' Elen whispered. 'You will smudge them if you don't, and there you will be at the governor's house, or wherever Mor will lodge us, with smudges on your cheeks. Are you in love with this Dylan?' A sudden, hideous thought struck her. 'Is *he* the man you saw at midwinter?'

Gwenlliant shook her head violently. 'No. He was fair, fairer even than Flavius. But Dylan troubles me, draws me, and I – will you help me?'

Elen had never been able to resist Gwenlliant when she appealed to her. She opened her mouth, then shut it and her eyes in quick thanksgiving that, up ahead, Mor was shouting commands and the line of march was grinding to a stop.

'We're stopping!' Elen laid fingers across her cousin's lips. 'Cousin, you heard your brother. Captain Dylan will visit us tonight. Let me watch, and then I shall tell you what I think.'

Gwenlliant flung herself into Elen's arms, kissing her so gratefully that Elen disentangled herself from her grasp. *I do not want her power, at least not the power that means that one day she will wear a crown. But her power to love and to draw love . . . ahhh, what would I give for that?*

What indeed, Elen? she asked herself, suddenly chill with fear and self-distrust. *To win her brother, would I really conspire to thrust her into the arms of a man who may just have conspired against her mother's very life? Before I do that, I shall swallow fire . . .*

Or will I?

Chapter Nine

The governor's house that Mor had appropriated for his mother's use stood in the centre of town. It was built in the Roman style – cold stone facing outward, and within, high-ceilinged rooms surrounding an atrium that should have been cool. But no breezes wafted through it to freshen the air that hung above the dining couches, and appeared to make the very figures of Antony Cosmokrator and Cleopatra, reclining on their barge in the mural on the far wall, sweat. And for all the water in the *impluvium* at the centre of the atrium, the dolphin that ramped and sprayed on the mosaic in its depth might have died of thirst.

Angry voices from the dining room made Elen pause before she entered it. She could hear mother and son arguing in intense, controlled tones that meant a serious problem, not argument for sport.

' . . . don't like it at all,' Mor was grumbling, and pacing as he complained.

'He was aimed at me. You can imagine, son, that I like it even less than you,' Olwen retorted. 'Yes, I can imagine how Marric will react to that scarab with Irene's cartouche on it. But he won't blame you.'

('Better hush,' Elen whispered to Gwenlliant, restraining her with a quick hand on her arm from running in on a very tense scene.)

'I am not a boy, or a trooper, to fear blame, lady,' Mor's voice stiffened with offended pride. 'The ship's captain was under my orders, acted as my agent. What was an assassin doing on board his ship? And now, you say, the man is dead? Convenient?'

'Sometimes, my son, I think you have lived so long in your father's Empire that you do not want to trust anyone. The assassin died at Dylan's hands. Which, I may add, he almost lost fighting the man; his blade was poisoned.'

'So you wasted healing on . . .'

'I *wasted* nothing!' Olwen snapped. Elen peered around a corner at the Queen as she held out a hand to her son, who moved jerkily to take and kiss it. Beneath the bronze of his tan, his skin was yellowish, and lines of strain pulled down at the corners of a mouth that should have smiled, should have been generous, but had been forced prematurely into expressions of suspicion and restraint.

His father asks him to bear a great deal – or he chooses to, for his father's sake. As if sensing the same thing, Olwen's next words came in a softer voice. 'Mor, your Dylan is of the Iceni, did you know that?' She laughed. 'All the tribes are alike to you? And I took such trouble with your schooling before I sent you to your father, too. Very well then, to put it simply: I cannot believe that a man of the Iceni would conspire to murder me.'

'He will be here this evening,' Mor spoke, almost to himself. 'To think that I – *I* – praised him and invited him here myself!'

'It was well enough done,' Olwen told him. 'You can question him without arousing suspicions. And if he is the man that I – and, by the way, your sister . . .'

Mor snorted derisively, and Elen once again restrained her cousin.

' . . . think that he is, he forced himself not to spoil our reunion, little knowing that we might contrive that for ourselves by blurting out what he cannot help but feel to reflect upon his ship.'

Mor shrugged, as if setting the question aside until Dylan appeared.

'Gwenlliant, Elen, you may stop lurking in the hall now,' Olwen called, amusement in her voice.

Elen suppressed a smile. Olwen called the Empire suspicious and devious? Not even Elen's own mother could have manoeuvred the Prince more adroitly or made more skilful play of her finely trained voice . . . finely trained, in any case, Elen realized, by Alexa.

'We weren't eavesdropping!' Gwenlliant announced, and entered the room in her usual rush of brilliant energy. Both she and Elen sank on the nearest couches with sighs of relief that only deepened as servants offered them towels and water scented with roses and lemon. They exclaimed in undertones because the water was even cold.

'Enjoy it,' said Mor. 'They have probably used the last of the ice for tonight's dinner.'

'You have had trouble here,' Olwen did not even bother to phrase that as a question. Her sandals clattering on the tiles, she flung her cloak on to the nearest couch. Mor gestured, and the Queen made a most unregal face (*that was so like Olwen*,

98

Elen thought), and waited, tapping her foot, until a servant took her cloak, painstakingly folded it, then exited, soft footed, followed by the others. Then she turned to her son.

'What did you see?' Mor asked.

'Did you see the town?' she demanded. 'That was all I needed. The front streets were splendid, but the back ways! The filth, the heat, the flies! I wonder that no fever has broken out.'

'It has,' Mor said. 'But I detached the army surgeons to set up a clinic in the town and aid the local physicians.' He laughed, a short bark that lacked humour. 'Given the choice between fever and an Egyptian healer, most people take the Egyptian healer.'

'So the citizens are troubled? I saw many faces sullen beneath their smiles. Are they turning on one another too, then?'

'At least they cheered for you and the girls lustily enough,' Mor said. 'Even they couldn't resist that. But I had guards posted, in case . . .'

'In case of what?'

'We have had several riots,' Mor admitted. 'Water riots, mainly. You wouldn't think that there would be any lack of water here. In point of fact, there is not. But the standing pools have been brackish, and I ordered the aqueducts shut. Then . . .' he shook his head angrily, his eyes flashing ' . . . a rumour got around that some of the Finns who came here with old Audun Bearmaster's people had been poisoning wells.'

'The Bearmaster's clan wouldn't do that!' Gwenlliant exclaimed.

'Who says that they would?' Mor whirled round to confront her.

'Who started the rumour?' Olwen asked quietly, watching her son.

'Can't tell,' Mor said. 'The Saxons blame the Egyptian traders who came up by way of Massilia. The local Celtoi – your pardon, my mother – who were born here blame any outsiders. Including the Romans whom I used to supplement my troops from the city.'

The Prince stood with his back to his mother, stripping off rings and armlets and casting them, with a vehement clatter of weighty metal and a flurry of sparkles, on to a side table of golden pine.

'Your father does that, too,' mused the Queen. Her eyes were very far away and very fond.

'Does what, Mother? Stands with his back to you? Forgive me again; I hadn't meant to be rude. Father would thrash me if he knew.'

Olwen laughed. 'No, my son. No sooner than your father walks into some place where he can be away from people, he pulls off any jewellery that he has felt compelled to wear. And then,' Olwen smiled reminiscently, 'he dares to tell me I do not travel in proper state.'

Mor grinned, and Elen forced herself not to look away from the flash of white teeth in his tanned face, the sudden, mischievous gleam in his eyes that made him look very young . . . but not a boy. Never a boy. At that moment, the boy whom Elen remembered so tepidly vanished from her thoughts forever. She ached – with envy, as she thought – when his mother smiled and opened her arms.

'Now that we are away from all that proper ceremony, I can greet my son properly.' Mor smiled again. Eagerly, he went into his mother's embrace. Olwen laughed as her son's arms closed about her and as he lifted her off her feet, 'To show you that I can,' he laughed before his grin faded. For an instant, he laid his cheek against her hair where it flowed down over her shoulder and breast.

'An army, yes, I can command an army,' he muttered. 'But a town . . . mother, I cannot do all that needs doing, not by myself.'

'I am here now, Mor. And, though you share blood with these people, you do not know them. Not as I do. Before we leave for Byzantium . . . and perhaps we may delay for a time . . . we shall see what is best to do. First, though, we must have those backstreets cleaned and stop the threat of riots.'

'That's why I used the Romans,' Mor said. 'They appear . . . immune to the rumours. Even to gossip about sorcery by the Finns or the Egyptians . . .'

Both the Finns and the Egyptians, Elen thought with an inner gleam of mirth, *were* races known to be adept in secret powers.

As if sensing her thought, Mor gestured impatiently. 'If the Finns could have saved themselves by magic, more of them would have been alive now. Osiris' blood, men would have paid gold for a soft breeze, let alone a favourable wind. And as for rain –! No, they have no power here. Perhaps they are too far south?'

Olwen sighed. 'You sound half Roman yourself, Mor. All pragmatism, no power.'

Mor shook his head. 'The garrison is filled with fighting priests. Priest-ridden, my father calls the army. But when they call, he bends his head as quickly as any man. *He*, the priests tell me, could summon their power, could *be* an adept of some power did he only choose to. I, of course, have no such potential and therefore am not priest-ridden at all. For which I thank all the gods most devoutly.'

Gwenlliant laughed merrily, Elen with some guilt. Olwen looked sad. 'Your tasks might be easier if you could sense which people . . .'

'As you did this afternoon?' Mor asked. 'I know. But I cannot regret freedom from magic; it appears to be more burden than blessing, if you ask me. There have been secular emperors before . . . my grandfather . . . that is, the Emperor Antonios. But I am ready to be schooled,' with the easy grace of a panther, Mor flung himself down on the couch nearest Elen.

'Because of the foul water, my army and I have become accustomed to drinking wine unwatered,' he held out his cup to Elen as if to tempt her, then smiled into her eyes until she flushed like a much younger, more foolish creature and looked away.

'No?' he asked. 'Well, back to the Finns, then. You say that they had power, and have power no longer?'

Olwen nodded. 'The harvests throughout the Isles are fading. I have done what I can, but it is like the canker, which eats away from within. By the time the sufferer looks pale and thin, it is too late to cure him. I fear that the same is true here. And,' she took a deep breath, 'it is true for me, too. In normal times, I might have expected five, eight, ten years more. Now . . .'

Mor heaved himself to his feet. 'Lady,' he stated flatly, 'if I travelled west to bring you on a farewell progress through the Empire that you swore to serve . . .' His voice cracked. Rising, he walked too quickly for propriety out into the atrium. Gwenlliant followed, and Olwen sighed.

'What am I going to do with them?' she asked.

Elen, reclining nearby, felt that she must answer. 'Love them, lady. What else is there?'

When the sun set, Gwenlliant vowed that she had seen a flash of green light at the horizon. No gulls called from the shore, and the imported nightingales in the governor's gardens were still. The heat seemed to force even the noises from the street into a parched, exhausted silence that one longed for the rumble and flash of heat lightning to break.

Though a wind stirred in the atrium, the dining room was hot and dusky. Only one lamp, wrought of glass streaked with red and indigo, burned, but it filled the room with the scents of sweet oil and oily smoke, and sent flickers of light and shadow dancing up the wall to give eerie life to the figures in the mural. From their cushions in their barge, Antony and Cleopatra seemed to study their descendants with the same attention that Elen, reclining on her couch, studied the room.

She arranged the folds of her white, pleated dress, designed as closely after the ancient garb of Egypt as possible without leaving her bare above the waist. Very much aware when Mor's gaze slid up the slender line of her arm to her shoulders, covered only by gilded leather straps, Elen tried to focus her attention on the centre of the room where Olwen and Gwenlliant sat, the lamplight turning their hair to molten gold.

It was like a theatre. Even as Elen watched, Mor's aide, Flavius, leaned over Gwenlliant. 'Your brother told me, Princess,' he said with a smile that showed in the darkness only as a flash of teeth and eyes, 'that if Gesoriacum grew any hotter, he would allow us all to pretend that we were in ancient Egypt and to wear only kilts and, to greet important guests, jewelled collars. Now, if you and your cousin wore such garb too, that would be a sight well worth seeing.'

Gwenlliant laughed, of course, one hand at her breast in mock modesty, as Mor shook his head at his sister and Flavius Marcellinus. Elen watched them narrowly. Marcellinus, a few years older than Mor – what was he to her cousin? He was more friend than aide, that much was clear. 'My father sent you with me to make me attend to duty, not to charm my little sister,' Mor laughed. 'A fine conscience you are! What would *your* father say if he heard you?'

'More than I want to hear, my Prince,' Flavius Marcellinus grimaced. 'Far more. Majesty, I appeal to you. Do I deserve such a sentence, after all my years of loyalty?'

With a nod of apology, Olwen turned away from the governor of the town, whom she had been thanking for the loan of his house, which she praised lavishly. 'We could make it a bargain,' she remarked. 'Mor's silence in return for your own.'

'Majesty, if I gave offence . . .' Even in the half light of the dining room, Elen could see him blush.

'Offence? Penllyn may be misty, but do you truly think that we muffle ourselves to the eyebrows all the time? Your suggestion was most practical – ' Olwen's smile broadened and turned just a trifle ironic – 'if not, shall we say, disinterested.'

Elen flicked a cautious glance at Mor, then looked down quickly. He was watching her and smiling, as if approving Flavius' observations. She copied Gwenlliant's earlier gesture of a hand raised to her breast; the room had grown no hotter, the air no more thick with smoke and dust, but a sudden vision of how it might feel to recline, dressed only in what Flavius Marcellinus had described, beneath Mor's eyes. There was a sinuous luxury to the idea – and far more.

She reached for her cup, fine Alexandrian glass beaded with cool water, with a hand that trembled. Not for the first time, she envied the ease with which Gwenlliant fell in and out of love – or what she laughingly called love. Today, Dylan had the power to wake her dreams and to make her cry; tomorrow, perhaps it might be Flavius Marcellinus: but she was warm, heart-whole . . . except, of course, for her dream of a man who had staved off the advances of the Lord of the Wild Hunt . . . for dream Elen believed it. She fanned herself with her free hand, careful not to look at Gwenlliant's brother. *This is a fever*, she told herself. *If I were Gwenlliant, I might recover.*

In the absence of servants, the town's governor, a blunt, middle-aged man whose prominent nose, small stature and common sense betrayed his Roman origins, reached for the wine and water, but Olwen forestalled him. 'Let that be my task, sir,' she said, and the man's plain face suddenly kindled into grace from the afterglow of her charm. 'I thank Isis that you are here, Majesty. For though the Prince can uphold the law, my town needs care more than correction.'

'I am here to help you,' Olwen told him.

For an instant, the fragrance of spring lilacs wafted through the room, and Elen shivered a little.

'All shall be well, and all manner of things shall be well now that the Queen is here,' the governor replied, bowing from his couch. When he raised his head again, his eyes shone with the adoration of a much younger, much less pragmatic man.

Would anyone ever match that charm of Olwen's? At least Elen need not envy Gwenlliant the burden that she would face for the rest of her life: of following Olwen and of trying, all her life, not to fail too conspicuously.

A flicker of white and lamplight startled them when it appeared at the door as the major domo entered, bowed, and announced the arrival of Dylan, the Iceni captain whom Mor had invited to take wine with them. Carefully, he limped into the room.

Mor leaned forward, poised like a hunting cat stalking his quarry, but Olwen held up a hand for him to wait. She gestured at a nearby couch and, smiling, offered him wine. Refusing both seat and drink, he stood tensely at the centre of the room.

Mor rose too. 'You are seen, Captain,' he acknowledged the man's salute coldly. 'Tell me, where have you seen this before?'

He threw the scarab bearing Irene's sigil upon the table, where the lamplight turned the ruddy stone into a burning coal from which Gwenlliant averted her eyes.

'Prince Mor,' said Dylan harshly, 'I stand before you a man disgraced. You trusted me with the welfare of Her Majesty the Queen and her daughters . . . I mean, the Imperial Princess and Princess Elen, and instead of guarding them with my life and my crew's, I allowed an assassin to ship out with us . . .' Awkwardly, he dropped to one knee, his lame leg, shorter than the other and slightly withered, splaying out behind him. 'I swear by any gods that any of us honour that I had no knowledge of that, that I have never seen that sigil before, and I am willing . . .' he drew a ragged breath ' . . . to stake my life upon that oath.'

'And if I do not believe you?' Mor asked, his face a mask of anger, arrogance and, yes, fear for the safety of his mother, his sister, and even of Elen herself.

'Then, Prince, I have lived long enough among Romans to know that my life must pay for your disbelief. I am ready now.'

With a mercurial change of expression and mood, Mor was on his feet, striding over to the exiled Iceni. 'Get off your knees, Captain. Horus hover over you with His wings, my mother and my sister have dinned your innocence in my ears: shall I call the imperial ladies liars?' The hands that Mor clapped on Dylan's shoulders helped him rise without putting him to the shame of reaching for support.

'Now,' said Mor, 'sit and drink with us, and accept my thanks for saving Her Sacred Majesty's life.'

Olwen reached for the heaviest of the bracelets that bound her wrist, but her son's upraised hand stopped her as he made to lift a necklace from around his own neck and toss it over Dylan's head.

'I beg you, no, Imperial Highness,' Dylan protested, twisting away from the glitter of massive gold and garnets. 'I hold myself guilty until we . . . until *I* . . . find that killer's masters and make an end of them.'

Gwenlliant smiled radiantly; Flavius Marcellinus and the town's governor nodded approval. Mor laughed, his anger vanished as if it had never been. 'Ah,' he said, 'there speaks all the pride of my mother's people. She says that we are akin?'

Dylan's eyes went hooded, unreadable, and he bowed his head. 'I would not so presume, Highness,' he muttered. Uneasy before the Prince, he fingered the heavy links of his neckchain.

As if ashamed of his earlier suspicions, Mor poured a cup of wine and brought it to Dylan himself. 'Drink, man!'

Having no other choice, Dylan took the cup, raised it in brief, ironic salute . . . *in Gwenlliant's direction*, Elen noted, *despite all his words that afternoon* . . . and drained it.

'Majesty,' he turned to Olwen. 'I beg you to hold me excused. I have not yet finished questioning my crew and the merchants with whom I deal here.'

Her smile was warm, and when Mor might have spoken to him, she held up a hand. With a careful bow, Dylan began limping from the room. Gwenlliant stirred, her eyes flashing angrily at her brother, but a sudden fierce, pulsing light distracted her.

'Look at that!' she cried.

The scarab that Olwen had turned over to Mor and that had lain forgotten on the table seemed now to have drawn the reddish lamplight to itself, into itself: from a bloodstone the size, perhaps, of a fingertip, it had grown larger and more brilliant, as if it had gorged upon the light, which was an angry crimson now, and Gwenlliant flinched away from it.

'Look to Her Highness!' Dylan cried.

'Sister, what is wrong?' Mor whirled to look at her, then at the scarab. Anger flared like summer lightning across his mobile face. 'We have had enough, I think, of your presence,' he spoke to the gem, which now pulsed sullenly. Even as he reached for it, Elen tore a strip from the flimsy stuff of her gown. Hurling herself from her couch to her knees by the table, she scooped up the gem in the white gauze before Mor's unprotected hand could touch it. It felt as if she held a hot, beating heart in her hand, a heart that sought for power wherever it might be found, that sought to drain her.

'Give it to me before it hurts you, cousin,' Mor commanded. Only then did Elen realize that she had gasped, was swaying from the effort not to cry out. She forced herself to shake her head.

'I tell you, you can trust me,' Mor said. Walking over to her, he pried her fingers off the gem and opened the ragged square of cloth in which it had been shrouded. The pulsing stopped and the bloodlight faded.

'I have no magics to draw on,' he said. 'And thus, no magics can draw on me. The ArchPriest of Osiris in Byzantium calls that a lack, but I think it will serve us well tonight, do you not?'

He stared down at the gem, his eyes kindling with their own fire. With the smooth, sudden movements that marked him as surely as the lines of brow and nose, he hurled the thing into the lamp. A jet of flame shot from it, then subsided. The governor could not restrain a low cry of protest.

'Sir,' Mor spoke to him, 'I had not thought that that gem might damage your lamp. My regrets – and a new lamp – should we discover that it is cracked.' Mor raised his voice slightly. 'Someone bring incense!' he called. A soldier in full armour, not the servant that Elen expected, entered the room with the incense that Mor demanded, then left. No footsteps, however, struck the marble and died away down the hall.

Unobtrusively, Elen rose from her knees and walked towards the atrium, her hands upraised in the opening gesture of the warding ceremony. The rip in her gown gave way further, exposing much of her legs, and the moonlight shone through her gown, picking out the lithe movements of her body, the delicate modelling of arms, throat and face as she raised her face to the sky and chanted.

She had practised the rituals for years, she *knew* that posture, words and tones were right. All about her, the air in the hot, stuffy room began to change, to flow outward . . . and then it ceased as if she had been swimming from deep water into the shallows and had found herself kicking into mud. Sweat trickled from her hairline down her face and ran over her shoulders. Her upraised arms were leaden, and her spine felt like a column of fire from the effort of maintaining her posture. For a second, her concentration broke, and the progress, the edifice of sound, power, and safety that she had tried to construct, began to crumble.

Olwen started to rise from her seat, and Elen forced herself not to moan in despair: not another time that she must drain strength from the Queen! Mor, already standing, was faster. As Elen swayed, he strode over to her and, as her arms drooped, he gripped her upper arms and supported them.

'*Now* go on,' he whispered, his breath hot against her face.

Elen closed her eyes, which stung from sweat, forced back the knowledge of how badly she was failing, of what a horror she must look, with stains on her face and her eyes rolling in her head, of her awareness of the young man so close to her. She gasped at the hot air, drawing it deep into her lungs, remembering the groves in which she had been schooled, and the sweet, intoxicating clarity of power well used.

The air in the room freshened as silver light welled from the moon to limn her. Mor dropped his hands, and now Elen stood without shaking, her voice clear and strong. As she made the final gestures, the light that haloed her faded, and she was once again herself. Mor reached out to catch her, but she flung out a hand to stop him and tottered under her own strength back to her couch where she stretched out gasping. Without being asked, Gwenlliant steeped a cloth in cool water and began to wipe her face and limbs. As the water touched her, Elen started to shiver.

Olwen took the cloth from her daughter. 'Fetch a robe,' she whispered. She laid her hand on Elen's brow. 'Foolish one, brave one,' she crooned. Mor knelt at Elen's other side and took her hand, raising it to his lips. As his mouth touched her palm, Elen flinched.

'But yes,' he murmured, cradling her fingers against his cheek. 'Rest easy.'

Olwen's fingertips slipped from Elen's forehead to her eyelids.

'No healing!' Elen muttered. 'Promise! You will need your strength.'

'Majesty . . .' The voice that forced itself into calmness belonged to the governor. Though Elen's eyelids felt gummed shut, too heavy to open, she knew when Olwen turned around and lifted her chin to speak to him.

But if the man hoped for comfort from Isis-on-Earth, he would be disappointed.

'Have your priests not told you that more than drought and riots hover above Gesoriacum? All over Prydein, magic falters and fails, And now, it seems, the same blight has struck the Empire. Gwenlliant, that robe! Do you want Elen to take cold?'

'Sorry,' said Gwenlliant. Her footsteps receded, then paused for an instant at the door. Once again, the air in the room changed subtly as Gwenlliant passed through the wards.

Elen let herself drift. True to the promise that she had exacted, Olwen made no attempt to restore her beyond washing her with cool water and insisting she drink from the goblet that her son held.

'Where *is* Gwenlliant?' Mor fumed. 'How long does it take to snatch up a robe and come back here?'

'Do not be so quick to criticize your sister,' Olwen said. 'I hear footsteps now.'

There were many footsteps, not the light, sandalled tread of a young woman, but the heavier steps of soldiers racing towards the dining room, and pausing there, unable to enter. Those steps were followed by the more deliberate tread of . . .

'Priests,' muttered the governor. 'What are they doing . . . ?'

Outside the room came the rumble of male voices chanting the counterspell to the wards that Elen had so painstakingly and painfully set. Hot air rushed before the priests into the room, where they stopped short before the Queen, the Prince and the girl who shivered on the couch between them.

'Most Sacred Majesty, Highness,' they bowed slightly, then nodded at the governor. 'It appears that we come too late to warn you to flee.'

'To flee what?' Mor demanded.

A priest wearing the insignia of the order of Thoth, noted as healers throughout the Empire, stepped forward to examine Elen.

Mor started forward, one hand on the hilt of his dagger, despite the governor's protest. 'No, you don't touch her, you don't move one step further into this room until you tell me. What is the problem now?'

Dark circles underlay the priest's eyes. At some point, his robes might even have fit him, but now they hung slackly, bunching over shoulders and chest into untidy folds.

'What is the point of fighting now, Prince?' he asked. 'What we face is plague.'

Chapter Ten

Gwenlliant hastened down the corridor, eager to find a cloak for Elen and get back to the dining room. Light from the single polycandelon hanging from the ceiling gleamed on mosaics and murals, casting a flickering life on the still features.

'Princess, may I speak with you?'

Gwenlliant stopped short. In that instant, her hands went cold and sweaty, her eyes filled, and her ears roared. That was Dylan's voice, Dylan who had rejected Olwen's hospitality, Mor's attempt to honour him . . . and herself, though Goddess only knew why Gwenlliant found herself drawn to him like a moth to a flame. Her pride still writhed as she remembered his conversation with her, 'Princess, I am not a fit companion for you. You do neither of us any good by seeking me out.'

She forced herself to take several more steps forward, her back self-consciously straight. Princess he had called her, and princess she would be. What other choice did she have?

'Please, Gwenlliant.'

At the sound of her name, at the gentle, almost beseeching tone of Dylan's voice, her hurt pride healed somewhat. She turned in a flurry of soft, gauzy draperies.

'Elen is ill, I must bring a cloak for her. Come speak with me while I fetch it,' she told him, and quickened her pace. Despite his limp, he kept pace with her. The flickering of the polycandelon made it hard for her to read his face. At least, that also made it hard for him to see how she had flushed, and that her eyes had filled with tears.

He hesitated on the threshold of her room, and she hissed in exasperation as she darted in and flung herself on to her knees beside a half-unpacked chest, trying in the dark to identify, among fold after fold of fine cloth, the heavier folds of a cloak. Ah! There it was.

As her fingers tightened on the cloth, drawing it out from under the other garments, Dylan knelt behind her. He laid one hand on her shoulder and cupped her chin in his other hand, turning her face up to his, then bending to kiss her.

Gwenlliant gasped and brought her hands up, the cloak clasped in them, between herself and Dylan. His lips tasted of wine, of salt and iron, and hers parted beneath them. When she broke free, he reached to draw her wholly into his arms. She managed enough self-command to break away.

'The cloak for Elen, remember?'

'I saw her after you did, Gwenlliant,' he told her. 'She asked me to tell you not to trouble yourself and to say to you, "You know how much I detest people hovering about me".'

'That is Elen, all right,' Gwenlliant laughed. 'Though I suspect . . .' No, she would not discuss her cousin Elen, she would not discuss the way that, even through her own preoccupations, she could see Elen and Mor drawn ineluctably together, not even with a man whom she found more attractive than any man . . . *since midwinter, when the Dark King wooed me and I fled with the fair prince who called him enemy.*

The memory still had the power to turn her weak. She sighed, and Dylan, thinking that she sighed for him, embraced her.

'Let us leave this place,' he whispered against her hair, his breath hot in her ear. 'The gardens, perhaps? Somewhere that we could . . . speak without worrying about five serving women or six kinsmen intruding upon us. One thing I have always liked about the Empire – they value privacy here. And they understand secrets.' He murmured that against her throat, and she shivered.

Dylan took the cloak from her hands and rose slowly, then assisted her to stand. She swayed, and he put an arm about her, guiding her back down the shadowy corridors. Gwenlliant thought that she saw one of the serving women that he had disparaged, and laughed under her breath. She was no soft, sequestered kitten of the Empire, but a free princess of the Celtoi, who came and went – and chose – as she would. And because this town lay in her brother's keeping, she would walk in it unafraid with whatever man she chose. Defiantly, she tossed her head at the woman and the reproofs that she imagined.

Out the doors of the governor's house Dylan led her, but not to the gardens, the leafy darkness and privacy of which made Gwenlliant's knees go weak, but down a side street. She put up a hand to stop him, and he smiled down at her.

'I have a better place in mind,' he told her, leading her away from the house with a speed surprising for a lame man who admitted that he walked more easily on shipboard than on land. The moonlight seemed to be diseased, reddish. It cast an unhealthy light on her hands as she held them up, and made the heavy chain that Dylan wore about his throat look as if it were wrought of bronze, rather than gold. *Slave-metal, all of it, her father often called the heavy jewellery he had to wear on state occasions.*

'Where *are* we going?' she demanded. She planted her feet firmly in the hot, dry dust that puffed up even from the stone-paved streets.

'Where do you think?' he laughed. 'I did not lie to you, Gwenlliant, about wanting to speak with you. And once we finish speaking . . .' He laughed throatily and pulled her close. 'But as I was leaving the governor's house, one of my sailors brought me information about the man who tried to kill the Queen, and I came back to show it to you . . .'

'Why me? Why did you not show it to my mother and my brother?' Bright Gwenlliant knew that she was, trained in arms she was, too, to some extent; but no quality of hers yet equalled her mother's statecraft or her brother's war-training. *Or Elen's wit.* Elen had distrusted her attraction to Dylan, calling it infatuation, a term that still galled her.

Perhaps if Dylan's information were good, if Dylan and Gwenlliant together tracked down the people who had loosed the assassin on board his ship, Elen might admit that her feeling for Dylan was more than infatuation, and the others would see that she was more than a passionately selfish and wilful child.

Dylan laid his hand over his heart, as if taking some kind of strange oath. 'Princess, must I swear to you that . . .' the light shifted, and Gwenlliant's doubts seemed as ephemeral as the moonlight or the dust in which she walked. At this hour, only one or two people were out: men hastening to their homes or from one tavern to the next; one woman, and best not speculate . . . no, that could hardly be true; she was carrying a child.

'The light,' she mused.

'What of it? Come with me,' said Dylan, and tightened his grip on her fingers.

Gwenlliant gasped; the woman who carried a child had dropped to her knees, then collapsed on the street.

'Wait one moment,' Gwenlliant told Dylan. She freed her hand, shook it, mildly surprised at the strength of Dylan's hand-clasp. It seemed to be more a restraint than a caress: odd, seeing that she had accompanied him willingly, even happily. She shook her hand as if letting him know that she found his grasp overly possessive, and hurried over to the woman.

Kneeling down, Gwenlliant turned her gently. When she fell, she had protected the babe with her own body. Though it squalled fiercely, it . . . no, he . . . appeared to be unharmed (though its swaddlings were damp), and she soon lulled it back to sleep.

'Hold the child for me while I check on his mother, will you?' she asked Dylan, raising the child in her arms.

He backed away. 'Not I. I might drop him.'

Granted, some men *were* afraid of children, though not in any family Gwenlliant knew well. Her own father adored them, and when he could not be with her, Elen's father practically raised her. (If the truth be known, in fact, he probably had a gentler hand with children than did Alexa.) Gwenlliant sniffed at Dylan's qualm. That was, she told herself, as she always did, a most unprincesslike noise. It was also a most unseductive noise, and here she was, postponing a time when . . . she rolled the child's mother over and gasped at the heat of the woman's skin. Her face was flushed and mottled, and she shivered with fever. The woman's heartbeat was too fast, and when Gwenlliant loosened her clothing, it fell open and she saw the first dark swellings . . .

Gwenlliant recoiled. She had never seen plague before; thank the Goddess in whatever manifestation she preferred that it came but rarely to the Isles of Mist. She herself . . . if it struck her, she knew that Olwen would heal her, though at what cost to herself . . .

'Dylan, it's plague. Run to the Temple of Thoth. Get a healer-priest!'

Deliberately, Gwenlliant settled herself more comfortably, sitting back on her heels. She took three deep breaths, as she had seen Olwen do all her life before she healed. Finally, she stretched her hands out over the plague-stricken woman, reaching for body-knowledge, awareness of the wrongnesses, the subtle signs, and the great ones, that the plague wrought in the linkage between the body lying before her and the soul that it housed. Body was, or should be, a healthy whole, united with the spirit that sought, in the woman before her, to escape what increasingly became carrion and not living flesh.

She shut her eyes, imagining the power of the earth beneath her as a pool from which she could draw, as a fire from which she could find warmth, and from which she could draw coals of power to heal this woman. The earth's power came but sluggishly, and Gwenlliant plunged more deeply, more urgently into her awareness that the power *was* there, and that she was fit to tap it.

'Gwenlliant, come before you too fall ill and die!' Dylan hissed.

Something was shaking Gwenlliant, and she pulled free. To her astonishment, over the stinks of sweat, of fear, and the infant's fouled swaddlings, she smelled ripening grain and spring flowers . . . *I almost had it!* she exulted.

'Just one moment more!' she hissed at Dylan.

Again, she closed her eyes. This time, when she quested for the energy deep within herself and in the earth, her mother, it was with more assurance. *Ah, this must be the power that Olwen felt when she healed! No wonder she prized it above any other gift and lamented as it faded.* The scents of spring intensified and a tingling raced up Gwenlliant's spine, down her arms, and into her outstretched hands.

She opened her eyes and her hands seemed, in the unwholesome moonlight, to glow the way a child's hands glow when they are held near a lamp. They felt suddenly heavy, suddenly right, and she dropped them upon the woman who moaned and twisted before her, dropped them and meditated on wholeness, upon health, upon union of body, soul and nurturing earth.

The woman sighed and lay still. Power flowed from Gwenlliant, then, abruptly, ceased.

She sagged, and Dylan caught her, wrapping her in the cloak that he had never dropped. As he tugged her roughly to her feet, he seemed careful not to touch her with unprotected hands.

'Why did you break in? I almost had her!' Gwenlliant complained. She laid trembling fingertips on the woman's brow, which was cool and sweaty. The fever had broken. Despite the uncertainty of the light, Gwenlliant thought that her skin looked less mottled, less diseased.

'Look, she sleeps now. Whatever you did, it worked. Your brother's guards will find her. Now come away!' Dylan himself looked greenish, and Gwenlliant reached out with that new strength that made her feel sure, for the first time in her life, of her power to heal. He jerked his head away and gasped for breath, then hurried her away from the woman as if he could not bear to remain nearby.

This was not the ardour of a lover, or the eagerness of a man who felt himself wronged to clear his name by showing her evidence. Drained after healing the plague-stricken woman, Gwenlliant stumbled and felt Dylan buoy her up, as if they swam together as they had after he and that assassin had plunged overboard.

He was not limping! That awareness brought Gwenlliant up short. They had walked almost a hundred yards, and in all that time Dylan had not limped.

His pace slowed in the next seconds, and the limp was back. Gwenlliant glanced down. Surely, something was different. Now, Dylan limped *on his* left *leg!*

She pulled free of him. 'This is not wise,' she told him. 'I think we had best go back to the governor's house. You have only to ask for me there.' And, to salvage whatever might be salvaged from this disaster of a tryst, she added, 'I am not fickle, not easily frightened.'

But she was lying, and she knew it. Dylan had changed from the man she had laughed with on board his ship.

Dylan smiled at her. 'My shy one,' he murmured.

Why had she ever found that voice seductive? She blinked, trying to see Dylan more clearly despite the moonlight and the haze that overhung the streets down which he still ushered her. Already they were close to the outskirts of the town.

It was the healing, she realized. The healing had given her, if not wisdom – that would have been far too much to ask, that Gwenlliant, who never thought when she could feel, might be wise – truer perceptions than she had ever had. Before, she could sense how others felt. Now, she sensed whether or not they were true, were sound – or good or evil.

And the man who stood before her . . . Gwenlliant drew a faint, whimpering breath . . . man? Dylan's face wavered in her sight, almost as if the familiar, attractive features overlaid another face that she did not find attractive at all.

'Ah, my Princess,' murmured Dylan. 'As a token, then, let me give you this.'

He pulled from around his neck the chain that he always wore beneath his tunic and, as Mor had tried to do that very evening, made as if to toss it over Gwenlliant's head.

Swinging from it was a heavy round medallion that caught Gwenlliant's attention and, having caught it, would not relinquish it. She could barely discern the markings on it, but she thought that it was no medallion of any god or goddess that she knew; and, thank you very much, she wasn't about to wear an amulet of an unfamiliar power that she was certain that she did not trust. She caught it in her hand, and gasped as it scorched her palm.

Dylan pulled it out of her grasp.

'What was that Set-begotten thing?' she cried, truly angry at him. She backed away, her hand dropping instinctively to the dagger . . . *but*, she wailed inwardly, *she had dressed lightly, formally, for her first dinner on shore with her brother, and she had not worn it!*

'You should not blaspheme, Princess,' said the man from whom all traces of Dylan's countenance had fallen away. Gwenlliant had heard of simulacra, men forced by dark powers to assume the guise of other men, but had never believed them. 'For you will soon be facing His priests and the heirs of our rightful empress.'

'The Goddess of Battles eat your soul!' Gwenlliant snapped, and turned to run.

But Dylan's limp had vanished from the man along with his semblance. Though Gwenlliant ran as fleetly as a lifetime of prowling the heights of Penllyn had accustomed her, he was faster yet, and not encumbered by linen skirts.

'Get away from me!' she cried, but, on the deserted street, no one heard her.

He had his hands on her bare shoulders, was spinning her about. She screamed with fury and sank her teeth into his left wrist. He slapped her, and it felt as if she had run headlong into a tree. She staggered and, in her last moments of consciousness, felt the weight of folds of cloak – that damned cloak for Elen! – hurled over her head as one might bag a fowl. She had time for a mental scream of fury and terror, and then all time vanished.

Chapter Eleven

'Plague,' repeated one of the priests, 'and it appears to have struck to the core of our Empire. What times do we live in when a princess of the Imperial line can be stricken with plague?'

Plague. At first it had just been a sound to Elen, as she lay shivering in the exhaustion that follows magic, '*If you are fool enough to overspend your power*'. Elen had heard that scolding before, from the ArchDruid and from her mother. Finally, however, the priest's words sank home like a dagger that is poorly aimed but, for all that, fatal nonetheless. She shuddered again, this time with honest fear rather than from the aftermath of the magics she had been foolish enough to confront unprepared and alone. Once again, she could almost hear the cultured Greek in which her mother expressed her most scathing ironies, '*So, instinct made you ward an open room unaided? Very noble, I am certain, for beasts who have but instinct to guide them. Try using reason the next time . . . if your folly permits you a next time.*'

'Plague?' Olwen looked at her hands as if she did not know whether she expected to see them disfigured or whether healing would be demanded of her on the spot.

'It is this dust, this heat,' she murmured.

Though the priests looked clean, the aura of sleepless worry and sickness appeared to cling to them; and they crowded close to the Queen, as if her mere presence could comfort them. 'No, Elen, lie back down. I assure you, reverend fathers, this is not plague. My niece has but over-spent her strength. How long since the first case of plague was seen? Have there been any deaths?' She turned to look down the long corridor. 'Elen, you are still trembling. Oh, *where* is Gwenlliant with that cloak?'

For a moment, everyone in the dark dining room spoke at once. Even the moonlight that filled the empty *impluvium* appeared sinister, red tinged, and the very shadows seemed threatening. Plague . . . a man had collapsed in a tavern, raving from fever. Hours later, the buboes had appeared on him. He was dead now, *and at peace*, Elen, who had read Galen and the works of other healers, thought, *and none too soon*. Hours after that, the woman who had tended him collapsed too; and people who had drawn too near either of them threatened to panic and run through the streets, spreading contagion and death, until the priests of Thoth had emerged from their shrines to minister to the dying, the sick, and the merely terrified.

'Guards!' Mor shouted, far too close to Elen's ear. Nail-soled sandals clattered on the marble. The noise was dizzying and she swayed slightly, her head spinning. Were those sparks she saw, rising from the marble, or simply flaming spots dancing before her eyes? Olwen touched her cheek. Despite the night's fierce humidity, Elen smelled flowers and the cool air of home. She shook her head at her aunt. How should she know where Gwenlliant was? She had fainted, remember?

Gwenlliant? The room went dark and spun about Elen. Eagerness . . . growing bewilderment and anger . . . a sudden, stifling weight, like a . . . a cloak flung over her head, then true darkness. Elen flung out a hand and Olwen clasped it absently.

'I want you to help these good priests,' Mor ordered hoarsely. 'Let no one leave the town, except . . . Flavius, a word with you. You will prepare to ride within the hour, and you will take the imperial ladies with you. Upon your soul, Flavius, upon your soul, swear to me that you will guard them as I would.'

Elen levered herself up, pushing against Mor's hand when he tried to restrain her, until she could stand. Another instinct flickered her thoughts, and she drew energy from the ground itself up through her body until, at the back of her skull, it bloomed into a strength that she knew she would pay for later. At least that sense of being *somewhere else* had vanished.

But, should she wish it back? That idea haunted her.

'Damn you, my Prince!' Flavius Marcellinus snarled. 'You

really think that I am going to leave you here to face plague, riots and Set-knows-what sort of priest-ridden – your pardon, holy fathers – mischief? What am I to tell your father? And – the gods preserve me – what am I to tell mine?'

'That lo, there you are, obedient to commands,' Mor told him glibly.

'They all *died* at Thermopylae!' Flavius said. His sun-flushed skin had turned pallid, and sweat beaded his hairline and ran down clean-shaven cheeks. He fell to his knees. 'Never mind what your father or mine might say if I left you! Prince, I beg you, don't send me away.'

'Not "damn you, my Prince"?' Mor asked. 'Flavius mine, I am the last man in the world to stand on ceremony, but it does strike me that "damn you, my Prince" hardly seems respectful address. To say the least. But you can atone by obeying me in this. I realize that I am a poor substitute for my father. But I have sworn to do as best I can, even if it costs me my life.'

The officer seized Mor's hand and laid his face against it.

'Mother, Elen,' Mor turned to them. 'Flavius will convey you and Gwenlliant to Byzantium as soon as I prepare a letter to send with him.'

'No,' said Olwen. 'Mor, how can you close Gesoriacum's road yet allow your own family to flee?'

'As Isis on Earth, you, of all people, must be spared,' Mor protested, though he flushed darkly.

'Of all people, I am the one that Gesoriacum is least able to spare,' she said, drawing herself up. Though she had long since plucked the flower crown that she had worn at dinner from her long braids, a fragrance of lilacs and roses wreathed about her, and moonlight caught and tangled in the richness of her hair.

'But . . .'

'But, nothing!' Olwen snapped. 'There are no high queens in Penllyn. The Goddess avert that such a thing exist ever again! But Byzantium has an Empress; and whether or not that is a role that I would have chosen, for good or for evil, I am she. I am this land's mother, my son, just as I am mother to my own lands and my children. When my child tosses with fever, is that a time when I should abandon it?'

Mor opened his mouth to protest again.

'That is enough argument!' she ordered, stamping her foot. There was a distant, responding grumble of thunder at the horizon. 'We have spoken!'

And Olwen hated the plural that Empire imposed on its rulers, Elen knew.

For a moment, Olwen drew herself up, Empress and Goddess on Earth, taller than mortal, gleaming in the flickering light of the last remaining lamp, as lovely and as inflexible as a statue of Isis herself. Then she sighed and subsided again into mere humanity. 'And how should I abandon Gwenlliant? Has anyone seen her?'

Sobbing rose from behind the ranks of soldiers and priests. 'Oh, lady, lady,' came a loud cry from one of the serving women, who then began to keen.

'What is it?' Olwen whispered. 'Let her approach!'

Daringly, one of the governor's serving women was edging past, in among the priests and soldiers, her face working, her mouth trembling.

'You saw her where?' Olwen demanded sharply. 'Leaving the house with a tall young man who limped?'

'Oh Majesty, Goddess, I went to her room,' wept the woman, 'and I found . . . I do not know what it is, like a glede though it does not burn; but, this much I know: if I touch it, I am certain it will cost me my life.'

'I must see this,' decided the Queen. 'Mor, Elen, attend me. Flavius, of your kindness, I shall ask you to conduct my niece to Byzantium, and to bear a letter to His Most Sacred Majesty.'

Flavius bowed low. Elen, opening her mouth to protest, gasped. That sense of being in two places at once had returned. 'A man with a limp?' Mor asked. 'You . . . you . . . and over there! Search the docks and taverns for Dylan, one of my captains, you know, the one from the Isles of Mist, the one who limps? Bring him to me.' His voice softened to a feral snarl. 'Undamaged.'

As Elen followed the much taller Olwen down the corridor to Gwenlliant's room, her dizziness abated.

'Why did you not stop her?' the Queen demanded of the serving woman.

'*I* stop a Princess of the Empire and the Celtoi to forbid her from seeing whatever man she pleases? I would not dare.'

Mor growled. There was no other way to describe it. He strode back and forth in the darkened little room, effortlessly avoiding its few pieces of furniture, and Elen thought of an angry hunting leopard. 'Priests,' he whispered, 'one of you, remain. The rest – do me the favour of returning to your temples and your healing. You have my thanks and prayers.'

Elen's fingers tightened convulsively on the necklace that she always wore. Tonight it dangled beneath her elaborate collar. Its links cut into her hand, and the pain triggered alertness, suspicion . . . and foreboding. She had long known that she had inherited her mother's knack for sensing things of the dark. She opened her mouth to speak, and emitted only garbled noises. As Olwen turned, sparing her one quick, worried glance, Elen's mouth jerked and her hands fluttered.

But I am no prophet! the last vestiges of her sanity keened in her skull before lightning and the dark took her. She heard a voice cry out, recognized it, with vast astonishment, for her own, and reeled, to be steadied against her aunt's side.

'The blood moon near midsummer . . . havoc with the wards . . . power fading . . .' that last complaint, Elen was certain, came from a priest. Then all was blackness once more, pierced only by her aunt's appalled cry . . .

'To the shattered circle, go! And behold, there is a middle way between the hungry king who waits in the earth, and the tree of leaf and flame . . . let those who tread there . . .' In a kind of abstract wonder, Elen listened to her own voice spin moonshine that no bard would have dared to mouth.

'Another scarab!' Mor growled. 'One of you, take charge of that thing!'

'I have it, son.'

'Does it bear Irene's cartouche too?' He would much have preferred assassins, Elen suspected, to a war in which magic was the chief weapon. Irene had all but destroyed Marric, his father, and Elen's own mother; and Mor was still young enough, she realized suddenly, to measure himself against his father, who – hard as it was for him – had been a legend before he even ascended the throne. How could he war against her or her heirs-in-spirit?

How indeed, if they could not be found?

'My daughter,' Olwen whispered. 'They have stolen her.'

Elen whimpered, then bit her lip, despising herself for her weakness. She felt groggy, sick, and she coughed, as if too long stinted of fresh air. *Oh, they will kill me when they find me!* the thought came. It was not her thought; and that realization forced a gasp from her that the Queen did not hear.

– *Gwenlliant*, – Elen called. – *Where are you?*–

But that second, inner consciousness had faded.

'It is no weakness in your defences, Mor, but in mine. As my powers wane, this is what happens. The enemy strikes within our best defences to snatch away our dearest ones . . .'

His senses as feverishly honed as a hunting cat's when it has been starved to make it hunt more fiercely, Mor whirled as he heard heavy footsteps that had to be those of armed men.

'*There* he is!' Mor's shout of rage had elements of ferocious hunger. 'You! You damned traitor.'

As his soldiers hustled in the limping Dylan, his mouth working and bloodied at one corner, his head down to protect it from random blows, Mor strode towards him, hands grasping his shoulders. 'What did the damned witch's heirs pay you to betray your Empire, coward? My mother, my cousin, my sister – you had only to look at them, listen to them, and know they could never harm you. Take a second look at this room, from which you lured my sister. Do they desire her death – or mine? What is their price?' Mor shouted.

'Prince,' Dylan shouted back, 'the last I saw of the Princess was in this very room. I will swear that by Llyr, my patron, or by Horus, your own.'

– *Amazement . . . fury . . . to be tricked so easily. Fool! Lured by your own dreams to your own destruction.* –

– *Cousin*, – Elen shrieked inside her head, – *where are you?* –

'Liar!' Mor shouted. 'The servants say they saw my sister smile and leave with a man who limped.' He gestured at Dylan.

Olwen's hand again touched Elen and, in her heightened consciousness, she sensed how power flowed imperceptibly from the older woman into her body, restoring her to herself. 'I need you back now,' Olwen whispered.

She started forward. 'Mor, let him speak . . .'

'Prince,' Dylan tried again, 'only this afternoon, I told the Princess that I was no fit . . .'

'That is true, Mor,' Elen put in quickly. 'I saw her weep.'

'What can he say but lies?' As Mor shook Dylan, he saw the heavy, red-gold chain that the captain wore. 'Was this part of your price?' he demanded. 'Was it? Then I think that it is only just that it be your death, too.'

He pulled the chain free of Dylan's clothes and began to twist the flat, heavy links tightly around his throat.

'Lady,' Flavius spoke quickly, warningly. Elen had heard of Mor's father's rages. They were inherited from Alexander himself; she had seen Alexa's own angers, which her mother had spent half her life fighting until, these days, they were but a pale shadow. If this, however, were not the full-blown madness, Elen had no desire, ever, to witness it.

Mor's face was pale, his lips paler. The pupils of his eyes had constricted until all his world centred on the man he shook and strangled by his heavy gold chain. Dylan's face had already turned the colour of porphyry, and he gasped for breath.

'What did they promise you for your betrayal?' Mor gasped, as if he, as well as Dylan, were strangling. 'Women? My sister, damn your stinking soul? Gold – or how about a chance at a leg that works normally?'

'Stop that! You call your Empire one of law, but you would slay him without a hearing, without a trial?' Olwen stood at Mor's shoulder, trying and failing to gain his attention. 'Your father acted thus once, do you know that? He killed a Druid, one of the order of bards, and he has grieved for it all his life . . . Must you add sacrilege to bad temper?'

Her sharp glance struck Elen. Alexander, she thought. After he killed Kleitos, he almost ran mad; and Alexander is our ancestor. *What can I do?* she thought, but stepped forward anyway. Dylan had fallen sideways, limp, and still Mor shook him as a ship's cat might shake her prey.

'Mor,' she said, very quietly. 'Not this way.'

She put out her hand gingerly, and touched his fingers where they twisted on Dylan's throat, bruised and bleeding from the pressure of the metal links. She could feel his fear for his family, his army and the town, his helplessness even in the face of the rage that overrode his judgement, and tightened his grip despite his better judgement.

'Stop, Mor. No need to kill him. Here, take my hand.' *Take it as you did that day in the heights. Let me help you.* As if he had suddenly been doused with icy water from the Cynfael, Mor gasped. His fingers tightened one last time. The soft gold broke, and as the chain came free in Mor's hand, he stepped back, leaving Dylan to collapse on the floor, where Olwen knelt to assure herself that he still lived and could answer questions.

Attached to the long, heavy chain was a medallion. Chain and medallion puddled into Mor's hands, and he held the necklace up to the light. Stamped on the medallion was a strong profile that even Elen remembered . . . 'My father's face,' Mor muttered. 'Where did he steal this?'

The Emperor had many such necklaces made and might give them as a reward, or as a sign of his favour. Dylan coughed weakly and struggled up to his elbows.

'Before you talk, wait . . . be still . . . there now,' Olwen murmured. The air stirred and freshened as her power flowed into Dylan, healing him.

'Mor, can you let Dylan speak without trying to kill him?' she asked, her voice cold with the suppressed anger rare among Celtoi. *Perhaps she learned that from my mother, or from her husband*, Elen thought.

'Lady, why do you defend this . . . offal?' Bewilderment began to emerge from the insensate rage that had thickened Mor's voice. One hand outstretched, the broken chain dripped from it, the medallion hanging from the chain swaying, in the lamplight, from shadowed disc to gleaming, miniature sun, 'He stole your daughter, my sister . . .'

'Did he? I would condemn no man on the evidence that we have heard, or not heard, given your outbreak of violence. How can you expect to be master of an Empire if you cannot first master yourself?'

Mor sighed. 'I am tame,' he muttered. 'Ask what questions you will.' He drew a deep, sighing breath, almost panting as he fought to return to sanity and the rational control expected of Hellenes. Flavius walked over to him, a cup of watered wine in his hand, and stood close to him, his hand clasping the Prince's shoulder reassuringly. The madness, the plague, the weakness in their defences that enabled Irene's creature to steal Gwenlliant: perhaps the scarab was responsible for weakening Mor's control, too.

Mor patted his friend's hand, then looked to Elen. 'Thank you for stopping me,' he said simply. Then he sat on his heels, close by his mother and by Dylan.

'Very well, then,' Mor began. 'You live, for now. Where did you get that necklace.'

'From my mother,' spat the captain.

'And where did your mother get it?' Elen sensed that Mor's patience, his indulgence of a man he fully hoped to kill, would be temporary, and hastened Dylan to the questions that Mor truly wanted answered.

Dylan sat up slowly, one hand rubbing his throat in the old gesture, as he reached up to finger the necklace that Mor had ripped from him. Instead, he touched a faint red mark, all that remained of the bruises and cuts that Mor had dealt him, using the necklace as a noose.

'Again you heal me, lady,' he murmured to the Queen. 'And now, I fear I bring you unwelcome news. Myself. My mother received that necklace from the man whom she swore was my father.'

Mor's hand opened, and the massy gold fell into Olwen's outstretched palm.

'Your mother was of the Iceni,' she said, clearly weighing all possibilities. 'And you asked about Queen Luned as might one who knew her, and who cared for her?' Abruptly, incongruously, she laughed.

'Marric told me that she had set him on the road to Penllyn, that she had told him of me. I had not thought . . . but why not, knowing the two of them? No wonder, Dylan, no wonder that I was drawn to favour you . . .'

Aye, and Gwenlliant too, Elen thought. She had been drawn to him, attracted past reason, past even Gwenlliant's usual brief tempests of infatuation. Not to the brother she knew, but to a dark stranger whose injuries called out all her warmth, all the healing gifts that awoke in her, and that terrified her as they woke.

Mor stood upright, spitting out words in Hunnic that drew raised eyebrows from Flavius.

'At least,' he breathed, 'I didn't murder him. Thank all the gods for that. The punishment for fratricide . . .'

'I know,' Elen said. 'My mother warned me.'

'Seeing that you grew up with Gwenlliant . . .' There was no reason, could be no reason for them to smile at one another so warmly. Yet they did, and they drew closer to one another.

Olwen hushed them both. 'Why did you never make yourself known?' she demanded of Mor. 'My husband would have loved more children than I could bear; I would willingly have welcomed you, and he would have . . .'

'With *this*, Queen?' Dylan cried, his voice cracking like a much younger man's. 'My mother told him that she would return the medallion round the neck of their son. But as what would he have welcomed me? As a scribe, a cripple, a useless mouth: his lame son. In the course of one fever, one wretched little fever that seemed so light that I barely bothered to put on a cloak, I went from being my mother's and sisters' pride to an object of pity. After that, how could I remain among the tribe? How could I gain power in any tribe, imperfect as I was?

'So I went to sea. At least, there, I made my own way, and did not need to see the pity, the disgust in my father's eyes.'

There it was, if you had eyes to see it, Elen thought. The angular bones of the strong face, the stubborn jaw, the passionate dark eyes, and the mouth clamped thin on memories that brought no joy. No wonder Gwenlliant had been drawn to him, though the brother whom she had known all her life left her unmoved. No wonder he had seemed familiar to her. Blood called to blood.

No one, not even Mor, thought to protest. The explanation was too complete, the resemblance too apparent.

Olwen shook her head, and a tear rolled down her face. 'Oh, you baby,' she whispered. 'You utter, total fool. He would so gladly have loved you. As would we all.'

Dylan hung his own head. Humbly, he held out his hand,

palm up, as if begging his own medallion back. 'That is why,' he whispered, 'I had to stay aloof from Princess Gwen . . . from my half-sister. I knew she was attracted to me; yet brother with sister is the Sin, we say in the Isles. Had I grown up with her, with all of you, that would never have happened. I would have known you all, loved you . . .'

Mor, whom Dylan might have displaced, laid a hand on his shoulder.

'I was ten when I caught the fever that twisted and withered my right leg, leaving me as you see,' Dylan said. 'Right then, I swore never to make my father acknowledge me, a cripple.'

'You might have done him the courtesy of letting him decide if you were a burden or a disgrace, a wreck or not,' said Olwen. 'Your loneliness is your doing. You yourself crippled your mind. Before that, only your leg was lame.'

'I know that now,' Dylan said. 'Suffer me to go. I swear to you, I shall seek out your daughter . . . my half-sister, and if I do not, may the sea that I have so loved drown me!'

Wordlessly, Olwen poured the necklace into Dylan's palm, held out to receive it as humbly as if he begged by the docks. Its clasp needed fixing. Gently, he stowed it in his tunic.

Mor raised an eyebrow in silent question, and Olwen nodded. 'Let him go.' With a kind of rough sympathy, Flavius bent to help Dylan rise, but he jerked away, almost convulsively.

'You learn to keep your balance at sea,' Dylan remarked as he struggled to his feet and limped down the hall, his long, uneven shadow jolting darkly before him.

'Have him followed,' Mor muttered at Flavius. 'No, don't you do it. I told you, I need you to escort the Princess Elen to safety.'

Olwen embraced Elen. 'Do not fear contagion, child,' she whispered. 'I have strength enough to ward you and Flavius from it.' Indeed, Elen thought, Olwen seemed to glow. A sheen transformed her face and cast new radiance on her braids, and the fragrance of summer flowers was very strong. *She draws on all her reserves at once*, Elen drew one of her mother's most private fears from her memory. 'I must go directly to the temples to aid the healers. I shall have no time to write as I should. But give . . .' her eyes filled . . . 'give Marric my dearest love, and tell him that I do this for him, too.'

Elen, standing close to Mor, jolted back to furious awareness as she was mentioned. 'I won't go!' she announced. 'There is plague here. With the Princess gone, who but I can assist the Queen? And . . .' she drew a deep breath and cast back in her mind for some of the deepest, most arcane learning she had garnered from her mother . . . 'although the priests of Osiris or Anubis might be able to track down whatever created the simulacrum of Dylan, you will need my help if you want to follow Gwenlliant.'

'Can you hear her thoughts?' asked the priest.

Elen nodded and spoke the words that she knew would test her, body and soul, and perhaps cost her both of them. 'Yes,' she murmured. 'I believe that I can.'

Chapter Twelve

Someone must help Dylan! Gwenlliant had dived into the water after him. Now he had caught her in a deadly, panic-stricken hold, and they would both drown. She tried to flail out with her hands, but he had clutched them beyond her power to break free. She was drowning, she was stifling, panting for breath in the dark . . . and then the hot, cumbersome folds of the cloak that the Dylan-simulacrum had hurled over Gwenlliant's head to subdue her were pulled loose, and she drew welcome breaths of hot air tainted by the smells of dust, sweat, and lathered, frightened horse, as if she had been fleeing enemies through a desert and come upon a hidden pool.

Below her, the ground seemed to rise and fall with the horse's hoofbeats; the saddle, over which someone had flung her after she had fainted for lack of air, was doing its best to hack her in half at the belly; and she didn't know whether a headache, or nausea a thousand-fold worse than seasickness, would end her miserable life first.

She tossed her head to shake matted, sweaty strands of her hair free of her nose and eyes, only to find herself grasped by it, and hauled upwards, gasping. At least, that ridge composed of the saddle and the horse's spine was no longer cutting her in two. Now she found herself incongruously supported against the chest and shoulder of the very man who had led her from her brother's house and stolen her from Gesoriacum. Her hands, bound at the wrist, balled into fists; she could neither attack him nor seize the horse's reins.

She felt her kidnapper's chuckle rumble in his chest as much as heard it above the hoofbeats, the swish of leaves, and the rush of the hot summer wind as they rode. A splash of moisture caught her in the face; the horse was lathered and the froth that trickled from its jaws was tinged, in the reddish moonlight, with a deeper colour. So, he had stolen her from the protection of a queen, an imperial heir and a governor? That said more about her own stupidity than about their protection, she decided, in the harshest self-condemnation of her life. And, to take her to wherever he needed her to be, he would kill his horse?

Best to let him under-rate her, she thought, and permitted a little moan of pain and returning awareness to escape her dry, swollen lips. Thirst . . . awareness of how dry her mouth was obsessed her, thrusting her earlier discomforts from her mind. They were trivial, not worth thinking about, much less whimpering over; but if she could only get to water! She would kill for it.

'You are an excellent actress, girl,' her captor told her, 'but I knew that you had waked from your nap when you started to fight against the cloak. Why do you think I lifted you? *This* position, at least, is minimally interesting for me, though I would have sworn that had the real Dylan tossed you up before him on a horse . . .'

Gwenlliant tried to swallow past what felt like half the Arabian desert in her mouth. 'Forgive me, Princess. You must be thirsty.'

The man reined in his horse, and the poor beast's head drooped immediately to its knees. He unslung a leather bottle from his saddle and held it to her lips. Watered wine ran down over her chin and neck. Gwenlliant swallowed once, convulsively, and gasped both from the fire of the wine and the fact that some of the fluid went down the wrong way. She coughed, spraying wine and water over herself and her kidnapper, then drank again. That swallow had to be the finest drink she had ever tasted, assuaging her thirst and restoring what few wits she might have had before this ride. She took another gulp and tried to spit it at her captor.

'Manners, manners,' scolded her captor, and reslung the bottle.

Refusing to look at him, Gwenlliant glared at her bound hands. That sibilant accent of his: had she ever heard it before? And the way he, when disguised as Dylan, had stood too close to her, had grasped her so possessively that it had aroused *her suspicions . . . not quickly enough*, she thought, abruptly, murderously angry at herself as much as at him. The man rode well, effortlessly, in fact, in the mode of the Eastern Empire, with saddle and stirrups. And he was Irene's man – or the servant of her heirs, as he said. His breath smelled of garlic, overlaid with the cardamom that he must have been chewing to mask the garlic. Irene had come from Syria, therefore perhaps this man too . . . perhaps he despised women (except for his dead and damned mistress); perhaps she could exploit that.

'Do not even try to plan an escape,' he warned her. 'You are wild, and as desirable as I was told the women of the West are. I could enjoy taming you. But I would far rather go on living.'

Gwenlliant clamped her lips on at least three Arabic curses that she had heard her father use when he thought she was not listening.

'I could give you any treasure you asked for,' she tried, cautiously.

'I told you, Princess, I would far rather live than be briefly wealthy from your ransom.'

'My father and brother will find you and kill you,' she said.

'If I betray them, my masters will eat my soul. Let your brother and father come, let your witch of a mother come and test her failing magics against our own,' said the man. 'My

Empress's heirs are very hungry, for power in this world, and souls in the next.'

What heirs? Irene had had one son – one *legitimate* son, whom Alexa had killed.

Intrigued, determined to learn what she could of her enemy, Gwenlliant asked, 'Who are her heirs?' but, as if signifying that negotiations were over, the man kicked his horse into a stumbling trot, cursed, and then lashed it to greater speed. Gwenlliant felt its gasps for breath through her legs where they rested against its flanks and the very leather of the saddle.

So much for trying to bargain. Gwenlliant found herself amazed by her own sardonic amusement. She had always loved her father's story of how the ship that was taking him to be sold in Alexandria had been captured by pirates, and how he had vowed to win his freedom, hunt them down and hang them all.

'I will see you hang,' she muttered.

Another chuckle, smug and assured, told her that she had been overheard, and she thought hatred at her captor, hatred and anger, red fury . . . *if I can sense how others feel, if I can heal them*, she wondered suddenly, *could I also not use that gift as a weapon?*

Not if you have any sense, she told herself. Often and often, her aunt had warned her of what came of turning power to the dark. But Alexa, in desperation during the wars with the werefighters of Jomsborg, had taken her power and twisted it, and she had survived to warn against it.

Think of anger, Gwenlliant told herself. *Think of anger as a weapon.* Alexa had once described her own rages as red fire and shrieking birds with sharp beaks and sharper talons. She tried to summon those images, but her anger faded. To summon it again, she would need her own images. *Think of anger again. Think of it as a knife, a weapon to strike down those who oppose you. Think of anger as queensblade, the black dagger that her mother carried, that her mother would one day turn on herself and pass on to her daughter, assuming that her daughter lived that long . . .* Gwenlliant's breath came in quick, fierce gasps, and her eyes felt as if they were fire itself before she shut them. *Think of queensblade, think of a dagger striking down the people you love the most, a dagger of fire, cutting senselessly away at whatever you care for . . .*

– *Gwenlliant?* –

So intent was she on her hatred that she heard her name three times before she realized what the sounds meant. Her concentration had hurled her awareness into that plane of consciousness on which, occasionally, she and Elen had toyed with underhearing. How much more clearly, more easily it came to her now!

– *Who calls Gwenlliant?* – she thought defiantly.

Fear and furious aggravation answered her. – Elen, where are you? –

– *Following you, Mor and I. Show me where you are, and I will tell Mor, who knows these lands.* –

Her captor must think her sunk in despair, perhaps even weeping. Carefully, she shifted her position until she could see the track on which their horse faltered.

The horse stumbled, and its rider swore, then lashed at it once again. It screamed and arched its head, trying to bite the puny, cruel thing that forced it on and on . . .

'You're going to kill that animal, and then how do you get me to whomever owns you?' Gwenlliant spat, despite her resolve not to speak with the man.

'You waste your pity,' he told her.

Her awareness remained fractured: one level of her mind recorded images – the shape of a rock, the twist in the trail, a sudden clearing where no trees grew and little else (– *Mor thinks he has it!* – came Elen's quick call); another level attempted to maintain her seat as the horse plunged and tried to summon the strength to buck; a third level simply and purely hated.

A dagger of flame, queensblade transformed to punish the enemies of the land, striking down this fool that touched its heir . . .

Behind her, the man reeled as if struck in the heart. Gwenlliant felt his hand go up to clasp at his medallion for protection.

'So that's your little trick, is it?' he gasped.

Once again, he reined in and unslung a leather bottle, not the same one from which Gwenlliant had drunk before. He unstoppered it, and she smelled the flat heaviness of a drug. Mandragora or poppy, to make her sleepy and docile. If she drank enough of either, it would kill her. She did not think that her captor would dare permit her to escape him thus.

– *Fire, hate, a dagger . . . Elen, Mor, he seeks to drug me* – He pressed the bottle to her lips and forced her to swallow. Desperately, Gwenlliant twisted away, trying to spit out what washed into her mouth, to spew out what she had already swallowed, but even the fumes from the bottle were over-powering, and she . . .

– *Courage, Gwenlliant!* –

She took that cry with her down into thick darkness, a field of black poppies into which, from the heights of her rage, she fell and fainted.

If Elen could reach Gwenlliant's mind, then, naturally, she must be one of the hunting party; equally naturally, she must be able to ride. Bolstered by Olwen's cool appropriation of the governor's youngest son's hunting clothes, by the tales traders told of women in Ch'in playing polo in men's clothing, and by her own absolute refusal to chafe herself raw in skirts, Elen had quickly and calmly pulled on breeches and boots, strode out to where Mor waited with the horses, and promptly wished that she could hide herself in the cloak that she carried without looking like a blushing, simpering fool. Women, she knew, did *not* ride thus in Byzantium – and all too clearly, Mor was appreciating the innovation.

Squaring her shoulders somewhat in defiance, Elen glanced about for a way of climbing on to the horse to which Mor gestured. He flung its reins to Flavius and himself lifted her on to its back, his hands lingering on her waist and hip just an instant too long, his admiring grin too broad, Elen thought, for the seriousness of the occasion.

As if sensing her thought, Mor's smile faded. 'An hour ago, you were collapsing on a couch,' he told her. 'Can you—'

'Can I ride? Can I keep the pace that you will set?' Elen demanded, to cover her own doubts. 'Can *you* find Gwenlliant without me?' *Let him not know how faint the linkage is*, Elen prayed. *I can hear her only when she wakes, and only then when she wills it.*

Flavius began to mutter something about doubling the size of the Prince's guard, the better to protect . . . whom? Prince Mor, or herself? Flavius had protested loudly against Elen's going at all, but '*I am going,*' Elen had told him, '*I am going to help Mor rescue my cousin, and then I myself am going to kill her. Slowly.*' Even Flavius, who was the youngest of what seemed like seven brothers, understood family loyalty such as that.

'The city,' Mor mused. 'Plague-struck, and I ride away from it . . .'

'Leaving your mother, the Empress, in command, Mor, do not forget that,' Elen said. She squeezed his hand. 'Now, do we stand here worrying all night, or do you show me this pace that you fear I am too weak to keep . . . now!'

Mor flung himself on to his horse's back in what had to be a trick he learned from the Huns, and out they rode towards the gates of Gesoriacum. Flavius had argued that the hunting party should head for the docks. After all, he said, Dylan was a sailor. That, Mor snapped back, was precisely why they would *not* head for the docks. The sailors all knew one another. Seeing Dylan with a young woman, conscious or not, would cause gossip that ultimately they would be able to overhear. For that matter, seeing anyone with a girl like Gwenlliant would cause talk, especially if she were recognized. At that point, Flavius had flung up a hand in mock-surrender, and Elen had realized that the argument was a mock-battle, useful for refining their thoughts. Her own instincts were to head for the great forest that covered most of Gallia, *and Goddess spare me, for I shall not, if I am wrong.*

As if rumour of Gwenlliant's disappearance had spread with the deadly speed of plague, men and women milled about the governor's house and in the dusty streets. The tang of salt filled the air, warring with the fumes of incense that poured from houses and temples as people prayed and fought the plague. At the horizon, heat lightning flashed and rumbled, but never a drop of rain to make the heat less oppressive. Their passage raised a hot wind that passers-by flinched from.

Elen reined in before they rode past a knot of people who crouched over a woman and child.

'Why do you stop?' Mor demanded.

Elen shook her head. 'I do not know for certain. Just ask them what ails the woman lying there?'

Mor had to bend in his saddle to hear the reply of the one man brave enough to speak to what was, after all, Horus incarnate. When he rose again, his face was puzzled. 'He says nothing at all is wrong with her. She had felt herself ill, had started for the Temple of Isis with her son, and fallen . . . see, it is further down the road. When she woke, she found these people bending over . . .'

'Gwenlliant,' Elen said. 'She must have seen her, healed her.'

Light glittered up at them from the pavement, and one of the guard dismounted to scoop it up. Elen held out her hand for whatever it was: one of the earrings Gwenlliant had worn, gold and emerald, at dinner. She *must* have seen this woman, healed her, and only then discovered that 'Dylan' was no friend, no hoped-for lover (or unknown half-brother, Elen thought mordantly) and, Gwenlliant-fashion, put up a fine fight before she was overpowered. She closed her hand upon the tiny, precious thing and felt a flash, even more precious, of its owner's essence. For a moment, Elen closed her eyes. By the time that she opened them, she was sure of her course.

'We are falling behind,' Elen murmured at moonset. They were walking the horses at that point in order to let them rest: walk for an hour; mount and walk them further; trot; gallop; and then walk them again. Once deep into the forest, the horses must last. If they killed these mounts, no one knew where they might find – or steal – others; and larger beasts than man stalked the woods.

Incongruously, Mor laughed, 'Achilles and the tortoise,' he said. 'They hasten; we move slowly and steadily to the same goal – and beat them to it.' They walked on for several steps. 'As much as it goes against my instincts to compare any of Irene's slaves to Achilles. And assuming that we – can you . . . ?'

'Have I found any trace of Gwenlliant?' Elen asked. 'Not yet.

When we next ride, though, I will tie myself to the saddle and send my mind ahead to quest for her.'

'Do you put yourself in danger if you do that?'

Elen allowed herself to nod. She hoped that she looked neither reluctant nor self-sacrificing before Gwenlliant's brother. She was furious with her cousin – no unusual occurrence – yet that had nothing at all to do with her obligation to protect Gwenlliant if she could; with her life, if she must. After all, though Elen herself bore the style of princess, she stood in relation to her cousin as Flavius did to Mor. Gwenlliant was *her* princess, heir to Penllyn and Byzantium both.

Mor shook his head. The preposterous thought flitted through her mind that he was reluctant to save his sister at the risk, or cost, of Elen's life. 'There are dangers,' she told him, 'in these woods themselves, you know. Your own father was attacked by bears.'

'During the Jomsborg Wars,' Mor agreed. 'We are hemmed in by dangers. On board ship, there are assassins; in Gesoriacum, poisoned wells; in the very streets, rumours about the poisoners, riots and plague. Now, we enter the forest itself, and, lady, if it comes to safety, I frankly prefer the woods to the haunts of men.'

Elen fell silent, mulling over tales she had heard from her parents and the Druids. The Forest, she had learned, just like the various planes of being, had its own otherness, its own marvels, and its own threats. She leaned against her horse's flank and tried to listen with ears and the other senses of her underhearing.

'Elen?' Mor had his hands on her shoulders, was steadying her against him.

She shook her head. 'This prophecy makes me too weak,' she grumbled. Despite the heat of what was close to Midsummer's Eve itself, she did not move away from him, did not even try. She glanced at him, forcing herself to make the glance briefer than she wished. How a silent boy could turn into a man whose sheer, glowing presence reduced her to witless admiration: best not to let him even suspect; never let him know. But even in the pallid light before dawn, even worn out, he was beautiful.

'Did you . . . ?'

'Yes, yes!' Now that her strength recovered, she grinned at him, her eyes dancing. 'About an hour up ahead, they paused and turned south and east. We can follow them.'

Mor tightened his hold into an exuberant hug, then examined her face, nodded to himself, and swung her, protesting, into her saddle. 'You weigh nothing at all. From here on, even when we walk, you will ride each of the horses in turn,' he decided. 'And no, you do not ride because you are a woman. You ride because you are our lodestone and must be spared.'

Chapter Thirteen

Gwenlliant was thankful to wake. Not that the drugs that she had been forced to drink gave her dreams that were, as she had expected, spectacularly and hideously lurid: but they were all the more terrible for their very monotony. As she dreamt, she felt herself floating at times, and at other times, trudging through a world of greys: forests of tree trunks, and no leaves anywhere; rocks crumbled and fallen, not with the splendour of boulders toppled by a shore, but grotesque, partially melted or tilted at absurd angles to the grey, starved land; riverbeds flowing with iridescent scum, rather than cold, clear . . .

Oh sweet Goddess, water! Gwenlliant, struggling out of the greyness back to her sense, longed for water the way her abductor, it seemed, longed to be possessed by Irene's ghost or her heirs. His horse stumbled, and Gwenlliant fell forward. Had she not been bound to the saddle, she might have toppled to the ground, there to have broken open her skull on one of the thousands of rocks that littered the land, like gigantic stone avatars of the mushrooms and puffballs that feed on waste.

Despite her previous resolve not to show herself sick or afraid, she bent over the saddle and retched on the ground, not that there was much to bring up. Nor did her kidnapper offer her the skin of wine and water again. That, in itself, warned her of what her fate was likely to be. Not for the first time, she wished that she had worn a dagger the night before. But for the first time, she understood why her mother bore queensblade: against something that she personally considered worse than death itself.

An aching head and a glare in the east warned her that the sun was rising. Midsummer, she thought, though the land through which the dying horse plodded seemed one that would never know the promise of spring, the richness of summer, the ripeness of autumn – or even the silence of winter that led to rebirth.

She stifled a moan and let herself fall back, her head drooping against her kidnapper. Pleasant company, she must be: her hair matted, her breath noisome with drugs, wine and sickness – and he was welcome to it all! She closed eyes that felt somehow too large for their sockets and concentrated on deep, rhythmic breathing. If the Goddess were kind, she might escape into a reverie. She dared not hope that she might escape into that other plane where her mind could range as free as her body was constrained.

And she was, indeed, right not to hope. Her thoughts beat themselves against the cage of her mind and the drugs, and she had to fall back, acknowledging – but only for the moment – that she was beaten. Whatever they wanted her for, they could not keep her drugged all the time. At some point, her mind would belong to herself once again, and she could try to call Elen.

It occurred to Gwenlliant that Elen, in her position, might not be as helpless, that there were rituals that might counter the drugged stupour in which she had ridden and the sickness as it wore off. Perhaps she might try to heal herself of it, she thought, but a spasm of dry heaving warned her against such an attempt right now. Later, when she had more power . . .

There had been power in this land once, she knew, power in the forest that stretched over all Europa. She could feel only scars now in the land, scars that ached as the land remembered, as she passed, when its power had been reft from it. Some might yet remain, as it did to the west and in the Isles, but here it flickered near extinction. Perhaps, she thought, it would be kinder to allow the spark to die than to attempt to rekindle it.

'Do not despair yet, Princess,' said the man behind her. 'You may yet be rescued. Certainly, I hope that your kin will try; we need them.'

Gwenlliant did not waste strength by spitting at him, assuming that she had strength enough to do so. She let herself drift into a trance of vacancy, and woke only as the horse stumbled to its knees this time, and she was cut free from its saddle and dragged away.

'On your feet, Princess,' her companion said, and hauled her to them by an arm. Her nostrils flared, and she swept one quick, frightened look about the clearing in which she stood. Here, indeed, lay the blasted grey stone of her drug-induced nightmares. Toppled in the centre of the clearing was a heap of stone that once must have been a trilithon; stumps of rock still guarded the perimeter, some blackened from lightning or fire, others crumbled, two or three leaning over like the last teeth in a derelict's mouth. The shafts of dead wood outside the remnants of the stone circle – Gwenlliant blinked. Yes, surely those had once been hawthorn trees. Then this place was – or had been – a death nemet, and she had no iron about her.

She hoped that the Goddess would pardon her for the oversight. Her own death surely would atone for it.

The pain of circulation returning to her legs made her buckle and stagger. Her eyes went dark for some time. When she regained awareness, she felt herself bound again and braced, this time against the cool rock of the last menhir left standing in what must have once been a formidable circle.

'The horse,' she muttered. 'Someone knock it on the head and end its pain.'

'This horse? Your tender-heartedness is touching, Princess. This horse's pain cannot end, because, you see, it cannot die. It cannot really live, either, yet it serves us well enough. It serves – as will you and your kin.'

'I shall see you all in the nether worlds first,' she told the voice. Her head hurt too much for her to try looking up. And it was easier, she admitted to herself, to say that than to confess that she feared what she might see.

Then she forced herself to raise her eyes.

The man who stood over her, who gloated over his plan to use her to ensnare her family, was unremarkable. She might have passed a thousand like him in the streets of Gesoriacum: for all she knew, she might have passed him, although not in the purple that he had dared to assume. The imperial colour was unflattering to him, and the collar of crystals and rubies that he wore over it only accentuated the stoop of his shoulders.

'I am Ctesiphon, son of Ctesiphon, grandson of Irene, Adept and Empress,' he told Gwenlliant.

'I doubt it,' she snapped. Ctesiphon, whose son he claimed to be, had died young, killed by Alexa, who he had tried to rape. She was not, Gwenlliant knew, proud of her fratricide, but she had paid for it, *'and,' as she often said, 'The Goddess knew, only Irene deserved more to be murdered.'* Seeing this spindly fraud posing as the late princeling's bastard, Gwenlliant could agree eagerly.

The man who stood at his side was far more imposing. Gwenlliant had to force herself not to shudder as she met his ophidian gaze. Like 'Ctesiphon', he wore the purple, but his in the form or a priest's robe; and the shade of purple he chose was a porphyry shade precisely the colour of dried blood.

Behind him stood ranks of other men and women. Most were robed in black; a very few wore that same porphyry shade. Though they came of many races throughout the Empire – she could discern Egyptians of both the Upper and Lower Kingdoms, Hellenes, barbarians from Thrakia, even one or two who might be Celtoi or men of the North – their faces all bore the same mark: eyes that watched her, that devoured her presence, her youth, her energy.

That they seemed so ordinary was truly the hideous thing about them: men and women with no great gift for virtue, or, for that matter, no great inclination to evil either, who had surrendered themselves – submitted any part of themselves that might perhaps have taken joy in a Midsummer dawn or a young woman's courage – to the serice of this . . . this effete princeling who called himself heir to Irene. Whatever else she had been – regicide, perhaps, sorceress, adulteress and killer most definitely

– she had been more than he, and far more than the crowd that
so avidly watched Gwenlliant.

Abruptly, even her sickness and fear seemed to her altogether
admirable, because they were human. These creatures had made
themselves nothing, and were like the vandal who, wanting light
by which to eat or slay the wounded, burns the library that
might have enabled him to grow food or heal the very people
he strikes down. Having no life or dreams themselves, they
sought to destroy those things in others, and then, because their
sameness was all that would remain, they would boast that it,
not the gods, was divine.

Gwenlliant began to sweat with honest terror. In Penllyn,
much of the land's life was vested in its queen; in the Empire,
the rulers were father and mother to their land. It did not
matter, she realized, whether such rulers practised magic or not:
for all intents and purposes, they *were* magic. And these people
sought to slay them and take their power for themselves.

Once or twice she had heard speculation about what life might
be like in a world from which all magic had departed. Olwen
had flatly stated that it was preposterous and a waste of breath
even to discuss it. Alexa, always heretical, had laughed and
posed an additional paradox. 'Consider,' she said 'a world in
which Antony Autokrator had lost to Octavianus. What a prosy
bore it would have been. Do you truly think that any magic
would have survived in such a world? Certainly, not among the
rulers. It would have all diffused and been lost the way that dye
from the murex, used to tint silk, produces purple, but nothing
at all if it is wasted in the sea.'

If Gwenlliant ever escaped from this shattered death nemet,
she would tell Alexa that her dream of a Roman-dominated
world was a bard's wedding song compared to what the world
would actually be like with the human automata that sought to
rule it now. Irene had been fired by passions – for power, for
her son's future, for men's adoration and desire. These creatures, who called themselves her heirs, sought only annihilation
for all not of their band.

Impossible to believe that Irene had given birth to any one
among them. Heirs could be spiritual heirs, as hard as it was

for Gwenlliant to imagine that any of the priest's followers had spirits.

'My kinsfolk will kill you,' she told the imposter and the dark priest.

'Do you think that they will succeed?' The priest, not the princeling, asked that question. Gwenlliant firmed her lips. As she suspected, then; priest, not Prince, held the reins here.

'I know that they will try.'

'Let them. Before we are done with you, who so arrogantly call yourselves Imperial, we shall have the very Emperor himself kneel at our feet and grind his face in the dust.'

'And, for all that,' Gwenlliant cried hotly, 'he will remain Emperor – and a better man! – than you will ever be.'

She felt power flow out of herself, and a rumble of satisfaction from the people hovering at the priest's back. *You get no more from me!* she resolved. Once or twice, Gwenlliant had seen a cat toy with a mouse. Although she loved cats, she had made it a point of pride to interrupt the cat at its sport and allow the mouse to run free. Now she herself was the mouse.

He waited for an answer. When she gave none, he tugged at her hair until she raised her chin merely to end the pressure that threatened to tear her scalp. 'No,' she retorted. 'I do not. You are like that . . . that horse. You cannot be killed because you are not truly alive.'

'We shall wait for your kin,' he told her. 'Oh, it is safe enough to tell you that. If you appeal to them, we shall simply reel them in the more quickly. And once we have your brother and your cousin, we shall demand, as the price of your ransom, that your parents come here and bow before us. And then . . .' for the first time, the man's breath came faster, and his pallid face acquired colour and at least some species of animation, ' . . . and then we shall have all our desire; and all of *you*, ruling in the sunlight, shall be the nothing that you have always been fated to become.'

She dared a glance at the man at whose side the dark priest stood. Did Ctesiphon, if that was what he wanted to be called, truly imagine that this priest would permit him to rule? Or perhaps he simply meant to rule through him. It hardly mattered. What did matter, even if it cost Gwenlliant her life, were the kinsfolk who must be pursuing her.

Stay away! Gwenlliant flung all of the strength that remained to her into that cry to Elen, wherever she might be. She felt no answer, except for pain that nearly shattered her skull.

The midsummer sun rose higher and higher in the sky. Ordinarily, it would be cause for celebrations, for needfire kindled all over Prydein and in the Empire. Today, it was cause for a dull headache and terrible fear. When the sun set, the gods only knew what would become of her. And she suspected that those gods that knew had nothing to do with Isis and Osiris, save to name them as their mortal enemies.

For a time, she toyed with healing herself of the dizziness with which her captor's drugs had left her. Gradually, the foul taste in her mouth faded, and the stubs of the stones that she could see stopped jiggling up and down, partnered by the flares and spots of light that danced in her eyes. Then she must have dozed or swooned. For, when she woke this time, she felt stronger. Most of the congregation in that desecrated nemet was gone. She writhed, trying to settle herself as comfortably as possible, then gasped as she felt the rasp of a sharp blade along the leather strips that bound her to the standing stone.

Midsummer dawn was a hazed-over smear when Mor signalled for the guard to mount up again. Though all of them were experienced scouts, nevertheless, the creak of harness and the rattle of their weapons seemed to carry in the silence of the withering forest. Elen put her head down and tried, for the last time during this rest halt, to touch Gwenlliant's thoughts. She rubbed her temples and wished that the cloak that she had made her pillow did not scratch so. Her head ached with her efforts to concentrate, and, she began to think, with more than her own pain.

'Can you find her?' Mor's voice in her ear, and his hand, warm on her shoulder, roused her from her abortive trance. He helped her to turn on to her back, and she snatched the luxury of a moment to watch him. – *Do you know what is happening, cousin?* – she thought at him. She was particularly with her mind, but Mor simply looked at her before he traced first the hollows beneath her eyes, then her lips, with a gentle fingertip.

'They will see us,' she shaped the words soundlessly and won a smile from him.

– I wish we did not have to move now. – Hardy she was, with the discipline of one Druid-trained. But that was not a soldier's training; the frenzies of the day, the night's ride, and the constant, anxious questing for Gwenlliant had drained her past the point at which Alexa would have insisted that she rest. *I know I am drained, Mother*, she told the silent, accusing presence in her mind. *But I am unlikely to have time to do anything about it. Suffice it to say, I know, and I will be careful.*

But if there were no need to move now, and no guards breaking camp about her, she knew that she would have smiled at Mor, put her arms about his neck, drawn him down to her, and rested content. He claimed he had no powers, none like hers or his mother's or sister's, not even the fight against his own magic that had tormented his father lifelong. But, she had noticed, people stood stronger, rode harder, lasted longer in his presence. As she herself did. Even these few seconds, with him kneeling above her, made her sure that she could ride.

As she sat up, he shook his head regretfully, and Elen wondered just how true his claim not to hear thoughts was. Surely he possessed at least some measure of his mother's and sister's empathy.

He aided her to her feet, hand clasping hand, and did not relinquish his grasp even when she was in the saddle. 'You have to mount,' she warned him. 'See, your men are waiting.'

Still he looked up at her, as he had ten years ago, from the crumbling brink of a cliff above a river, when she had commanded him to hold on, and risked her life to help him hold on until help arrived. 'If we come out of this alive . . .' she began.

Again, his grin flashed. 'We did before. Do you doubt us?'

No, but I doubt . . . Memory, long-suppressed, struck her with the force of overwhelming necessity. After Marric had brought them down from the hills, Elen riding his horse, Mor, with his broken ankle, cradled in his father's arms. Gwenlliant clinging to his leg, Olwen had tried to separate them in order to heal her son and allow Elen to sleep. Gwenlliant, who had cried herself into exhaustion, had gone off to bed with astonishing docility. But when Alexa tried to lead Elen away, she had fought; and Mor had woken at her screams and tears, thrashing and crying out. '. . . *Let the girl have her will. Elen saved my boy's life, you know that, sister,*' she had heard the Emperor tell her mother.

Alexa – even now, Elen remembered her relief that her mother had not been angry at her – had bent and kissed Elen's forehead. Lamplight had shone on her dark, glossy hair. '*I know, Marric. I am proud of her. But when she has rested, I shall send her to Deva. No, do not argue. I think I know what is best for my own child now. It is almost autumn; you and Mor will sail soon, and they should not miss one another too much.*'

'*You would not consider, you and Gereint, bringing Elen to Byzantium for the winter?*'

Alexa's reaction had been passionate and quick. '*So Mor will not be alone? How can you even ask? It is one thing for Elen to be brought up with Gwenlliant. They can be sisters to one another. But Mor is to be raised as Horus on Earth, and* my *daughter* is *not in the direct line. I do not want them to grow so close that . . .*'

'*That was your choice, Alexa.*' Elen had tossed restively, and it was the Emperor's own hand that tucked the sleeping furs more firmly about her. For a miracle, neither adult wondered if she understood their rapidly spoken Greek.

'*My choice, yes! And because of it, I must make sure that Elen has a life of her own to go to when she and your children are grown. Or have you forgotten the fates of minor royalty, brother?*'

The Emperor and his heir had left Penllyn early that year, well before autumn, and now, finally, Elen knew why. Alexa had been afraid, had waited and thought, and finally, after ten years, determined to give her daughter a chance to reclaim what she herself had renounced. She was crafty beyond her daughter's capabilities; and at this moment, Elen wanted only to hide in the shelter of her skirts.

The reason for Alexa's fear and planning now stood looking up at her. His trust and courage shone in his dark eyes just as it had when he had tried to order her to leave him, to spare her the sight of his body falling and breaking on the rocks. Only now, he was a man, and their parents were far away, their wishes and plans further-seeming yet.

'No, I could not reach Gwenlliant,' she told him gently. 'Let us go.'

Mor mounted quickly. He had put away his flamboyant, Hunnish tricks like parade armour until a time of peace. They walked their horses down a narrow track, and the dusty leaves on the trees about them changed and paled from deep green to sickly yellow and dead browns and greys. Finally, the trees bore no leaves at all. This forest bore as much resemblance to the rest of the forests of Gallia as the necropolis of Byzantium did to the city itself.

Despite the flat glare of the sun through a grimy haze, thunder rumbled overhead. Elen raised her face to the sky. Rain would be welcome, rain would settle the dust, to help Olwen, Olwen back in Gesoriacum with the priests, battle plague as she and Mor sought to battle whatever it was that turned this forest into a waste. But only the hot wind raised by their passing touched her cheeks.

Against the guards' protest, she and Mor rode at the head of the tiny troop, men fanning out to either side. She had forbidden them, for their souls' sakes, not to scout ahead, then apologized with a glance to their commander, who had only smiled.

'My father passed this way during the Jomsborg Wars,' Mor said. 'In fact, somewhere near here is the site of a major battle. But this isn't how he described the land to me. This very waste . . . once it was overgrown with trees. Good hunting, too, but tell me, Elen, have you even heard one bird?'

She shook her head, listening to Mor, but absently, as she followed the trail, leaning over her horse's neck to search for hoofprints, droppings, perhaps even a rag of cloth or a gem to signify that Gwenlliant had passed this way.

There! Something shone, and she called out. Mor swung down to retrieve am embroidered scrap of soiled white cloth that might have come from the hem of Gwenlliant's gown.

'That way!' he pointed towards where a new track in the blasted woods appeared to open.

Elen held out her hand to take the scrap of cloth. Then she

recoiled. 'Mor, look at the gold stitching on this. How could Gwenlliant have sat a horse, torn at her hem, and tossed this scrap – the first one that we have seen – down for us to find, all without someone noticing?'

'Get back!'

Mor hurled his full weight against her horse, forcing it sideways, just as a tree limb, high overhead, cracked from its rotten trunk and toppled down on them. Her horse bucked, plunged, and came up, trembling, against a tree trunk about as wide as Elen's wrist. It promptly cracked, and the horse tripped.

'Quick!' As the horse fell, Mor snatched Elen from its back, saving her from a fall that would probably have killed her had the horse pinned her with its weight. It fought back to all fours and ran, followed by Mor's own mount.

Overhead pealed more thunder. Lightning hurled down upon them like a barrage of spears, followed by the snapping of branches and trunks, and a smell of smoke wherever it landed. All around Elen, men dismounted, snatched their cloaks from their saddles, and wrapped them over their horses' eyes.

'We may not be able to keep the horses,' Mor observed. 'Get your packs!' he ordered his men, shouting over the cracks of trees and the bolts of lightning that cast glowing violet afterimages across the now dark sky.

Mor held her tightly, one hand pressing her head protectively against his shoulder. She squirmed in his arms.

'We must get away from these trees,' she whispered.

'The lightning? Good thought!' He signalled for the guard to follow them towards a clearing, and set out almost at a run, dragging Elen with him.

A slender white figure stood in his path, long hair blowing in a wind that no woman on earth should be able to feel, her hand upraised in warning.

'No! Not that way!' Elen cried. She let herself fall limp, bearing Mor to the ground with her just as the earth rumbled and what looked like an open patch of ground suddenly churned before them. One man and two horses, not as quick as she, screamed as the ground engulfed them, roiled again and again. Over the shouts of the remaining guardsmen came the shrieks of panicked, plunging horses and the crash of more trees falling.

Elen flung her arms over Mor's head, as if that might protect him from a falling branch, and burrowed her face against his shoulder. They clung to one another until the tremors subsided.

Gradually, sunlight filtered through Elen's eyelids, as tightly as she had squeezed them shut. It took a moment or two for ears, stunned by the fury of lightning, snapping trees and earthquake, to adjust to a silence that was the absence of noise rather than actual deafness. Mor raised his head cautiously, then moved away from Elen. Rising, he brushed earth and splinters from himself, then, absently, raised her to her feet.

The ambush, for such it was, had no doubt been intended — it had spooked their horses and cut them off from their escorts. They were quite alone, except for a thrashing horse pinned beneath a fallen branch. Mor released Elen's hand and walked over to examine the beast, the snapped wood about it, and the snapped foreleg that rendered close examination senseless. Shaking his head and sighing, he laid his head against the horse's.

'It may lash out at you,' Elen called, but Mor gestured confidence at her. He seemed to speak into its ear. Then he drew one hand down the horse's nose. Still speaking in a low steady voice, never taking his gaze from the horse's wide, fear-glazed eyes, he drew his dagger and opened the great vein in the injured animal's throat.

For a moment, he stared at the dagger as if he wanted to hurl it from him. Clearly, then, he reconsidered and cleaned the knife on the horse's saddle-blanket before taking the leather bottle and packs that were slung there. When he came back to Elen, his eyes were wet, his lips set in a narrow line, and his only words to her were, 'How did you know?'

She reached out for the water bottle and took a careful, grudging sip. 'As above,' she said hoarsely, 'so below.' The sky . . . the lightning was so violent that I expected that the earth must answer. As it did. But it was not only I. Did you see her?'

'See who?' Mor forced the words out as his jaw worked with the effort not to weep over the horse, so senselessly dead.

'A woman in a white robe, tall, with silvery hair. She warned me to go no further. Didn't you see her?'

Mor shook his head. 'You *know* I have no such powers,' he reminded her.

'I know you say so.' For a moment, cousin glared at cousin, and then Mor grinned mirthlessly.

'Very well, then. I did not see anyone. I heard you scream to stop. So I stopped. Did you recognize this apparition of yours?'

'My mother's spirit guide, I suspect. Her name is Stephana. I have never seen her manifest before. Goddess only knows what it cost her. But she must have intervened to save . . .' shyly, Elen looked up at Mor. 'You would be especially dear to her.'

Mor glanced away. 'I know the name. One of my nurses, Daphne – you know her?' Elen nodded her head – yes. 'Daphne used to tell me about her, that she was a seeress, that my father loved her, and that Irene cut her down. Always, our parents and their friends step in to save us. Do you think that we will ever achieve anything of our own?'

His face paled and twisted with the intensity of the question, mate to her own determination to have some sort of life for herself, to make some choices not manipulated by her mother's decisions, or compelled by her father's unquestioning love into paths that he thought were safe for his only child. But this was not the time or place, if ever a time or place would come, for her to reassure him. She answered with the stark truth. 'Not without Gwenlliant.'

She sat on a fallen log and forced herself to reason rather than to feel. She could not find Gwenlliant any place in this waste. Yet power crackled deeper in its blasted heart, power that must come from some source, power intensified by Midsummer, by the summoning of whatever dark agents Irene's heirs served, and even by Gwenlliant's presence, at best as hostage, at worst as sacrificial victim.

'A core of power,' she mused. 'Mor, tell me, remind me, please, of the Jomsborg Wars. There was a battle hereabouts, was there not?'

'Aye,' Mor sat down beside her, astride the log, hacking at it with his dagger. 'When my father . . . there is no tactful way to say this. When my father journeyed west to Penllyn because he hoped to bring your mother, Alexa, back to Byzantium, he encountered two Aescir not far from here who had been wounded by Jomsborgers in the guise of black bears. They all retreated into a . . . what so the Celtoi call a sacred grove with standing stones in it?'

'A nemet.'

'My father said that it was a death nemet, in more ways than one.'

'A hawthorn grove?' Elen shivered. There was a hawthorn nemet near the queen's maenol, a nemet into which Olwen must . . . but Mor was speaking again.

'A hawthorn grove. But the priests that served it had been slain by Jomsborgers and their bodies left in the grove. My father and his men men took shelter there. The priests warded it, as you warded the governor's house.'

Elen nodded. A death nemet, and a desecrated one at that. It *had* to be the source of whatever power had assailed them.

'But then they found that their enemies had sealed them within their own wards. I do not know the words for what they did, but one of the Aescir hurled himself against the wards and sacrificed his life so that my father and his troops could break free. Elen, Elen, when you prophesied, you spoke of a shattered circle and midsummer night!'

'Can you bring us to this place?' Elen demanded.

'I can try.' Mor looked grim. Behind his words, behind his dark looks, fit match for his name, was the awareness that if he did not try, and did not succeed by that night, there might be no chance, and no reason, for any actions ever afterwards.

Chapter Fourteen

As the thongs that lashed Gwenlliant to the standing stone parted, she bit her lip against the sting of blood returning to her hands and wrists, then drew a deep, deep breath. It was pure pleasure to breathe even the dusty, lifeless air of the defiled nemet without leather strips cutting across her chest and pressing in upon her ribs. Her ankles had been but loosely tied, thank the Goddess. If she could balance, she thought she could run.

She tried to flex her swollen fingers and suppressed a groan.

'Just a moment longer, Gwenlliant,' came a treacherously familiar man's voice.

The man who had cut her free limped around the base of the pillar and knelt beside her. He wore one of the black robes that she had seen on the unholy congregation that had watched her so avidly; a rusty splash across the breast told her how he had obtained it. Small loss, she decided.

'The last time you asked me to go with you, this is what befell me,' she spat at Dylan.

He lowered the hood of his robe to let her see his face, unshaven and drawn, the eyes red with exhaustion and fear.

'Not I, Princess,' he whispered. 'Let me beg forgiveness later. Come on!' He forced himself up, then, careful to avoid her swollen hands and wrists, dragged her upwards by her forearms. Laying an arm about her shoulders, whether to give support or to gain it, he drew her towards the perimeter of the circle, into the shadows cast by the withered hawthorn trees.

The robe, as much as his limp (his lame leg truly was the *right* leg, Gwenlliant observed), cumbered him, and he paused to throw it aside.

'Where is your horse?' she breathed.

'What horse? There was a storm earlier today, all lightning, but no rain. The earth quaked and my horse threw me. It is by the Goddess' mercy that both my legs were not crippled . . .'

'That may yet be arranged, sea captain,' came a chill voice. 'Take our little Princess and her gallant rescuer back to the standing stones to wait until nightfall.'

Four men in black robes like the one Dylan had discarded glided out to pin their arms behind their backs. Dylan hurled himself at their feet, tripping three of them.

'Run, Gwenlliant, run!' he cried.

She ran, but over the pounding of the blood in her temples, the crackle as her thin sandals crushed the dry underbrush, she could hear blows and the grunts of Dylan's breath. He had followed her into danger; could she do less for him?

Two more robed figures appeared to either side of her. Had she only her normal strength or even decent sandals! she lamented to herself. She might elude these people, then double back and release Dylan. But stubble pierced her feet, her foot caught on a loose stone, and she went sprawling with a cry not of pain but of pure fury.

They pulled her to her feet, but Gwenlliant tore free. 'Do not touch me,' she flared. 'I can return to my prison unassisted, and so can Dylan.'

'A loving sister,' purred the priest's voice. 'You should be proud, captain. And you, Prince Ctesiphon. Quite an estimable little family party, especially when the two others arrive.'

'They are a cadet branch,' sniffed Ctesiphon. 'Their parents were offered power but, being weak, let it slip through their fingers, as *I*, rest assured, shall not.'

'Rest assured,' the priest agreed suavely, 'that I believe you.'

Gwenlliant stopped where she stood, and her two guards almost walked into her. '*My* brother?' she let her voice turn to pure ice. 'My brother is heir to the Two Lands, not a sea captain with a bad leg, whose mother does not say who fathered him.' *Dylan, forgive me!* she thought, wondering all the while if, for once, the priest spoke the truth. Perhaps, though, her scorn would convince the priest. Her guards reached out to take her by the shoulders, but she rounded on them furiously and they fell back.

They pushed Gwenlliant and Dylan down by the menhir to which she had been tied before.

'This time, watch them,' ordered the priest, 'or more than one of you will die for his stupidity.'

'Watch us if you must,' Gwelliant snapped, 'but take yourself back a decent distance. The air is already foul enough without your breath to add to it.'

'Most unwise,' murmured Dylan, 'but Goddess, if I had half your spirit!'

'Apparently, you may,' Gwenlliant breathed. 'What was that wretch talking about when he called me your sister?'

'Oddly enough, the truth,' said Dylan. Holding up his hands

in an elaborate gesture that declared himself unarmed and harm-less, he reached into his tunic. Two of the dark robes drew closer, then stopped as all they saw in his hand was a simple, but heavy chain.

'The necklace that I always wear, Gwenlliant. Take it, look at it.' He poured the links, warm from his body, into her hand.

'A commemorative medallion,' she observed. 'Dated from my father's reign, stamped with his portrait and the Horus Hawk on the obverse. Where did you get this?'

'From my mother,' Dylan said. 'She was Luned of the Iceni. When your father first travelled to Prydein, he guested in the South, where he met her. She agreed to set him on the road to Penllyn; apparently, she also agreed to other things. A persuasive man, your father. He gave her this necklace as a remembrance, and she promised to return it, if she conceived, round the neck of their son.'

'Then . . .' Her cheeks flamed, and she knew that if she did not think before she spoke, she would stammer out something idiotic and probably insulting. 'You are older than Mor, who is heir. Why have you not . . . ?'

Dylan glanced down at his leg. 'I got this in a summer fever when I was a boy. You know our laws. No imperfect man or woman may rule. How could I go to the Emperor of Byzantium himself and present myself, cripple that I am, saying, "Hello, father"?'

'My father would not have cared!' Gwenlliant cried, then glanced around and lowered her voice.

'So your mother said, too. And then,' he turned his face away, 'I met you, and I knew that depriving myself of a father was not the worst test that had befallen me. Do you see now why I tried to warn you away?'

'They say,' Gwenlliant forced a tiny laugh that almost turned into a sob, 'that in the Empire, half-brother and -sister, if they are royal . . .'

'And not half of the Celtoi, too. You have been reared to marry your brother Mor, Gwenlliant.'

Despite herself, she grimaced. 'It would not work, you see,' he told her, his mouth wry. 'I may not be purely Celt, but I have been purely stupid. I might have grown up with you, I see that now, and I would have spared us all a great deal of pain. But I was proud, like all my tribe. It was only when I first saw you that I regretted all those years of empty pride.'

Her mouth twisted in anguish, a babyish gesture that she had never lost. 'Ah now, little one, don't cry. Not here, of all places. Come, let me . . .' He drew her to rest with her head against his shoulder. How strange that she had longed for him to hold her in just this way, but how different it was from all of her fantasies. His arm about her shoulder was comforting . . . *brotherly*, as well it might be.

Gwenlliant sighed. 'I wish you were miles away from here, and safe,' she told the man whom she must now learn to regard as brother, not lover. 'But forgive me if I say I am glad not to be here alone. You will give me courage.'

He laid his cheek against her hair, matted and full of withered leaves and stalks as it was. 'They are searching for you. Try to reach out to them. Or if you cannot do that, lean on me and sleep while you can.

'Gwenlliant? One last thing,' Dylan said, jolting her from the incongruously comfortable drowse into which she was sinking. She blinked up at him. 'This is for you to keep.'

Taking her hand, he poured into it the chain and medallion, and sealed her fingers around it. Then he shut his eyes and turned his face away.

Gwenlliant's eyes burnt. Then she remembered what she had told the dark priest: that her parents might come and abase themselves in the dirt – but that they would lose none of their royalty by so doing. She thought of how Alexa had prostrated herself before Olwen, then swept from the hall, her dignity augmented, if anything. She herself, if she were to figure in a rite of sacrifice, she prayed that she could endure with the dignity appropriate to a princess of Penllyn and of Byzantium. At least her parents should have the comfort that, unsatisfactory as she might have been in life, her death was worthy of the examples that they set.

'They are here.' As much as Dylan's low-voiced words, long shadows falling across Gwenlliant's face woke her. Behind, long, dusky shadow streamed out from the standing stone against which she had lain; lesser shadows clustered or capered as black-robed figures moved to and fro carrying torches, braziers and blades. She decided that she would not ask what they were to be used for.

Arms folded across his narrow chest, Ctesiphon stood looking down at her and Dylan, still huddled together. 'Very touching sight,' he commented.

A sudden, ludicrous thought struck her. *Sweet Goddess, let him not tell me that he needs a consort. If he does, I am sure that I shall laugh in his face and die all the more slowly.* She stifled a sharp, hysterical laugh, and felt Dylan's hand touch her hair reassuringly.

Narrowing her eyes against the dying sun, Gwenlliant looked Ctesiphon over. 'Don't you believe in *washing* your sacrifices? Or is the god you serve as grimy as it is unclean?'

Then it was Dylan's turn to choke with suppressed laughter. 'Celt to the core, aren't we? It would be better to die clean.'

'I promise you,' said Irene's heir, 'you will not care for much longer whether you are clean or dirty. Ah, there goes the needfire!'

At the centre of the circle, just behind a pile of rubble that once, perhaps, had been a trilithon, flame roared up into the still, twilight sky, scattering sparks over half of the circle. Dry as the air was, it was a wonder that the entire forest did not blaze up like tinder, and that might be the kindest fate . . . *not the burning*, Gwenlliant thought, shivering despite the nearness of the fire. *Far better the blade than the burning.* She wished that Dylan had not dropped his dagger when they were recaptured.

'So you are all assembled,' came the smooth voice of the dark priest, like oil poured on the needfire. 'Good.'

'Priest,' began Ctesiphon, 'shall I begin?'

'You may indeed,' said the priest. 'Though I doubt that you will take much joy in the manner of your beginning. Seize him!' he commanded the acolytes robed in that dark, dark red, who advanced, despite his protests, and bound him fast.

'But I am of the blood of Irene . . .'

'Are you? Or are you simply a man weak enough not to work when he can lie or trick? Such a man may not rule. And if you are of Irene's blood, then you too are royal; and, as I told you, we need those of the blood, *all* those of the blood, for the ritual that will transfer power. You may, however, in light of your claim that these others are of bastard or cadet stock, go first.'

As if weary of debate, the priest pulled his hood down over his face, Only his eyes glowed in the firelight. 'Take him,' he ordered his servants. They moved forward as men who had no will but their master's.

'And do not let him scream for too long.'

Nor did they. Very quickly thereafter, two of the black-robed tossed myrrh into the fire to cleanse it of the smell of charring flesh and bone.

Then the dark priest turned back to Gwenlliant and Dylan, as they stood, their hands clasped, pressed against what now seemed like the comforting solidity of the menhir at their backs. Heat lightning flashed overhead, heralding a fierce, blue-white bolt that sizzled down into the needfire. The priest sighed in satisfaction. Reaching within the folds of his robes, he drew out a curiously twisted horn, placed it to his lips, and blew a long, mournful note.

The ground before the needfire trembled; Gwenlliant could feel the vibrations underfoot. Then, with a crack as sharp as the sound of the levin-bolt, the earth parted, revealing a passage lined with stone blocks and leading into blackness.

'A blood sacrifice always opens the way. Is that not true?' asked the priest. 'His blood was weak; but it served to draw the true blood that my king needs once again to be whole.'

Dylan's eyes widened, and his eyebrows raised. 'Never think that I meant to restore Irene's line to the throne. A sorceress, and unreliable, like all the Levantines,' he remarked. 'Easy enough to use that fool' – he flicked a contemptuous gesture at the needfire – 'to hire assassins, spread a legion of rumours, even to strew a few scarabs where I wished them to be found. But I have no will but my king's, and he is weary of seeing humans arrogate to themselves the honours that rightfully should be his.

'Come with me.' He led the way to the stone passage. It reminded Gwenlliant somewhat of the ancient room that underlay the *gorsedd* back home, the airless chamber in which those seeking full initiation must survive a night. Alexa, she knew, dared it, and perhaps Elen, who never spoke of such things to her. She herself: it was no shame to admit to fear of such things. Even the Emperor, her father, feared them.

Hot wind, fanned by the fire, brought the blood to her cheeks. She tried to think back to the last time she could breathe, the last time she was cold and the air tasted sweet. She had hurled herself overboard after Dylan. Sun on the blue water, in the blue sky; cold water dripping from her hair and down her back; salt on her lips; a brother beside her – no bad memories to take with her into the dark.

Despite her resolve, part of her mind gibbered like dead souls without a coin for passage, longing for release.

– *Hold, sister!* – A vision of hands clasping hands buoyed her, and she sagged, for one weak second, in pure relief against Dylan.

'We do not want them here,' he muttered. 'Can you send them away?'

But the priest gestured, and whatever barrier had rendered impossible earlier attempts to reach Elen vanished. Now, it seemed, Gwenlliant, who dared not reach her, could not help but succeed.

– *Do not fear for us. We are coming.* –

'Good,' said the priest. 'They shall follow us into the earth.'

He raised a hand, and a black-robe placed a torch within it. Holding the torch high over his head, he led the way down into the earth. His acolytes massed behind Gwenlliant and Dylan, who had no choice but to follow.

'We are going,' he whispered, 'to the stars. Follow close behind me. Although the Guardian here is old, he is still faithful and will punish any affront to Stone-King.'

Guardian? Gwenlliant thought. Stone-King? She needed Elen, with her knowledge, here . . . *no, what I am thinking? Elen, stay away!*

– *Quiet, cousin. We are coming.* –

'Do you realize,' murmured the priest, 'how few people have your bloodline's privilege actually to merge with the earth and stone here, to return to the Mother, and to meet the King?'

He began to chant. Though the language was one that Gwenlliant had never before heard, visions oppressed her consciousness, almost dousing it: stones laid in the earth, walling in a chamber in which the bravest and strongest vied to be interred beside their king, an ageing, though still vigorous man, weathered after his decades in the sun. His hair and beard were as black as his eyes, which appeared to be vastly enlarged, much more so than figures in even the most impressive mosaics. Their eyes were circled by dark tesserae; this king's eyes, black and lustrous, were ringed by intricate tattoos of black and indigo that made them seem twice their size, and spiralled, snakelike, from their corners down upon his cheeks.

They saw him as a youth, gripping a staff until it snapped while the tattoos were etched into his flesh; as a warrior, a husband to his wives, a father and a priest. Last of all, they saw him chosen to be the king in the earth. Though his hair was still black, and his back straight, he himself led his funeral procession into the tomb and enthroned himself in a stone chair between the pillars at the west of the chamber. The bravest of his warriors pledged him with a drink that smelled heavy, then stretched out across the threshold; and Stone-King watched his breathing slow, then cease.

Silence then; and he waited as the torches guttered out and the air turned foul and thick. Then there was nothing for a long time, long even as rocks and tide measure time, until a rumbling above the tomb cracked open the sealed passageway, and the priest who became his creature found Stone-King's crypt.

'How many people,' whispered the priest, 'venture through the earth to the stars? Only those who are chosen worthy, who themselves become as gods and oversee the land with Stone-King. All magic that lives beneath the sun shall sink below ground, and all power shall be his. Glory to Stone-King!'

Gwenlliant dug her nails into her palms and glanced at Dylan. He nodded at her. No point in prolonging this, none at all, and they might save Mor and Elen.

'To Set with your clamour about glory to Stone-King!' he cried, loudly and deliberately in the cheerful accents of the dock. 'I spit on you and I spit on him too!'

Overhead, the stone quivered, and a trail of white dust trickled down at his feet.

He could not truly be there, in the beehive chamber with

them, could he? Gwenlliant thought. But ageless king or hallucination, the man she saw, wrapped in his ancient leathers, his
eyes marked with the tattoos of a vanished race, threw back his
bearded head and laughed with all his heart.

Chapter Fifteen

'Up ahead!' Mor whispered and pointed.

Mor must have eyes like the hunting leopard whose silent,
vicious skill he possessed. Though she herself could not see the
petrified hawthorns or the blackened, crumbling remnants of
the standing stones, she shivered at the greenish radiance that
she detected rising from that place.

'Quickly,' she tugged at his hand. 'Don't you hear the
chanting?'

'Let me go first,' Mor ordered. Metal hissed out, and Elen
thought that in comparison with the ghoulish candles formed by
the shattered stones of the circle, the light that rose from his
sword was a clean, lunar radiance. The chant rose from within,
rising above the heavy odours of smoke, of charred flesh, and
of myrrh.

'*Scent, sight and sound,*' she heard the ArchDruid's voice,
'*can be deadly weapons.*' And she remembered her mother's
stories on the subject – drawn from the fragile papyri that, once
a year, a most trusted priest brought her from Byzantium – of
the ancient people, now sunk beneath the wave, who were easily
spellbound by such things.

Mor gasped.

'Do not let yourself be drawn in. That is for barbarians, for
men and women who lived so long ago that they were less
separate beings than part of one mind. *These* barbarians have
made themselves sink to that level. Come!'

Flinging her arms wide in a gesture of summoning, Elen led
the way, and Mor followed, his sword drawn as if he walked in

triumph through the circle that had been the site of one of his father's strangest victories. The worshippers, masses of robes in heavy fabrics of black and porphyry, parted to allow them passage to the ragged patch of darkness that led . . .

'I can feel them, Mor. They went into the earth itself.' His sigil was the hawk. From the instant that Elen had seen him at the harbour, she had known that he belonged in the air and the sunlight. And he was no magician trained. For that matter, she herself was but half-trained. She lacked the years of study and of ritual; and above all else, she lacked the consummation of the descent into the earth.

'Isis stripped herself at the gates of hell to seek out her brother,' Elen muttered to herself. 'Can I give less than all that I can give?'

As they walked by the needfire, its light twined about them, striking answering gleams from the rich darkness of Elen's hair, and turning Mor's upraised sword into a golden torch that showed the way to a rough-hewn stair that led them into the pit.

Elen drew a deep breath of the air, which was as heavy as she expected, tinct with funerary spices: nard, nitre, and myrrh. Mor's sword illumined the heavy folds and twists of the rock that made up the oppressively low ceiling of the tunnel. She took a cautious step downward, then another. She could tell by the motion of the air in the silent chamber that to her right lay a low tunnel that surely led to another room. And in that room . . . she sensed the presence of another figure, a human dedicated in life and death to guarding this shrine. What could make a man or woman choose that type of fate?

It was hard to see, harder to breath . . . she was gasping, she was doubling over, and then she heard Mor's voice, quavering at first, then growing in strength. 'If thou findest me, O Eye of Horus, make thou me to stand up like those beings who are like unto Osiris and who never lie down in death. Let not Osiris, triumphant, triumphant, lie down in death in Annu, the land wherein souls are joined unto their bodies. If thou findest me, O Eye of Horus, make thou me to stand up like unto those.'

In the presence of Mor's faith, Elen's qualms melted from her. Here was the challenge for which, all her life, she had been schooled; for which, the Druids had taught her, she had probably been born. And, praise Isis, she was equal at least to the attempt of the ordeal. Taking a deep breath of the air, she let her voice ring out in counterpart to Mor's, 'Hail, ye gods, who row in the boat of the lord of millions of years, who tow it above the underworld, who make it to pass over the ways of Nu, who make souls to enter into their glorified bodies, whose hands are filled with righteousness, and whose fingers grasp your sceptres, destroy ye the foe.'

Elen sensed a flicker of curiosity, even of interest, as Mor, himself, a creature of the sun, took up the litany, 'The boat of the sun rejoiceth, and the great god advanceth in peace. Behold ye gods, grant that this soul of Osiris may come forth triumphant before the gods, and triumphant before you, from the eastern horizon of heaven, to follow unto the place where it was yesterday, in peace, in peace.'

Odd, Elen thought, and oddly moving that a Prince so fitted to war would speak of peace with such longing. She took up the chant in her turn. 'May he behold his body, may he rest in his glorified frame, may he never perish, and may his body never see corruption.'

The voice that replied was rich with age and with laughter. 'May I do so indeed, strangers. Who calls upon Stone-King?'

Gwenlliant whirled round to see her brother and cousin standing transformed. The stone cell was no longer black, for her brother Mor carried a flaming sword. He stood in shadow, but light from the sword fell across Elen, turning her entire body the colour of the great electrum statue in the innermost shrine of Isis. Her hair streamed free about her shoulders and down her back; silver strands seemed to separate from it and encircle her face.

The dark priest shrank away from Mor's sword and from his face, as motionless and resolute as the great statues of the kings, carved into the living cliffs at Abu Simbel or in the Necropolis as Byzantium.

'Priest and Priestess; Prince and Princess,' Stone-King nodded to them, a greeting of equals. 'The stars have, I am told, changed their places in the sky since I last saw them, and I thought none like you yet remained above me on the earth.'

For a moment, Elen met Stone-King's glossy black eyes fully. It took all her courage not to draw back against Mor, whose body felt like a wall at her back. For a moment, she stared; and then for another moment. Her fear vanished. Stone-King's eyes were too glossy. They flicked from her to Mor, standing so protectively behind her, his sword raised as if to guard her or to salute the ancient King, to Gwenlliant, standing hand in hand with Dylan, both battered, but defiant, then back to her.

Very slightly, he shook his head, as if in appreciation of what he saw. *Can he possibly be lonely?* Elen asked herself. Although she *saw* Stone-King as localized in a body, all her training reminded her that he was discarnate, eternal (or almost so). Why would such a creature long for human contact, human comfort?

Then she thought of Stephana, her mother's guide, standing in the road, waiting, perfected spirit though she was, to warn Elen. Her eyes went to the heavily robed priest, who knelt glaring at the four figures who refused to grovel before his uncanny master. *If this were all I saw of humanity, I should be lonely too*, Elen thought. *Sweet Goddess, centuries of adoration, abasement and demands for vengeance. It is a wonder that Stone-King has not turned mad or malignant.*

Then she saw the look that he turned on the heavily robed priest. *Perhaps he has*, Elen thought.

'My servant,' he turned to speak to the dark priest, who bowed his head on the cold stones in abject fear, 'you did not tell me that such men and women yet existed, not this Prince and Princess, nor the child with the hair like flame and her own brave defender. I have seen only suppliants before, who demanded aid and counsel.

'But that is no matter. I welcome you to this, my kingdom, and would gladly show you what once I ruled.'

Stone-King gestured, and the wall behind his throne, between the light pillar and the dark, turned all to smoke. When it cleared, Stone-King's world stretched out before them . . . *and the sun, somehow, seemed much younger as it shone down upon broad-leafed trees and huge, round stones, gleaming from the crystals they contained as the sun looked down upon them. The forest stretched from the sea as far as their bravest warriors and wisest shamans could envision. In one clearing, though, was Stone-King's realm, such as it was: a gathering of some fifty round-walled huts; a temple of two rooms, one an outer court, the other a shrine in which a priestess sat between a horned altar and a cleft in the rock from which, when smoke emerged, she prophesied, and the villagers rewarded her, her cat and the temple serpent with fresh milk.*

'Ahhhh,' Stone-King seemed to smile as they looked upon the priestess, her eyes marked as were his, but with a blue that matched their colour, which resembled that of a torch's most secret fire or that of Elen's own eyes. She was tall and slender, her face stamped with divine madness and the saving grace of humour.

'We had many children, that priestess and I,' remembered Stone-King. 'Brave sons and strong daughters. But she grew old, old; and finally, she died. And I was old, too.

'After she joined the Mother – long since, for she was wiser far than I, she has passed within the world and into the sea of stars – I tarried. Sunlight was yet sweet, even to an old man's aching shoulders, and so were my grandchildren chubby, valiant children who listened to an old man's tales. But how might I expect others to merge with the earth while still young enough, strong enough to profit her, if I myself turned away?

'My children painted me with red clay. Wailing, they led me here, where they had carved out my long, long home and made it brave (for I saw it with eyes that wished to see all before the light failed) with noble pictures of bulls and hunts, all of the joys that I had won during my life. They led me here, and sat me upon my throne. They wept, but then they went away. They could not have wept for long.

'The sun went out for me, and then the torches; and finally, all life and light together. It has been long and long that I have stared at the walls of this, my temple. My guard is humble and will not converse: humility he calls it; I, pride. I miss the light; I miss the village; I miss the women with hair the colour of fire or the sharp black glass that, they say, is hewn only for kings from a burning mountain's fire. But I have seen, ah, I have seen stars such as no living man can describe. Soon, I shall pass free of this chamber and walk among them.'

In the play of fire and shadow cast on the rough walls by Mor's flaming sword, they saw yet other shadows, carved and painted figures of fleet horses or deer, leaping felines, and strange composite beasts, all surrounding a tall figure whose face was indistinct, but whose breasts and belly ripened with the promise of rich life.

Then those figures too faded. Beyond them lay only the dark.

'Like a sea,' muttered Dylan.

'Nut, who overwatches the sky. That silvery arch – look, do you see her?' whispered Elen.

'No,' Mor whispered hoarsely. 'Where is the sunrise and the Boat of a Million Years?'

'Ah, dweller in the light,' murmured Stone-King. 'And you, little flame-hair. What do you see?'

'Stars, oh look at them!' gasped Gwenlliant. 'Like flowers, wherever I glance, they blossom, red and yellow, green and blue; but the fairest of all are white. What holds you back?' Gwenlliant's voice was breathy, but alive with the curiosity that was the heritage of the Celt and of the Byzantine and that conquered her fear.

'My children,' said Stone-King, 'those that seek me in the dark, weeping; those others that have not yet merged with the Dark Mother. How can I . . .'

'Lord, you would not betray us, leaving us wandering above the earth in darkness!' shouted the dark priest. 'You swore that you would aid your children, avenge us on those that destroyed so many of your children and displaced the rest.

'See, I have brought these four to you, four great with power. But devour them, and see, we shall be strong enough to devour stronger yet than these. We shall devour all their magic, and then we shall be as gods . . .'

'What vengeance?' cried Gwenlliant. 'The vengeance that tries to slay a mother or snatches a daughter from her brother's house? The vengeance that spreads plague yet forbids a healer to minister to it? Did you *know*, Stone-King, of what use you were made?

'*Did you?*'

'They are not innocents!' spat the priest. 'Deny me if you dare. Deny that you have hated, lusted, envied . . . look you, Majesty, look at these children who would flatter you and win your favour. Ask them . . . *ask* them what they would do to seize their heart's desire.'

He gestured, and Elen's eyes darkened . . . *to rule, to walk boldly before the man, or men, whom she wanted, and have them follow . . . to find freedom from the constraints of study and the Druids' Isle, to speak without thought or controlling her passions* . . . She sensed Gwenlliant's own desire, twisting about Dylan, standing near her side, and felt her own loins heat. But that was not Gwenlliant's truest desire . . . *take the knife, let Mother live to hold a grandchild. Yet I have no grandchildren, and likely am I to have none.*

Then there was Dylan. As keenly as her awareness of her own body came awareness of Dylan's: the pain of a withered leg on a rainy morning at sea; the cautious building up of muscles and skills; the even more cautious avoidance of men who protected him, women who laughed when he would approach them. Anger, finally, and a desire never again to be outcast, even by his own doing.

'Innocents, are they?' demanded the priest. 'Each of them toys with such acts as would add life upon life to their time within the circles of the world, if they did not extinguish their souls. And you call them innocents? Stone-King; Old-King. Perhaps what they say about the grove above ground is true; and all its strength is gone and it should be torn down.'

'No!' Mor snapped. 'This is distortion. Keep still. Until I command you, or you have aught worth saying, you must keep still. But, one thing more. You must answer my sister.'

'I aided those who begged me,' Stone-King spoke slowly. For the first time, his deep voice was uncertain. 'After time that I could not count, time in which the carvings of my tomb wore away into smoothness, people at last called upon me.'

Elen had thought that the grove in which the circle lay was a death nemet because of the hawthorn trees that had once grown there. Perhaps not, though. Had the Druids known of Stone-King?

'For the first epoch, I mourned. When I lived in the light,

there had been times when my power wore hard upon me; yet now, in the darkness, I found that I missed being needed. Then, for a long, long time, I went mad, and swore vengeance upon all my sons and daughters who had allowed me to lock myself in darkness. When my grief and rage wore themselves out, I swore that any man who came to me would receive the wish of his heart if he would help me gain mine: escape from this tomb.'

'And did any come?' Mor dared to ask.

Stone-King nodded grimly. 'He who calls himself my priest says that they came about twenty years ago. Even through the rock I felt it: madness overhead, hatred of the land and its creatures. Overhead, men lay trapped in the circle of standing stones that I had felt when sages caused them to be built. I waited for them to call me, for there were those among them whose power I might well have drawn on, men worthy to serve me.

'They used those powers and found their own path, though – ' Stone-King laughed harshly, 'I helped to stir the earth, though they knew it not. For many, the path led simply to a grave even more strait than the one that I had endured since the sun was young and bright. For one: let me say only that my Guardian welcomed his spirit.'

'My father told me that he ordered the Aescir who led the charge buried in the centre of the circle,' Mor said.

'Your father sent that man to me? Then *he* has my gratitude. We were silent, my Guardian, his companion and I, until this man, who now calls himself my priest, called upon me and promised me aid, strength to pass beyond the earth out to the realm of stars if I would only aid him and his. They called me their father and begged me to devour their enemies and set their power at naught.

'Are you those enemies? I thought better of you, you with your hair like harvest, and of you, with your sword, who could be a son of my loins. But the other two, sea lord and priestess . . . perhaps the priest is right; perhaps you are magicians arrayed against my children. What would you have of them?'

'Our freedom!' cried Elen.

'Wait,' said Dylan. He held up a hand. 'What would you have of us, Great Lord?'

'The flame-hair has spoken truthfully. What keeps me here? Only the cries of children. I have fulfilled my vow. I set a watch over them, then go my ways . . .'

'As a foolish mother does, leaving the child to the nurse, while she drinks wine!' interrupted the priest as he knelt with his face against the cold, rough stone floor of the chamber. 'My enemies are not yet devoured . . .'

'Silence!' cried Stone-King. 'In those years that I have spoken with you, never once have you asked of *me* how I fared, what I required: no, all was talk of sacrifices and destruction. Never once have you done me the honour to stand erect, to honour me not with self-abasement but with respect. I have wearied of it, as I have wearied of power that is stolen, not freely granted. Now, I am ready to move on. But before I do, I must select a guide to oversee those weak ones among my children, who must have their father's stick hung above the fire to remind them to be good.

'Who will descend into the earth to guard my children in my place?' asked Stone-King.

Chapter Sixteen

For a moment, all were too astonished and appalled to speak. Stone-King continued, 'There is my Guardian,' and there is the man who joined us, when the ground first split, and before my servant there found me; but they are not kin.'

Elen could have laughed or sworn with frustration. By Stone-King's own standards, his questions were logical, even loving. If the best thing in the world was, as her own priestly teachers told her, to meet the Goddess, then his question made the most profound sense, not just to the logic in which she, as half-Hellene, had been trained, but also to her instinct, that ancient part of the brain that lodged at the base of her skull, the brain that shuddered and whined to be free when the Atlantean fervour of the chant rang out above ground. Still, if it freed the others . . .

'No!' screamed the priest.

'Dylan . . .' Gwennlliant whispered. Another trickle of whitish dust fell from the ceiling, where tiny fissures had now opened. Elen followed Gwenlliant's half-sketched gesture. Whatever action they took must come rapidly, or they all might be entombed with Stone-King, would they, would they not.

A sudden fury twisted in Elen's vitals. Would they die for this folly, because a great, weary king had been deceived and his deception was leaching her aunt's realm, and her uncle's, dry of all virtue? She thought of Olwen, wearied, her power and her life waning as she aged prematurely; of Marric, as Alexa had made of Alexa herself, who, if she had forced her daughter to stark discipline, did so because she preferred that to the madness in their line. And for what? For an impostor, the dupe of a false priest and coward . . . Her hands clenched and, for the first time in her life, she longed for the deadly ease with which her mother, at her age, drew upon battle magics, or even for a dagger. She, though, she was no warrior, as were Mor and, for all his protestations, Dylan, nor had she gloried in her own arms training, the way that Gwenlliant had.

But she too could fight, though her weapons were sharp wits, forged into plots and words.

'Majesty,' she spoke quietly to Stone-King. 'You have been deceived, but your companions under the earth are blameless. I beg you, when you pass within the worlds to the stars, let your guard and servant accompany you.'

'Kindly thought and spoken. But who will guard this place after they are gone?' asked Stone-King.

Elen's eyes flashed, and her voice went furious and unforgiving. 'Him!' she cried, and pointed at the priest. 'The man who deceived you, who used another as a dupe to convince you that he had enemies whose power you should steal for love of him, who loves only annihilation! He has done . . . in a thousand years of life, he will never be clear of the shame and guilt. In two thousand, in ten thousand? Ah, who knows? He has called himself your child. Give him the chance to be your good child and let him inherit this, your realm.'

Stone-King nodded, his indigo-circled eyes glinting with appreciation. 'You have the wisdom of the priestess I remember,' he said, and gestured. 'Well, servant mine, you often said that there was nothing that you would not do for me.'

Once again, the false priest shrieked.

'It is just,' Gwenlliant told him. 'You took that fool who called himself Irene's heir and, when he thought to call upon the power you led him to believe was his, you yourself fed him to the flames.'

'No!' cried the priest.

'You?' demanded Stone-King. 'You, who offered me gifts of lives and souls, you refuse to enter the earth as I have done? You, who told me how utterly unfit your enemies were to be aught but swept from the earth and devoured? I have heard them speak, heard them battle over which of them will offer life and eternity so that I may go free.'

'But I fear the dark!' shrieked the priest.

'Do you now?' asked Stone-King. 'Well enough, then. You will have ages to cure yourself of that fear until you too are ready to pass within and enter the realm of stars . . . if ever you do. I have spoken. You shall sit in this throne when I have discarded it.'

'Elen?' Mor's appalled whisper, his hand on her shoulder drew her back only briefly from her contemplation of her enemy dwindling and fading beneath Stone-King's commands.

She shook her head, then briefly rested her cheek against his hand while she listened as the priest's wails died away to sobs, and then to an uncomfortable silence, as of a man bleeding to death after a sword thrust.

'After all of that,' muttered Gwenlliant sardonically, 'who would have thought that *he* of all men would have been afraid of the dark?'

Finally, Stone-King turned back to Elen.

'It was well done,' she told him.

'How strange it was. He had no need of fear, yet fear he did . . . and fear he does. I myself fear that with him as a companion, the years will be as heavy as the rocks overhead. It would be better alone, than with him. I am glad that my guardians will fare with me, after all. But tell me, Priestess, you with your wisdom and your harsh justice, and with your eyes the colour – or so I remember – of the sky: you would not consider joining me too?' Mor's hand tightened on her shoulder, and he started to draw her back against his body.

Elen leaned against him, but smiled sadly at the ancient King. 'My fate is tied to this world.' Mor drew her wholly into his arms and whispered to her. Abruptly, she turned aside, her face going livid at his words.

'No!' she cried.

'You heard him call me son,' Mor muttered. 'You also heard him speak well of my father . . . of *our* father. And I am sworn to protect the Empire, even if . . .'

'No, indeed,' Dylan interrupted. 'A son of the Emperor might indeed serve, but not you.

'Sir,' he spoke to Stone-King. 'You face a sea of stars. You cannot traverse it without taking with you a skilled captain. I am such a man.'

'No . . . brother,' said Mor. 'I forbid it. I said that I would offer my life to save the Empire, and I am offering.' he began to step forward, his sword held out at Dylan, but the sailor, as he moved towards him, feigned a stumble, a cunning feint that brought him up, in a stagger that was no stagger, beneath and within Mor's guard. In the instant that Mor hesitated, one hand out to aid his newly found half-brother, Dylan punched Mor, who fell against the wall, then to the ground.

More fissures appeared, this time spreading over walls and ceiling. Elen dropped to her knees to wrap her arms about her cousin.

'I am sorry,' Dylan said, low-voiced. 'But there are no cripples on the sea, on any sea; and I would do anything to be whole once more.'

He turned to Stone-King. 'Sir, I am ready.'

Stone-King held out his hand for the sailor's, and Dylan took it.

'My blessings upon you, children!' Stone-King raised one hand high in benediction. His voice rose to the intensity of a chant. 'The flame-hair herself will shed light upon the world that you,

Prince, will guard beneath the gaze of the lady of the moon.' For the last time, Elen saw herself reflected in his eyes: a small beauty, all black and silver. Even her dark hair was laced now with silvery strands.

Then, like the wall when Stone-King had shown them his realm and village, the King and the lamed sailor seemed to become translucent, to dwindle, and finally to swirl out of existence. For a moment, Elen gasped at the beauty of the stars that she saw through their eyes for the last time. Then the stars too faded, leaving only the wall; and the cracks that now patterned it entirely were widening. The rock itself was crumbling.

'Such stars . . . like a breeze on a summer's night, when Arktos' Wain guides the boat . . . and no duties call, so I can sit and rest, forget my leg . . .' Dylan's voice was wondering, dreamy. Then it changed. 'Brother, sisters, the rock is crumbling. Leave this place while I can still save you. We are moving further and further away from the haunts of men.'

Then his voice sharpened, became the voice of the Dylan that they had all known. 'Gwenlliant, get *away!*'

'Come on!' Gwenlliant hissed. 'Are you going to let him waste it?'

She turned and fled upward along the track, Mor and Elen right behind her. Mor paused only long enough to rub his jaw and salute the west wall of the chamber ironically.

'I shall tell our father that you were a hero, Dylan – and worthy to be king,' he said.

Gwenlliant shrieked as a chunk tore from the living rock of the chamber's walls. When the white dust from its fall settled, she was nowhere in sight. All that seemed to remain was a kind of white radiance, the after-image where once had stood a girl they loved.

'Gwenlliant!' Elen screamed. As if her scream beat against the crumbling sides of the tomb, more rock came loose from the walls. Jagged cracks split open overhead, and the floor rocked beneath them.

'Come, Elen,' Mor grabbed her wrists. 'Goddess forgive me, but we remain, and we must try to live.'

Elen sobbed. She knew that below ground, where the polarities of male to female were reversed, female was the active, male the passive polarity. She might not be the priestess that Stone-King had called her, but she was learned in the mysteries.

But Gwenlliant – never to see that bright hair again, never to quarrel with her, never to appreciate the way that Gwenlliant threw . . . had thrown . . . her whole heart into whatever she did. A sudden overwhelming urge simply to lie down in the cavern, much as had Stone-King's guardians, possessed her, and she staggered. She had no heart to go on.

'No heart, have you?' nagged a voice within her skull. 'Go on despite the lack.'

Though the grip of Mor's fingers on her wrists was the least of her pain, it, as much as the dusty air, the perilous footing, and the almost-certainty of another boulder smashing down upon the two of them, obsessed her. '*Go away, Elen, I can't hold on. Go away and leave me. I don't want you here.*' That day out on the cliffs, Mor had faltered and despaired. When he felt certain that he would fall, he had tried to send her away. But that time, Elen had clung to him until he could be pulled free, back into the sunlight.

'*No heart? What about him?*' demanded that inner, ruthless voice that was not Alexa, not Olwen, not Stephana, nor any of the other terrifyingly wiser, older women who had tested and lectured her lifelong. '*For just such a moment,*' that voice added. In the lower world, it was the woman who took the active role, agent of earth, of the darkness that means silent, secret growth, like a seed in the earth after it is planted but before it buds in spring. It was for her to usher Mor into the light, and indeed, he watched her as if she, and she alone, held his safety in her two scratched hands.

Once again the ground rumbled and cracked open. This time, Elen caught her foot in the narrow, jagged space between two rocks. She gasped and cried out thinly – a despairing, exhausted sound – before another earth tremor brought her to her knees.

'Elen!' Mor shouted, and bent to free her trapped foot. Only a faint, graveside radiance came from the hilt of the sword that he had scabbarded, as if whatever virtue had made it flame had been drained by the time – how long was it? – that they had spent in the earth. A jolt hurled him against the rock wall, and he muttered an oath. The pressure of strong fingers against her ankle hurt, but she forced herself to ignore it, and worked her foot.

'Try to help me get it free!' he gasped.

'You go on, Mor. Climb back into the light and leave this place before it collapses in upon itself.' And because, truly, she saw no escape for herself, she spoke of the thing that neither had yet mentioned. 'This time, your father cannot come in time to climb down and save us. Go back to him. Tell him that I return you to him, with my love.'

Mor had his arm about her shoulder, was trying to pull her from the rock. As well try to cut a slave's shackle with the dagger that she used for meat! She sobbed, and laid her head down against her knees, huddling into as small a compass as possible, making herself less of a target for falling rock.

'No,' Mor told her. 'I will not let you give up. Elen, you must rise!'

As if the harmonics of his voice set off the worst tremors yet, up ahead, a huge boulder jolted loose from the spiralling corridor. Crying out in involuntary terror, Mor thrust himself between Elen and the rolling, grinding rock.

'Light!' He gasped. 'Look! The earth is cracking open. They want us gone.'

A shaft of light pierced the earth, touching them as they huddled in fear of the next hail of rocks or of a crack that might yawn open and engulf them deep within the earth.

'I'll try to work you free,' he told her. 'Help me!'

The next tremor sent them toppling, to come up sharply, Elen beneath Mor, against the shaking stone. Her ankle suddenly felt light, suddenly ached as blood rushed back to throbbing, robbed sinews. Was this how a slave felt when his collar was removed?

'That did it! I'm free!'

He struggled to his feet, holding out his hands for hers.

'Can you put your weight on it?'

She wanted to refuse. Some hateful, dark-obsessed part of her wanted her to lie down and die right there.

'Elen,' came a voice that she barely recognized as Mor's. 'By my patron, I command you!'

The light shone down on Mor's hair and face. It was not the

brilliance of fire, not the spectral phosphorescence of underground, but true, brilliant daylight, thrusting down to crown him, to guide him back up into the light that was the natural province of Horus on Earth. It was not Mor who commanded her, bur Horus Himself. She thought that high overhead, in the open air that she had despaired of ever reaching, a hawk shrieked and circled at dawn, swooping down to catch its prey and snatch it – 'Up!' urged Mor. 'Up into the light!'

With her last strength, she flung herself into his arms and fell forward, sending them both falling up the spiral path, up towards the crack in the rock that widened, miraculously, as if it birthed them from the earth itself.

Chapter Seventeen

As the passageway to Stone-King's discarded tomb toppled in upon itself, Elen flung herself away from the shuddering earth and rock, but her injured ankle gave way, and she stumbled to her knees. 'I can't lose you now!' Mor panted, and dragged her up the last few crumbling steps and into the light.

She gasped as she looked up at the sky, for the light was unlike any dawn that she had ever seen.

'Elen?' Mor was at her side, his now-gentle fingers probing at her ankle. The touch hurt, and she flinched, then put away the pain to stare about herself, rapt.

What glowed overhead was not the sun but a kind of silvery radiance that cast gentle light and shadows over the forest that surrounded them. Somehow, they had been transported from a withering forest, sweltering in a breathless, fever-stricken summer, to a living wood, glowing in a season that remained eternally poised between spring and summer.

They stood in a clearing that Elen recognized. But it too had been transformed from a desecrated fane of shattered standing stones and dying hawthorns into a pleasant lawn, the soft green of the grass broken up in places by reddish rocks and patches of coppery soil.

'Not of . . . this world at all, Mor,' Elen breathed.

'Is this the Horizon? How can it be?' Mor asked too quickly. 'I see no shore, and if we had died, how could your ankle hurt so much? Unless . . .' he shivered, 'we are dead and we do not know it.'

Elen shook her head. 'We would know *that*,' she told him absently. 'We are not dead, but look at that sky! All silver and rose. This must be the Horizon. And, oh, Mor, look at that tree!'

Her eyes filled with tears as she gazed at the tree that blossomed in the centre of the clearing. In the world they knew, in the clearing that they had entered with such risk, a huge grey trilithon had once occupied that very spot. Later on, when the stones had fallen, it became the burial place of an Aescir lord, whom even Stone-King delighted to honour. Then it too was corrupted, and became the focus for rituals that had reached their consummation in the burning of Irene's false heir and the punishment of the priest who had exploited him. That was in the land that they had known.

But now that place had undergone the same metamorphosis as the rest of the nemet. At the centre of the clearing glowed a tree unlike any Elen had ever seen, unlike any of the others in the wood that surrounded them. Like the hawthorn, this tree's trunk was tall and straight, but its bark was dark, almost black. As for its leaves – ah, there lay the wonder. Staring at the tree, Elen sighed in pure satisfaction. Though until that very moment she had never seen such a tree, she was certain now that in her dreams she had wandered into this place, had sat beside such a tree, had yearned to turn from it just long enough to see the awe that she felt reflected on a lover's face, then return to contemplation of the tree.

Around its trunk twined a golden serpent with wise, gleaming eyes, a twin to the *uraeus* that the Emperor, who was also Pharaoh, wore in the great temples on the most sacred holidays. Its branches seemed to fan out in two intricately laced patterns. On the left-hand branches there budded green leaves and white blossoms, and a whole summer's freshness and perfume lay upon them. To the right shone leaves wrought of verdant fire. On their outer side, the flame leaves were the colours of emerald, and on their paler, inner sides – revealed whenever the tree stirred in some subtle, fragrant breeze – they were the shade of peridot. Gleaming among the flames were what appeared to be pomegranates of a redness and a ripeness that Elen had never seen.

Abruptly, she was aware of her own hunger and her own thirst. What would happen, she mused, if she plucked one of those pomegranates and shared it with Mor? Would they, like Persephone, be bound in this place? Temptation washed over her, and she trembled. *Never to return, never to face the pain that lay ahead, never to give up power or love or face the dusty years again. . . .*

Mor's hand fell upon her hair. What if she tricked him into sharing the fruit of that tree with her? They might have eternity together, but it would be an eternity tainted by deception.

Erupting from the tree in a flurry of gold and bronze came a huge hawk that circled over Mor's head, then disappeared into the silver haze of the horizon. Another bird roosted amid the leaves of flame, its plumage a miracle of opalescent indigos and purples. The flames burned and flickered in the gentle wind of the place, but did not consume leaf nor tree, no, nor the ripe pomegranates that glistened amid the leaf-shaped flames. And the phoenix, staring at them from its nest of flame, inclined its crested head.

'Is that a phoenix?' asked Mor. 'Perhaps, even if we *are* dead, we can return to life.'

'If we were dead,' Elen told him, 'I would not be as thirsty as I am.'

Running through the clearing was a spring so clear that she saw individual pale crystals gleaming in the pebbles and boulders strewn over the white sand of its bed. That spring . . . if it cost her her life, she must drink from it. On her hands and knees, Elen crept over to the spring. She was sweating and whimpering by the time that she reached it, and she flung herself down upon the grassy bank and laved her hot face in the water. It was so cold that her teeth and the skin of her cheeks ached, but it was as fresh, as clean and as delicious as any drink that she had ever imagined.

She sighed with the pleasure of that drink.

'Elen in the name of all the gods . . . !'

It would have been so easy to sink back into the comfort of the springy grass that bordered the spring, to fall asleep gazing at the interplay of flower, leaf and fire. Instead, she allowed Mor to draw her to her feet.

She thought that she could put a name to the god or goddess whose face manifested itself from the silvery haze overhead and smiled down upon them. For a moment, she and Mor stood hand in hand, meeting the being's eyes. She savoured the strength of his hand, then tore her glance away from the tree, and the being that regarded them so steadily, to look at Mor. He, too, had been transformed – from cheerful prince, who had turned grimly responsible the moment that his people or his family were threatened – and now seemed to glow. The warmth and the intensity that had drawn her and woken her desire shone so brightly that Elen felt her knees grow weak. She glanced above the tree to the creature that watched her so lovingly and saw, in its glance, the same love that lay in Mor's. Then her grasp on consciousness slipped, and her mind was overwhelmed by the power that she contemplated. She yielded, and her will and senses were engulfed.

Darkness lay over her, and rain pattered down upon it. One or two drops touched her face; they had woken her. Overhead pealed thunder, and the rain intensified. She was back, then, back in the world into which she had been born: a world of rain, of darkness, of thunder . . .

But there was fire in it too. Close beside her, his knees drawn up, sat Mor, tending a tiny fire that glowed in a pit that he had hollowed out and lined with flat stones. Over it roasted two birds that he prodded with the point of a dagger. Beyond the shelter of the cloak he had slung overhead from low-hanging branches came the stamp of hooves, doubly loud in the damp air. Shadows from the hanging cloak hid his face, but there was no mistaking the way that his eyes kindled into joy when she looked at him.

'Elen?' Mor's voice might have been just a rasp of breath, but the fervour in it warmed her. 'You have slept since dawn, and I . . .'

He broke off. 'Thank Isis that you wake. I . . .' His face twisted with a grief that, clearly, he had no way yet to express. Elen ached to draw him into her arms and comfort him for his sister's loss, but she knew that she must step delicately. If she had a need to nurture, he had a need to protect: he would tear free of any attempts to smother him with pity that he could not accept.

'Do you remember this place?' she asked.

'Hard as it is to believe, I think that we are near the hawthorn nemet,' Mor told her. 'While you were . . . sleeping, I explored. That was how I found the horses. I am no magician, Elen: you know that. When I see the land about me change, what else can I think except that we have journeyed? But now, I would stake my life on the belief that we have moved not a single step.

'What do you make of it?' His words came rapidly. 'You are more familiar with this type of thing than I.' *Be more familiar; make this right for me*, he pleaded with her silently. 'In the world we know – or knew – this was a blasted shrine. At the Horizon, this is the site of the Great Tree. And now . . .'

'A very beautiful, very fertile land,' Elen told him. Then, more practically, 'How long has it rained?' she asked.

'Since dawn, when I woke here. Rain,' he breathed. 'Thank all the gods. In Gesoriacum, too, it will be raining. Perhaps the plague will cease. My mother will be pleased, at least for the moment. It should ease her tasks there.'

He smiled, a fleeting glimmer of the brilliant grin that Elen remembered and that had made her think of sunlight on water . . . best not think of sun on water, or she would think of Dylan, and she would weep. And she had no desire to weep. She could not remember having ever felt so happy, or of lying in such comfort as she did now, under a cloak, in the rain with horses nearby, a fire cooking game that made her want to seize it and eat it half-raw, so hungry she was. Sitting beside her, his eyes never leaving her face, was the one man who had ever made her pulses kindle into flame. She could see herself in his eyes. She knew herself, and she was not that lovely, not that warm, especially not now, exhausted as she was by the pursuit of Gwenlliant, which had ended so sadly, by the night's sorcery, even by the vision of the Tree and the being that had blessed them both.

But Mor thought that she was. Lifelong, she could warm herself on the fire in his eyes and heart.

She stretched, the better to savour her well-being, and made a new discovery. Beneath the cloak in which he had wrapped her, she was naked. She sat up somewhat cautiously, eyeing Mor. 'You appear to have put the time to good use,' she said, surprised at how reproachful, even embarrassed, her tone was.

'I found our pack and riding horses,' he said. 'Just as well: we were both soaked to our skins, and our skins were fairly filthy, too. Since, in this current version of the place, a stream runs through the clearing, I bathed in it. Yes,' he added, somewhat shamefacedly, 'I bathed you, too. I have to admit that I hoped that might awaken you. You had been asleep for too long. And I wanted you to wake.'

'I wish it had,' Elen said.

'So do I,' Mor told her. 'You are very lovely when you are clean.'

Elen smiled, then looked away. Looked down and, if the truth must be admitted, she blushed, abashed as she had never been in the many . . . *let us be honest again: not 'many', several, perhaps, but not many* . . . times that one of her age-mates among the Celtoi had persuaded her to let him look at her, to let him touch her. They had been comfortable enough companions, and their touch had neither hurt not displeased her, but when they had sought out others among the young women, she had not been sorry. None of those young men were Mor.

Abruptly, her memory of Alexa's words to the Emperor rang in her memory. 'If they are ever to have separate lives . . .' Alexa had seen her and Mor after Marric brought them down from the hills, had watched them, and, subtle beyond Elen's experience, had detected the bond that terror and shared endurance had created between them. For whatever reasons of her own – her brother's throne, her own hatred of crowns, her desire that her daughter grow up as a young woman who could choose

her life, not have it imposed upon her like bejewelled slavery –
Alexa had tried to break the bond. Tried and failed: moments
after seeing Mor for the first time in years, the old oneness had
reasserted itself, and more strongly than before.

Tears filled Elen's eyes. *Mother had to fight for her own life;
she wanted me to have mine.* Thus, she had fought any influence
that might shape Elen's judgement . . . any but her own. Still,
she could not blame her mother for that, or for trying, with her
usual inspired craft, for what she thought would give her
daughter the most freedom. Then, as it became clear that any
'own life' for Elen lay outside Penllyn, she had changed her
plans, conquered her own fears and, regardless of how she and
Gereint would miss their daughter, sent her with Olwen and
Gwenlliant to meet Mor once again.

Had Alexa created the fears that drew them together? Not
she. Ingenious she was; tortuous she was; malicious, she could
not be. No wonder Elen had cared little for any of the young
Celtoi. The bruises that she had born from Mor's almost toppling
into the abyss forced a bond more direct than any marriage gift.
Elen looked down at her wrists again. Marked with bruises from
the handclasp that had saved her life, they were very slender.
Mor put out one finger to trace the line of her arm to her bare
shoulder, and she purred beneath his touch. Surely, he would
raise her chin now, kiss her now, and she could finally draw him
to lie beside her. Her breathing trembled, then grew more rapid.

But Mor let his hand, then his head, rest on his knees.

'Mor?' In the rain and the darkness, even his flare and brilliance were doused. She could feel his doubt and indecision as
if they were her own. As, in a way, they must be. Those hours
by the cliff, that night in the chamber beneath the stone circle
had made them one being.

'I vowed,' Mor's voice was a reluctant whisper, 'I vowed to
Stone-King that I would take his place. But . . .' he shuddered.
'Elen, how could I vow that? I never thought that I would say
it, but I *hate* the dark now, so much do I fear it. And Dylan:
he promised and he kept his word.'

Elen nodded. 'You would have kept yours too, had it been
required.'

'But he was not afraid.'

She raised an eyebrow. 'Was he not? Stone-King showed him a sea of stars that he could not resist. But I think, however, that he was more afraid of the life that he had known: pity, pain, a fight to be treated as a man and a commander.' She ached to reach out to him, embrace him and draw him down beside her. But not because of his fear. He would reject consolation for fear, she knew. For a moment, the need to hold him overwhelmed her and made her breathing ragged.

With the passionate control that the long ascetic years of study had given her in suppressing her emotions, Elen denied herself the satisfaction of reaching out to him. Not yet, she told herself. He, who had thought never to fear at all, had feared the dark. But that was not the reason for which he clearly was suffering, nor the only reason why she longed to hold him.

'And then, of course, there was . . .'

Gwenlliant. The name of the girl, the sister and cousin who had not escaped with them, ached like the socket of a tooth that has just fallen loose. Mor winced away from that thought for what; Elen was willing to wager; was the first time in his courageous, sunny life. They might have been raised apart, might have seen very little of one another, and what they had seen, they usually quarrelled over. But Dylan had met her, loved her, and found the courage to push her away – much to her sorrow.

Gwenlliant, even more than his new-found fear, was the cause of Mor's sombre mood. Gwenlliant? Unable to use the magic that slumbered in his blood, Mor was certain that she was dead. After all, what he saw, he knew; and he had seen rock crash down where she stood. Elen probed with her mind, prepared for the ache of a mental bond untimely ripped free. Instead, she felt a laugh bubbling up, and stifled it, lest Mor should think her monstrous.

'Gwenlliant is not dead,' Elen let the words fall into the soft patter of the rain. 'We have spoken together in our minds so often that if she were dead, Mor, I would know it.' *And so, for that matter*, the undervoice commented wryly, *would you, if you could bring yourself to wake and face your own powers*. He might think that he possessed none of the magic of his line; but Elen knew better. Mor had no need to perform magic; he *was* magic – and, love-besotted though Elen might be, she could not delude herself about that.

Mor sat bolt upright, his hands on her shoulders, pulling her up. The cloak fell away, leaving her bare to the waist. 'Alive?'

She nodded, happily, and knew that her smile was only a tallow dip in comparison with the full sun of Mor's.

'Can you find her?' he demanded.

When she nodded once again, he flung his arms about her, hiding his face on her left shoulder and weeping for relief. Elen sighed with contentment. Now, at last, she was where she had wanted to be, and his arms felt just as strong, just as good as she had imagined.

His weight bore them back on to the pallet that he had made for her while she slept. and he laughed and wept until he was quiet. For a long, long time, she stroked her cousin's hair, twining her fingers in the dark curls, massaging the iron-hard neck until he sighed and relaxed.

When the shape of his mouth, where it lay against her throat, firmed and changed, she knew it and shivered in anticipation as he kissed up the line of her throat to her lips.

'This isn't how I wanted it to be,' he told her, running his hands down her back until she pressed against him.

She supposed that he had been well-schooled in love, as in all other things. 'Not how you wanted it?' she taunted him gently. 'How long have you planned this?'

Mor kissed her mouth leisurely, expertly, and grinned at her, pleased by her response, before he answered. 'I have always wanted you. Do you know, when I was a boy, I was in love with you? You were so little, so self-contained and perfect, a woman already, while I was still tripping over my feet or my sword. I used to dream of you. And, as I grew older . . . and less clumsy, and I learned more of women, I tried to imagine what would please you.'

'And?'

'I'll show you,' Mor said.

Again he kissed her slowly, parting her lips with his own. With one hand, he began to stroke her, hot, practised caresses that made her arch upward towards him, her hands sliding beneath his tunic to rub down his back and legs. His skin was warm and very smooth, despite the one or two scars that her fingers probed, making him shiver with her touch. In Byzantium, no doubt, there had been women, hetairai and nobles . . . he was like his father in that way, a man whom women loved easily. He had desired her lifelong, but now that he had her, naked in his arms, she feared that he would find her clumsy, a dream that faded and spoiled upon waking.

When he moved away from her, she died a little, sure that somehow, her awkwardness had betrayed her and would leave her bereft. But he touched her face, then looked down at her, his fingers stroking what his eyes, too, caressed.

'Lovely,' he whispered. 'Elen . . . you do know what you are doing?'

'Not well, but enough.' She turned her face into his shoulder. She had been raised among Celtoi; he had not. Perhaps he was disappointed not to be first with her. He had been stroking her breasts, but he had stopped. She twisted against him, wanting the touch of his hands and lips once again.

'Good,' Mor said. 'I was afraid that you were virgin. Gods help us both, Elen, I didn't know how long I could hold myself back. I was afraid that I might hurt you.'

He hugged her with more passion than skill and more enthusiasm than either. She laughed and returned the embrace with all her strength, digging her fingers into his ribs until he laughed, then retaliated by trapping her beneath him, pinning her hands over her head with his own, and, with his legs, separating and immobilizing her own.

She laughed breathlessly in his face, then tilted her head to kiss his mouth as she wriggled in a pretence of wanting to be free of the full weight of his body as he played at subduing her.

'Damn these cloaks!' he muttered at the folds of cloth that separated their bodies. 'I caught you! But I cannot get at you!'

'Yes, you have me. What will you do with me?' she asked. Held as she was, this was her triumph as well as his.

'What I have done all my life,' Mor said. 'Love you.'

Somehow, before his hands and lips drove her to sobbing madness, she managed to ease his tunic over his head. She started to pull down his leggings but lacked the will to move away from him long enough to do so. It was he who undressed himself, then pulled the cloak from where it had lain between their heated bodies.

Once again, he held himself away from her and smiled into her eyes.

'They will call you Helena in Byzantium,' he observed. She flushed at the name, which had belonged to the greatest beauty in their race's history, past or present, and which therefore suited her not at all.

'*They* may do so. Not you.' If she could not tease him, jest with him, she would burn up like incense in a fire just from the sight of him. And the touch – she laid her head against his body, shutting her eyes as she explored him with her fingers, while her mouth explored the hollow of his throat, which trembled as he spoke.

'If I cannot call you the name by which the Empire will hail you, what can I call you?' His eyes were warm and wickedly knowing. 'If I cannot call you by name, what can I do with you?'

For a moment, Elen recoiled from him. When he touched her, when he entered her, she would explode; she knew it. Loving Mor would be like death. Part of her, the silent, solitary, waiting part, would die – but she would have this radiance, this heat in her blood and his, for the rest of their lives. They had always been as much one creature, body and soul, as they had been two separate entities. And then they were again, and she ceased to think or fear.

Much, much later, Mor lay beside her, one hand stroking the curve of her side, coming to rest upon her hip, then moving on to her belly before it touched her lower and more intimately yet.

'Will you let me touch you that way?' she asked, surprised at how gentle, even shy her voice was.

'If you want to.'

She let her hands rove over him. 'I want to now. I want to know how you are made, what you like . . .' As her hands sought out his own pleasure, he gasped.

'We will have a lifetime to learn that of one another,' he spoke, his mouth against hers, his tongue moving in rhythm with his hands and body.

'Helena,' he murmured.

Elen let the mockery go unpunished.

Heavy with the day's rain, Mor's cloak slid from the branches on which he had hung it, and a stream of water fell from its drenched folds on to the tiny fire below. Hot coals hissed, and smoke poured up from the firepit. Drowsing in one another's arms, Mor and Elen woke coughing.

'The fire!' Mor cried. He tried to lunge at it, to snatch the scorching, smoking wildfowl from their spits, and found himself tangled in Elen's hair and arms. She reached out and batted the spits free of the now dead fire.

'Burnt,' she judged. 'But we ought to be able to eat them.' She stretched luxuriously, satisfied to notice that Mor's attention shifted from away from the fire and the dangling cloak back to her.

'Stop trying to tempt me!' he snapped, laughing. 'Or we'll both drown, if we don't die of fever or starvation.'

Elen laughed back at him and knelt, the better to help him anchor the cloak on the branches. She shivered as the raindrops touched her, cold, welcome on her heated skin.

'The rain seems to be slowing,' Mor told her. 'Over there. Can you see where the clouds are breaking?' Picking up one of the burnt fowl, he tore it in half and handed the less charred piece to her, muttering to himself all the while. 'Gods, how could I let a fire go out? Sleeping on watch! What was I thinking about? And now I'm starved, aren't you?'

Juice from the bird dripped down Elen's chin as she stared at him helplessly. Tears poured down her cheeks as she struggled to swallow the too-hot bite that she had ripped from the wild-fowl. She flung herself face down, laughing until Mor bent over her, as concerned for her as he had been irritated at himself a moment before, and turned her over.

'I expect,' she gasped, 'I expect that you were distracted. This way.' And she pulled him down and kissed him. His mouth tasted of ashes now, of seared wildfowl, as well as – no point in trying even to think what his mouth reminded her of. He too was laughing too hard for passion, and soon he rolled on to his side.

'For the rest of our lives,' he said quietly. 'We know how lucky we are.'

It was not a question, but, nevertheless, Elen nodded confirmation. With hunger, rain, cold and laughter, the world came flooding back in on them. For the first time, she thought of Mor's father's reactions, and she shrank in on herself somewhat. Mor touched her cheek. 'My mother knows. Your mother . . .'

'Sent me,' Elen whispered.

'My father has always thought of you as another daughter. Now he has his wish.'

'Gwenlliant!' Elen cried. 'We have to find her. What must *I* have been thinking about?' Even as she pushed away from her lover, she was laughing. 'Mor, where did you throw my clothes?'

So clever Mor, and so sly, undressing and bathing her while she slept. Now, if only he had managed to toss her clothes into a dry place, or if the packhorse that he had found had fresh ones! On her knees, she rummaged through the various piles of fabric, the wet, the dry, and the merely wrinkled. She heard herself grumbling about princes who had cubiculars and underofficers, all manner of underlings to spare them nuisances like lost clothes. Mor grinned at her and forestalled her as she snatched up a tunic she would have much preferred to discard than to look at, even less put on once more.

'Beloved,' he said. His voice, as much as the title, halted her in mid-tirade just as hers had earlier called him back. Elen sighed. She might lack – as a matter of fact, she recalled, she did *not* lack the power of prophecy – but she needed neither sorcery nor wild magic to look into a future in which she and Mor could each hail the other back from quarrels and non-essentials simply by invoking their bond. The thought drew tears to her eyes, and she laid her cheek against his shoulder for an instant while his hands soothed down her hair and back.

'Do you know,' he asked, 'that your hair has silver in it now? And I thought that you were only a year or two older than I.' Because he lifted a lock of her hair and kissed it, Elen decided that she would not punish him for that question – unless, of course, he were foolish enough to ask it again.

'We have to find Gwenlliant,' she reminded him instead. 'Think how frightened and sad she must be.'

Freeing herself, not even with reluctance (for hadn't they the rest of their lives – *and all the worlds thereafter?*), she struggled into her clothing.

'Gwenlliant be . . .' whatever churlish wish Mor had for his sister was muffled as he tugged on his own garments, then stepped outside the tiny shelter.

'That is hardly just,' Elen pointed out as she rolled up blankets and fought them back into a shape in which they could be loaded on to the horses. Gwenlliant had probably been out all night in the rain, while they slept. Ah, *there* was a pack with fresh clothes. Best leave them for Gwenlliant. She gasped as she stepped too heavily on the foot that had almost trapped her below the ground. For the next several days, she supposed, she would have to limp.

Mor regarded his cloak with distaste and left it hanging from the branches.

'Don't try to mount by yourself. I'll lift you,' he offered, overtaking her as she limped towards a saddle horse.

Just how weak did he think she was? She started to bristle, but his hands worked their usual spell on her.

When Mor himself had mounted and turned back to her, humour warred with bewilderment in his face. 'Ah . . . you *do* know where my sister is?' he asked.

For reply, she tossed her reins to him and shut her eyes. Carefully, she shut from her mind the pain of her foot, the joy of Mor's touch – *does this count as a wedding night?* – that thought glinted in her consciousness, then had to be laid aside. The years of caring and feuding and, more recently, the under-hearing that she and Gwenlliant had learned together gleamed in Elen's mind's eye like a ball of silver thread that she cast out. It flew glittering from her mind, offering comfort and love the way a fisherman might lure a fish. The speed with which it soared dizzied Elen somewhat. She flung out a hand and felt, rather than saw, Mor take it. His horse pressed against her own, and he laid an arm across her shoulder, tacit permission for her to draw on him for strength.

There was a tug on that mental line.

– *Gwenlliant?* –

Elen picked up wonderment, and the tug firmed into a steady grasp.

– *Where are you?* – She cast joy, fear, grief at the other girl, who promptly dodged past the emotions she projected to touch Elen's mind with a skill that astonished her.

– *You and Mor. That is good.* – Satisfaction, as well as grief, quivered between them. – *Had Dylan not been my brother, we might have been like that.* –

The linkage firmed into the sure and easy mental speech that they had shared. – *Have you been weeping all night, then, out in the rain, cousin?* –

Faintly wicked humour flicked across and above the undercurrent of Gwenlliant's mourning. *Why, if it comes to that, Elen, I warrant that I slept more soundly than you or Mor, even though* – (the mental sigh was profound and profoundly sad) *I slept alone.* – She cast a visualization of the shelter in which she rested . . . shelter?

– *You fell in with some of Mor's soldiers?* – Elen asked, too incredulous even to mark Gwenlliant's amusement down for future revenge.

'Have you found her?' Mor asked, and Elen nodded.

– *Show me where you are?* – she demanded. With a docility that she distrusted, Gwenlliant visualized the clearing in which the soldiers had built a shelter for her and mounted guard about it. She recognized that place by a stream, right before the place where the forest began to wither.

– *Mor's Flavius Marcellinus insisted on sleeping across the threshhold, if lean-tos have thresholds,* – Gwenlliant told her. – *When the storm broke, Mother sent him after us.* –

– *We will come to you as quickly as we can,* – Elen said, and opened her eyes. She could hardly wait to see Mor's face when she told him . . . or Gwenlliant's when they finally met up with her again.

Finding the clearing which Gwenlliant had visualized proved to be harder than Elen expected: the forest was withered no longer. But even as the first guards stepped on to the narrow track and lowered spears before Mor and Elen, and as horses up ahead nickered in greeting, 'Elen!' she heard, and a swish and splash as Gwenlliant ran towards her.

Elen slipped from her horse, careful to land on her undamaged foot, and ducked under the nearest spear just as Mor shouted at the man who held it. She held out her arms in time for Gwenlliant to hurtle into them with such force that she nearly fell.

The taller, younger girl wrapped her arms about Elen. She was shaking now, all her mockery and humour abandoned the instant that she saw Elen and knew that she no longer had to act like a brave, resourceful princess before her brother's troops. She shook with sobs, not all of them her own: to Elen's astonishment, she too was weeping, with joy at finding Gwenlliant safe and in sorrow because the girl, quite clearly, mourned as she had never, in her careless, happy life, mourned before.

Elen tried to say something, anything, but a gust of tears choked her. Then Mor's arms encompassed them both. If he too wept, he concealed it well. 'So glad . . . you are alive!' Elen forced past the tears in her throat. 'But how . . . ?'

'Your foot!' Gwenlliant, typically, was distracted. 'Oh, it hurts you. Sit down, right away, and let me heal it.'

She pushed Elen down on to the wet grass and had her low riding boot off on the instant. Her fingers probed Elen's swollen ankle lightly, though any touch at all made her hiss with pain. Mor knelt behind her and let her lean against him, his arms circling her waist.

'How did this happen?' Gwenlliant asked.

'I caught my foot between stones as the tomb collapsed,' Elen said. No one needed an explanation of which tomb she meant. 'Mor pulled me free.' She permitted herself an upward glance at Mor – just one, because Gwenlliant had lost Dylan, and it was cruel to flaunt her love for Mor, and his for her, before the girl.

'Is it broken?' Mor asked.

Gwenlliant shook her head. 'Just badly sprained. Even if it were broken, though, I could heal it,' she announced. 'I healed plague.' Unabashed pride shimmered in her eyes.

'The woman lying in the street with a child. You healed her!'

Gwenlliant nodded vigorously. 'She was the first. That was

when I knew that whoever lured me from the house was not Dylan . . .' her voice trailed away. 'Let me heal this.'

Flower scents wreathed about her, and Elen felt her ankle heat beneath Gwenlliant's touch, felt the ache and swelling subside under a touch that, in its own way, was as comforting as Mor's arms about her waist.

Gwenlliant gasped and released her foot. For a moment, she knelt with her head down, as if catching her breath after running. 'How is that?' she asked, and the glow of pride was back.

Elen flexed her foot, then embraced her cousin once again.

'When the rock fell,' she said, 'we thought that you . . .' She broke off. What they had thought was too horrible to be spoken of here in the sun, with Gwenlliant seated on the damp ground, the fragrance of flowers rising from her hair and flesh, and with Mor rising to return Flavius Marcellinus' salute, then catch him in a rough, brother's embrace.

'So did I, sister,' said Gwenlliant. It was a measure of her own terror that she chose the more intimate term. 'But . . . just as I breathed dust and expected to be ground down into dust myself, I was snatched away . . .' Awe rang in her voice. 'Oh, the shore, with the sand like gems, and the lapping, gentle waves! I saw neither moon nor stars; the entire sky was alight, and a bird flew across it, singing. The woman who pulled me free . . . she was very tall, and her hair was silvered. Like yours is now, Elen. I thought she might be the Goddess and started to kneel, but she laughed at me and pointed me away from the water where I saw . . . I cannot speak of it, but when I saw the Goddess Herself and her consort, I realized . . . no, I cannot speak of that. But there is . . . this.'

She reached into the bodice of her gown and drew out a gold chain of heavy links, Byzantine work, from which hung a massive disc stamped with the likeness of her father, the Emperor. 'It was Dylan's,' she reminded them.

Mor touched it with one finger. 'Here is where I tried to strangle him with it, and it broke.'

'It is not broken now,' Elen pointed out, touching a link where red gold mended the breach.

'I wish I could make it up to him . . .' Mor sounded deeply unhappy, and Elen touched his face.

'You can,' said Gwenlliant. For the first time that Elen could remember, she was completely grave, completely dignified, and it became her like nothing else she had ever seen.

'Dylan tried to rescue me, but we were recaptured. Before we were, however, he gave this to me, and told me that his mother had once promised to return it to our father round the neck of his son. Here, Mor. You wear it now.'

As Mor bent his head, Gwenlliant threw the necklace over it. Her brother turned away, turned even from the solace that Elen longed to offer him. Valiantly, to draw and hold the attention of the others present, Gwenlliant forced herself to chatter on. 'When I woke from that place, I heard horses. At first I hid. Then, as I saw the arms and standards, I realized that mother had sent out a party to bring us back safely. And here . . . here we all are. Is it well?'

Her voice quivered, and she sounded very young and very lost.

'Yes . . . sister,' said Elen. 'It is very well.'

Over her head, Elen could hear Flavius Marcellinus brief Mor, 'When the rain hit, Her Sacred Majesty turned to me, laughed, and said, 'they must have done something right.' Immediately thereafter, no new cases of plague were brought into the temples.'

'My mother,' Mor asked. 'How is she?'

'The Queen, your mother, fainted once she healed the last person who was brought in . . . a child, I think, with a broken wrist: nothing at all to do with plague.'

'She fainted?' Mor demanded.

'It happens if you overspend your power,' Elen told him, looking up. 'She will be all right.'

Gwenlliant's eyes were grave and dim. By that token, Elen knew that her words were a lie. Olwen had overspent her power when it was already on the wane. It would not be all right. It would not be all right at all.

'Her Sacred Majesty has given me dispatches to put into your hand for the Emperor. I am ordered to escort you to Byzantium with all haste. No need to return to Gesoriacum, were her words. Here are the letters, Prince.'

Stiffly, Marcellinus handed them over, and Mor bowed his head, kissed them, and tucked them into his tunic.

Gwenlliant and Elen clasped hands, and their eyes met with perfect understanding. *Olwen thinks that she has drained herself of power, and dares not confront thus her husband.* The logic was as clear to Elen as if her mother Alexa stood there, explaining it. Olwen expected to sacrifice herself come Beltane; Marric would forbid it – and they would fight, once again, about what could not be changed. She glanced at Olwen's son and daughter. *They know too*, she thought.

For a moment, all were silent. Then, with deceptive lightness, Mor turned back to Flavius Marcellinus. 'I hope,' he remarked, 'that you do not expect us to travel like this' – he gestured at his worn clothing – 'all the way East.'

Chapter Eighteen

Not for the first time that hour, Marric, called Autokrator of the Romans and Lord of the Two Lands, growled to himself that he actually had less freedom than the tradesmen who, no doubt, had lined the Mese to cheer as Prince Mor came home. Unharmed, for which Marric praised the gods sincerely and thanked the priests less insincerely than usual.

Granted, though the boy entered through the Silver Gate, this was not a Triumph. He had arrived by sea the night before and ridden to the gate for his grand entry, his and his sister's. Reports were – and had followed them all the way from Gallia – that they looked well. But Marric had not yet seen them.

Even though he were Emperor and Pharaoh, with all the constraints of his office, he might well have demanded a horse and ridden down to the harbour to embrace his children the way old Caius Marcellinus had. If he had been willing to submit to the usual complex escort, or the fanfare that the Emperor's slightest movement made, turning even the simplest ride or walk into a parade, he might now have embraced his children. The clamour and boredom were small enough prices for the end of an isolation that had grown day by day since he received the crown from the now ancient High Priest of Osiris. He could have shrugged them off.

But if the turmoil that accompanied his slightest move detracted at all from the city's fondness for the Prince and Princess who would rule it one day . . . no, in that case, Marric would fret in his quarters in the palace compound, cause his Master of Offices to threaten to resign, and hound the Master's agents until they decided that apoplexy might be preferable to ambition. And he would probably agree with them.

Marric strode over the mosaic tiles to the garden and stared out, but it was not flowers that he saw. At this point, Mor, accompanied by his sister Gwenlliant (a-horse, Marric was privately willing to wager, if he knew his hoyden of a daughter) and their cousin Elen, would be riding down the Mese. No doubt, half the citizens of Byzantium were screaming themselves hoarse, to the great delight of tavern owners and physicians. Marric grinned to himself. If Mor had resisted wearing full parade armour, he would be astonished. A handsome brood, his children, his and Olwen's; and, the last time he had seen Alexa's girl, she looked as if she might grow up pretty too.

Sending Mor west as provincial governor with an army, and ending his tour of duty with orders to bring his mother and sister home, had been a good deal to ask of the boy. Marric could hardly blame him for the plague in Gesoriacum that had made Olwen decide to remain there, pleading responsibilities to the townsfolk (a good ploy, all the better for having so much truth in it): if *he*, after more than twenty years, could not impose his wishes on Olwen, how could her son? He shrugged. Luring his wife to Byzantium by offering her her son's company had been a good ploy too; no point in blaming either himself or Mor that it had failed.

He sighed, then reached around to rub the small of his back. *Getting a little old to have Horus as a patron, aren't you?* he asked himself. *Time, perhaps, to move on to Osiris, grave-wrappings and all.* Let the city cheer a gallant young prince. Marric had been a gallant young prince once; their season was damnably short – and his had been shorter, and wilder, than most. So wild, in fact, that his father had sent him away to the most rebellious of the eastern themes, a kill-or-cure measure that had damned near achieved both, for him and for his sister.

She had summoned him back to Byzantium in terror for life, throne – *and soul*, Marric recalled, though that was not a thing she had mentioned. While trying to flee the city and return to Marric's army, he had been captured by Irene, his father's minor wife and, as Alexa had warned him, a sorceress. Failing to seduce him, she had ordered him sold into slavery in Alexandria; and the marks of that were on him yet, body and soul.

Twenty-five years later, the body was still holding up decently, he thought. Granted, it was more a collection of scars than not, now, and most of those scars ached at dawn and if he rode or sat too long without stretching; but he survived. Though his shoulders had thickened and he must now ride a much larger horse than the high-bred Arabs that he preferred, he had not, praise the Goddess, grown fat or bald, like one of the priests. *And I haven't the bulk of old Audun either. Yet.* His hair had greyed but not receded by much; he wore it short now, in a style that his army had adopted. And he had refused to grow a beard like an old man, preferring, instead, the clean-shaven comfort he had, perforce, learned to appreciate first in Alexandria, then in summer campaigns in the Middle Sea.

The first years of his reign had been marked by intense campaigning, first against the pirates based at Cyzicus, and later in the eastern themes that had fallen away from the Empire during Irene's usurpation. After his journey west to bring back his sister, a trip that culminated in imperial involvement in the Jomsborg wars and his marriage – as strange a marriage as had ever been – to Olwen, one of the petty queens of Prydein, he had, by negotiations, guile and threats of violence, returned to the Empire other themes that had long withdrawn their allegiance. It had taken him over twenty years; but he would leave his son an empire greater and stronger than the one he had fought to win.

And he would rather die than detract one whit from that son's popularity by racing down to the harbour as if Mor were a boy for whom Marric had been afraid. Let Mor ride through the city while 'the old Emperor' sat serenely in the palace, awaiting his son, his daughter (whom he confidently expected to wed Mor in accordance with the example of Isis and Orisis themselves), and their elder cousin, herself a princess of their line. Lie though it was, that story made for good theatre. Since his coronation, Marric had not been serene. It was part of Irene's death curse that, as long as he ruled, he would never know peace.

Odd, he thought, stretching under the light mail that he wore, even in his private chambers, how that curse twisted and turned. He had children whom he would cheerfully have died for, but not enough; a sister who should have been his bride and empress, who repudiated the honour; a wife who had only to enter the city to make it fall at her feet – and she wanted only to die. He would have to consider what was best to do; Olwen's last letters from Gesoriacum had spoken only of plague and of her obligations as Isis on Earth, not of any other plans. Celt she might be, but she could hold her counsel; and she had lived with Alexa for long enough to plot like a proper Byzantine. He would have to speak with his children to know her mind better. His girl Gwenlliant, who would inherit in Prydein, ought to be a good source.

Now that is a truly despicable idea, Marric my lad, he told himself. *Set the daughter to spy on the mother. Despicable, and knowing my girl, impractical too. Maybe you are getting old.*

Of course, Alexa was the best source of intelligence that any man could have. Clever, even crafty, and fiercely protective, she had sent him reports on his family for many years; but those reports, too, had ceased as Alexa found that her loyalties to both ruling houses to which she owned loyalty conflicted.

He slammed his fist on the doorpost and swore under his breath. Damn Caius Marcellinus, anyhow! He could trust the old patrician with his city, with his whole Empire, while he rode off on campaign. Marric grinned, as he always did, at the thought of his Civil Service's wails on that particular subject. The old Domestikos, senior general of the most aristocratic regiment in the Empire, had stood by Marric when he had had to hide in a safe house, supported only by priests and one sorceress. He could trust Caius to meet him blade to blade in the Mangana and to scratch Marric a good one if he showed signs of slowing down; he could trust him with his son. But he could not trust old Caius not to dash down to the harbour – all the while his Emperor, whom he had served with body and soul lifelong, prowled his quarters, a prisoner of his own exalted rank – to see his youngest son the instant that their ship docked.

But then, he had never been good at waiting. Stephana had always said so. Even this many years after the death of the woman who had been lover, inspiration and seeress to him, thinking about her made him smile and would have made his eyes mist, had Irene's curse left him capable of tears. Most of the sorrow was gone now. What remained was his profound guilt that she had died in pain because he was too stupid to guard her as she had deserved: the rest of his memories of their months together were bittersweet. Except the last time that he had seen her – in Prydein. She had not been bittersweet then. Osiris in Glory, she had not even been alive then, but had appeared to him at his sister's guide-in-spirit to warn him of his fate if he persisted in his vow to wed her.

After all, what was one broken vow more or less? He had already slain a Druid, lay under Irene's curse, and – though he but suspected it – had been sick almost unto damnation from a curse cast upon him by the Jomsborg skin-changers. It made for good theatre. The trouble was, good theatre was not especially good living. 'Count no man happy,' he reminded himself, 'before you have seen the day of his death.'

Measured by that standard, his score was about even.

Uproar from the city swelled to such an extent that even in his secluded chambers, Marric heard it. Though the cheers and screams had to be in his children's honour, the sound nevertheless turned him cold. He had heard it the night he took Byzantium. He had heard it the day that he had brought Olwen – surely the strangest lady ever to wear the moon crown – into the city in triumph. The shouting meant exultation, meant the near-worship that he always reminded himself meant nothing at all. But it could also mean sudden death: the city's mobs were a fickle and lethal beast.

From across the garden courtyard, he heard sandals slapping down the marble and tiles. Varangians materialized from hiding places in the garden itself: a convention that allowed them to satisfy themselves that he was guarded while allowing him to pretend that he retained some privacy. (Olwen protested the arrangement bitterly whenever she was in Byzantium.) That commotion had to be the cubiculars tending to last-minute arrangements he had ordered for the children's rooms: fresh gilding, new furniture and, for the two girls, an entire new staff, supervised by Daphne, whom he had bought in Alexandria to tend his lost Stephana and who married a guardsman and, despite her marriage, remained in Imperial service. He could not remember his father attending to such details: after all, that was what pedagogues and servants were for. Perhaps, had his father been less remote . . . well, Olwen might complain about the ways of the Empire, but she had never faulted him on his devotion to their children.

Footsteps in the corridors outside his own rooms drew him back from the gardens. He forbade himself to do another thing that he would have liked: fling open the doors, race down the hall, and embrace Mor and Gwenlliant. Instead, he straightened his robes dutifully and walked over to sit in a huge, centrally placed chair of ebony and ivory, inlaid with gold. Had his son and daughter been younger, he might have dispensed with ceremony; had they been older, they would have been as impatient of it as he. Rather than make them feel as if he thought of them still as inmates of the women's quarters, he must treat them like visiting ambassadors – and he hated it.

The doors were flung open. Dimly, he supposed that someone had announced, with a flurry of titles, Mor Marric Alexandros, and Gwenlliant (mispronounced a different way each time); he heard only a blare of sound, because his eyes were fixed upon his children.

Three there were, instead of two, all gorgeously dressed and jewelled for the occasion; and, he reproved himself, they were not children, but a man and two lovely young women. The man entered first, as if nothing else would satisfy him that the room was safe for his sister and cousin to enter. Mor looked fit enough, Marric dared to allow himself to think. He tried to keep his hands immobile on the sphinx-carved arms of his chair, tried to suppress the way he wanted to laugh and shout at his boy. Horus on the Horizon, Mor looked magnificent, tanned and glowing from the sea voyage from Massilia; and, as Marric had suspected, he wore full parade dress. He came to formal military salute, and his eyes blazed with . . . thank all the gods, humour too. He knew and enjoyed just how absurd this charade was. What an emperor Mor would make!

It was a pity – the thought flashed through Marric's mind – that he would not live to see it.

Marric returned Mor's greeting and then, finally, could rise to catch his son, just as he started to bow, in the hug he had been longing for. He had so much to say to Mor! What came out of his mouth, naturally, was none of what he needed to say, but strangled laughter and a hope that neither of them broke a hand on the other's mailshirt. Long after propriety demanded that Mor step back, the boy clung to him. *We have a story here*, Marric thought, in the first stirrings of disquiet, and ruffled his son's hair before releasing him.

No need to be formal with Gwenlliant, however, even assuming that she would tolerate it. 'What a beauty you are, daughter,' he told her, and held out his arms. She might resemble Olwen down to the sweetness of flowers that clung to her hair, but Gwenlliant was as rebellious and as noisy as he had been at her age. The Celtoi counted that a great virtue among their women. Though it went hard with him to agree with the Celtoi on any point of conduct – and never on court etiquette – in this case, they were right.

'What?' he whispered. 'My wild bird, my tiger cat, in tears?' He tilted up her chin, smiling into the amber eyes, flicking away tears from her cheeks before bending to kiss her on the brow and to embrace her once again.

'Oh father, father . . .' she began, and broke off, crying again.

'This is not,' he whispered, 'simply that you are happy to see me. Well, I have you safe, and I will hold you. Just tell me what the trouble is, dear heart, and I will fix it.'

She shook her head frantically, and what sounded like 'You can't!' was muffled against the purple silk that he wore over his mail. Stroking her hair, he looked over at Elen, who hung back beside the door.

Why were all three of the children acting so strangely? The last time he had seen Elen, she had practically raced with

Gwenlliant to see who could fling herself upon him first. Now, she watched him with her eyes huge with tears, her lips quivering. Her face, which should have been tanned from her time at sea, was very pale. Marric shut his eyes in pain. *Afraid of me, child? Of me? The first time I saw you, you snared your fingers in the necklace that I wore; and it might as well have been my heartstrings that you caught.* As she ventured forward slowly, hesitantly, he saw that she was wearing that necklace . . . as if it were an amulet.

As if sensing her fear, Mor turned and took her hand, leading her to Marric. He forced himself simply to rest his hands on her delicate shoulders and kiss her forehead; as he touched her, she trembled and would not meet his eyes.

And am I so suddenly a monster? he thought. Quickly, mercifully, he let her escape to Gwenlliant's side.

'Well,' he grinned at the three of them, 'now that the formalities are over, sit and have some wine. I imagine that the city is no less dusty than usual?' Light talk might help them relax, help them say what, clearly, they could not be at peace until they said. And not to be at peace was a fate that he would wish on no one, least of all the children.

He reached over and poured from a silver pitcher, the work of Persian smiths, and about the best thing he knew – barring their horses – of that entire tribe. 'The water is in the pitcher at your right,' he told Gwenlliant, who, he hoped, did not plan on drinking unwatered wine while she was in the city, and handed each a cup.

Mor drew a deep breath, and Marric looked at him expectantly.

'I have letters from Her Sacred Majesty,' he said, and withdrew them from a pouch. Marric glanced down at them: no scribe's hand, but the work of Olwen herself. Her hands were deft, clever . . . Goddess, he wished that she had chosen to come east. There would be time, and a decent privacy, in which to read his wife's letters, he told himself, and laid them aside. For now, it was more important to fathom why Mor had presented the letters when Marric was certain that he had meant to say something else instead.

'You are here until spring,' he told the two girls. 'That is very good.' At least, he thought, Elen would stay through the winter. As for Gwenlliant, if the gods were kind, she would wed Mor soon, and then Marric would have them both here forever. And if they were all very, very lucky – and if Mor were his son in more than looks and his skill with armies – Marric shook his head from side to side, aware that he was grinning foolishly. But he could just hear Olwen tell him, 'You are an even bigger fool as a grandfather than you were as a father.' Isis grant that he could ensure that she live to rebuke him.

'You shall have your old rooms,' he smiled at his daugher, 'though they have new furnishings and mosaics in them. Elen, you will share them, as you did last time – and shall I call Daphne to look after you? She has a new baby that you will like to see, too.'

Elen and Gwenlliant looked at one another. Then Elen flushed and looked down, and Gwenlliant glared at Mor, who gulped his wine, poured another cup, then resolutely set it aside.

Bless his volatile little daughter! Marric thought then. Clearly, Gwenlliant had run out of patience and was going to blurt out whatever it was that had turned three loving children into such strained, frightened adults.

Sunset flared, casting odd lights and shadows over the three of them. Marric blinked. For a moment, he could have sworn that Elen glowed.

Then Gwenlliant tossed her hair, which was richer and more luxuriant than any ornament that the most skilled goldsmith could even dream of. It caught up and cast around her slender shoulders all the light in the room, a cloak fit not just for a princess, but for the empress herself. The fragrance of roses hung about her, and she smiled – with a compassion unsettling in a girl as young and as heedless as Gwenlliant – at Elen and at Mor, who had risen to his feet, one hand clasping a heavy chain that he wore.

'Father, before you go any further, you must listen to me,' she said, her voice sweet and earnest. 'Elen doesn't want to share my quarters, can't you see that? She wants to stay with Mor. And he wants her. Forever.'

Chapter Nineteen

Only half a lifetime spent as emperor prevented Marric from spilling wine over himself or inhaling, rather than drinking, from the cup that he had raised to his lips as Gwenlliant spoke. What was it that she had said? *Give your father a moment, girl, I am no longer young and quick*, he thought at her ironically, and was shocked to see her raise an equally ironic eyebrow at him.

Mor and Elen? Not his sister as his bride, but his cousin?

Alarmed by his long silence, Elen rose convulsively from her chair, pushing it clattering to the floor. But Mor caught her before she could flee from the room, encircling her with his arms and bringing her to stand before his father.

'I have watched you, Father,' he said hesitantly. 'You cannot have failed to suspect that something is amiss with all three of us. We are not clever enough – not even my Elen – to conceal it from you. Even had we wanted to try.'

Elen looked up at Mor and her lips moved in a whisper of distress. Mor only tightened his arms about her and stood watching his father, as calm now that he had committed himself as he had been agitated before.

Those women set this up! Marric thought. His first impulse was to bellow in outrage and delight. But was that quite fair? Ten years ago, when Gwenlliant ran to him shrieking of disaster, he had swung down and rescued his son from a rock face. To the end of his life, he would never forget the moment when he saw the boy dangling above a drop that seemed to stretch like the abyss of Tuat itself. Flat at the lip of the cliff lay Elen, her hands grasping his son's, her face white, her eyes rolled back in trance. So that was how Mor had had the strength to hang on! When he had brought his son to safety, he had to pry free Elen's fingers from his hands, reassure her that Mor was safe, before she would let go. And once she had, she had collapsed.

Alexa had been prompter, wiser than he. 'They did not just draw on one another for strength,' she said. 'In some way, they became one another.' She had looked very sombre, and she had separated her daughter from his son almost immediately to give them, she stated at the time, a chance at independent lives.

Well, they had chosen. And Elen, if she resembled either of her parents, was no fool. What about Mor, though? The boy wanted this, Marric thought. The boy wanted *her*. His sister's daughter. Well, what of it? His father and mother had been cousins, not brother and sister; and they had been well-mated for as long as Antonia remained alive.

Gwenlliant gave a sort of choking cry, and Marric turned to the girl who had just been deprived of the Empire that should be hers, as well as her brother's, by right. 'Child, does this grieve you?' he whispered. She shook her head fiercely.

'I'm *glad* for them,' she whispered huskily.

But this was not how he had planned his children's futures, he reminded himself.

Then he looked at Mor and Elen, and all his plans faded. The sensuality between them was palpable to anyone, especially anyone with his long experience: he would have expected no less. But the polarity that flowed between them, making them one creature in spirit, quivered in the air and reminded him of desires and hopes that he had long since put away. He smiled as he saw how protectively Mor's arms held the girl, and how her hands, resting on his, restrained them from the quick, casual caress of side or breast that they clearly sought, even in Marric's presence. He had had Mor schooled in pleasure as well as war; apparently, his teachers had done their work well.

The fools, the little fools he told himself. All that love, all that longing – and they wasted even an instant in fear of him. Before he was fully aware that he was going to, Marric chuckled. Elen, startled, looked up and met Marric's eyes for the first time.

Her father Gereint, he knew, had blue eyes, but Elen's eyes were the smoky blue of a candle's flame, hot and intense with desire . . . and with something else. Marric studied her and almost gasped. Her dark hair, flowing down over her shoulders, glowed as the silver strands within it almost seemed to move with lives of their own. And Mor held her as if she were the greatest, most delicate treasure in all the world.

Once Marric too had treasured a woman with silvery hair and

eyes like blue fire. He could remember holding Stephana as if she were silver or fine Egyptian glass. And she had loved him. In all the years, he had never doubted that. But she had been well along in her tale of lives, and badly crushed by the one in which she had saved his life and learned to love him. Because she loved him, she had been almost willing to postpone her freedom from flesh. To this day, that realization shook him to the core. But Irene had struck her, and he had freed her from any more pain, though her death took with it the greater part of his heart.

Almost, he could imagine that Stephana's eyes, infinitely wise and loving, smiled at him from Elen's, and that she was his lost love's daughter as well as his sister's.

Even if that were not true, how could he reproach his son — or the girl herself?

Again, Marric shook his head and chuckled. This time, he smiled, too, and was glad that it came out unforced.

'Daughter,' he called Elen.

'I *told* you,' Mor whispered in Elen's ear, while Marric waited for him to finish. Elen gasped and flushed, beginning to believe that she might not be cast out.

'I have always had one regret about you: that you were not daughter but niece. Now, it seems, you have removed any sadness that I might have had.

'Mor,' he jerked his chin to one side, ordering his son to release his bride. Absurdly, his son's reluctant obedience reminded Marric of his first glimpse of Elen, moments after he had been reunited with her mother. '*My dear*,' he had told Alexa, who had feared to let him hold her baby, '*I am hardly a Spartan father.*' He had not wanted to acknowledge Elen's existence, meaning as it did, the ruin of his hopes; but he had held the child to please its mother, and she had reached up and grasped his necklace . . .

Marric had taken it off and given it to her to play with, he remembered, and she was wearing it now.

Marric held out his arms, and she ran into them. 'Elen,' he told her, 'welcome, welcome a thousand times, dearest. Don't tremble like that. I am glad that you and my son have chosen each other' — *or glad enough to reassure her, in any case.*

She looked up at those words. 'Truly?' she asked.

'Truly.' Marric bowed his head. He meant to kiss her cheek, but at the last moment, his mouth grazed hers, and the surge of warmth and of pure power that rocked him made him release her to Mor's jealous grasp. Marric stepped back in surprise.

There was magic there, and great strength; and power flowed around Elen like a cloak or the flickering halo cast by the silver in her hair. *The gods grant that Mor have – and keep – what I could not hold*, Marric prayed. He looked at his son with new respect: Mor might be no magician, but if he could inspire the worship that shone in Elen's eyes and not be overwhelmed by how much more than mortal she was likely to become, he was even more than Marric had thought that he was.

Thus, Byzantium would have its Isis on Earth in the next generation too. Judging from the nimbus of light that flickered about her, she would be an Isis of considerable power, fit consort for an emperor. But, judging from the way she had responded even to Marric's light kiss, Mor was a lucky man.

'You still wear the necklace that I gave you when we first met,' he told Elen, as tenderly as if he spoke to an Elen who was still an infant. 'Let me hold it for a moment? I promise that I will give it back.'

She let him lift it, warm from her flesh, from her neck.

'Come here, both of you,' Marric ordered. 'Give me your hands. I must confess, that for the first time in my life, I am delighted that the old Osiris priest assures me that I am both priest and king. But, if you tell him that I said that . . .'

Serious again after the mock-threat, he took and joined their outstretched hands, then bound them together with the necklace.

'The rites that the priests use to join Isis to Osiris on earth are long, complex and – as I remember from my own experience with them – moderately public and, therefore, immoderately embarrassing. They are also inordinately long. But, as a priest and king myself, I can anticipate them somewhat. At least this way, you can claim one another, assuming ' – he flashed a frank grin at them – 'that you haven't already done so before they take place.'

Mor grimaced, and Elen, for all her magic, looked away. *If*

*you wanted maidenly modesty, my dear, you should have wed
into another family. Just wait until you learn what lies in the
formal rites!* They had caused even Olwen to flush, years ago.
Well, if Marric's humour was the most ribald that they encountered during their wedding ceremonies, they would have gotten
away lightly. But the time for wedding jokes had not yet come.

He bowed his head and concentrated on the two hands that
the pearl and gold chain bound together, on the current that
flowed up from his spine, down his arms, and into the joined
hands and through the pair that stood before him, uniting them.
Mor turned to Elen and, with his free hand, tipped up her face
and kissed her. Marric studied the tenderness of that gesture
with an expert's approval, then unbound their hands and laid the
necklace over Elen's head, touching the silken, almost magnetic
warmth of her hair.

'I will see the pair of you again in the morning,' he told them.
'Elen, this palace is your home now. Whatever in the heir's
quarters that you may wish to change . . . or we can discuss that
later.'

He expected Mor to draw Elen away to his quarters and into
the sort of consummation that Marric would insist upon if the
choice were his. Instead, the boy held his ground.

He whispered something to her. Her eyes glowing in the
twilight, she slipped her arms about him quickly with an
expression of such trust that Marric, once again, longed for the
capacity to weep that he had been denied for half a lifetime.

Mor's face went sad as he walked towards Marric, pulling the
necklace, that he had earlier toyed with, from about *his* neck.
'I was asked,' he told Marric, 'to give this to you.'

Gwenlliant shook her head at him.

'No, that's not quite right,' Mor added. 'I was told that this
necklace would be returned to you around the neck of your
son.'

'Sweet Goddess.' Marric dropped into his chair a little too
heavily for dignity, but not quickly enough. Without even
looking at it, he knew what he held: a heavy chain bearing a
medallion on which his portrait was stamped.

Her name had been Luned, he recalled, *a tall warrior-queen
with hair like darkest wine. And what was that tribe that she had*

205

ruled? The Iceni. Some kind of kin to Olwen, as it turned out. She had been one of the first people whom he had met after landing in Prydein, only moments before what had to be the worst storm he had ever weathered in his life tossed them practically into one another's arms. That night, and several nights that followed, Luned had been all to him that any woman had been since Stephana's death: passionate and forthright. It had been she who first warned Marric that Alexa might not thank him for taking her away from Penllyn; she who directed Marric to Penllyn; even she who had first told him of Olwen. And it was she who hoped for a child from him.

They had reached Iceni land, and Marric and his troops prepared to turn west towards Penllyn. The Iceni supplied them with food, some remounts, and guides for the journey. Then, just before Marric mounted, Luned reached up and kissed him. Her lips were dry, the kiss but a formality, but her eyes were very warm.

'Remember what I said. All of what I said, Marric.'

He reached for her, to take her wholly in his arms despite the assembled warriors. When she eluded him, he lifted a chain bearing a large medallion from about his neck.

'It is not a trinket,' he reassured her as her eyes flashed, 'but a token of rank in my home. My remembrance to you, or a gift to a child.'

He clasped her hand about the medallion. 'See, it bears my likeness.'

Luned shook back her hair. 'I shall remember you without such baubles. Please the Goddess, I shall return it to you, round the neck of my son.'

Very gently, as if he touched Luned's strong, beautiful face instead of the metal representation of his own, Marric caressed the medallion, warm from contact with his son's – his living son's – body, with his fingertips. In a moment, he thought, the hurt would start, as it did with wounds. For the first few instants after a sword cut or blow from a whip, you felt no pain. Then, if you were unfortunate enough not to faint or die, the pain struck and you had to try not to scream. He had bitten his lips raw against the pain more times than he could count, and now he must do it again.

The anguish hit then, and he closed his hand on the chain to give himself a more manageable pain. His eyes burned, but remained dry.

'Luned?' he murmured.

'Dead last spring, in a raid,' Mor said.

'The gods receive her at the Horizon; she was a valiant lady.' *You would protect me out of my strength*, she had accused him. Yes, he would have done so, whether or not she wished it. He would have been wrong, he told her – but would he? She was dead now, who might have lived far longer had she not been a warrior as well as a queen.

'And my son?' he asked Mor, who would have been younger than this son of Luned's whom he had never seen. 'Why did Luned never send him to me as she vowed?'

To Marric's astonishment, Gwenlliant knelt at his feet and took his hands between her own, cupping them under chin. 'He told us that she tried, Father. But he would not go.'

'Why should my own son hate me?' Marric whispered. 'I would have welcomed him.'

'Father, when he was a child, a summer fever left him with a withered leg, and he refused, he said, to show himself, damaged as he felt himself to be, to the Emperor, and claim him as a father.'

'Ah *gods!*' Marric whispered. He tried half-heartedly to withdraw his hands from his daughter's warm, compassionate grip, but she held on to them. To his astonishment, strength and healing flowed from her hands into his, warming them. The fragrance of lilies and roses that wreathed her intensified. *She has her mother's gift*, Marric realized. *My daughter has come into her own magic.*

'His name was Dylan, Father, and he took to the sea as befits that name. He was our captain when we crossed from Prydein to Gallia. He saved mother from an assassin's knife. And he saved the rest of us from . . . her voice faltered, and Marric's heart broke within him. Celt that she was, Gwenlliant could not want the brother with whom she had grown up as a lover or husband. But this stranger, who was also her brother . . . tears ran down her face, but still she gazed up into Marric's eyes, putting her own grief aside to assuage his.

'What would it matter to me if he were crippled?' Marric cried. 'I would have acknowledged him and loved him. Did you say that to him? Did he know that before he died?' The ache in his eyes burned like sea fire now, or acid, and he cursed Irene anew for the tears he could not shed.

'He told me,' Gwenlliant said, 'that he had been a fool. He might have known all of us, and we might have . . .' her voice quavered . . . 'loved him.' For an instant, her control snapped, and she cried out, 'What do you expect of Celtoi, father? You know how proud we are!'

Marric gathered her close. If she had been any younger, he would have lifted her on to his lap right then.

'I promised him that I would bring you this necklace,' Mor said, 'and he asked me to tell you of him. I promised him that I would tell you that your son Dylan, my elder brother, died a hero in this world, and will rule in the other world as a king. I only thank the gods that he had the courage to take upon himself a fate that I shrank from . . .' In a few quick words, Marric learned of the ancient entity called Stone-King and the bargain that he struck.

Elen slipped her arm about Mor's waist and rested her head against his shoulder, trying to comfort him with her very presence. 'It is getting dark,' she murmured. 'Shall we light the lamps?'

Gwenlliant shook her head vehemently. Her tears fell on Marric's hands, and suddenly, he knew what to say. He pried her hands open and poured the necklace across one palm.

'You keep this, daughter. One day you will hang it around the neck of a son of your own. I swear that to you.' He flicked a glance at Mor and Elen, who stood embracing once again, all but unconscious of the fact. 'I shall see you in the morning; Gwenlliant, unless you are worn out, I hope that you will dine with me.'

She laid her gleaming head against his knee. Absently, he stroked her hair. 'Poor child,' he murmured. 'You have had a rough time of it.' First, Olwen's illness, followed by a crossing, and by falling in love – for all the signs were there to see – with the one man in the world (aside from Mor) who could not joyously embrace a girl as beautiful in form and spirit as his daughter. He would see that she ate and rested; and then, when she was ready, he would ask her if she wanted to tell him the entire story.

But she had travelled far; this was not the proper time. 'I imagine,' he said slyly, 'that the trip to Byzantium must have been fairly boring, to say the least, with those two as your only company.'

That won a faint laugh from his daughter. 'They tried their best not to show that what they really wanted was to dally in their cabin,' she stated with the candour that had been her most disastrous accomplishment since her childhood. 'Though I was not convinced, I appreciated their courtesy. But I am glad to be here with you.'

'Do you regret that Mor chose another to be empress?' If it took Marric the rest of his life, he would make it up to her – conquer more countries to give her an empire of her own – anything.

A vehement headshake set that fear to rest. 'Oh, but father,' Gwenlliant sighed, 'when I was little, I used to believe that there was nothing that you couldn't do. Please, can you make that be true again?'

And that, of course, was the one gift that Marric could not give her.

Chapter Twenty

Absently acknowledging the usual number of salutes, Marric hastened into his rooms and stripped the usual amount of splendour from fingers, wrists and neck. *Less* than the usual amount, he conceded with an inner chuckle. The entire city had been too preoccupied by the spectacle of Mor and Elen to notice that, throughout the winter, Marric had withdrawn to the shadows. Mor and Elen glittered throughout the city, enthroned side by side (and hand in hand whenever possible): young, vital, supremely dramatic.

For Marric's entire reign, Byzantium had not had an empress resident in the palace. With a realm of her own to guard, Olwen had come and gone on her own occasions. And, although her hair might have made her a wonder to the dark, intense city-dwellers who thrived on novelty, her name was hard for them to shout in the streets. Elen, now – or Helena, as she had reluctantly allowed herself to be called – she was daughter of a princess whom the oldest in the city or the biggest liars claimed to remember. And, as exotically beautifully as Olwen was, Elen looked like one of their own.

Marric could not remember a winter as pleasant and, even for him, as peaceful as this past. With Mor and Elen taking on more and more of the ceremonial functions, he found himself increasingly free to tend to the real task of ruling his Empire: not Triumphs or battles. Where divine right and Imperial privilege left off, law had to begin, or privilege became licence. It was a truth that his own father had tried to teach him, a truth, Marric privately suspected, that could not be taught, except by example and by ageing.

Despite the comforting warmth rising from the hypocaust, Marric shivered as he laid aside his *paludamentum*. Knowing his habits, his body-servants had laid out a robe for him and vanished. Marric shrugged into the garment, cut in the rich Persian style: heavily furred, elaborately brocaded, and far more flamboyant than he would have worn had he been left to his own choice. Which, of course, he hadn't. Gwenlliant, with the Celtoi's magpie eye for bright colour and, he had to admit, beauty, had chosen it for him and teased him into wearing it.

And now – he had even admitted it to her, too – he found that he liked the robe. The lamps and polycandela in his study gleamed on the metallic threads in its silk, making him feel like the focus of all the light in the room as the day faded.

The hour before twilight had become his favourite time of day. When he was a youth, he had preferred the nights for carousing or for making love; as a young man, dawn and noon were for battles or a day's work; but now, as he grew older, the early evening was a time for rest and for contemplation – and for his daughter Gwenlliant to join him before dinner.

This past winter, she had retreated with her father into the shadows. Those Byzantines who might have looked forward to the flame-haired princess' more dubious exploits – such as driving her brother's chariot, or riding in boy's garments through the city ('You told me that ladies do so in Ch'in!' she had protested when vengeance for that particular misdeed struck), or the vivid talk and laughter that distracted spectators in the Hippodrome from the performers – were disappointed. During this past winter, Gwenlliant had shown a maturity and sobriety that should have made any parent rejoice, but that, instead, grieved Marric deeply. Like him, she mourned the loss of Dylan. Unlike him, she knew what she was mourning. The loss had drawn them more closely together, at least.

Now he heard rapid footsteps outside, a quick laugh, a joke too fast for him to catch, as Gwenlliant greeted his guards, and she rushed into the room. The lamps immediately seemed to burn brighter, and Gwenlliant drew their light to herself until she glowed like a mosaic wrought of light and living colours and textures.

She let her smile fade, as if it were like the purple itself that she assumed in public and could not wait to throw aside, then hurried over to him and kissed him.

'Tired, Gwenlliant?' It pleased him to lead her to a chair, to tend her as if she were a child – or the great lady which, actually, he had to admit that she was. He had asked Flavius Marcellinus to look out for her when he could be released from Mor's service, hoping perhaps that the young man, so loyal and pleasant, might draw his daughter's attention. He was not brilliant, but he was steady and kind; and Gwenlliant had need of such qualities. As much as Marric favoured the lad, he would have had words with him if he had permitted his daughter to tire herself.

She shook her head wearily, then laughed at the contradiction. 'I went today to the Temple of Osiris,' she told him. 'The high priest is ill; I thought perhaps that I could heal him where the priests of Thoth failed.'

She looked down, laced her hands together to still their trembling, and shivered. 'I failed too.'

Immediately, Marric was out of his chair. He laid his robe about his daughter's shoulders and hugged her until she sighed and relaxed against him. 'That was kindly thought of, Gwenlliant. But you cannot heal age.'

'He told me that too.' He felt, rather than saw, the girl's nod of agreement. 'He told me that he will be glad to rest, that he is so weary . . . and,' she shuddered hard, 'I felt it. For the first time, I understand what "weary unto death" means, more than a sad phrase that bards use.'

'Then why trouble him at all?' In the next moment, Marric bit his lip, angry at himself. He had not meant to criticize Gwenlliant for what, after all, was the best gift that she could offer.

'You ask me that, Father? *You?*' Gwenlliant replied.

Marric flung up a hand, acknowledging a shrewd hit. 'We are much alike, child.'

'That is what Aunt Alexa says.'

'It is clear that you listened to her well. What else did she say?'

'That the gods . . .' Gwenlliant's eyes, so like Olwen's amber ones, went soft and vague as she drew Alexa's words from her memory, ' . . . the gods are sly. They give my brother a son according to his heart, and a daughter according to his nature. I think that it sounds like blasphemy, but . . .'

Marric laughed, 'But it is, nonetheless, true.' He poured wine for her and, because she was drained by her failure to heal, watered it carefully. 'Not a word more until you drink.'

'But I did it for you, Father. Because you rely on the high priest so. Because you need him – and you will need him more . . .'

'I said, not another word!' Marric held up a finger. 'A fine father I am, insisting that my young daughter drink.'

That won the laugh from her that he had hoped for. If it had more of duty than of mirth about it, well, at least it was a laugh.

He considered summoning a cubicular to light more lamps, then fumbled out flint and steel from the kit that old army habit insisted he keep close at hand, and kindled them himself. The gold mosaics on the walls reflected the light until the huge room glowed with peach and amber light that, for once, made it look comfortable and homelike. He seated himself and pretended to be busy with letters while covertly studying Gwenlliant.

She was more sad than weary, he realized. Her mood must not come from the attempt at healing. Marric's heart grew cold as Gwenlliant reached into her pouch and drew out a parchment. It was torn and stained as if she had crumpled and hurled it from her. Carefully, she unfolded it and handed it to Marric, who took it with the care he would accord a dagger.

But the dagger he had in mind was one that no man had ever touched: cast from a fallen star, black-hilted, too harsh to take the life of aught but a wolf's-head – but destined to draw the blood of queens. *She is our daughter, Olwen. Can you not let the curse end?* he wished at his absent, stubborn queen. Bad enough that she was probably fool enough to die of her stubbornness . . . he jerked his thoughts away from the danger point at which he would, once again, decide to meddle in the ways of gods and, once again, pay for it with a piece of his heart.

Still, he could not help but look at the letter as if it were the summons to a battle. To a battle that Gwenlliant, not he, must fight, he knew. That knowledge cut more bitterly than any sword, axe or whip: she faced violence, and he, who would have died to spare her pain, could not shield her. He knew that, just as he had known, in his deepest heart, that Stephana had been too badly hurt to want to live, that Alexa would never return with him . . . his eyes stung, tearless, as if burnt by acid.

'You had to have known!' Gwenlliant broke into his reverie.

Marric nodded. Just that morning, he had had a twin to that letter, when the messenger from the western themes presented himself.

'What does your mother write?' he asked.

'You know,' Gwenlliant looked down.

'I had hoped, if you were happy, that you might stay . . . stay here with me,' Marric admitted. Even after his plan to wed son and daughter to one another went awry, he had laid his snares carefully, baited with everything that Gwenlliant loved: fine horses, finer clothes and – much to his lasting satisfaction – the chance to spend long hours with the priests of Thoth, learning to turn the healing power of her mother's line into a sure art.

'I *have* been happy here,' Gwenlliant muttered. 'But I have known that as soon as it was safe to sail, I must go back.'

'And face . . . do you know what?' Marric asked. 'You do know what your mother plans, don't you? And you must also know that I had hoped to bring her here to persuade her to live.' Tomorrow, he realized, or even five minutes from now, he would be bitterly ashamed, but now, his frustrations leapt out at his child. 'What if she can no longer heal? What if she can no longer conceive? Sweet Isis' breasts, what of it? We *have* our heirs – and no one could ask for finer ones! They, however, they could ask for more, for seasoning, wisdom, the teaching that rules can pass on before they go to the Horizon after full lives. She has years yet, years of service, years that you and I . . .' his voice strained, then stopped altogether for a mortifying instant ' . . . who love her cannot sacrifice.'

He saw the child waver, her lower lip drooping as it did when she was sad, then followed with his last question.

'You know what she plans. Gwenlliant, in your heart of hearts, are you truly ready to be queen?' he asked.

His daughter burst into tears and flung herself at him. 'When you ask me that, I know that you are right. This is too soon. But when mother writes to me of the blighted trees, the miscarriages, the burnt villages that must be rebuilt and blessed, I feel in my heart that she is right too. I don't want to die,' she cried. 'And I don't want mother to die! But this is Penllyn's way!'

Olwen, Olwen, my dearest. I do not want you to die either, but I could cheerfully strangle you right now! Marric thought. Desire, fury and fear raced in his blood, as they always did at the thought of his queen. For so many years, they had sparred and competed with one another in every place but their bed. So many years, though, had worn the old angers smooth and covered them, as an oyster covers grit with precious nacre, with acceptance, humour, affection . . . call it love.

Perhaps it was not the protective, passionate tenderness that he had felt for Stephana. Even as Marric clasped his daughter in his arms, he remembered:

214

*He had been a proud, arrogant fool, and now Stephana was
dying in his arms, dying in pain.*

*'Pull the blade out,' his master-of-arms had always taught him,
'and the man dies mercifully.' But this was a woman, his woman.
His beloved. But he could see from the nature of the wound that
he could not help her to live. Thus, he must help her to die. 'You
will indeed be the death of me,' she had once told him. He did
not want to be responsible for her death. But he was. And he
couldn't deny her easy passage.*

*Kissing her, he gathered her close. 'Don't look, beloved,' he
whispered, and laid his hands over hers on the dagger's hilt. He
used all his strength to draw it quickly from the wound. As the
hilt, unshielded by contact with her flesh, blistered his palm, he
hurled it from him.*

Marric's love for Stephana had been a fire that had burnt him
even as it warmed. His love for Olwen – call it a hearth fire;
she had not been his first love, nor he hers; but they had learned
to value and trust each other, and their love for their children
had taught them to love one another the more.

Unless he could find a way to stop it, Olwen would die in the
nemet, he knew; and this time, he would not even be there to
aid her passage. Instead, that duty would fall to the child in his
arms, who would take Olwen's place as queen thereafter and,
one day, stand as sacrifice and sacrificer in her place.

What sacrilege will you attempt now, Marric? Olwen's rebuke
echoed in his ears and, deep in thought, he remembered
Stephana's accusing glance the night he had slain Kynan the
bard.

'Father,' Gwenlliant was whispering, 'oh, Father, I am afraid.
I do not want to go back there, but it is my home. I do not
want to see . . . what I must see, but I miss mother; and it
would tear my heart in shreds to betray her. We have a story at
home . . .' *Home*, Marric thought. *Not Byzantium, but Prydein.*
' . . . of Ganhumara who failed and fled, rather than slay herself.
I will not flee, but help me, help me to do what is right!'

Help her to do what was right? Gwenlliant's cry conquered
Marric utterly: craft, guile, even love fell away from him in the
face of her appeal.

'I would have kept you here,' he told her. 'As I would have

215

tried to keep your mother. I would not have been right, but I would have done it.' He smoothed Gwenlliant's hair and kissed her forehead. 'Do not worry, child. I will not hold you against your conscience – or against, I find, my own. I shall send you back to your home with an escort fit for a queen!'

He forced himself to smile at that. 'Unlike your mother, you will not protest at that.'

'I am not ready; you know I am not,' she whispered against his shoulder.

'I know; and I will help you.'

'Do you think that I could stop . . . ?'

Oh, this one *was* his child in heart and mind, willing to dare the gods to protect whomever she loved. 'It might be, daughter, that you could succeed where I have failed. There is no curse on you. But, Gwenlliant, this thing too you must know. I have spent my entire life battling against the fates of everyone whom I have loved. When I have stepped into their paths, the gods have not been kind.

'I have an empire to guide and heirs to train; if I am to succeed in my tasks, I can no longer badger and defy the gods. But I should be very glad, Gwenlliant, if your mother could live, at least to see a grandchild. I should be eternally grateful if the cycle of blood could stop.'

But if you fail, child, as I have failed, the gods grant that I do not outlive you.

Gwenlliant tightened her arms about him. 'Up, then, child. We have grieved long enough. If you are to learn to be a queen, you must learn to lay pain aside when there is need.'

Gwenlliant scrambled to her feet and pulled her gown smooth. 'How?'

Taking care that his face was shadowed until he could control his expression, he brought out a gameboard. 'Chess is one way,' he said. 'The game of battles. It disciplines the mind.'

Obediently, Gwenlliant sat opposite him and tried to play, but her pawns rapidly headed into death country, as a Ch'in trader called it, and her queen followed too quickly.

'I am sorry,' she whispered. 'I am very stupid today.'

'Then we do not have to play,' he told her. 'I shall resign the game to you.'

She put out her hand to stop him when he moved to overturn his king. 'Aunt Alexa says that one must always play out the game.'

Marric raised his daughter's hand to his lips. 'Then I shall be wrong again. It will not be the first time, as your aunt and mother will no doubt tell you. If you will not play chess, Gwenlliant, sit with me now until dinner.'

She rose from the chair opposite what she perceived to be the endless expanse of carven table that divided them and dropped lithely at his feet, laying her bright hair against his knee; and he stroked it until the amber light turned violet and the lamps, one by one, sputtered and went out.

Chapter Twenty-one

The track to the tidal cauldron at Talebolion seemed filled with rocks, roots or brambles, each determined to bar Gwenlliant's way. For at least the fifth time, she forced herself up from her knees. Her grimy hands plucked some painful burrs from her sandals and tattered cloak. It had been fine once – fit for a princess, not the renegade that she had made of herself.

They will jeer at me as they do at Ganhumara. The bards will make satires. I have been false to all that I have been taught. But mother will live . . .

Rock outcroppings and thistles had made rags of her clothing and scratched arms and legs until they bled. *If the land wants blood, let it take mine!* Gwenlliant hurled her thought defiantly at the shadowed trees with their stunted leaves.

But queensblade, her mother's black dagger, lay in its scabbard at Gwenlliant's waist, not Olwen's.

Watching out for another loose stone or exposed root, Gwenlliant worked her way down the Cynfael's banks towards the crags of Talebolion where the river flung itself far below into a boiling tidal basin. Edged with knife-sharp rocks, Talebolion would keep what it gained forever. If Gwenlliant drowned the royal dagger within it, her mother could not enter the hawthorn nemet at Beltane – only three days away – and there sacrifice her life for the land's sake.

Her father had said that he would be eternally grateful if Olwen could be spared. He had also said that he was too old to fight the gods, and she had seen the lines, the weariness on his face, marks of his years of battles. *Father, I do this for you too*, she thought. *Let the blame fall to me. All I want is to save mother's life*, she told the moon. *Goddess, why is that so much to ask? What are you, that your daughters must die in the hawthorn grove?*

But a cloud veiled the moon, as if the Goddess had turned her face away. Gwenlliant's thoughts shaped themselves into a prayer, panted out to the painful rhythm of her blistered feet. Her nails cut into her palms – soft after her winter in Byzantium – cutting off her chant with awareness of this new pain and the darkness of the moon. To save her mother, Gwenlliant had made herself outlaw. She could hear the bard's satires already: they would call her Ganhumara's daughter, not Olwen's, for Ganhumara, who had fled her realm with her lover, abandoning it to war that she might live a few wretched years longer, was the mother of all traitors – if of nothing else.

But her mother would live. Gwenlliant was glad, glad, glad that she had stolen queensblade. Hot tears surged into her eyes, and the drying riverbed quivered into dark rainbows. She waited for the wind to clear her vision. The rocks and mud of shrinking Cynfael were treacherous to walk if her eyes were blinded with weeping. Should she fall and break her ankle, here she'd lie until she starved, unable to save herself. Or to rid Penllyn of queensblade . . . *queens' bane would be a better name for you*, she told the dagger. She rubbed one hip, bruised and aching from the fall off her pony – she who rode so well. (Don't think of the pony now, or you'll weep again!) Tumbling clear of the poor beast's hooves, she had driven the dagger's black hilt so hard into her flesh that she winced now at every step.

If only Cynfael still flowed deep, as it had in her childhood when it nursed all Penllyn, Gwenlliant would have flung queensblade into it and rested content. But the winter's snows were scant, and Cynfael was almost dry. The narrow spring that remained might spew the dagger back on land for someone to return to Olwen's maenol . . . and to Olwen, who would promptly turn it on herself for the land's sake. But let the sea swallow it, and only fish would ever know what became of it. Let queensblade have their thin blood as a sacrifice, and welcome!

And afterwards? If Gwenlliant tumbled from the rocks, or if she escaped . . . where would she go? Her father ruled the Empire; tribes akin to her ruled throughout Prydein; and would the Aescir accept one who had turned against all customs as she had?

They would have accepted Alexa, she told herself. But Alexa had been sorry for her crimes.

Gwenlliant the thief, Gwenlliant the coward. She plodded onward towards the sea.

It was the flowers that had broken her courage. When Gwenlliant had returned to Penllyn, she had been resolute, determined to persuade and, failing persuasion, beg her mother to live. Failing that, she had known that she must enter the nemet beside her and witness Olwen's death.

Olwen's joy at her return had almost been reward enough. Her mother had embraced her, and Gwenlliant had realized with a shudder, *Why, I am taller than she!* During the winter in Byzantium, she must have gained her full woman's height; she had remembered Olwen, however, as being taller still. Olwen's body felt frail, thinner and somehow softer, its fine muscle tone flaccid after the summer and autumn in Gallia, fighting plague and rebuilding what had been cast down, and after a winter that had been cold and harsh, albeit dry, in her own realm. But her embrace had been strong with welcome and relief; and her relief had grown as Gwenlliant agreed that yes, she would accompany her about the realm, yes, she would learn from her mother all that she could so that she might rule well when her turn came.

But the flowers, the poor parched flowers!

Gwenlliant had become used, in Byzantium, to flowers in her rooms. She it was who had softened the stark palace corridors of marble and mosaic with clusters of blossoms and flowering plants; and her father had smiled at the change, smiled and asked if she, like her mother before her, wished to be known as the woman of flowers.

But Byzantium was rich with water; Penllyn was not. In Penllyn, no one would ever compare Gwenlliant with her mother, Olwen, and sing that where she walked, white roses bloomed; not one flower could she coax into bud.

That her flowers should thrive became suddenly important to her. Newly returned home, new to her healing powers, Gwenlliant was certain that could she but heal the gardens, the rest of the land must follow. And healing began with water. Accordingly, Gwenlliant had hastened to the artesian well near the kitchens. Even when all the other wells dried up the summer before, that one alone had supplied the entire maenol. But she had had to lower the leather bucket almost to the end of its rope before she finally heard a muffled splash, finally drew up a little brown, silty fluid . . .

Perhaps just one bloom . . .

A once-strong hand on the bucket's rope handle stopped her.

'Pour it back,' said the Queen in a voice that Gwenlliant had never disobeyed. 'We cannot waste water on flowers when we need food.'

'But my garden dies,' Gwenlliant could not refrain from protesting.

'So does mine,' replied the Queen.

Gwenlliant's eyes had flickered to the black dagger at her mother's belt, then beyond the maenol to the secrecy of the hawthorn grove, most sacred of all the nemets in Penllyn.

Olwen followed her eyes. 'Beltane comes with the new moon, Gwenlliant. My courses have stopped; I cannot bear. If Penllyn is to bear fruit this year . . .'

'No!' Gwenlliant, for all her resolve, had cried. 'You have years left!'

'Gwenlliant, you are the one with the years. Mine are all counted. You'll make a good queen, dear. I've taught you all that I know; and I am certain that your aunt and your father have taught you too.'

Sunlight had glared on queensblade, had drawn Gwenlliant's eyes the way an adder draws a fledgling towards its coils.

'You're *not* going into the nemet with that!' She gestured, revolted, at the dagger she had seen all her life. 'How can we know that the Goddess' law is still true?'

'That is your father speaking,' Olwen said in measured tones. 'But I am certain that he also tried to teach you that to question what must be is pointless. And this is what must be. Sooner or later, I must pass within the Goddess for the land's sake. That is the law; and for all your father's temper, he reveres law. Just give me your blessing, Gwenlliant . . .' to her horror, Olwen sounded almost imploring ' . . . and I shall pass content. But refuse, and I must go just the same. Daughter, we have had this talk before. Don't you see that Penllyn dies? The land needs young blood to rule it.'

Young blood. After Olwen's blood had glutted queensblade, Gwenlliant would have to wear it, until she too aged and the law compelled her to turn it on herself.

'Can't you wait just a little longer?' She heard the whining, bargaining tone in her voice that she had used as a child when she had pleaded to stay up later. 'Elen bears a child; you could wait for its birth at least. And I would be so happy if you could wait until I am a mother myself. There is so much for me to learn still, I know that now . . . I am not ready . . .'

'You are going to have to be,' Olwen told her firmly. Years ago, that same tone had ordered Gwenlliant to bed.

'But it's not fair!' Olwen protested. 'Why does Penllyn need you more than I do? Because Amergin declares that that's the law?' Hysteria welled up in her, turning her against people whom she had loved and trusted lifelong. 'He's old and cold, like all the Druids. They love power too much, and they use law like a whip to keep Penllyn in fear. The Goddess' law is cold. Any sort of land that wants its queen's blood – I say that it isn't worth it!'

'You blaspheme,' Olwen said in a voice so cold that Gwenlliant would much have preferred it if her mother had screamed at her or slapped her. 'All that we are is by favour of the Goddess. And see that you remember that, girl!'

'It's all so hopeless!' Gwenlliant had choked like a much younger girl, and fled back to her dusty, dying garden.

Amergin the ArchDruid found her there. 'Gwenlliant,' he ordered, 'turn around.'

She had shaken her head. 'Stand up and face me!' he ordered. She could not imagine disobeying him when he spoke in that tone: no one could. Reluctantly, Gwenlliant stood, her face half-averted and wholly rebellious. Why was it that when her father railed against fate, people thought that he was noble; but when she tried it, they treated her like a sullen brat? She was a grown woman, a princess, not a brat. That too was not fair.

'Your childishness has caused your mother much unhappiness,' Amergin informed her sadly.

And risks all Penllyn. Gwenlliant bristled more at the words that he forbore to speak than at the ones he had actually uttered.

'Tell me, Druid,' she demanded in the imperious tones she had learned in Byzantium, 'what sort of mother craves the death of a child?'

Amergin strode forward and grasped her shoulders, as if he would shake her into submission to the grisly law that doomed Penllyn's queens for a prayer of rain. Then he calmed himself and his hands loosened.

'I thought that I had taught you better, or that your family had. But as always: It is the careless weaver who must weave the same cloth twice. Sit down, and I'll try again.'

Amergin's patience humiliated Gwenlliant more than his anger. For the first time, she could fully understand why her father railed against the high priest of Osiris – and yet what bound them together. Her chin quivered, though, and she bit her lip, turning her face away lest Amergin see a princess weep.

'Because you were born royal, Gwenlliant, did you think that you would be spared the return of gift for gift? What we most love, we most pay for. You have seen that in your family. And if those examples are too familiar to you, consider birds or rabbits. Have you never seen them run before the hunter to lure him away from their young?

'Or perhaps you have seen pregnant women who are ill, starving perhaps, but whose bodies stint themselves to feed the child within. Even if it costs them their own lives.'

The mother in Gesoriacum had been burning up with fever, had fallen on the road, but she had taken care to cushion her child's fall with her body. Gwenlliant had healed her.

'If a common woman risks death for her unborn child, how

222

much more should a queen accept for the land that she has known and warded? The queen is the Goddess' favourite daughter, but the land's mother. Her fertility is Penllyn's and as her inner spring dies . . .'

'We cannot lose her!' It came out as a cry of pure anguish.

'Do you think that I want to tell you that you must?' Amergin's voice filled with deep pain. 'Do you think me cold, daughter? I simply submitted, for thus I was trained, to what *is:* not what pleases me, nor even what I judge fair, but simply what must be.' He had looked down at his hands, high-veined, long-fingered, and old, almost as old as the high priest's. 'So now, rather than oppose the Goddess' law, I must even submit to your hatred.'

The ArchDruid's voice had quivered, and Gwenlliant, hearing the hurt in it, burst into tears. With almost a mother's gentleness, Amergin reached out and stroked her coppery hair. 'Gwenlliant, child, are you ready to be queen? Gladly would I spare you this, but if we are to have rain, the land must be revived . . . and soon . . .'

Gwenlliant had been stymied on all sides. Even Alexa, on whose craft she had hoped to rely, had withdrawn to Deva for a time. Gwenlliant supposed that in the next few weeks she had run a little mad. That was when her great idea had been born. Ganhumara the Traitor, she remembered, had brought suffering upon the land because she had refused to use queensblade. But if Gwenlliant took it, if Gwenlliant stole it, Olwen couldn't use it because she wouldn't have it, Penllyn would be safe, and so too would Olwen. If Gwenlliant threw the dagger into the sea, the queens would have no sacrificial dagger. Lacking it, they would have to – at least, she hoped that they would have to – abandon the sacrifice. And no one would blame or harm Olwen.

Weighed against life itself, what was Gwenlliant's honour? She was a healer: her honour lay only in life.

Trudging beside the sluggish river, Gwenlliant cursed herself for a fool. Oh, it had been easy enough to slip into her mother's rooms while Olwen was bathing and the dagger lay unguarded.

She trusted me, Gwenlliant thought, twisting the knife – at least, though, it was not queensblade! – in the wound.

But not an hour out of the maenol, and they'd discovered the theft and set hunters on her.

How their horns had shrieked, like the Wild Hunt itself! Or was it the Hunt? Two winters ago, on the shortest night of the year, Gwenlliant had met the Hunt. Since then, she had encountered assassins, kidnap and the ancient rage of Stone-King. Yet she had survived all of them. She was not certain that she could resist the Master of the Wild Hunt should he ride towards her again . . . and she could not count on rescue by the man who had spared her the last time. Not now.

She jerked her pony's head round and galloped into the deep forest where the hunters' tall horses couldn't break through the low-sweeping branches. Even here, Penllyn's blight had spread: fallen trees blocked her way, forcing her from the road, deeper and deeper into the shadowy haunts of hungry wolves.

Horns howled out again. *I am being herded*, Gwenlliant realized. She pummelled her pony's sides, urging it to greater haste in the crackling underbush. Trusting her, it ran, as it had run two midwinters ago, when she had also fled the shrines.

As she twisted in the saddle to check her back trail, a gnarled root caught the pony's hoof. It stumbled and fell with a shrill scream. Just in time to avoid being pinned, Gwenlliant rolled free and winced as queensblade's hilt crushed painfully into the flesh of her thigh.

For what seemed like endless hours, she lay watching a dizzy, violet sunset whirl over her upturned face.

Come with me. She blinked and saw the narrow, imperious face of the Wild Hunt's lord.

No.

Look at yourself. Look at what you have done. Who would want you now but me? And I desire you . . . come with me..

No. She was a Celt, wasn't she? And hadn't her father always said that for sheer, dogged stubbornness, no one could beat the Celtoi?

Would he *take you back now?*

He forgave his sister. And if she could atone for what she *did, perhaps . . .*

Do you truly believe that?

Go away, ghost. I heal and spare the living; you have neither life nor breath.

I am leaving now – but I shall be back.

The horns rang out, sorrowful but somehow sullen. Gwenlliant knew that she would hear them again. Please Goddess (though she had little right to the prayer any longer) that she could resist the Lord of the Hunt when next he came.

The pony whickered again, and Gwenlliant dragged herself over to it. Saddle and stirrups were twisted grotesquely on its flank. 'Oh, Liatha,' she murmured. 'I should have taken a horse and not risked you. I should never have galloped on such rough ground. I have killed you.'

She laid hands on the broken foreleg and opened her mind for the healing magic. But no flow of warmth or power responded. *What did you expect?* She had prized her talent, late as it had blossomed, for healing; but her mother's life was worth losing it.

Gently, Gwenlliant removed her pony's saddle and bridle, then sat stroking its mane. As the sky darkened, she knew that she would have to move on. But she couldn't just leave the old pony, her oldest friend in the stables, to suffer alone until hunter, thirst – or wolves – killed her. It had been all her fault. She longed for Gwyn the hostler, who would do what had to be done, and spare Gwenlliant.

But Gwyn was at the maenol, assuming that he was not out searching for Gwenlliant. Liatha could not walk, and she must not be left behind to die a lingering death. Gwenlliant looked down at queensblade, the only weapon that she had.

Flinging her arms about the old pony's hot, sweat-lathered neck, she cried like the child who had learned to ride on her broad back many years ago, begging the pony's forgiveness until Liatha nickered at her, nudging her with a soft nose. Gwenlliant drew the black dagger, hiding it in a fold of her cloak so Liatha wouldn't see. The gesture reminded her of the ritual at Midwinter, when Amergin cut the mistletoe by stealth, and she shuddered.

Your hand can't shake now, Gwenlliant. Hold steady.

'Pretty Liatha, good girl,' Gwenlliant crooned, blinking back her tears in order to see the spot in the throat that Gwyn had once shown her.

Quickly, she made the merciful cut and jumped back from the pony's neck. She hurled the bloody dagger away. It quivered – a sweet, sated sound – in a nearby tree trunk. As the light dimmed in Liatha's loving, malt-coloured eyes, Gwenlliant laid her head against the pony's flank and wept herself out.

Finally she sat up, scrubbed her hands in the rough grass to clean the blood from them, and shivered. Near the pallid horizon, the waxing moon had emerged and was watching her coldly.

She stared back. *Well, Goddess, is that enough blood for you?*

The pulse of crickets frayed at her nerves. She hadn't turned thief just to give up here. She retrieved queensblade and wiped it off. Moonlight on its hammered surfaces caught her eyes.

Accept what must be, Amergin had said.

But her father had never done so.

Later that night, Gwenlliant wrapped her cloak about her. Twigs plucked her hood from her head and snapped off in her hair; brambles snagged her skirts and scratched her ankles. And queensblade, her pony's blood on it too, lay heavy at her side. Kinslayer carried by thief: the bards would enjoy that riddle.

A huge oak, two branches outstretched to grab her, loomed up on the path, looking like an avenging Druid. Gwenlliant cowered back, tripped on a loose stone, and crashed heavily. For some little time, she cried – for her mother, her pony, the smarts of her scrapes and bruises. But no more crying! She had wallowed far too long in self-pity. She was Gwenlliant, and she had to destroy queensblade. That was enough.

Over and over she chanted her name and purpose to herself and to the stars. Black clouds whirled away in the cold wind, and the Goddess' face rose still higher in its path across the sky: brilliant and reproachful. Under the moon's steady glare, what had seemed like a high, unselfish deed felt like treason.

Cynfael's course emerged from the forest and flowed past a hill. Half cut off by that channel from the rest of Penllyn, there nestled a tiny clearing.

Gwenlliant stared at it, almost too exhausted to believe that she had finally escaped the forest. Something darted past her feet, and she staggered, bringing up hard against a birch sapling, one hand pressed against her teeth. The Master of the Hunt again? If she didn't scream, perhaps it would creep away.

Thirstily the tall grass whispered and rustled. Towards her. Now she dared to look down. Almost at her feet crouched a rabbit, its coat matted and dull, its ears flattened against its head, and its eyes glazed and staring with fear. Why had it run *towards* her?

She glanced around quickly. A tangle of grass and tufts of fur softened a nest in which four finger-length rabbit kittens huddled, blind and vulnerable.

'I won't hurt them,' Gwenlliant promised. She stooped, extending her fingers, her hand palm out, to the doe who had sought to lure her away, but it jumped back, eyes flicking from her to its kittens and back again. 'See,' she cried. 'I'm leaving now.'

Carefully, she stepped past the rabbit, past the nest. The grass shifted again, and she knew that the doe had rejoined her litter. By now, she thought, Elen would be huge with child, a tiny girl like that. And she would never see the babe.

Keep walking, fool, she ordered herself, and continued down the hill towards the clearing. Years ago, someone must have started to fence it in, then decided that it was not worth the effort. But a few posts still lurched around a poor house. The night wind blew the smell of the sea towards her. No wonder the soil here yielded nothing but stunted trees and weeds and meagre seedlings: seawater had leached into the tiny, ragged fields.

At first, Gwenlliant thought that it was years deserted, but reddish light worked itself out to her through the cracked hide of its one window and the gaps in the poorly chinked walls. Outside the door, a goat with shrunken teats cropped at winter-dried tufts of sparse grass. What did the people who lived in that den do for milk or meat?

Gwenlliant too, since she must walk all the way to Talebolion, needed rest. And food. Poor as these people were, they were still people of Penllyn, and it had always been her country's pride that no stranger was turned away unfed and unwarmed.

She scrubbed her hands across her face, licked them, and tried again. She thought that perhaps her face might almost be clean now. Then she plucked the twigs and leaves from her dishevelled braids and twisted her belt around to hide queensblade within the tatters of her cloak. Hurt, hungry and bedraggled, now she would look like any other young woman who had gone astray. Even if these people knew that the Princess had run away, how could they think that she would turn up on their doorstep?

Now that Gwenlliant saw a promise of rest, she was surprised at just how unsteady her knees felt. *I must have grown soft in Byzantium.* She walked up to the door. No rich odour of boiling meat greeted her, and as she approached, the voices that she heard inside hushed fearfully. Almost timidly, she scratched at the warped planks of the door. Even its leather hinges were tearing.

'Hallo, the house?' she called. Her voice rose thinly, then – to her horror – broke. 'Please, anybody?'

'Be welcome to this hearth,' came a tired woman's voice, mouthing words by rote. Nevertheless, Gwenlliant pushed the door open and edged inside.

A few reed pallets lay on one side of a meagre fire. On the other side of the hearth, a rough-hewn table and benches were the only furniture in the cottage. Two children sat quietly, waiting to eat; another, only slightly older than his brother or sister, grunted as he heaved a heavy axe back on to the pegs driven into the wall to hold it.

Why hasn't mother . . . then Gwenlliant remembered. Olwen could not seek out every cottager in her land to make certain that they all starved at the same time. Perhaps after she threw away queensblade . . .

The woman knelt beside the hearth fire, nursing it with sticks from the pile of wood that her son had brought in, staggering under the load until he could drop it, and almost collapse beside it. In the corners of the room, firelight leapt to the night wind, cast shadow dancers on the crude walls. Behind Gwenlliant, the door slammed shut.

'Well, come in,' said the woman. Despite her rags and the stoop of her thin shoulders, her voice was friendly enough. She straightened and gave a last stir to the battered black pot which hung from a warped metal hook over the fire.

'Come and eat,' she said. 'You're just in time. The soup is thin, but no one at my hearth shall starve.'

Gwenlliant watched the woman's bony hands. Firelight shone through them as she filled the last bowl. Her ladle scraped on the bottom of the pot, trembling as the hand that held it shook. There were four bowls, Gwenlliant noticed, and now that she had come, there were five people to feed.

Do you steal food as well as daggers, Gwenlliant?

'No thank you,' Gwenlliant told the mother. 'There will be food for me at home. And I am already late.'

A haze of pity and dizziness blurred the sight of the mother and children who stared at the strange girl, as Gwenlliant, not daring to trust the voice that still might break and beg food from those with so little to give, backed towards the cracked door.

The wind cooled across her cheeks, reddened with sun and with shame. Then, by the cottage wall, Gwenlliant sank down, weeping for the starvelings within. This was spring. All over Penllyn, fields and orchards should quicken, yet that family had nothing. At that rate, they would never see autumn, much less survive a winter.

She huddled shoulders into her cloak, her hand brushing against the serpentine pin that fastened it. The gift of Amergin, it was of precious metal and amethysts. If she left it where the family might come and find . . .

And what then? she thought. *Men have killed for the price of a gem. Or what if someone saw it and cried, 'Look! The lost Princess' brooch! What have you done to her?' They might be punished, and they are innocent, innocent . . .*

Her charity might only worsen and hasten their fate. That was not good enough.

Unsteadily, Gwenlliant rose to her feet, regretting the gift that she dare not leave. Her feet lagged on the path to the sea. The wind took on a sharper edge, and she smelled the tang of salt, heard the rush of wave against rock. Her reckoning had been off; she stood nearer Talebolion than she had thought.

An hour's walk brought her out to the end of rock where the sea crashed against the high cliffs and gleamed, eternal and dissatisfied, beneath the Goddess' face. The wind blew and belled her cloak out from her body.

Will you join me now? Come, I worship you; we will have forever for me to prove it.

'Go *away!*' she snapped at the Master of the Wild Hunt. He had left his horse and his troop behind and had come up soundlessly behind her, his narrow, booted feet silent on the ancient rock. The moonlight glinted on his pale eyes and thin features as he reached out to clasp her hand and bring it to icy lips that sent a bolt of flame from her palm all along her nerves. She gasped and snatched her hand back from him.

But you need an ally, now more than ever. Behold! He thrust out an arm, and his cloak swirled about him. Gwenlliant followed his gesture.

'Goddess, help me!' she screamed suddenly. At the horizon showed sails, and on the sails, vivid in the bright moonlight, ramped black bears. Jomsborg had come again!

'No!' Gwenlliant shrieked. 'Go back!'

Now, will you ally with me? Say the word only, and I shall fall upon the skin-changers with spear, with hoof, and with terror, and drive them back for you.

She had no time to argue. She waved both hands at her enemies, took a rash step forward. But the wind forced her back and blew the waves into froth. The ships neared the shore. In moments, she realized, the Jomsborgers would drive their bear-prowed ships on to the land . . . on to *her* land . . . and change into the guise of black, hungry bears. Perhaps they would find the cottage in the clearing.

Not if I can help it. Gwenlliant thought.

And if you cannot? asked the Lord of the Wild Hunt.

'Then I die. But I die protecting my land.'

I shall stop you, he said, and clasped her close. His arms were strong, almost familiar: just as strongly, Dylan had stood between her and their enemies; Dylan, who had allied with strange, old magics – but for protection for all that he loved. She too . . .

But he sought to force her. Last time he had seen her, he had also tried to trick her. Perhaps this too was a trick.

She turned in his arms, her eyes marking out the path that would lead to the shore. Once again the wind blew, and clouds scattered. *Let me see truth!* she prayed.

Did it take magic to see truth? she asked herself with her next breath. The Master of the Wild Hunt sought to play on hatred and terror. She would have to think rather than simply react.

As if in response to that decision, she seemed to hear her father's voice. *Tell me, daughter, why would the Jomsborgers strike from the west? Their old base was at Wolin, to the east.*

Strange, indeed, she remarked. Too strange for her to believe. Show me truth, she had prayed. She had shown herself!

Perhaps that was, in and of itself, the magic for which she had sought.

The Goddess' face gleamed above the water, revealing that the sea was empty of ships. It held only the reflection of the Beltane moon.

'Liar!' she cried, and pushed free of the Wild Hunt's lord. Vulnerable to her, he staggered on the narrow path, and she flung out a hand to steady him.

Did you think that I would fall? His laughter was ironic, cutting.

It does not matter. I seek to save life. Even what passes for it with you.

So bright was that moon that Gwenlliant could see her face in the blade – in queensblade, which unconsciously she had drawn when she thought that Penllyn was in danger. She rushed down the path.

Till next time! the Hunt's tall master called after her.

Would there be a next time? What if there had been ships? She, as much as the Master of the Wild Hunt, asked that question. Well, if there had been, she would have rushed at them – one young woman against a fleet – and tried to protect her realm, even if she died in the attempt.

And what would have become of the Master of the Wild Hunt, had she let him slip . . . not that she could. She had no desire to see the Lord of the Hunt himself tracked, hunted, and slain like a stag, nor did she wish to ride with him. He had his place in the realm, deep within the forests, spreading panic to the queen's enemies, not lingering near living warmth.

You have your place, Lord; and I have mine.

Moonlight startled off the blade and spilled down into the sea.

Is that how mother feels too? Gwenlliant wondered.

Queensblade trembled as her hand shook. For an instant longer, she tensed, tempted desperately to throw it into the cauldron at Talebolion and end all questions for all time. But she would have used it to defend Penllyn. She would have died using it.

Lowering her head, Gwenlliant sheathed queensblade. She keened, a thing that they would not at all understand in Byzantium, but which she felt to be necessary now. Later on, she knew, she would have to be brave, even on Beltane when she would enter the nemet with her mother, but emerge alone, bound by the ArchDruid with crown and queensblade to Penllyn's service. Then, she would have to summon Alexa and comfort her, reassure (despite Alexa's idiotic policy that a young queen needed young advisors) her aunt, and then, finally, write to her father and brother in Byzantium.

She would have no time to mourn then.

Gwenlliant turned from the smell of brine, the crash of wind and wave, feeling infinitely tired, infinitely sad, but clear of mind, like one who had recovered from a fever that led her mind astray down dark, grim roads. Her shoulders ached, and she rubbed at them . . . *just the way she had watched her father rub at his*.

She was going home.

Her steps quickened, but she saved her strength. Penllyn would need its new queen too much for her to hazard herself by speed.

There was no choice. She would return home, as she had after the Midwinter when she had fled, and, as had happened last time, her mother would ask no questions, glad of her return.

When she returned the last time, her mother had slain the white bear, a quick, violent mercy. Gwenlliant fought tears, wishing, for an instant, that she shared her father's curse that had left him, lifelong, unable to weep.

But there was no point in wishing for a curse. She was heir to Penllyn, to the Goddess' favour; her blessings would be hard enough to endure. And she must endure them, unlike Mor and Elen, alone. The last time that she had seen the Hunt's Master, a young prince had rescued her, then disappeared. This time, she had rescued herself.

She had no choice but to go on alone and to rule. And because she had no choice, *I will care for you*, she promised the weary, sleeping land.

Chapter Twenty-two

This spring, Marric thought fondly, Byzantium was a city of mosaics. The great square, with its intricate pattern of flagstones, turned the space between the ancient Temple of Osiris and the recently completed Temple of Isis into one such mosaic. And the worshippers who thronged the square, some in their finest garments, others in robes of mourning, were another, living mosaic, even in the dark. The flames of the torches that many bore flickered like lamplight on the golden-tiled mosaics within.

Five days ago, throughout the city, all the fires had been quenched. For this was the time of the *Sed* festival, which commemorated death and rebirth. Though the holiday was sombre, now, during the ritual called the 'Lighting of the Flame', the city glittered once again, a fit reflection of Pharaoh's greatness, and of the gods'.

The Temple of Osiris shone with the greatest mosaics in all Byzantium. On one side of the massive, sloping wall, glittering tiles of golds, oranges and silver showed the Boat of a Million Years in its passage through the underworld and out into a dawn sky, triumphant in rose, indigo and electrum. Wrought on the opposite wall was the tale of Isis' descent to the netherworld. Stripped of her divine robes and crown, the goddess' form was very white against tiles that became darker and darker until Osiris was restored and stood in glory, a mighty statue clad in golden grave-wrappings that outshone any triumphal robe worn by prince, princess, priest or emperor.

He had seen much of those mosaics during the past five days of the *Sed* festival, and more of the halls and thronerooms especially (and – it was a pity, albeit unavoidable – expensively) built for the occasion. Though *Sed* festivals must be held at least every thirty years, it had been less than that since the last one. Marric himself had missed it, stationed somewhere along the frontiers, as he had been for much of his military career while his father lived.

But the priests remembered, as they remembered everything else.

For five days, the city had held the solemn spring festival: first, the processions under the aegis of Hathor in which Marric had had to wear the belt that bore her four faces and, in an absurd survival from the very-longest-ago, a bull's tail. But even that ritual paled before the one for which Marric now prepared. This time, he wore a stiff, archaic cloak, a garment that well expressed his mood as he walked towards the sanctuary of the wolf-god Upwaut, he who opens the way from earth to the Horizon.

It was not, however, he, Marric, or he, Upwaut, who opened the way, Marric thought. It was Olwen. Marric himself might mime death and symbolic rebirth; but Olwen had chosen to undergo both, or suffer the one in the hopes of the second. *At least I can share that much with you, walk with you, my spirit and yours, as far as I dare*, Marric thought. Though the *Sed* festival should have been held in early spring, yet, because Marric had had it in his power to change the date of the festival, he had done so – as far as he dared – to the time that, in Penllyn, they called Beltane.

He had had pleasant, occasionally passionate memories of that holiday; but never again, after tonight. Tonight the Druids would be gathering in the nemet: the Druids, his daughter, and – Isis breathe peace upon her – his Queen. Marric's breath came harsh and short, and he wrested his thoughts away from imagining the one sight that he had feared above all others for the many years since he had finally realized that Olwen had always meant to turn queensblade upon herself.

Ahead of Marric danced a priestess who clapped and called, 'Come! Bring it!' as he moved forward, holding flail, sceptre and a tiny scroll, in a careful, ceremonial walk. Before priestess and priest-king, a priest clad in hides bore the wolf-standard of the Opener of the Way. They turned into the temple. Now, the rituals required that Marric withdraw. Within the ritual, that meant symbolic death. After all, the Empire was old, the priesthood older still, and far more pragmatic. Too pragmatic to sacrifice Emperor and Pharaoh to renew the land.

Tell that to Penllyn, where they were not pragmatic at all, Marric thought. And thank the gods that ritual required he keep his face immobile.

Instead of retreating, however, Marric held his ground. 'I have run,' he cried, 'holding the secret of the Two Partners, the will that my father has given me before Geb. I have passed through the land and touched the four sides of it. I traverse it as I wish.'

Ahead of him, he could see his heirs. Prince and Princess shone as bravely as their honour guard. Even from his station at the front of the temple, Marric could sense the aura of joy, of sensuality, and promise that united them. He could be satisfied with that, at least. He heard delighted murmurs as they passed, hand in hand as they most often were. Had he dared disrupt the ritual, he too would have turned round to look at his son and . . . yes, Elen *was* his daughter now. Alexa had healed the old loss. The winter now past had been the easiest in memory, even in the memory of the ancient priest who now stood before the great statue of Osiris.

Gone were the leopard pelts, the gold sistrum and the turquoise and carnelian gems. The priest wore but a simple white robe, almost shroud-like, a twin to the garment that Marric himself wore. He too had laid aside the splendour of his office: *uraeus*-adorned crown, crook and flail, the sombre bravery of amethyst, ruby and amber at fingers, wrist and neck.

For this was the ceremony of renewal of his powers as king and – poor enough imitation that he was – priest.

Both of them had chosen to hold these last rituals in the great temple. Marric and the high priest would follow the trail of Osiris, step by step, in the ritual, down to the nether world and up into the glory at the Horizon, reflected here, in the temple in Byzantium, in brilliant, faceted stone. Chant and incense teased at his senses, then overwhelmed them quite: he was sinking into trance, his breathing falling, as if by instinct, into the rhythms that he had learned so many years ago. The chants ringing out from massed choirs of priests and acolytes took on added subtle harmonies that, somehow, he had never noticed in all of his years of performing this ritual, invoking rebirth for himself and his city.

Behind him, Mor stirred. Marric knew that he had received a sheaf of barley from Elen. She was doubly fruitful for the city, Mor had told him just yesterday, and he rejoiced at it. His son's footsteps padded down the temple towards Marric: tread of a panther, eyes of the hawk whose sigil he now assumed, bearing the barley that was the symbol of Osiris' resurrection.

The ancient priest, his skin resembling the finest, oldest of papyri, gestured, and a sub-priest threw another handful of myrrh on the nearest brazier. Myrrh: that was for death, for mourning, for embalming. Pharaoh was dead. Osiris was dead and should rise in verdant splendor. Marric should withdraw now, to emerge fully robed and be carried in a boxlike litter to the chapel of Horus, lifelong his patron, where he would once again receive crook, flail and sceptre, and where he must shoot an arrow in each of four directions before the final procession and proclamation of rebirth.

But – the thought pierced the haze of trance, chant, sistrum and scent – Olwen would have no such rebirth, at least not in the flesh. Olwen! He had thought that as the day passed, and no hint of what she had planned had touched him . . . perhaps Gwenlliant had succeeded where he had failed and persuaded her mother not to enter the hawthorn nemet for one last time; perhaps Gwenlliant had even twisted the magic to her own designs. He could always hope, and, as the day wore on towards twilight and this festival, he had dared to.

Had those hopes been premature?

Pain lanced through Marric's left side. As he watched, his hand began to open, nerveless, and he forced its grip to tighten on the scroll that he held. Then the pain returned, and he gasped and fought not to double over or sink on to his knees. Sweat poured down his face and dampened the shroudlike folds of his white robe. The heavy silk undertunic of black and silver brocade was choking him, but he dared not disrupt the solemnity by tearing at the tunic's austerely high collar. His hands seemed to freeze, and he felt himself trembling. He swallowed, and that hurt too, as if a knife stood in his breast.

Up ahead of him, the Osiris priest seemed to multiply. Two, then three of the old man shimmered in Marric's gaze, which narrowed and darkened. Never mind the sanctity of the ritual, which had not been interrupted for as long as Byzantium stood. Perhaps even Alexander had participated in it at Siwah; long before that in Egypt, while the pyramids were a-building – *and the sphinx was yet a kitten*, Marric told himself in what he knew was a pathetic attempt at levity – priests had shown adoring congregations their god and whispered the sacred, secret words: 'I am Barley.'

Pain stabbed through his chest, and he staggered back as if he had taken a knife in the heart. His mouth opened in a square of pure anguish, but no sound forced itself out. All breath, all movement had been arrested, except for the pain, worse than any he had felt since, twenty years ago, he had trampled the hag at the last battle against Jomsborg. A trickle started at the corner of his mouth: too salt to be sweat, and he felt himself topple . . .

. . . into a swirl of green leaves, of white flowers, their petals falling, turning crimson, falling on to a bed of green leaves while, somewhere, a young girl struggled neither to weep nor tremble, and a woman who was not yet old held aloof, her eyes as tearless as Marric's own. Even as he watched, those eyes widened into exaltation, focusing on the sheen of deadly metal as it plunged down . . . He had a moment's too-vivid awareness of tall, dark-leaved trees, of white-robed watchers, their eyes compassionate . . . and then nothing at all.

Sweet suffering Osiris, Marric thought, was this the pain You felt when Set's knives pierced You? Using the new senses that had come upon him at the culmination of the *Sed*-ritual, he called frantically, *Olwen! Beloved!*

Or, asked the quiet, inexorable voice that had goaded Marric since childhood, was what he felt the mortal agony of Olwen as she turned queensblade on herself in the hawthorn nemet?

He struggled to groan, but his throat seemed to be filled with blood, and he gagged on it as he sagged to his knees, his hands tearing at the fabric at his chest, as if they could remove the dagger . . . there was no blade, no dagger . . . but he felt its rough-carved hilt burn into his palms, remembered armsmaster's words that a lifetime's endurance could not leach of pain. 'Pull out the blade, and the man dies quickly.'

He could not pull out the blade. But he must, if Olwen were to live. . . . if Stephana were to live. He must!

You must not! came the cry.

'Father, no!' Elen's voice, terrified and grief-stricken. Slippered feet ran forward – *be gentle with my grandson!* Marric longed to warn her, and she was propping his head against her breast, aware, with a curious, twinned awareness, that Olwen rested against another strong, lithe young shoulder, and that the girl who held her was weeping too.

'It is Beltane,' Elen whispered to the Prince, kneeling resplendent at her side. Marric heard his breath catch, just this side of a sob. Mor. His poor son, who must learn now to accept that his mother had just slain herself. They were more truly mated than Marric would have thought, for her sacrifice to be stopping his . . .

'Stop it!' Elen cried. 'Listen to me. Come back to me! You cannot join her—'

A crown of golden hair above amber eyes, flickering and changing, even as he gazed, to silvered braids and smoke-blue eyes . . . both smiling at him. *Come away.*

'No!' Elen's voice was shrill with anger and grief. 'By your curse, by your life, by your oaths, I call you back!' she cried. He felt her bend over him, heard her mutter, 'My mother breathed life back into her brother; perhaps I—' she broke off. 'Father, come back to us!' she cried, then began to weep. Mor took up the prayer, seconded by the weak voice but sure power of the ancient priest.

The faces rushed past him, following the trail of leaves and rose petals down into . . . blackness, silence, peace.

Peace? No, Marric could not enter there, not any place wherein peace remained. *Are you trying to flee again?* came the acid mental 'voice' of the high priest. He lashed out with sudden quick fury.

'Get me wine!' he heard Elen command. 'Sweet Isis be thanked, he begins to stir, to warm . . . ah, look at his poor hands . . .'

'Look to the priest!' Mor cried, then dashed forward to catch the elderly high priest before he fell to the pavement.

'We'll lose them both!' Mor's voice, and there was fear in it! Fear? His son? Then Marric had failed at his tasks and must . . .

'By your curse, by your duty . . .' Elen's voice, hard with fear and desperation, broke ' . . . by your love, come you back, Father, come you back!'

She sobbed rackingly. She might hurt herself and the child, Marric thought. Sighing, he let his eyes drift open. His lids were terribly heavy, and the light, splintering from the thousands upon thousands of tesserae, hurt, but not as much as the sight of Osiris in Majesty, the Boat of a Million Years rising into the dawn behind him.

'Like your mother . . .' he muttered at Elen. 'Simply drag me back from peace. If I did not love you, that would be a hard offence to forgive.'

'Do you deserve peace?' Elen retorted through her tears. Strange. Alexa had asked him the same question. Or perhaps it was not that strange.

'How is . . . the priest?' Odd how his voice rasped. He had fought all day and not felt this drained.

For the first time in his life, he saw the high priest of Osiris make a gesture that was not premeditated and perfectly controlled. Though his hand shook, he held it out to Marric, who flung himself on to his belly beside the old man, took his hand in both of Marric's own, and winced as the blisters on his palms pressed against the hard bones and raised tendons of the high priest's hand.

Laying his cheek against it, he tried to will strength into the priest. He had no strength to give, and no tears either: thus, ultimately, he simply lay there, his face pressed into the high priest's cupped hands until, tenderly, Mor helped the under-priests separate the two of them and bear them out of the temple into the inner precincts.

'Let me help you carry him.' That voice, harsh with suppressed grief, belonged to Caius Marcellinus, who, for the first time in his life, broke ranks and stepped into the ritual, interrupted now past repair. He knelt, and just as Marric had done with the high priest's hand, Marcellinus laid his wet face against his Emperor's lax fingers. *After all these years, Caius mine, of fighting against and for one another, we are brothers. Do not fear, I shall not die on you this time. Not now that Elen has pulled me back.*

Sweet Goddess, the command in that child's voice and hands! If he followed Olwen out into peace, out where Stephana no doubt would greet them both, she would weep; and she carried an heir whose health must not be endangered.

There had been a time when Marric would have fought like a starving leopard for his own life; he remembered, but how distant that now seemed!

His eyes rolled open as they carried him down the corridors towards the priests' quarters. They ached, and he had no tears to spare, no tears at all, for his wife, who had sacrificed herself. 'Your mother . . .' he whispered to Mor, who pressed Marric's shoulder.

Mor nodded, then cleared his throat, so Marric would know that he had been understood. 'I am sorry, my son.'

His head rolled to one side. To his astonishment, he saw that the Osiris priest mouthed the same words . . . but at him. And when the men who bore his pallet started down a corridor different from that chosen by Marric's bearers, he held up a frail hand that Marric reached out to clasp.

He knew these precincts. Years ago, he had strode boldly down the centre of their corridors – brave with paintings of the Eye, of hieroglyphs of the founding of the city – towards the high priest's quarters, determined to claim initiation, gain it, and return to his safe house, preferably before noon. It had taken half a life for him to realize how preposterous his hopes had been. Incongruously, he laughed.

The old priest's eyes lit.

'At how foolish I was, so many years . . .' Marric started to explain, and the old man's eyes smouldered more intensely. Hard to believe, when one stared into those eyes, how old, how weak, feeble and febrile, the priest must be. He was naught but pale skin stretched taut over fine bone.

The bearers took one more turn.

'Stop!' Marric husked. The rituals. They were broken and must be resumed. 'I must be robed, must enter the litter . . . let me down,' he ordered Caius.

To his astonishment, the old general turned towards Mor, who dashed one hand over his eyes.

'He has to try,' whispered the boy . . . no, his son was no longer a boy.

Gently, Caius Marcellinus eased Marric down on to his feet. He flung a hand out against the wall, hoping for its support and for restoration from the coolness of the stone; but his knees buckled and the stone was warm, almost as warm as flesh.

Up, up, *damn you!* he commanded himself. But for the first time in all his years as Emperor, he was disobeyed; and, after years of testing and of fears, his body finally betrayed him, and he sank to the floor.

But there was one more thing that he could do. He gestured at the crown. 'Take it,' he whispered to Mor. 'Take my place. Father and son; we are one creature in this.'

'Father, I can't leave you.' His son stared at Marric, begging for a solution. *That would require magic; and I have ever been a failure where magic was concerned*, he thought. He tried to lever himself up, but fell back, gasping.

'How can I leave him like this?' Mor whispered at Elen. She simply pushed the regalia into his hands, then helped to settle Marric's head against Marcellinus' shoulder. A tear fell on to Marric's face, and he glanced up to see that her face was very white and set. 'I shall be with him,' she whispered. 'You do as he has bid you.'

Mor strode back towards the central temple; Marric's bearers drew him further into its hidden ways.

Down the right-hand way lay the great sarcophagus of basalt and porphyry in which those who were fit dared the path of initiation. Down this middle corridor lay the high priest's rooms. Marric remembered them. Once before, Marric had been laid on a mat and offered a bitter herbal drink that, once again, he shook his head at.

'You need it.' A measure of control had returned to the high priest's voice; as he had before, he reproved Marric, who took up the cup of dark, acrid fluid, and drank.

Words of twenty-five years past flickered through his consciousness. *'It appears that I cannot even bear an initiate's diet.'* he remarked, pulling the words from memory.

'How long,' whispered the priest, answering with memories of his own, 'how long, I should like to know, have you been the high priest of Osiris to decide what you – *you!* – can and cannot bear?'

It seemed to Marric that as the old man talked, as the old man criticized Marric, his voice grew stronger and stronger. *Perhaps if I provoke him, he will recover and live a while longer.*

And do you care if he lives? came the thought. Yes! For he is older than my father, and, since my father passed to his Horizon, he has been priest and father to me. In fact, Marric realized, though his father had always been intent on Marric as his heir, it had been the old priest who had seen Marric as he was – ardent, eager boy; rebellious youth; arrogant warrior; and now, last of all, an emperor.

'Not last of all,' said the priest. 'One more transformation remains?'

'To become an adept-emperor?' Marric made his voice sceptical. 'I have not the virtue of the old priest-kings in me. You saw.' Half a lifetime old, the memory of his humiliation before the basalt sarcophagus in which priests were initiated into the Mysteries heated his cheeks as it always did. 'The instant that I saw the Watcher, I panicked. I am not fit for initiation.'

The priest snorted, a sound so derisive and so familiar that the acid, tearless burning started once again in Marric's eyes.

'*I* decide that. And I never said that you were unworthy. Just premature.' He shut his eyes, as if vastly weary, but, in the next instant, waved away the handful of priests who hovered over him with medicine and prayers. 'Premature,' he added. 'By the Boat and the Horizon, you were ludicrously premature! But now . . .'

Marric shivered, despite the fine fleeces that had been laid over him. 'But now what?'

'But now,' mused the priest, as if he were drifting away from Marric down a river that only he could see, 'but now, I think that your spirit's wings are strong enough for you to fly.'

It was Marric's turn to snort. 'And what for?' he demanded.

'For peace. Not your Empire's peace. Your own.'

The answer was stunning, unexpected, and infinitely desirable. But he had his reply ready. 'Irene said that as long as I wore the crown, I should have no peace.'

'As long as you wore the crown,' agreed the priest. 'Mor is a man grown now, and Helena . . .'

'How do you know?' Marric demanded hotly. 'What makes you so certain that this time I could triumph when last time I barely escaped . . . escaped, that is, with my life, my life and not my integrity. Not a day has passed that I have not felt myself shamed by that day.'

'Shamed? And I was thinking that you had finally abandoned your follies, my son. You, shamed? Not a man in a thousand would have dared what you tried, all unprepared; of those, fewer would have come back to the land of the living. My own son . . .' the old grief, as fresh now as it must have been when first the high priest realized that only a corpse, and not a living son, would be lifted from the sarcophagus.

'How do I know? Blood calls to blood. And we are of one blood, thou and I. My son . . .' the voice lingered over the words. 'We are indeed kin. I am your father's uncle. And *his* father's elder brother.'

If the high priest – whose name Marric had still never learned – was uncle – son of the elder brother – to Marric's father, then, 'You should be Emperor, and not I!' he gasped.

'By blood alone, aye. But by calling, by commitment, and by love: I chose the life I needed; and it drew me here. You, however, have served as Emperor long and well. They of Hind have a saying: Twenty years a child, twenty years a soldier, twenty years the head of a household; and thereafter, it is time to mend one's soul before faring forward. Thus I tell you, Marric, who should have been my son: it is time to fare forward. Neither Byzantium nor Prydein are countries for old men. It is time we admitted that and let our tasks pass to our heirs.'

'To abdicate . . .' It sounded like retreat or, worse yet, abandonment, if not outright defeat. Marric feared the idea, the very word itself as, in all his life, he had feared only magic.

'When you could not walk, when you feared that you could not do what the Empire needed, you passed your crown to your son. I watched: the decision cost you not at all. So, why not let the boy keep it?'

Put that way, the idea seemed so simple, so seductive. Simply let Mor keep what he himself had granted him. Too simple, probably.

Could this be another test? Not so, for the ancient priest was smiling.

'What would I be, if I were not Emperor?' he asked the old man.

'At peace, perhaps?'

He thought of himself crowned, seated in his throne between mechanical lions, a flowering tree at his back, ambassadors prostrate before him. Was it the Empire that he loved, or the vision of himself as its ruler? Empire would survive without him; he had his heir; and his heirs had – let Isis-Hathor be merciful – the promise of a child themselves.

He had fought for that crown. He had bled for it. He had wept for it, then wept no more. And he had served it all his life. Was it not he who had compared it once to a slave's chain. He had worn both, and the crown was far heavier.

It had seemed all eternity until he had freed himself of his slave's chain back in Alexandria.

What if . . . oh, what if he removed the crown now?

Unfamiliar, astonishing tears prickled at the backs of his eyes.

'*As long as you wear this crown, you will never know peace,*' Irene had cursed him. That was the only truth that she had spoken. To serve the crown, he had lost Stephana. He had been willing to abduct his own sister. And in all the years of hard work and occasional glory, he had never once known peace.

He thought that, perhaps, he had finally earned the chance.

'Very . . . well,' the words were a gasp. 'If I abdicate, what then?'

'Then, my son, I shall be your initiator. There is yet enough life in this old man for that. You asked what you would be if you were not an emperor. Once you receive initiation, you will know.'

He had strength enough to relinquish Stephana, to relinquish dream after dream, to stand aside as Olwen sacrificed her life for her realm. He had been given, against all hope, the chance to mend a shame of twenty-five years' standing. Would it be on this challenge that his integrity would quail?

He gasped, then said the words that would give himself away, separate him from what had been the greatest part of his life for almost a generation. 'How will it be accomplished if I choose to abdicate? For I so choose.'

He visualized himself laying aside the serpent crown, letting it rest on a silk-velvet cushion dyed with Tyrian murex and woven with gold thread. He imagined Mor taking it up (as even now he did) and setting it on his head; with his Isis at his side, wearing the great moon crown that Olwen – no, he gasped at the sudden shrewd pain; no, that was wrong, for Olwen was dead now.

His wife was dead, gone to the Horizon . . . no, the Celtoi did not believe that. What, then, did they believe? Did it matter? Soon he would no longer be Emperor.

Tears prickled at his eyelids, made him gasp somewhat; and he fought for control.

'Let them come. Be a child again, Marric.' Even his royal Horus name was gone too. The high priest took a deep breath. When he spoke again, his voice had the resonance of ritual. 'Do you, Marric of Byzantium, Marric son of Antonios, of the line of Alexander, Lord of the Two Lands, renounce the crown?'

He was not making the decision any easier than he had to, Marric thought. He nodded, but a simple nod was not enough for an act of the magnitude that he had described.

'I renounce it,' Marric said finally, and bowed his head.

The tears in his eyes threatened to overflow.

'It is finished then. And it is well finished,' said the priest.

Then, to Marric's horror, he wept: wept for his wife, wept for his children, catapulted prematurely into power, wept for his sister, and for all of the silent, anguished years.

Though he remembered those years as having contained much joy, they must have been underlaid with pain too if he had stored up this amount of grief.

The old priest gestured. Marric heard noises as of a pallet being lifted and moved away down the hall. 'Let your father rest now,' rasped the high priest's voice.

Mor? His son had come back, and needed him? Had he given back his crown, thinking to win release of cares? Then he had been wrong. In telling Mor of his decision, in burdening his son with the crown, Marric faced his hardest task yet.

Best face it now. He opened his mouth to call to him, but only a strangled groan emerged. He rolled on to his belly, biting his wrist against the tearlessness that usually made him sweat with pain, just as he had done all the years of his reign.

But it was tears, not sweat, that rolled down Marric's face now: natural, effortless tears that eased scars that he had long forgotten, and went on for longer than he would have dreamed possible.

Marric, former Emperor of Byzantium, turned his face to the wall of the temple, and he wept.

Chapter Twenty-three

Mor's outrage echoed off the mosaics in the Emperor's study, its doors and windows carefully shut to make eavesdropping marginally more difficult. Ostensibly, Marric admired the mosaics, every tile of which he had known from childhood. Actually, he studied his son as he might study an opposing general. A lifetime of battles fought and won replayed in his mind, tinged now with guilt. Of all of them, he thought, this one had caused him the most anxiety; for if he were to win it and go free, he must defeat his only son, who must then assume Marric's burdens.

Better you learn defeat from one who loves you, son, Marric thought at Mor. But Mor could not hear him, deaf, as always, to powers that were of the spirit, rather than of the mind and body. Mor's wife, Elen, however, turned briefly, awarding Marric a level, understanding blue gaze, unblinking as a cat. *Teaching the lesson of defeat had been hard; watching his son try to master it was worse.*

'Why must you abdicate? This makes no sense!' Mor shouted, slamming both fists down on the carven table that had been a gift from a Persian ambassador. Silver cups rattled, and Elen moved deftly, unobtrusively, to still them as Mor paced up and down in the Emperor's study, a room, clearly, he had neither expected nor wished to inherit for quite a while.

He had staying power, Marric would concede him that, though nothing else.

'*Why* must you abdicate?' his son demanded again. 'And don't talk about your age, either, sir. I've watched you at practise; I've sparred with you, and you're not slowing down. All you have to do these days is ride on to a battlefield. I've seen it. Some poor infantryman screams, "Run, it is the Emperor!" and the officers promptly ask for terms. Set take it, how do you expect me to match that?'

'Which question do you want me to answer first?' Marric asked. 'Or are they both rhetorical?'

The need to be cool, rational, when his son's fear and uncertainty made him want only to hug the . . . no, he was not a lad; he was a prince, a general, and soon to be a father . . . tore at him. Now, Marric was justly, ironically punished for his rejoicing that Mor seemed blind to magic; his son simply could not understand the logic behind Marric's decision to leave his crown behind to seek initiation and peace. *At his age, I wouldn't have understood it, either.*

Mor whirled and glared at him. 'I had hoped to have years yet to learn from you.'

'And so you shall,' Marric said. 'It isn't as if I am going to die. If I had been killed in one of those battles you speak of, you would have had to assume the crown on the battlefield. And then,' he added, 'the Empire's foes would have said, "Look, the cub tries to roar like his father. Let's test his fangs." But if I resign the Empire to you, well, if I do that, they will think that you must be Alexander come again!'

Two long strides brought Mor head to head with Marric. 'That's what I mean. I cannot plan like that yet!' His fists slammed down on the table once again. 'I lack the craft!'

'Then you will learn it!' Marric's fists slammed down beside his son's.

'How can I, if you're not beside me?'

'Now, *that* was a good ploy!'

Elen laughed softly. Immediately, both men whirled to confront her, scowls black on their faces. That made her laugh again. 'You are so much alike,' she explained, and walked over to the window.

'It is stuffy in here,' she said apologetically. 'I was hot.'

No wonder, Marric thought. As Elen's pregnancy advanced, she had refused to wear the starched linens and sheer cottons that a summer in Byzantium made common sense. Instead, when she could, she wore the heavy skirts and tunics that she had brought from Prydein. Given the choice, she dressed as simply as Marric himself. A pity, that was: he enjoyed watching her bloom as her pregnancy progressed.

'Let me open that for you, Ellen,' Mor said. 'It is too heavy for you now.' After years of hearing how strong the women of the Celtoi were, how pregnancy did not hinder them from lifting, fetching, or carrying, Marric watched, amused, as Mor opened the window for Elen, tenderly settled her in a chair, and kissed her sleek, dark hair, which gleamed almost iridescent in the sunlight.

Her interruption – as that crafty child intended! – broke the tension between father and son. 'If you think that your burden is too heavy for you,' deliberately, mercilessly, Marric picked up on his son's words, 'remember that you will have Elen to help you. You should also remember that you *are* my chosen heir. Do you trust my judgement? Then believe that you are fit to rule.'

'Your decision . . . was it that attack you had the day . . .'
Mor's voice almost cracked, 'the day of the *Sed* festival?' Fear
whitened his face. 'What else did the physicians tell you?'

Marric laughed. 'That I am likely to live for many, many
years. But not as an emperor any longer, Mor. You know Irene
death-cursed me never to know peace as long as I ruled. I am
tired, Mor. I have fought throughout my reign so that you might
bring peace. I need that peace too, now.'

Mor turned his back on his father and wife. Guilt stabbed
through Marric, as sharp as the pangs he had felt the day of the
Sed festival and of Olwen's death. *It is not enough that I defeat
my son. Now I must hammer my own slave chains upon him
too.* He would have died to spare Mor pain, any pain but this,
he realized, and shook his head, in grim understanding of the
choice that, years ago, Stephana faced and that, only this year,
Olwen too suffered.

He opened his mouth on an apology, but stopped. Mor had
turned back around, and the expression on the boy's face tore
at him. 'Son of Re,' he said, using the most formal and rarest
of Marric's titles, 'I beg you.'

Damn this business of weeping! The tears always started to
leak out at the wrong time. He reached out and caught his son
by the shoulders lest, in the next instant, the boy tried to drop
to his knees. Set take it, his son should kneel to no one! Marric
set his jaw and blinked fiercely. 'Emperors do not beg, son.
Believe me. It does no good.'

Mor's expression changed little beyond a raised brow that
stabbed Marric to the heart. 'You think that I did not try?' he
asked, hurt turning his voice sharp.

'Did you?'

Gods, did the boy really think that he had let Olwen disappear
into the nemet without trying to fight two sets of gods? He had
even tried to tempt his daughter to defy the gods, and that was
a dangerous habit to lead a child into.

Marric pressed his hand against a sudden ache in his chest.
Then anger rescued him from his sorrow. 'Say that again . . . if
I ever hear that again, tall as you are, father that you are about
to be, emperor as I am about to hallow you, I will thrash you
within an inch of your spoiled life!'

Mor glanced at his wife and flushed. It would go hard on the boy to be shamed in front of Elen.

Marric forced himself to laugh sharply. 'Elen grew up among Celtoi; no doubt, she'll tell you that she's heard far worse, isn't that right, child?'

Elen averted her eyes, unwilling to admit to anything that might let Mor think she sided with her father-in-law against her husband. Good girl! Instead, she glided over to Mor and slipped her arm about his waist.

Hugging her to him, Mor looked down. 'Forgive me, father,' he muttered. Then, clearly, he had to force the words out. 'Has . . . your decision aught to do with mother's death?'

Marric inclined his head, unable to speak at all.

'Father, I am not ready, I've told you that.'

'And I've told you that I shall be with you when you need me.' If he had to, he would beg his son to release him. *Emperors do not beg*, he reminded himself of his own maxim. *But I no longer am an emperor*.

'Mor,' Marric said softly. 'You are young, it's true. But you are young enough to enjoy ruling this Empire. Though I have laboured lifelong to put it in good order, much remains to be done. But the *Sed* festival gave me a sign: it is no longer my burden. I will do what I have to do,' he added. 'And so will you. But I would . . .' damn his own voice for cracking like an unfledged boy's! . . . 'welcome your blessing.'

He would never know whether Elen gave Mor the shove that sent his son forward to embrace him. But they were hugging, thumping one another on the back; Marric could feel Mor's sobs in the muscles of his back. Tears burned down his face, too.

As he held his son, he spoke to Elen. 'You will tell your mother?' he asked.

She nodded. 'Yes, though she will be sad if she does not learn of your action – and your reasons – from you.'

Mor broke out of Marric's embrace. 'How will you explain to Gwenlliant?' he demanded.

Elen flashed Marric a look that clearly meant *let me handle this*. 'Love,' she said, walking over to take Mor's hands in hers, 'after this past Beltane, do you think that Gwenlliant truly needs any explanation? She will understand.'

Marric raised an eyebrow at the girl who, almost imperceptibly, raised her chin at the door. *Thrown out of my own study, by Horus!* he thought. *No, that is not right. It is the* Emperor's *study.*

He walked towards the door, hearing the rustle of Elen's heavy skirts as she turned to her husband, the catch of breath as he swept her up for a long, comforting embrace. He started to close the door gently behind him, then paused. There were no guards, no servants in sight, or, presumably, in earshot; he himself had sent them away.

Though he was no longer emperor to be eavesdropped upon, he himself could listen . . . *eavesdrop upon my own son?* A decent man, he thought, would be ashamed of the idea. Nevertheless, Marric smiled wryly and pressed his back against the door, which he left slightly ajar, just as if he had eavesdropped lifelong. His sister and his daughter (if not his son) would be proud of him.

For a long time, the room was silent. Then Elen gasped and pressed her hands against Mor's chest, pushing him away. 'Let me go, my love.'

'Why do you want me to stop?' Mor asked, his voice husky. He reached for her again, and Marric shut his eyes.

'Because we cannot simply use our bodies to escape what your father has handed us. We must talk about it.'

Mor mumbled something that Marric could not hear. Again, he edged around, hoping to catch a – *have I truly sunk as low as to spy upon my own son?* Though abdication and his son's fears were no matters for humour, he found himself grinning.

Mor sat, hunched over the table, with Elen bending over him. Small as she was, her dark hair flowing down over her shoulders, nevertheless, she seemed protective of her husband.

'Yes, I know how hard it is going to be. But for both of us, not just for you. Mor, beloved, never forget that there are two of us to carry a burden that for most of your father's reign, he carried by himself. And the crown has weighted him down; you have seen it. Regardless of what he says, when he collapsed at the *Sed* festival, I was afraid. Mor, I don't think we have a choice. If you stop – if you *can* stop – him from abdicating, I fear you will become emperor in any case, and soon.'

Mor flinched, and flung up a hand.

'Elen, I am sorry. You have married a coward,' Mor's whisper was chill with self-contempt. 'A selfish coward. I do not want father to die. But Horus guard me, I do not want to rule yet either.'

The girl bent over and kissed his hair. For an instant, she seemed to try to rock him as if he were the child that she had yet to bear. 'Knowing what I am, how can you stand to touch me?' he demanded, pulling away, holding himself rigid.

Rebuffed, Elen straightened up, her eyes flashing.

'Be assured, *husband*, I know what you are. If you did not fear this task, you would be a fool or mad. And I have not wed a coward, a fool, or a madman!' Elen snapped back. 'Mor, quick! Take my hands. Hold on to them, that's right, the wrists too. Now, remember all the times that *this* has saved us when we have been in danger. We were both bred for this, Mor, bred and trained to rule. Somehow, we will survive . . .'

'As long as you are with me,' Mor told her and raised her hands to his lips. Then he took her in his arms, pressing his cheek against her hair. *So then, they will manage*, Marric thought. *She will be his wisdom, and he her courage. Alexa trained that girl well.*

As Elen's words died away into a murmur that quickly changed from comfort to pleasure, Marric smiled and, at last, turned away from their door.

In the inner precincts of the Temple of Osiris, chant rang out joyously through the ancient corridors, counterpointed, as it so often was these days, by a string of objections from Marric. Even as he voiced them, he was aware that he himself had chosen to lay aside his crown, chosen to seek initiation in the temple, chosen to be schooled once again. But it was hard for him to obey after spending a lifetime in command, hard for him to follow after years of successful generalship, and hardest of all to find himself a slow, reluctant student, when teachers had always praised his quickness and abilities.

'I will not take priests' vows,' he announced now, too defiant by half, he knew, for a man in his position. *Especially not vows of celibacy*, he qualified his refusal mentally. 'And I certainly will not shave my head.'

The high priest sat upright despite the obvious frailty that caused him to wrap himself in shawls even during the height of the summer. Except for the fingers of one hand, which stroked the long, elegant back of a purring cat, he was motionless. The chant rang down the corridor, but he ignored the music that he once had led: like Marric, he had resigned all offices.

'The gods forbid,' he observed, 'that we try to barber the lion.' The cat rolled over and cast a baleful blue gaze at Marric. Light winked from the gold earring that gleamed in one notched ear, shone in its eyes, and began to kindle in the ancient, deep-socketed eyes of the priest, like a guttering flame seen through thick, dark glass. 'Your vanity is harmless. Keep it, my son.'

That subdued Marric for the instant. He had expected, perhaps hoped, to be challenged, and to buoy himself up by sweeping aside any petty resistance just as he had when, as Emperor, he had swept aside all opposition in the high, imperious wake of his will. But the priest's very composure made him feel as if he had hurtled against a door, determined to batter it down with his shoulder, only to find it opening in welcome. Words and thoughts stumbled through the gap that the priest had opened, and paused.

The high priest gently laid the cat aside and started to rise. When Marric made as if to assist him, he waved him dismissively back to the low stool on which he sat. Slowly, painstakingly, he moved until he stood at Marric's back. Throughout his life, there were but few people whom Marric trusted at his back: his father, his children, Olwen and Alexa, at times, Caius, during battles, Stephana, and now the high priest.

The old man touched Marric's shoulders and silently began to rub the tension from them. Never before, since the years when he had chastised a fidgeting princeling, had the old man volunteered to touch him. The aged, fragile hands were surprisingly warm and strong.

His very lack of resistance and his calling Marric 'my son' disarmed him further. The old man had lost a son to the very ritual for which Marric now prepared. That son, he was sure, had learned and obeyed readily, and would not have panicked at the sight of the Watcher as Marric himself had done. *I am like my son*, he realized. *I too fear cowardice worse than pain or death.*

'If I fail,' he whispered, his head down so that his words could scarcely be heard, 'if I fail, what happens?'

The hands soothing the knots from his scarred shoulders barely paused, though Marric knew that his muscles had turned as hard as porphyry from tension.

'You will not fail.'

Marric rose in one fluid, easy motion. 'I gave my son Mor better advice than that before his first battle; and all his enemies could do to him was thrust a sword through his gut!'

The cat on the high priest's chair purred, and Marric felt his anger – lifelong his camouflage for fear – evaporate. The air in the priest's cell was warm, stirred ceaselessly, gently, by an unseen agent; he had broken into a light sweat . . . just as he had that time before he became emperor when he had come, all brashness and fury, to the high priest and demanded to be initiated then and there.

How could he have been so stupid? That memory had the power to make him writhe, especially now that he realized the magnitude of his risk. *I could not have risked initiation as an emperor*, he told himself. *Had I failed, the omens for Byzantium would have been dire.*

– *You call* that *reassurance?* – came the priest's thought.

Thinking back, perhaps he had sought initiation for the power he had hoped it would give him to use against Irene. Or, just possibly, he had wanted it as one more bond with Stephana. Sweet goddess, sweet lady – he had always confused Stephana, with her delicate, lunar beauty and her subtle strength, with the Goddess; and she had died for his confusion. He had never forgotten her, but now, he hoped, he understood her, as he had never done before. His love for her had been lifelong; hers had been the love of a creature who stands poised for a great journey, yet who turns at the threshold to glance back, perhaps to caress a much-loved pet (as the high priest now stroked his cat) before walking out into the night.

Lovely, wounded Stephana: that swine of an overseer that he had killed in Alexandria had been right about one thing. She did seem to him to be made of silver . . . like the image that glowed in the inmost shrine of Isis. And now he had Olwen to remember too, Olwen who was all fire and life and green leaves – though her leaves had fallen last spring.

'Never question your genius for life,' the priest said, repeating words from that very meeting so much now in Marric's thoughts. 'It is your greatest gift.'

Marric rounded on the man, again aware of his age. He was little more than a collection of stick-like bones and tendons, joined by the parchment skin and the blazing spirit that transfigured his skeletal face and form into a timeless, sculptural beauty. The cat purred once more and the chant grew louder, more exultant. Ramping at the limits of Marric's awareness was what he thought of as the rest of the old man's entourage: a jackal, a hawk, a sleeping serpent, all bathed in the gentle lunar glow of this cell. Already, he realized, he was able to see halfway into that other world that he must walk if, after a lifetime spent at war with his birthright, he were to achieve it.

Thirty-odd years ago, he had treasured the gift for life of which the priest spoke. Now, he almost feared it. What if it forced him back into his flesh when his soul sought to range freely over the Planes?

Why did the old priest not speak? Perhaps he was dreaming. Old men often fell into such slumbers. Old men? Marric himself was now at the age where he might have done so after too lavish a feast . . . the *old* Emperor, growing lazy, growing sleepy and fat after his years of battle . . . had he not chosen this way instead. And better so, he told himself. Lay his gold on one single chance, and either triumph or go out in a blaze of lightning. Thus he had always done.

Maybe the priest remembered his son too. Why had that man not survived initiation? The words trembled at the tip of Marric's tongue, but he forced them back guiltily. A decent man would not ask such a question. But he was not a decent man; he was a badly frightened one. He himself did not know what it was, thank Osiris, to lose a son, but Caius did: just one, out of his eight, but he still mourned the lad, still fought and refought the battle in which he had been slain.

'You want to know why my son died, don't you?' the priest said.

Marric flushed and looked down, ashamed.

'It was not, please believe me, that my son was weak. From the time that he entered temple service, I knew that his spirit burned too hotly. Life in the world might have anchored him, but he was, after all, my son, of *my* line; and I well-knew why I had renounced my own claim upon the serpent crown. Once he released his hold upon his body and stepped out on to the Planes, he simply saw no reason to return. And thus, he did not. I do not call that failure,' said the priest, 'but triumph.'

Marric grimaced.

'Yes, but for yourself, for your line and your father's, such would be a failure. Do you understand me yet? *Your* line is tied to the earth, therefore fittest to rule it.'

He paused, as if allowing Marric to meditate upon his words. Then, almost in a whisper, he continued, 'Death during initiation is a quicker death than most, but harder and more frightening. I saw my son's face when we lifted the lid of the sarcophagus aside. He looked transfigured. But I have seen others, too. Some screamed and frothed at the mouth before they smothered; one ran mad. Well,' he replied to Marric's hand, thrown up as if acknowledging a hit in sword practise, 'you did ask.'

'Does the Watcher devour them?' he rasped, almost in a whisper. He could imagine how the lid would scrape away from the tomb itself, how the priests would lift out the contorted, macerated husk, then wash down the stone to prepare it to receive its next . . .

'Stop it!' cried the priest. 'Turn such thoughts aside.'

'Lest I bring them into being?' Marric asked sardonically.

To his alarm, the priest nodded.

'Another question,' he murmured. 'Those who fail. Does aught remain of them? Of their souls, I mean?' Once he had met a magus, practically the only Persian whom he had ever trusted. The man had been one of the most popular – and, astonishingly, most honest – ambassadors in Byzantium, which he had left to face combat with a demon. If he failed, he had told Marric once, after too much wine, the body's death was the best that he could hope for, and annihilation of his soul far more likely.

'My son would not have taken such a risk,' said the high priest. 'We both knew that he would probably not return to incarnation. But I saw his face, remember, when we moved aside the stone. And it was not the face of a man who had lost his soul. Nothing good is lost forever, I believe that. But, Marric, I promise you, you shall not fail.'

After the many tearless years, Marric now found it far too easy to weep. He leaned his brow against the stone wall, his hand tracing the wing of a hawk carved into it until his eyes stopped burning. The pressure of callused finger against smooth stone reassured him. A faint rustle, as if of a falcon's wings, drew his attention, and he glanced up sharply. But, though he scanned the room as if it were enemy territory, he saw only the priest, calmly seated, patiently waiting for Marric to return to his lessons, and the cat, which purred and pressed against his leg.

'You shall not fail, Marric, because you are now my heir. All that I have will be yours, if you will but consent to learn it – and to sit down!'

The command was absurd in this context. Marric grinned, sat, and steadied his breathing, slowed it, and, moments later, had entered a deep, anodyne trance.

The cat purred about his legs, and all through the temple, the chant that was the anthem for the coronation of Marric's son swelled in triumph.

Chapter Twenty-four

The autumn winds blew from Asia and across the pavement that stretched before the Temple of Osiris. Clouds scudded in their train, amber from the setting sun, pierced by the spires of Byzantium and the comforting shape of the dome that crowned the newly complete Temple of Isis. The Golden Horn had never looked quite as golden, quite as precious to the man who strode across the marble slabs.

A cry from overhead made him glance up sharply. A hawk circled high above him, sunlight glinting off its wings and breast. Though the winds were chill and the man wore only a simple kilt, he paused, drawing himself up as if he faced an emperor. He raised his hands to the gleaming raptor, who swooped down almost to eye level. The light that surrounded it grew brighter and greater, then spilled over to encompass the tall, still man with the scarred back, who watched the hawk until it screamed and flew away.

For a moment longer, Marric stood, until a gust of wind drew his mind back. His shoulders ached from the cold. Well enough: he shut his eyes, breathed deeply and rhythmically, summoning warmth. But there was no need to waste energy that he would need tonight, he thought. Nor any need to waste more time.

He had said his farewells just as if he went into a battle in which he was uncertain of victory: had finally received Mor's forgiveness for absenting himself for his son's coronation; had embraced Elen, cautious because of the life that she carried. He had even visited his white bear, old now, its fur thinning, its bones evident despite the heavy padding of muscle and fat. But the cold had begun to revive it, and it had risen to its full ten-foot height as Marric had come in, growling a welcome and inviting him with massive, outstretched paws to come and wrestle.

Twenty-five years of tussling with his white bear, and he had never had a scratch. *Ah, old friend*, Marric had told him, *it is too late in the year now, but this spring, when the Bearmaster comes down from the North, you will have company. Perhaps a female, eh? Would you sire a cub or two before you set off on your own journey across the ice? You're strong; you could last for years. As could I . . . I hope.* The bear moaned happily and hugged his special friend, almost, but not quite, cracking his ribs. Then, man and bear released one another, the bear to return to whatever dreams of ice, prey and mates pleased him most, Marric to turn back to the temple to prepare for his initiation.

He returned to his cell and bathed hastily, knowing that priests and underpriests would come for him at sundown. He had expected almost bowel-loosening fear. Instead, a kind of quiet spread out from some previously unknown centre, flooding over him. These last moments of solitude reminded him of sea battles after the orders were given and his ships manoeuvred into position, when all that he could do was wait to see if his plans were better than his adversary's. And this was no battle. He had no adversary, the high priest kept reminding him.

Marric chuckled, a deep, rich sound incongruous in the tiny, barren cell. Knowing how much more he had to learn, he himself would have been glad to postpone his trial, but now it was the priest who insisted upon haste. Considering how the old man had failed over the summer, that was understandable. He had already waited half a normal lifetime too long to initiate Marric.

He drew a deep breath, mildly annoyed that it came out somewhat shaky. The evening chants echoed down the corridor. He had time for perhaps one last meditation before the procession arrived. He glanced around the cell, scrupulously clean, but bare of any ornaments beyond a crimson rose, its petals full-blown and starting to fade, and a green branch. He sprinkled water over both of them, then, tenderly, he touched them, savouring the feel of life beneath his fingers. All summer, such things had aided him in his meditations. If the high priest suspected what they meant to him, he had kindly let the matter pass.

Light winked from overhead and drew Marric's attention to his hand. How could he have forgotten the ring that shone there, the ring of his union with the Empire? He had worn it since he was acclaimed; its twin gleamed on Mor's hand even now.

The chant grew louder and louder, rising as the priests neared his door. They would be carrying the high priest in a litter, he supposed, assuming that the old man permitted it. He tried not to think of them as a funeral procession in which he would walk to his tomb. The sarcophagus that he must enter was no tomb but, instead, a portal to a different kind of life. *Sweet Goddess, let it be so!* he prayed hastily. His breathing had quickened once again, and he slowed it.

Once again, light glinted on the ring of his coronation. He

stared into the depths of the huge, dark amethyst, carved with the hawk-sigil, but he found no visions there. How should he? That ring represented his past: a sign of long, honourable labours, that was true, but of labours that were now complete. Sounding out now, counterpointing the chant, came the rattle of a sistrum and the silvery tones of flutes and cymbals. They would not play such instruments at funerals, now, would they? Priests regarded initiation as a joyous occasion.

He glanced down at his ring. Could he take it with him into the crypt, as a talisman and reminder of his courage? Abruptly, the stone appeared to turn dark, lifeless.

'Just as I thought,' Marric said.

As the procession reached the hanging mat that served his cell as a door, Marric pulled off the ring and let it roll on to the table beside the rose and the green branch. An underpriest rolled up the mat, and Marric stepped out to salute the high priest in his carved and gilded carrying chair.

Though the priests were splendidly robed, Marric himself wore only a linen kilt. How not? To the priests' way of thinking, he had yet to be born into their life. He suppressed an impulse to the sort of bleak humour with which he had always greeted battles, but saw the high priest's eyes kindle, responding to what he had considered unsuitable to speak. To Marric's astonishment, the old man almost grinned. *My uncle, I wish we could have been of an age*, he thought, which *did* wrest a grin from him. Though his smile made him look like a death's head, there was no mistaking the warmth in it.

Then the high priest gestured to his bearers, who set off again. The chant resumed. Marric let the procession sweep him into itself, and followed the high priest down the twists and concealments of the corridors, always down, and into the temple's core.

The room in which lay the basalt and porphyry sarcophagus of his ordeal was small and square. Older than the rest of the temple, its stonework did not shine with its own light. Instead, attendants thrust two torches into heavy, stubby sconces set into blocks at the wedge-shaped door. The torchlight wavered with that movement, then flared up, red at first, then refining itself to yellow and, at last, to nearly pure white. The light sent shadows dancing over the lid of the sarcophagus where Osiris, in his wrappings, received adoration, where Isis in her moon crown stood beside Horus, waiting for Marric.

The chanting swelled. Under its influence, Marric took a step within the room. Involuntarily, his thoughts recoiled, fled far above that place far underground to the city itself of towers and fortresses, where light gleamed hearteningly in each window, then outside the walls to the sea, to the borders of Empire. He had known many things, many places in his lifetime, but their centre lay far below, in this tiny, rough-hewn chamber.

Now the chant began to fade. The high priest himself watched Marric. He could still refuse the test. Long ago, he had stood here, he had insisted on standing here, and he should have refused it. The high priest gestured, and the chant died. He would not have it said that music seduced any candidate into the basalt tomb. If Marric entered it, he must do so of his own will.

Torchlight blazed up still further and cast light on the figure carved within the tomb itself, just where a body would be placed: a serpent, crowned and winged. That was the sigil of triumph and enlightenment. If Marric chose, henceforward, it – rather than the hawk – would be his sigil. The hawk circled, ever-restless, ever-hunting: it knew no peace. But this creature had the peace of the Horizon, a peace that Marric craved.

He entered the chamber and laid himself down in the sarcophagus. He had time for astonishment that its stone did not chill his back. He took one last, deep breath, cast a final, near-frantic glance about the room. As the strongest of the underpriests levered the sarcophagus' lid over his face, he saw the high priest raise a hand in blessing. – *Remember*, – the thought entered his mind, – *you will not be alone.* –

His senses, honed to wildcat sharpness, fastened on the grating of rock against rock, the smell of incense and ancient stone, the rasp of his own breathing. Light exploded in his head as his eyes protested the darkness of the tomb.

And Marric remembered his first battle, when all the drill, all the practises, the thrashings, the fears suddenly melded into grace and skill. *I understand this too!* he thought.

His mind's frantic quest for light subsided; his body's hasty, wasteful breathing slowed. Marric moved slightly, shifting on the warm stone as he might turn more comfortably in his own bed, drew three deep breaths, and then freed himself of that time and that place.

Marric found himself standing in what seemed like a gigantic sphere, though where its walls began, he did not know. Instinctively, he knew that he stood facing east. Behind him, the sphere glowed, as a sunset more splendid than any he had ever imagined while he walked within the prison of his body and his sense, turned the world into a gigantic fire opal. Cool water lapped at his ankles, and he glanced down. Nacre gleamed beneath the waters: he stood in the shallows now, on the shore of an unimaginable sea.

He was not imagining this place. This, he knew, was the Horizon. Once before, he had seen it, had seen the two pillars, one of jet, one of alabaster, that loomed up forever without visible bases of capitals. Then, he had prostrated himself before a pair of gods who stood between those pillars. Now, the space between them was empty.

Where was that divine pair and its shadowy court now?

The last time that Marric had come this way, memories of his life had assailed him, and he had fought them. Now, however, his only thought was that he must once again receive blessing from the God and Goddess who had, years ago, restored him to life. Nothing else mattered.

He glanced up, hoping that the hawk might come to guide him, but no shrill hunting cry pierced the serenity of wave and sky. How could he expect it? Marric thought. That visitation at sunset when he returned to the temple had been the hawk's farewell to him.

No barrier rose against him as he strode towards the pillars. Instead, he heard baying and howling, as if some watchdog sensed an intruder and came to drive it off. Watchdog? Marric thought. Say rather jackals, for a pack of them came toward him from the left.

Some instinct told him that once he passed between the two pillars, he would be safe. His memories of hounds, of hunts, assured him that if he showed no fear, the pack would pass him by, but if he ran, they would hunt him and pull him down. He kept walking towards the pillars, which seemed to grow no closer with every step that he took. In fact, were they retreating from him? Could that truly be?

'I have not done evil to mankind,' he found himself chanting, 'nor have I harmed animals, nor committed falsehood in the place of truth.'

His voice took on greater and greater strength as he prayed. The jackals whined, then subsided, to slink at his heels. Gradually, even the pillars towards which he marched seemed to stop their retreat.

Memories of past battles, of ships dying in flame, of men screaming, their mouths gouting blood, of sharp-edged weapons thrust at his heart, and more fearful memories of chains and darkness rose up from the sand to assail him. *Master of no man, least of yourself. Give way!* they seemed to cry.

Marric set his teeth at those memories. He had won those battles. He had freed himself and his friends. He had even mastered himself, finally, and conquered his fear of the darkness. *I am a match for my memories*, he thought, just as he had thought the last time he had dared this journey.

But he was older now. Self-mastery had brought him humility, if nothing else. The pillars seemed to be closer. He felt as if he had been marching towards them for hours, but many times throughout his life, he had endured forced marches. He could survive this one. Still, as he approached them, he continued his prayers. 'I have not known evil, nor have I acted wickedly.' Ten more steps! Ahead of him, the jet and the alabaster appeared to glow with an inner light . . . welcoming him?

'I have not caused misery or affliction, nor have I done what is abominable to God.'

'– *Have you not?* –' came a voice that caused Marric to recoil in a passion of terror and guilt.

Between the pillars, either to welcome a guest or to turn away the intruder that, abruptly, Marric felt himself to be stood Kynan, bard and Druid. His broken harp was slung over his shoulder, and the wound that Marric had dealt him in haste and disastrous error still dripped blood.

He reeled, and the opalescent sphere that was the Horizon

and his testing ground seemed to shake. Marric found himself struggling for breath . . . he was stifling, he had to get out . . . in an instant, this place that was but a hallucination of a mind starved for air would break apart, and he would awake to madness . . . or not awake at all.

Now another figure joined Kynan. 'Did you really expect to elude my curse so easily?' Irene's voice! Even after so many years, he knew it. She held out her hand, and a youth limped over to take it, his posture just as wretched, his mouth as petulant as Marric remembered. 'Is that not so, my darling? Now, at least, we shall have our revenge.' They moved to stand before the figure of Kynan. Hand in hand, they advanced upon Marric.

Oh no, you won't! Marric thought. He had been justified in taking the throne that was rightfully his from a usurper. And, if he had assumed bloodguilt because of Alexa's killing of their half-brother, he had paid for it, time and again. *This is illusion*, he told himself, and took a step forward.

They vanished, as he thought that they might.

But Kynan remained, and his terror returned. Of all of the things Marric had ever done that woke him in the night, sweating and remorseful, of all the foolish, wanton, or deliberately brutal acts that he had committed as man and emperor, the slaying of a bard and Druid who sought only to defend his queen was surely the worst. Even Stephana had recoiled from him.

The Druid held a reddened hand to his chest, caught the blood that dripped there, and hurled it, as he had done so long ago, in Marric's face. The fire, ah, the burning! he gasped; and cracks formed and widened in the opalescent sky.

That is not how it was! Marric told himself. *Kynan forgave me, even as he died. He flung his blood upon me, not as a curse, but to make me see clearly.*

The 'ground' began to rock, and Marric stumbled to his knees. '*Let me see clearly once more!*' he begged the figure of the Druid, his judge and, in this place, his adversary, his Watcher.

The figure nodded. Kynan had forgiven Marric. But had Marric ever truly forgiven himself? Or had he gone through his life priding himself on the drama of being a man accursed, barred from his birthright, even as he despised himself for the fears — not the blood curses — that, in truth, kept him from it?

Throughout his life, he had played many roles: rebel, warrior, slave, lover, emperor. *But the play is over now, Marric. Take off the mask and see clearly.*

He grinned at 'Kynan'. As he recalled now, he and the Druid had always liked one another, even though their goals made them seem to be enemies.

Take off the mask. He rose from his knees. The tremors ceased and, gradually, the sky resumed its former splendour. Crystalline music seemed to well from the water of the sea itself, while the silvery music of flute, lyre and cymbal tantalized him from behind the figure of the Druid.

Let the dead be dead, he told the figure silently. *You did not die forever; you simply changed form. And we both know it.*

He was not surprised when the figure returned his grin and held out his arms in welcome.

As Marric stepped between the pillars, light and sound exploded about him. The music blossomed into an exultant, brilliant chord that, by comparison, turned even the music at his acclamation, the crowning of his queen, the births of his children, into discord. When he felt himself embraced, he opened his mouth to comment ironically to the Druid . . .

. . . but found himself, instead, clasping a slender woman whose crown of silvered braids shone with a light of their own that her blue eyes suddenly eclipsed.

'Stephana!' he cried, and her mouth closed upon his as it formed her name. Her lips were cool fire; as they opened beneath his, fire lanced through him, not just the desire that she had always woken in him, but a sureness, a power that he knew now he would never lack.

When he could finally see past his tears and hers, he realized that he stood in the midst of the court that, many years ago, he had perceived as shadows. Now, he himself was a part of it, and it beggared any court he had ever seen or imagined. As the courtiers formed a double aisle, Marric wrapped his arm about Stephana's shoulders and started down it.

So many of the people past whom he walked looked familiar . . . were familiar . . . a small man with a scholar's bad vision, a huge Aescir, whom Marric remembered from Gallia, an emperor and empress who smiled at him with, for the first time in their lives, no reproach, a golden-haired queen who stood amidst white blossoms and who blew him a kiss. Beside her were two men, one in Druid's robes, the other, much younger, standing somewhat crookedly because of a lame right leg, but with welcome shining in a face much like Marric's own.

So many people to greet, to love – yet, in the east, behind the figures that Marric approached, rose and violet were replacing the pallor before the dawn. Stephana slipped from his clasp and gestured: he must walk the rest of the way by himself and do his own homage to the God and to the Goddess.

But before him stood one last figure: the high priest.

'Did I not tell you that you would not be alone?' he asked, and his voice was stronger, more joyous than Marric had ever heard it.

'Should you have come here to greet me?' Marric asked. Leaving the body took will and strength; while no one could doubt the high priest's will, he had been a dying man.

'To see your Triumph? Perhaps not. But just as you laid aside your crown my work was done. And now, finally, I can greet my son and follow where he leads. There he is!'

As the high priest disappeared in a burst of white light, and Marric prostrated himself before the pair whose faces were sometimes his parents', sometimes his and Olwen's, and yet at other times, his son's and Elen's, the dawn rose . . .

No time, no time to greet the spirits whom he had seen, not even the son whom he had never known . . .

It is all right, Marric, a voice echoed within his soul. They will wait for you; and on your last day, they will meet you at the shore. . . .

. . . he heard rock rasp against rock, sandals slap against cold stone, and he opened his eyes. Lithe as if he were not old and scarred, and had not passed an entire night lying on cold stone, he sat up and swung out of the sarcophagus, one hand stroking its rim as he might gentle a horse after a long, arduous journey. In the doorway, two priests knelt beside a figure lying face upward, its eyes open, its mouth smiling.

So, the high priest too had found his heart's desire. The priests would never understand or forgive him if he laughed. But as he took the white robe that one of them handed him and knelt to lay it tenderly over the high priest's outworn form, he was smiling.

Chapter Twenty-five

No one in Penllyn could remember a Beltane season this warm or this fair. The fields were already heavy and green with what promised to be a rich harvest, except where wild flowers sprang up, too lovely to be scythed down by even the most careful farmer. The trees were heavy leafed, the animals robust. And many new children had been born.

But Penllyn's queen had none. Try not to think about not having children, Gwenlliant's most treasured advisor, her aunt Alexa, had counselled her when she despaired of ever choosing a father for the heir whom she must speedily produce, or risk her land's well-being.

'That is foolish,' Gwenlliant had retorted. 'To not think about something, I must first think about it!'

Alexa had only laughed, and advised her to distract herself. Thus, because the day was fair, Gwenlliant sat outside her hall, in the centre of the queen's maenol, where she could watch the people over whom she ruled. A bard sat near her, singing of a queen so fair that where she walked, white flowers sprang up. Gwenlliant's face grew sombre. That had always been a song about her mother, Queen Olwen, who had passed within the nemet to the Goddess' peace last Beltane; Gwenlliant missed her sorely.

But the bard, sensing her unhappiness, changed his rhymes craftily and his tune to a ribald ditty. Gwenlliant found herself laughing and blushing, and when the bard returned to the other, older song, he added pink blossoms to the white, and she did not silence him.

She leaned back on her arms, staring up into the sky at the clouds. Penllyn's sheep were fat, it was true, but if they had fleece that rivalled those clouds, why then Penllyn would be rich enough to buy all the Isles of Mist. Assuming, of course, that the kings and queens in Prydein could agree on prices for their realms, or, indeed, anything at all. The thought made her smile.

It seemed a long time since she had lain back in the sun and watched clouds, as once she had with her cousin. Elen, now (to her mother's fierce joy) the absurdly dignified Empress of Byzantium, would watch ambassadors, or children: she had borne a son at midwinter. She and Elen had fought with and loved one another too long for Gwenlliant to begrudge her cousin anything at all, but *when shall my spring come?* she thought, translating the Roman words effortlessly into her birth-tongue. *When shall I become like the sparrow and cease to be mute?*

Gwenlliant's sigh came from the heart. If Alexa saw her now, she would scold her for not distracting herself successfully enough. Even doing accounts would be preferable to a scolding, *or to this greensickness*, she told herself.

Forgetting that, as queen, she might send a child to fetch her work, if she chose, she rose to seek out the chests in which she stored her records.

'Queen Gwenlliant, Queen Gwenlliant!'

Shrill and pure as a hawk's cry, the girls' voices called down from the hilltop where, once, she and Elen had watched the clouds. She started forward, hand to her mouth in fear, as the girls ran down the side of the slope so quickly that, at any instant, she expected them to pitch headlong and roll the rest of the way. Then she laughed. Her own feet remembered every step of that hill, every loose rock or outcropping, and precisely where it was safest to race. Were it not for her circlet and her skirts – and the black dagger belted at her side – she might have joined them.

'What is it, my dearests?' Gwenlliant contented herself by calling up at the running girls. How their hair glinted, copper and flaxen, in the light!

'They're here! It's here, Queen Gwenna, it's come at last!'

'*What's* come at last?' she cried.

Down at her feet the girls tumbled, like kittens after an hour of play, their faces red, their eyes shining. 'That's right,' she told them, 'catch your breath first, then give me all the news.' She knelt and smoothed back their hair from damp foreheads, first the flaxen braids, then the copper mane so much like her own when she was that age. ('Though,' she knew her aunt would say, 'how much older truly are you?')

'They're here, *he's* here,' gasped one of the girls. 'And he brought a white bear cub for you!'

Abruptly, Gwenlliant stood up, her heart pounding. She knew that her face flushed more than could be explained by a morning spent in the sun, and her blood coursed hot and cold at once through her veins.

'Aunt!' she called, her own voice hawk-shrill. 'Tangwen and Teleri say that the Bearmaster's here!'

Alexa might complain that she, like her brother, was getting too old to do more than retire to Deva and meditate, but no one had ever called her deaf. 'Audun?' she demanded. 'Gwenlliant, it can't be!'

Then her eyes went strange in her head, and Gwenlliant braced herself either to hear prophecy or to pick her aunt up if she swooned. Instead, Alexa tilted her head as if listening to an unseen companion (which, in Alexa's case, was usually the truth), and the green eyes lit like sunlight on a field after the rain. She launched herself at Gwenlliant, tugging her sleeves down upon her arms, straightening her belt, and twitching at the gold apples that bound her waist-length braids.

'Queen you may be,' Alexa laughed, 'but you have a smudge on your face.'

'Aunt, you are not a waiting woman,' Gwenlliant protested.

'You won't have one,' retorted her aunt. 'And you should. Think of Elen, in Byzantium, with a palace full of them.'

Gwenlliant made a rude noise at the idea. 'Think of you, fleeing all of them!'

'While you're thinking, wipe your cheek!' commanded Alexa. 'You are too old and too tall for me to wash your face, and – ' her own face lit with joy '– you truly will want it to be clean.'

Clearly, one of the paroxysms of energy that, from time to time, made Alexa the scourge of every person in the maenol who hoped for a moment's rest when she had other plans for them, was on her now. 'Gwenlliant, you sit back down there. The sunlight looks wonderful on your hair. Tangwen, you run to the well and fetch Prince Gereint. Teleri, inside with you and tell the women to plan a feast!'

'But Princess,' wailed Tangwen, the braver of the two girls, 'we want to see him. He's young and . . .'

'Not another word!' ordered Alexa. She clapped her hands, a gesture from the women's quarters in the imperial palace which, after a lifetime in Penllyn, she had still never managed to unlearn, and the girls went flying.

Relegated to the ranks of the girl-children sent to fetch, carry and obey without question, Gwenlliant found herself laughing. 'Young?' she asked. 'I would hate to think that they were losing their sight.' Audun was ancient, the oldest man, except for the high priest of Osiris who had died last autumn, that Gwenlliant had ever seen.

A cloud passed overhead, and its shadow flickered across Alexa's still-lovely face, draining it of animation. For a moment, but only one, she looked the full toll of her years. Then she sighed, shaking the mood from her just as the sun came back out.

'They're coming!' Like a girl Gwenlliant's age, she stamped her foot, determined that Gwenlliant sit where she was displayed to best advantage. 'Look, the gates are opening! Oh, sweet Isis, niece, set your circlet straight, can't you?'

'And what about yourself?' Gwenlliant demanded, even as she did as Alexa wished.

'Who will look at me?' Alexa shrugged. 'But, if you insist . . .'

'As I do . . .'

'Very well, then.' Alexa drew herself up, twitched the flow of her skirt into proper order, tossed back her braids and smiled, as dignified, as imperial – that was the only word for her – as if she wore the purple and the gems with which she had packed off her only daughter to ensnare an emperor's heart. She swept over to stand beside Gwenlliant, her face set in the distant look that stared out of every mosaic that Gwenlliant had ever seen.

Then, relenting, just before the troop that they could hear took the last turn of the path that led up to the queen's hall,

Alexa bent to embrace Gwenlliant. 'No more fears, now, not ever!' she whispered fiercely.

At least, not for many years. That thought lay unspoken between them. *And perhaps, even then* . . . 'You are so much your father's daughter,' Alexa murmured.

Before Gwenlliant could demand what she meant, Alexa had motioned her to silence. 'Not another word!' she hissed.

A clamour of happy and excited people ushered a train of packhorses and merchants into the open space before the queen's hall. Frisking at the heels, though never beneath them, of the foremost horse, a fine bay, was a white bear. If it were not, perhaps, the cub that the girls had exclaimed over, it was an animal still lean with youth and wearing a garland of flowers, red and pink and yellow.

But the tall young man who reined in his horse so quickly, and leapt down to untie the bear's tether from his saddle, bore no more resemblance to Audun than a girl-child does to her great grandam. He had fair hair, and eyes the colour of sunlight on indigo. Those eyes met hers, and Gwenlliant felt the heated bemusement of desire. Once again, waves of hot and cold swept over her. Cold . . . she had seen this man before, yes, and more than seen him.

'You,' she whispered, and he nodded, holding out the hand that held the white bear's leash. She put out her own hand, not to take possession of the tether, but to clasp his.

'I have dreamed you,' Gwenlliant said. Her eyes filled with tears. 'I have dreamed you twice. And I don't even know your name.'

She was behaving disgracefully, she knew. At any moment, she half-expected, half-hoped, that Alexa would step forward and rescue the situation – and Gwenlliant herself.

'I am Arinbjorn,' said the stranger whom Gwenlliant felt that she knew. Surely, she had lain by his side, warm and in a green clearing, though it had been a winter's night; and he had pointed out in the stars the pattern of the Great Bear and the Lesser.

'And you are Bearmaster now?'

Sorrow, akin to what Gwenlliant felt every time she thought of her mother, shaded his face. Unlike some of the Aescir, who were ruddy and bluff, he was very pale, and his features had that sculptural perfection that became attractive, rather than frightening, only when he smiled. And, despite his grief, he was smiling at her now.

'My eldest brother is Bearmaster now. I was the child of Audun Bearmaster and his wife Gerda's age.' Behind Gwenlliant, Alexa caught her breath in a sob.

Arinbjorn bowed to her. 'You must be Princess Alexa. Before my father went to the Ice, he charged me to ask you, "Did he choose well for you?" '

'He knows he did,' Alexa murmured, a tiny, strangled voice.

'My Queen,' Arinbjorn turned back to Gwenlliant. 'My brother Thorbjorn is Bearmaster in my father's place now. He begs that you accept our sister in fur into your household – and that you forgive him for sending me, rather than waiting upon you himself. He and his wife have just had their fifth child.'

'He will choose well for you too, Gwenlliant,' whispered Alexa. A kiss and a tear fell upon her hair, and then her aunt was gone, running towards Gereint in a welcome, and for a comfort that had always made Gwenlliant wistful. *Oh, perhaps now, Goddess, please* . . .

'Did you have a quiet journey?' Gwenlliant asked at random. She gestured, and Teleri edged forward, followed by several other girls from the maenol, bearing water, wine or ale to the men and their horses.

'We had one stormy night as we crossed into Penllyn from the south,' Arinbjorn smiled into her eyes. His hand tightened on hers, and no words that he could speak were as important as that touch.

'Bandits?' asked Gwenlliant. 'There have not been bandits . . .'

'The village where we sheltered warned us that the Wild Hunt rides thereabout during the storm. But I have no patience with unquiet ghosts, do you? We waited, my friends and I; sitting, drinking and laughing before a fire, we waited for this Hunt of which the villagers spoke. And do you know, it never arrived?'

He laughed, a warm easy sound that, for all his pale looks, reminded Gwenlliant of sunlight sparkling on water in the summer.

'I am not surprised,' she said. Then, with as great an effort as she had ever made in her life, she recalled herself and her duties. 'Come and refresh yourself. I will order quarters and baths prepared—' *and I will personally kill any of the women who offer to bathe this man!*

Arinbjorn was smiling again, as if he understood even those words that Gwenlliant managed not to speak. She spared a moment's thought, a moment's sorrow for Dylan, gone now to a destiny that she could neither imagine nor share, before she turned back to her guest.

'How long,' she asked, her voice breathless, 'did your brother give you leave to stay?'

'Seeing as I am the youngest, and can best be spared, I could stay at least until harvest,' said Arinbjorn.

'Perhaps I can persuade you to winter with us.'

'Queen,' said Arinbjorn, 'you have no need to persuade where you can smile.'

Tears stood in Gwenlliant's eyes. Once again, Alexa had been right. But at that moment, the bear, as if indignant that she had ignored it, butted against her. Had Arinbjorn not caught her, she certainly would have fallen in an ungainly mess of skirts and braids. 'Oh, you wretch!' Gwenlliant cried and knelt to hug her new companion. Had Arinbjorn not taken her breath away already, she certainly would have lost it then.

Steadying herself against Arinbjorn, one hand grasping the bear's tether, Gwenlliant rose and gestured towards her hall.

'My lord Arinbjorn,' she spoke formally, 'I welcome you and your companions to my hall, and I ask no better than that you regard it as your own home.'

'What more can I ask?' Arinbjorn smiled into her eyes and led her inside.

Epilogue

'Come on!' Marric urged his companion, Caius Marcellinus, towards Byzantium's eastern gate, where the sun already turned the great city walls to gold and crimson.

'I have never left my post before,' the old, patrician general grumbled.

'And still have not,' Marric assured him. 'It is true that I am no longer emperor, and you are no longer domestikos of the scholae, but your place is still at my side.'

He pulled up his hood, lest he be recognized, pressed heels into his horse's flanks, and headed for the gate. Long, long ago, he had ridden this way with just such a small guard and found the road filled with beggars. Now, the deserted homes had all been repaired; the people who walked the streets on their way to market looked well-fed and intent on whatever task they had in mind. Byzantium was a city of plenty now. *Perhaps Mor, or his son, will have the leisure that I never had for art or contemplation. Please the gods, let them be men of peace.*

That was a new prayer, and a strange one, coming as it did from a man who had, lifelong, been a warrior. Marric had no idea if it would ever be answered. But that was no longer his affair. Free, for the first time in his life, he planned to fulfil a long-deferred dream. By autumn, they would be in Persepolis, the city that Alexander sacked as a gesture of triumph. And who knew what land they might seek out thereafter? Hind, perhaps, where the descendants of King Poros still ruled. Or, as Alexander failed to do, they might travel until they reached the Endless Sea.

Marric smiled and led the way to the gate. Standing guard there was an officer whose features and heavy clothes marked him clearly as an Egyptian, far too old and too advanced in rank to hold that post. Marric peered sharply at him. As Marric approached, his hood fell back, and the man presented arms and a most disrespectful grin, remembering a time when Marric had ridden out with a friend and a priestess to seek an empire.

Now, he sought – what? He had had his empire, and he had won his peace.

And now what do you seek? he asked himself as his horse's hooves clattered through the tunnel that led through the wall and out over the bridge.

To see what lies beyond the life I have always known.

That was the only answer that he had for Caius Marcellinus.

Is that all? the former general had asked.

Is that all? Marric had echoed him. *It is everything!*

Remembering, he laughed.

'Are you going to laugh or to ride?' asked Marcellinus. 'Or have you reconsidered?'

Marric simply shook his head and grinned.

'And you trust the Persians enough to pass through their lands?' Marcellinus demanded, for at least the fifth time. 'With only these . . .' his gesture took in the smaall train of guards and horses that were the only escort to which Marric had consented.

'Not to mention our safe-conducts,' Marric said.

'I wouldn't mention those in any case,' Marcellinus growled, and Marric nodded agreement.

'I may not trust the Persians,' Marric said, 'but I do trust this!' He gestured, and light rose from his hands into a sphere of white radiance that expanded to encompass them all. 'I promise you, we shall resemble nothing more than a troop of merchants and the adept –' as always, he laughed when he applied that term to himself '– who travels with them. They are common, I am told, in the east. Now, do you ride with me, or shall I go alone?'

'I suppose,' conceded Marcellinus in a tone intended to counteract the smile on his face, 'that you are quite capable of arguing until old age overtakes us.'

'Old age?' asked Marric. 'I don't think that it ever will!' He shouted then, and spurred his horse out towards Asia.

Susan Shwartz
Byzantium's Crown £2.95

Book One in the *Heirs to Byzantium* trilogy

In the alternative history of *Heirs to Byzantium*, Antony and Cleopatra defeated Octavian at Actium and went on to establish a mighty empire with its capital the fabled Byzantium. For almost 1000 years their descendants have ruled as emperors and pharaohs . . .

After the death of his father it is Imperial Prince Marric who should rule in Byzantium with his sister Alexa. But in Marric's absence, his stepmother Irene has seized power.

Summoned secretly by Alexa, Marric returns to fight for their crown. Instead he ends up fighting for his life and soul. Captured by Irene, believing Alexa dead, Marric is tempted by the consort's magic powers, then sold into slavery.

As the Empire is devoured from within by evil and attacked from without by its former allies, Marric learns to endure slavery and, through the love of the seeress Stephana, to come to terms with his destiny. He also learns that for the first time in centuries, the Empire needs a ruler who can control more than mortal powers . . .

The Woman of Flowers £2.95

Book Two in the *Heirs to Byzantium* trilogy

Now the sorceress Irene has won the Empire through her powers of necromancy. The princess Alexa escapes her serpent clutches, travelling north under the protection of Audun, called Bearmaster, and his phalanx of white bear warriors.

Across wild waters, beset by the shape-changing battle hordes of Jomsburg's Reiver Jarl, they come to the northern fastness of the Aescir. There Alexa struggles to bring her fiery magic to Audun's aid, but as long as she remains with his people, the black bears of Jombsburg and the flame-tinged falcon of the sorceress will lay merciless seige to the Aescir.

So it is that Alexa journeys on to the Misty Isles of the Celtoi, where love seeks her out in the shadow of the standing stones. But Marric is coming. The prince who became a slave who became a warlord is destined to summon the woman of flowers back to far Byzantium . . .

Vernor Vinge
The Peace War £2.99

Paul Hoehler, mathematician of genius, had devised spherical force fields that allowed nothing – people, objects, light, air, radiation – in or out.

The ultimate defence initiative and supreme survival technology, it offered total power and the opportunity was not lost on Livermore Electronics Laboratories. Suddenly anyone in the vicinity of a government compound or a defence installation was 'bobbled', locked into a force field and lost to sight forever.

The new Peace Authority had global power in a world where war was obsolete. But outside the impregnable 'bobbles', mysterious plagues began their epic devastation.

And outside the 'bobbles', Hoehler, the man who had created the technology for total power, had become the Peace Authority's most feared enemy, the holder of the long-lost key of hope for a world dominated by soul-numbing repression . . .

'Well-written and thought provoking. The nuances of the future world . . . ring true'
SCIENCE FICTION REVIEW

Marooned in real time £2.99

The brilliant sequel to
The Peace War

The Extinction happened at some point in the twenty-third century. Beyond that point, all that remained of humankind survived locked in timeless limbo inside spherical force fields known as 'bobbles'.

The rebuilding of civilization and the rescue of survivors fell to the 'high-techs', themselves survivors of the technologically advanced decades just before the Extinction.

When they reached the 'bobble' where the last members of the Peace Authority lived on in stasis, one of the 'high-techs' was murdered, cruelly abandoned in real time.

Wil Brierson, the last detective in the world, was called in to handle the case. Seeking the murderer through a complex web of mysteries, he stumbled on a plan for a new – and final – Extinction . . .

'Highly recommended . . . scope and grandeur mark this as a high point in hard SF creativity'
SCIENCE FICTION REVIEW

Robert Silverberg
Lord Valentine's Castle £3.50

'In an archaic, feudal empire . . . Valentine, an itinerant juggler, discovers through dreams and portents that he is his namesake Lord Valentine, his body and throne stolen by a usurper. He sets out to win his throne back . . . Valentine and his companions trek across the forests and plains of Zimroel . . . to Allranroel with its labyrinth and then to the heights of power at Castle Mount. Silverberg's invention is prodigious . . . a near-encyclopaedia of unnatural wonders and weird ecosystems. Silverberg, like a competent juggler, maintains his rhythm and his suspense to the end'
TIMES LITERARY SUPPLEMENT

Alfred Bester
The Deceivers £2.95

Rogue Winter, King of the Maori Commandos, cruises the seedy Solar Circuit, from the Paradise of Carnal Pleasures to the torture chambers of the asteroid Triton, in search of his kidnapped lover, Demi Jeroux.

Snatched by the demonic Manchu Duke of Death, Demi is the pawn in a bitter struggle for control of the Meta-crystals, a secret source of unlimited energy lying deep beneath the surface of Triton.

Rogue is one of the few men alive capable of following the Manchu's trail. When he eventually confronts the Duke of Death, the future of the entire solar system will depend on the outcome . . .

Robert Heinlein
Red Planet £1.95

Through the amazing talents of Willis, an engaging Martian roundhead, two young teenagers in Syrtis Minor discover a plot by the Resident Agent General to make the colonists his slaves. The boys escape to warn their families in the South Colony and survive many dangers before finding sanctuary with the true Martians, who return the boys home to face arrest and disbelief. In a savage battle for survival everything depends on Willis . . .

All Pan books are available at your local bookshop or newsagent, or can be ordered direct from the publisher. Indicate the number of copies required and fill in the form below.

Send to: **CS Department, Pan Books Ltd., P.O. Box 40,
             Basingstoke, Hants.   RG21 2YT.**

or phone: 0256 469551 (Ansaphone), quoting title, author
             and Credit Card number.

Please enclose a remittance* to the value of the cover price plus :60p for the first book plus 30p per copy for each additional book ordered to a maximum charge of £2.40 to cover postage and packing.

*Payment may be made in sterling by UK personal cheque, postal order, sterling draft or international money order, made payable to Pan Books Ltd.

Alternatively by Barclaycard/Access:

Card No. | | | | | | | | | | | | | | | | | | |

_____

Signature:

Applicable only in the UK and Republic of Ireland.

While every effort is made to keep prices low, it is sometimes necessary to increase prices at short notice. Pan Books reserve the right to show on covers and charge new retail prices which may differ from those advertised in the text or elsewhere.

NAME AND ADDRESS IN BLOCK LETTERS PLEASE:

....

Name ————————————————————————

Address ———————————————————————

————————————————————————————

————————————————————————————

————————————————————————————

3/87